CW00520280

DEVIL IN THE DETAIL

SCOTT CULLEN BOOK 2

ED JAMES

Copyright © 2012 Ed James

The right of Ed James to be identified as the author of this work
has been asserted in accordance with the Copyright, Designs and
Patents Act 1988. All rights reserved.

No part of this publication may be reproduced, stored in or
transmitted into any retrieval system, in any form, or by any means
(electronic, mechanical, photocopying, recording or otherwise)
without the prior written permission of the publisher. Any person
who does any unauthorised act in relation to this publication may
be liable to criminal prosecution and civil claims for damages.

This is a work of fiction. Names, characters, businesses, places,
events and incidents are either the products of the author's
imagination or used in a fictitious manner. Any resemblance to
actual persons, living or dead, or actual events is purely
coincidental.

Cover design copyright © Ed James

OTHER BOOKS BY ED JAMES

SCOTT CULLEN MYSTERIES SERIES

1. GHOST IN THE MACHINE
2. DEVIL IN THE DETAIL
3. FIRE IN THE BLOOD
4. STAB IN THE DARK
5. COPS & ROBBERS
6. LIARS & THIEVES
7. COWBOYS & INDIANS
8. HEROES & VILLAINS

CULLEN & BAIN NOVELLAS

1. CITY OF THE DEAD (Coming March 2020)

CRAIG HUNTER SERIES

1. MISSING
2. HUNTED
3. THE BLACK ISLE

DS VICKY DODDS

1. TOOTH & CLAW

DI SIMON FENCHURCH SERIES

1. THE HOPE THAT KILLS
2. WORTH KILLING FOR
3. WHAT DOESN'T KILL YOU
4. IN FOR THE KILL
5. KILL WITH KINDNESS
6. KILL THE MESSENGER

MAX CARTER SERIES

1. TELL ME LIES

SUPERNATURE SERIES

1. BAD BLOOD
2. COLD BLOOD

For my parents.

PROLOGUE

Wednesday
18th August

1

Detective Constable Scott Cullen sat in the back seat of his Inspector's car, watching the mid-morning August rain pass overhead. It felt like they had been inside forever and they still hadn't come to fetch him. Maybe they didn't want him.

He was parked outside the house of Alan and Ailsa Miller, parents of Keith, a young Acting DC who had worked for Cullen. Keith was dead, murdered almost exactly two weeks ago.

Cullen blamed himself for the death of his colleague. He had taken some time off for counselling, returning to work that morning only to be forced into the confrontation he feared — meeting the family.

The Miller house was a Victorian villa in Trinity, an upmarket area of Edinburgh wedged between Leith, Newhaven and Granton — all noted for their teen gangs and other social problems. Cullen had taken Keith to be a typical Leith ned who had somehow ended up in the police. In truth, Miller's family had money — his dad was high up in an insurance company and his mother was a lawyer on George Street. Cullen assumed it was neglect and spoilt kid syndrome that gave Miller his outlook on life — being at school with kids who were in gangs wouldn't have helped.

A rap on the window jolted Cullen back to the present. DS Sharon McNeill.

"They're ready for you, Scott."

Cullen nodded and got out of the car.

"How was it?" he said, as they headed down the path to the house.

"Not great. The funeral doesn't seem to have closed things off."

"Not likely with a death like this." He stopped outside the front door. "This is your neck of the woods, isn't it?"

"It is," she said with a warm smile. "I grew up just down the road. Do you think we're ready to meet my parents yet?"

"Happy to," said Cullen, with a wink. "It's you that's stalling."

Sharon was Cullen's direct boss but more recently had become his... what? Girlfriend? Partner? Other half? Lover? Cullen liked none of the terms particularly but had settled on girlfriend. They had been an item for a fortnight but were yet to come clean to the powers that be. Cullen knew they would be separated into different teams in CID — one of them would draw the short straw and continue reporting to DI Brian Bain.

"Speaking of stalling," she said, "you'd better get in there. Bain's waiting."

"Fine," he said.

She led him through to the living room crammed full of ornate, dark oak furniture. Little light made it past the heavy curtains.

DI Bain sat in an armchair, his small blue eyes glaring at Cullen. He was mid-forties with a head of grey stubble, his left hand stroking his thin moustache.

Bain faced Alan and Ailsa Miller who sat on a large, red leather settee.

Alan Miller looked only slightly older than Bain. He had a full head of dark hair, with hints of grey around the temples. He was wearing a business suit, although Cullen couldn't tell if he'd come from the office or was still on leave.

His wife sat alongside fussing with a half-empty cafetière on the table in front of them. She looked older, as though she'd carried the pressure of her sons and her career. She wore a long black skirt and white blouse, her grey hair cut short. She clutched a paper tissue in her left hand.

Slouching on a dining chair and fiddling with his Samsung phone was Derek Miller, Keith's younger brother. He looked a few years younger than Keith and wore a t-shirt and hooded top — both Superdry — and G-Star jeans pulled low revealing the Calvin Klein logo on his underpants. Cullen hated this trend and in other circumstances would be tempted to pull the trousers up.

Bain gestured at a pair of armchairs next to the sofa, so Cullen and Sharon sat down.

Cullen tried to maintain eye contact with Miller's parents. He'd delivered death messages before in his career, for murders and accidents, but this was different — the parents already knew and the case was on the fast track through the courts. It was Cullen's fault their son was dead at the age of twenty-two.

"Detective Constable Cullen was Keith's mentor during the time he worked with us," said Bain. "He was with him when he was attacked and would like to say a few words."

Cullen looked up at Miller's parents — their eyes were all over him. Derek ignored him. He pulled out a sheet of paper with some scribbled notes. He had prepared a statement with Bain's help, neither of them agreeing with the sentiments but deeming it sufficiently sanitised.

"At the time of his death, Keith was an Acting DC but he was about to be made permanent," said Cullen. "It's a demanding role and Keith was learning to cope with the pressures. He brought many different skills and experiences to the job. Keith had a lot of exposure to senior officers in the police service and was well thought of right to the top."

Tears stung Cullen's eyes, genuine and heart-felt.

"Keith was also a friend. We shared a love of football, though we supported different teams. Keith asked me to go to the Hibs game against Barcelona the night before he died but sadly neither of us could make it."

Derek looked up. Miller had snuck off from a stakeout to go to the football. Derek had provided the tickets. Cullen hadn't told Bain.

"Keith died in the line of duty," said Cullen, his voice wavering slightly. "He died saving the life of another potential victim of the Schoolbook killer and his sacrifice helped secure sufficient evidence to convict. I know it is scant consolation but there are two parents in Glasgow who are not grieving and four sets of parents who have a sense of justice being done over the capture of their daughters' killer."

The Millers had stayed static throughout.

Cullen took a deep breath. "I hold myself responsible for Keith's death. I was the senior officer. We were in a suspect's house. We didn't have backup and I left Keith alone for a moment while I investigated a sound from the rear of the house. It turned out to be a hostage — who would undoubtedly have been killed. It was then I heard Keith scream. I returned to the living room and tried to help Keith, but he'd been stabbed in the stomach and was bleeding heavily."

"What were Keith's last words?" said Ailsa Miller, her voice a croak.

Cullen closed his eyes. "He told me to go after his attacker, who'd fled the flat."

"What exactly did he say?" said Ailsa.

"I think it was 'I'll be fine, go get him, Scotty'. In truth, there had been swear words in there. "I called DI Bain." He gestured to his superior officer. "I told him to get an ambulance over to the property while I gave chase." He looked up at them again. "That was the last time I spoke to Keith."

Ailsa Miller closed her eyes, tears sliding down her face. "Thank you." Alan Miller held her hand tight, whispered some words to her.

"You're a lying bastard," said Derek.

Everyone in the room looked around at the youth, now standing, eyes aflame. "I sat next to my brother at the game you said he wasn't at. Lying bastard."

Alan Miller was on his feet. "Derek, that's enough."

"This prick got my brother killed." Derek stabbed a finger in the air. "He's trying to convince himself it wasn't his fault but we all know it was. He got him killed."

Alan Miller grabbed his arm and marched him out of the room, through a set of sliding doors at the far end. The others sat in stunned silence.

A moment later, he returned wearing a false smile. "I'm sorry about that. This whole business has hit my son very hard. I'm sure you can understand."

"Of course," said Bain. "It has affected every one of us."

Alan Miller rubbed his forehead and sat down again. "Indeed."

Cullen cleared his throat — he wanted to say something not on Bain's script. "I've been seeing a counsellor to help me come to terms with this. He suggested I keep in contact with you. It might be mutually beneficial."

They exchanged a look before Alan Miller smiled. "Why, yes, I think that would be a good thing."

Cullen already had one of his cards in his hand and put it on the coffee table in front of them. "Here you are," he said, ignoring Bain's glare. "My mobile number is on it. Call me any time if you want to talk."

Alan Miller examined the card in detail then looked up at Cullen. "Thank you." He showed them out into the light rain.

Bain led them down the path to his car, his head down. Cullen could tell from experience that the DI was fuming. The driver door slammed.

Cullen and Sharon stopped by the car. "You did well," she said.

"Try telling him that." Cullen pointed at Bain. He got into the passenger side back seat, steeling himself for the inevitable onslaught.

Bain twisted round to look at Cullen. "That wasn't in the script."

"If it had been," said Cullen, "you wouldn't have let me say it."

Bain shook his head. "Enough with these games, Cullen, okay? You might think you're the big boy just now, what with catching that killer, but you've got to learn to toe the line."

Cullen didn't shrink back. "You need to learn to listen to me and DS McNeill."

"Leave me out of it," she said.

Bain turned round to face forward and shook his head. "This isn't the end of it, Cullen."

DAY 1

Monday
23rd January

five months later

2

Four slices of toast smoothly emerged from the polished steel Dualit toaster and Elaine Gibson tossed them into the clean, white ceramic toast rack. She put another four slices on then put the rack on the dining table. She sat down with her mug of coffee and set about spreading crunchy peanut butter on the wholemeal toast.

She yelled upstairs. "Thomas! Mandy! Can you hurry up?"

She took a bite of toast and sat looking out of the kitchen window, across the lawn at the Hopetoun Monument perched on one of the hills overlooking Garleton, ominous rainclouds looming in the west.

Her husband, Charles, came into the room, tying his necktie. "Morning," he said.

"There's coffee in the pot," she said.

"Ah, toast today. Good. I'm starving."

He poured a cup of coffee and started whistling. He sat down and buttered the toast, reaching for the jar of Marmite. The second batch of toast slowly emerged from the guts of the machine.

"Kids not up yet?" he said.

Elaine shook her head. "It's your turn today."

"I'll have my breakfast then I'll get on to them."

"Fine."

She finished her toast then added the new slices to the rack. She refilled her mug with coffee.

Thomas wandered in, mumbling something that might have been "Morning." He immediately set about the toast, gulping through two thickly buttered slices. Elaine almost castigated him again for not chewing but decided it would just fall on deaf ears.

"Have you seen your sister?" she said.

"No," said Thomas, through a mouthful of slice three.

"Charles..."

Gibson raised his hands as he stood up. "Fine, I'll get her." He left the room, heading upstairs.

"Won't be back till seven tonight," said Thomas. "Got ATC."

"Okay." Air Training Corps was Charles's idea to get some discipline into the boy. They, like many of their friends, had decided to send their children to the local comprehensive, the best in the area and at least equivalent to the private schools in Edinburgh, but they were determined he would get the same standard of extra-curricular activity.

"Any more toast?" said Thomas.

She reached over and put another two slices into the machine.

Gibson burst into the room. She turned to face him.

"She's gone," said Gibson, locking eyes with her.

"You're sure?" she said.

Thomas looked up at them.

"Yes," said Gibson. "I checked all the rooms upstairs. Nothing. And the front door is locked." He went over to the back door and tried it.

"I'll look in the conservatory," she said.

She rushed into the hall then into the conservatory, pulling her dressing gown tighter as the bitterly cold air hit her arms. She tried the French doors. Locked.

She checked the large cupboards in the hall, stuffed with shoes and coats but not hiding her daughter. She went back into the kitchen.

"It's locked," she said.

"Same with the back door," said Gibson. "The utility room is empty, too."

She let out a deep sigh. "Not again," she said, her voice a murmur.

Gibson held her shoulder. "Don't worry, I'm sure she'll be fine."

"Do you think she's gone to Susan's again?" she said.

Gibson nodded. "I'll check."

∼

MORAG TATTERSALL OPENED the gate beside the gatehouse at Balgone Ponds and walked through as though she owned the place. She led her greyhounds, Meg and Mindy, along what she still considered a public footpath.

The owners of the place — the *new* owners — had unilaterally taken the decision to block off the path and turn it into their garden. This irritated Morag and her neighbours in the cottages around the corner.

Every day she used the path to walk a series of dogs around the ponds, until *they* moved in. The only other way was through the hedge behind the gatehouse but she didn't want to cut her jacket or the dogs' paws on the hawthorn.

She thought about leaving the gate open but decided against such pettiness. Besides, it looked like they were away. She closed it and marched on.

She breathed in the fresh early morning air and powered on down the path. The dogs were pulling on their leads — she tugged them to the side and they obeyed. The sun was just beginning to rise from its winter slumber, appearing over the slight hills in the middle distance. The trees were bare and the path damp underfoot as it led down to the ponds.

She came to the downward slope and let the dogs off, putting their leather leads in her jacket pocket. They set off slowly — tails raised, heads combing the ground for trails, their muscular thighs bouncing along like they were shadowboxing before a fight, occasionally stopping and sniffing at a patch of ground.

As she overtook them, her thoughts turned to her itinerary — a yoga class in North Berwick in an hour and a half, then meeting Liz for lunch afterwards. She was looking forward to both.

Morag continued down the path descending to the level of the ponds. She walked on for a minute or so, lost in thoughts of getting around to Andrew's laundry and taking Meg to the vet for her boosters.

She couldn't see the dogs. "Meg! Mindy!"

She looked back the way she'd come. There was no sign of them. They'd no doubt seen a rabbit and run off after it. They'd only caught one once — she'd had to pull Mindy away from the squealing animal — but they'd given chase countless times. She turned back and retraced her steps.

She climbed the rise back to where she let them off. To the left, away from the pond, another path ran along the higher ground. She could see movement through the trees, grey like Mindy.

"Mindy!"

There was a rustling. Mindy raced through, coming right up to Morag. She grabbed her collar and put her back on the lead.

"Meg!"

Morag marched through the trees in the direction Mindy had come. She spotted Meg sniffing at a spot between two trees a few metres apart, in front of a row of rhododendrons.

"Meg, stop that."

Meg turned around, looked at Morag then went back to her sniffing.

Morag paced over to her and grabbed her collar. "Bad girl."

Mindy started pulling on her lead while Morag fiddled with Meg's collar.

Mindy lurched forward, almost pulling Morag's arm out of the socket, digging with her front paws at a patch of loose earth.

"Stop!"

The dog ignored her.

Morag saw some pink cloth. She gasped, letting go of the leads. Kneeling down, she joined in digging.

She scraped around the cloth, revealing an arm.

Morag rocked back on her heels, reaching into her pocket and fumbling with her mobile phone.

3

Cullen slammed his tray down at an empty table and sat, looking across the busy canteen. He let out a deep sigh before taking a drink of his black Americano.

"That's a beast of a sigh for a Monday morning," said ADC Angela Caldwell. She sat opposite him, placing her tray with more decorum than Cullen had.

She was tall and dark haired. She'd worked closely with Cullen before, being seconded to an investigation as a uniformed officer, and she'd recently been made Acting DC, the start of a training period to become a fully-fledged CID officer. Her management was assigned to Cullen as part of his own personal development plan. Though it was rarely mentioned, she was Keith Miller's replacement.

"Aye, sorry," said Cullen. The coffee was far too hot to drink so he left it, lid off. "Good weekend?"

"Not really, no." Angela took a sip of tea. "The house was still a mess after Christmas, so I was doing a lot of tidying. Not that *he* helped."

Cullen noticed she never referred to her husband by name, only *he* or *him*. He knew it was Rod but she hadn't called him that for a good while. "Sounds fun."

"Aye, had to go to IKEA for something to hold all of his bloody magazines."

Cullen looked away. "The joys of cohabiting."

"What about you?"

"We were out seeing Sharon's sister in East Linton," said Cullen.

"Didn't know she had one."

Cullen nodded. "Her husband is a boring twat."

"What's she like?"

"They look quite similar," said Cullen, "but they're really different. Deborah doesn't work. She gets involved with the church and local community groups and all that bollocks."

Angela laughed. "Doesn't sound like she's even from the same gene pool as DS McNeill."

"Tell me about it," said Cullen. "Rachel was glad to see her Uncle Scott."

"Are you a decent uncle?"

Cullen shrugged. "Not for me to say."

"I bet you love her, you big soft shite."

Cullen nodded. "I do enjoy seeing her. Maybe not her parents so much."

Angela raised an eyebrow.

"Sharon told me not to get any ideas," he said.

"Ideas about what?"

Cullen looked up. DS Alan Irvine. He was overweight, prematurely bald and Cullen's new DS. DCI Turnbull separated Sharon and Cullen when they finally announced they were an item and not just another in Cullen's long line of flings. Sharon initially appeared to have lucked out by getting away from Bain, but she now reported to DI Paul Wilkinson — 'out of the frying pan into the knackered gas cooker that doesn't give a shite' as she'd recently put it.

"Going to see the Scotland match in March?" said Cullen.

"Aye, I'm heading over," said Irvine. He put his tray on the table and sat down. He spat some chewing gum into a napkin then tucked into his fried breakfast, lips smacking as he ate. "It's Keith Miller's birthday today."

Cullen stared at his roll for a few seconds before picking it up and eating, avoiding eye contact with Irvine.

He was shit at remembering birthdays and would have let the fact pass by but for Irvine's typical Scottish lack of sensitivity. In a parallel universe somewhere, it would be Miller sitting beside them ogling the new girl in the canteen.

The counselling helped to a certain extent but Cullen still carried what happened around with him on a daily basis. Talking took the pain away inch by inch but still left a hollow shell of guilt. He had another session on Wednesday and the prospect of it gave him a tightness in his chest.

He finished his roll and got to his feet. "I'll see you in the briefing."

"There isn't one today," said Irvine. "The gaffer told us to get out to East Lothian. Place called Balgone Ponds. Some wee lassie has gone missing and Turnbull doesn't want the local CID making a dog's bollocks of it."

4

Cullen drove along the A199, the single carriageway that sliced East Lothian in two, the rain wriggling down his windscreen like snakes, wipers on full power. They descended the hill, the downpour slacking off as the vista widened, revealing Dunbar on the coast still basking in the winter sun — the rain hadn't made it that far yet.

Angela directed them from the passenger seat. "Just off here," she said, as they approached the turning for East Linton.

"You sure this is the right way?" said Cullen. "We should have turned up at Haddington and gone through Garleton."

"This is quicker," said Angela.

Cullen took them into the small town, coming to the old Victorian houses in the centre, turning left beneath the train line, the steel girders in stark contrast to the stone buildings.

Her phone rang and she quickly answered it. Cullen could hear the raised male voice bleed out of her speaker — Bain. "We thought it would be quicker," she said. Cullen heard Bain's voice getting louder.

He drove up the old high street, parked cars dotting the road, passing the shells of two closed pubs. He had to pull in to let an Audi come through, not that he had much choice. He almost stalled the car setting off again.

Angela hung up, angrily throwing her phone on the dashboard.

"Bain?" said Cullen.

"Got it in one. Said he'd been trying to phone you."

"My mobile's off while I drive. What was he wanting?"

"Just wondering where we were," she said. "I had to explain part of the reason we're not there yet was your car."

"Sailed through its MOT last week." His battered, bottle green Golf was seventeen years old and still running.

"Bribing a mechanic is a criminal offence," she said.

He laughed. "Yeah, well, I do have a mortgage deposit to save up for. And besides, we should have gone the other way."

"Aye right."

They left East Linton, heading up the steep hill, Cullen's car audibly struggling. He had to shift down to second.

"Do you know anything more about where we're going?" he said.

"Not much," she said. "He was just shouting at me for not being there already."

Balgone Ponds was roughly two thirds of the way from East Linton to North Berwick.

"Who's there with him?" he said.

"Irvine. Scene of Crime and Pathology are as well."

"That'll be why he's busting our balls," said Cullen. "He doesn't want us making him look bad."

"The girl is definitely dead," said Angela.

Cullen swallowed hard. "I thought she'd just gone missing?"

"She was found."

They came to a T-junction at the top of a hill, having driven for miles between empty fields. Angela navigated them to the right.

After another minute or so, Cullen spotted an entrance on the left. "Here?"

"No," she said. "Another couple of hundred metres on the right."

There was a gatehouse on the left, an ornate building that presumably once led to a country house.

"Just here," she said.

Cullen pulled off the main road, turning right along a lane lined with a row of five Victorian cottages. It was already rammed, two panda cars, an Astra and a certain purple sports Mondeo belonging to Bain.

Angela passed the map she'd printed to Cullen.

He pointed at it. "Should definitely have gone through Garleton."

"Whatever."

Cullen studied it — Balgone Ponds looked like some sort of nature reserve, two large ponds surrounded by cliffs on the south and west and a dense wood to the north, the whole area surrounded by fields. A small section of the John Muir Way ran through it, a mile of the thirty odd from Edinburgh to Dunbar. Angela had drawn an 'X' in red pen where they were to meet Bain.

"Come on, then," he said, and got out of the car.

They crossed the road and Cullen tried the metal gate. It was shut — he half expected it to be open, with a uniform in hi-vis gear ushering people through. Instead, there was an aggressive sign warning walkers off, insisting the gatehouse was closed to the public. What once was a path was now landscaped garden and drive, though absent of cars.

Cullen could make out the fierce glow of arc lights through the trees, pointing them to the scene of crime. "This it?"

"Think so."

"What do you reckon?" said Cullen, pointing to the signs. "Here?"

She frowned at her map. "Must be a way through up there. Bain mentioned something about the John Muir Way."

Cullen went back to his car and opened the boot.

"What are you up to now?" she said.

"Changing my shoes," he said. "It's pissing down."

He sat on the edge of the car and changed into a pair of hiking boots. He should really buy a pair of wellies.

She tapped her own feet — sturdy Dr Martens — then pointed at Cullen's discarded left brogue. "You're such a girl, Scott," she said, with a laugh. "I need to check one day that you don't walk to work in trainers and change into your heels when you get in."

"Can't imagine you wearing heels," he said, tugging the second boot on and tying the laces.

Angela towered over him. "Very funny."

They walked back to the gatehouse and followed the line of

the walled garden to a thick hawthorn hedge. There was a break at one end and Cullen squeezed through, helping Angela tug her coat free from the thorns as she followed. They kept to the John Muir Way for a hundred yards or so then came to a crossroads.

Angela directed them right and onto the path to the west, through the densely packed trees towards the ponds. They reached the Scene of Crime van, which must have ploughed along the path from the other direction.

Two masked figures in white overalls stood by the van, just inside the cordon. As they approached, Cullen recognised the first — Jimmy Deeley, the Chief Pathologist for Edinburgh, who regularly worked with Lothian & Borders police. A fat, bald middle-aged man, he was a good friend of Bain's, which meant he knew all the stories and jokes about Cullen.

"Oh look, Bain's got the Sundance Kid," said Deeley.

Sundance was Bain's less than affectionate nickname for Cullen, now spread wide through the force to Cullen's great irritation.

Cullen showed his warrant card to a young PC dressed in full Scene of Crime garb, and signed into the Crime Scene Access Log. "Any idea where the patron saint of policing is?"

Deeley exploded with laughter. "Just got here myself, so I haven't had the pleasure yet. I'm anticipating yet more requests to break the laws of physics to get my work done when he needs it rather than when it can be done."

The other figure pulled his mask down. It was James Anderson, one of the lead Scene of Crime Officers — SOCOs. He was medium height, dark-haired and with a robust goatee beard.

"What kept you, Cullen?" said Anderson, a smirk on his face.

"Bit suspicious you got to a murder scene so quickly," said Cullen.

"Aye well, I haven't spotted any toilets for you to chuck your guts up in," said Anderson.

"Hopefully no laptops to go missing either," said Cullen.

Deeley chuckled. "Boys, boys. We're supposed to be on the same side."

"You'd think," said Cullen, eyes lingering on Anderson. He turned to Deeley. "Where's the body?"

"Up there," said Deeley, pointing off the path into the trees, towards the north. Cullen could see a tent set up with some arc lights nearby, a group of SOCOs surrounding it.

Angela started off.

"Not so fast," said the PC with the clipboard. He held up an overall. "Get one of these on."

Cullen and Angela complied before following the trail towards the lights, finding Bain and another officer in full SOCO attire just by the inner cordon.

"Here they are," said Bain. "Batman and Robin."

Cullen and Angela exchanged a look.

"Robin was a boy," said Angela.

"I'm not calling you Catwoman," said Bain. "What took you?"

"His car," said Angela.

"Do we need to have another discussion about it?" said Bain.

Cullen didn't rise to it. "Care to bring us up to speed?"

Bain snorted. "Got here ten minutes ago. Policing is turning into a spectator sport, I tell you. Irvine's off making a nuisance of himself, just the way I like it." He gestured to the officer standing next to him. "This is DS Lamb, Haddington CID."

Lamb grinned at them. "Please, call me Bill."

He was a fit-looking man in his mid-thirties. He had one of those beards Cullen suspected Scottish men of a certain age thought added gravitas — the sort Billy Connolly had sported for the last ten or so years — a downward-pointing triangle of stubble underneath a thick moustache much fuller than the small grey pencil on Bain's top lip. Maybe it made them feel like rugged clan chieftains or Musketeers.

Cullen accepted Lamb's firm handshake then introduced Angela. Lamb looked her up and down slowly, not caring who noticed.

Lamb pointed at two men — thin, lean and tall — in their late twenties, both wearing smart casuals — jeans, jumpers and long jackets. "This is Stuart Murray and Ewan McLaren, my DCs."

He gestured at a younger woman — pretty with red hair. She wore jeans and a hooped jumper under a leather jacket. No matter what Cullen did, she wasn't taking her eyes off him. "This is Acting DC Eva Law."

They kept their distance and hung off Lamb's every word. Cullen thought it was refreshing they weren't in his face immediately, shaking hands and antagonising him in some territorial pissing ritual.

Cullen retrieved his notebook from his suit jacket's inside pocket. "So what's happened then?"

"A woman was out with her dogs first thing this morning, stays just round the corner," said Lamb. Cullen recalled the cottages they'd parked in front of. "They were off the lead and one of them bolted here. Uncovered a shallow grave." He took a deep breath. "It's Mandy Gibson."

"How did we get a match?" said Cullen.

"A high priority call came through," said Lamb. "They matched it up at Bilston. The mother, one Elaine Gibson of Garleton, called them at the back of seven to report her daughter missing." He closed his eyes. "Her father has just identified the body. Left a few minutes ago. We need to get some formal verification checks done, obviously, but he insists it's her. He was pretty shaken up, as you can imagine."

"Come on, then, Sundance, let's have a fuckin' look, shall we?" said Bain. "Get that genius brain of yours all over this." He turned and walked off towards the inner cordon.

Lamb shared a look with his officers.

Bain led them to a spot between two trees, surrounded by yellow police tape. Another officer stood there, his white scene of crime suit billowing in the wind. Cullen signed them in to the inner cordon, the area around the discovery.

"Who is the Crime Scene Manager?" said Cullen.

"Supposed to be Irvine," said Bain. "Can't see him, mind."

They signed another form and stepped over the tape, heading towards the arc lights. A hole had been dug and a mound of earth sat off to one side, a small tent erected in a vain attempt to keep the area dry and any forensics intact. The rain must have made the digging difficult, thought Cullen.

Mandy Gibson's body was still there, her arms and legs at odd angles to her body, her skin and hair covered in mud. She wore pink cotton pyjamas.

Anderson and Deeley appeared and Bain was straight in their faces. "I want an update from you two," he said, practically growling at them.

Neither of them wanted to go first.

"Not had much of a chance to look at her," said Deeley, eventually. "Does look like murder, though. There are signs of a struggle, we think."

"We think?" said Bain.

"I've not done the post mortem yet, Brian," said Deeley, "but there are bruises around her wrists, which would indicate that."

"How did she die?" said Cullen.

"Be able to tell you once the PM's done," said Deeley. "Be about one or two this afternoon."

"Time of death?" said Bain.

"Wait for the post mortem," said Deeley.

"Come on, just an indication," said Bain.

Deeley exhaled and scratched his forehead. "By the body temperature, I'd say it was more likely she died last night than this morning."

"Well, you'll just have to hurry up with the PM, then," said Bain.

Deeley shook his head, grinning.

Bain turned his attention to Anderson. "What can you tell me?"

"Nothing much, I'm afraid," said Anderson, eyes looking away from Bain. "The rain has removed any footprints."

"Anything else?" said Bain.

Anderson shrugged. "We're fighting a losing battle here. This is rapidly turning into a quagmire. I'd say your chances of finding anything are close to zero. Your only hope is Jimmy turns something up at the PM."

Bain locked onto Deeley now. "Well, we're all waiting on you, Jimmy."

"No pressure, eh?" said Deeley.

Cullen admired the way Anderson deflected Bain onto Deeley. He didn't know whether it was desperation or if he had something up his sleeve. The rain just got heavier, so Cullen very much doubted the latter.

"Right, off you go and get on with it," said Bain. "We'll be another couple of minutes here."

They stood and looked at Mandy's body, the tent struggling to keep out the rain.

"How old was she?" said Cullen.

"Thirteen," said Lamb.

"That's no age," said Cullen. "What happened after she was reported missing?"

"We received the call at about seven," said Lamb. "We got a squad together, managed to round up the night shift that was just leaving and some boys from North Berwick. We had a grid search around Garleton and the surrounding area."

Cullen had driven through Garleton once or twice before. It was a typical small Scottish town, not dissimilar to his hometown of Dalhousie in Angus. He gestured at the body. "Can't help but notice this is pretty far from the town. We're practically at North Berwick here."

Lamb nodded. "Like I said earlier, we didn't find her. A dog walker did. Morag Tattersall."

"Did she see anything suspicious this morning?" said Cullen.

"Nothing out of the ordinary," said Lamb.

"Is she still around?" said Cullen.

Lamb shook his head. "We took her statement then let her go home. She's not in a great state."

"Could you get me a copy of the statement?" said Cullen.

Lamb sighed. "Aye, will do."

Cullen looked at Bain. "You're being very quiet."

"It's called thinking, Sundance," said Bain.

"What do you want us to do?" said Cullen.

Bain took a deep breath through his nostrils. "Let me plan out a strategy here. Can you and Batgirl go off and speak to this woman who found her? I want her eliminated from suspicion."

5

"What are you doing?" said Angela.

Cullen had opened the gate to the gatehouse garden and was marching down the path, heading towards the front door. Angela ran to keep up with him.

"I'm wondering if they saw anything," he said, pointing to the house.

"Bain told us to go and speak to the dog walker, though."

"And we will," said Cullen.

He hammered on the front door. No answer. He squinted into the front room through drawn curtains but couldn't see anyone.

"Someone has either killed Mandy here or moved her here to dispose of the body," he said. "These people would be the first I'd expect to have heard anything during the night."

Angela took a deep breath. "This is your decision, not mine."

He smiled. "It's my arse Bain will kick."

He tried the door again. After another ten seconds, he headed round the back. A green wheelie bin was by the back door. He lifted the lid and peered inside.

Angela grabbed his arm. "Scott, what are you playing at?"

"I'm checking their bins," he said.

"What for?"

"To see if there's anything inside," said Cullen. "They're empty."

"So?"

"I'm just trying to check if there's anybody in," he said. "Like I said, somebody was here with Mandy, either dead or alive, and I would've expected the residents of this house to have seen or heard something." He checked the recycling tubs, empty as well. "Looks like they're away."

"Or the bin men have been," she said.

Cullen smiled. "We call them scaffies where I'm from." He looked into the room at the back, a kitchen fitted out to a high standard, dark oak freestanding furniture surrounding a wide Aga. It was spotless. "Nobody's home."

She rubbed her neck. "Good. Can we do what Bain's asked us to do?"

He looked in the window again and decided to give up. "Fine."

They walked through the garden and crossed the road, almost back to where they'd parked. Morag Tattersall's cottage was the house furthest from the road and looked like it had the biggest garden, with a reasonably sized landscaped area lying off to the side.

Cullen produced his warrant card and she let them in without saying anything.

The interior had a rustic style with exposed beams, pine furniture and checked curtains but also some very modern furniture. Tattersall sat on a reclining chair, black leather with matching footstool. Cullen knew them from IKEA — he'd been tempted to buy one himself but he wouldn't quite be able to fit it into his bedroom in the shared flat.

Her hands were still shaking, her fingernails encrusted with dark mud. According to the statement Lamb had given Cullen, she found the body at roughly eight thirty. It was only an hour later and the discovery must still be very fresh in her mind.

"I bet they need a lot of exercise," said Angela, pointing to the dogs.

Morag's dogs lay curled up on a leather sofa across from her. They were greyhounds, one black and one grey-brown.

"Not really," said Morag.

"My dad has two greyhounds," said Cullen. "They're the laziest dogs I've ever met. They go for a run on the beach then do absolutely nothing for the rest of the day."

His dad had kept a pair of rescue greyhounds for as long as he could remember, every so often replacing a sadly-departed old dog with a recently-retired young thing.

Morag looked at him and smiled, the first sign of any emotion.

Angela eventually managed to coax her into recounting her experience that morning and soon it came out in a stream — walking the dogs, Meg not returning when called, discovering the body, digging it out, calling the police, waiting for Lamb to turn up.

"Have you ever seen the girl before?" said Cullen.

Morag shook her head strongly. "No, never. The police officer said she's from Garleton. I rarely go there."

"Do you know anyone from the town?" said Cullen.

"There's a woman from my yoga class lives there," said Morag, "but she's barely an acquaintance."

Cullen decided it wasn't worth further investigation. "Did you see or hear anything suspicious as you approached the body?"

"Nothing out of the ordinary," said Morag. "I mean, it was very quiet — it always is — but the rain must have put most people off."

"Do you regularly walk at this time?" said Cullen.

"Most days, yes," said Morag, nodding. "Especially on a Monday — my yoga class is in North Berwick, so I walk the girls before I head off."

"Do you often see people on the walk?" said Cullen.

"Sometimes I do," said Morag. "There's a retired couple a few doors down who take their pair of Jack Russells around the ponds at about the same time."

Cullen noted it down. "And what about during the night? Anything strange? Any cars coming up, anything like that?"

Morag patted one of the dogs for a few seconds. "Not that I can think of, no," she said, her voice barely audible. "I'm not the lightest of sleepers, however."

"Do you live alone?" said Cullen.

"No, I live with my husband," said Morag.

"Could he have seen anything, do you think?" said Cullen.

Morag shook her head. "He's in London, I'm afraid. He's a management consultant, always away. He caught the train down last night from Dunbar at the back of six."

"That must be hard for you," said Angela, "especially at a time like this. Do you need anyone to look in?"

"Well, Andrew is trying to get away today," said Morag. "And my sister is coming over from Falkirk."

Cullen looked out the living room window — the view stretched across the hedge and fence to the gatehouse over the main road. "Do you know who owns the gatehouse?"

"Yes I do," said Morag, with a scowl. "Mr and Mrs Williamson. They just moved in a few months ago." Her face became even sourer. "They blocked the path off and turned it into a garden. It's a frightful nuisance."

"I see," said Cullen, wary of getting involved in a neighbourly dispute. "And do you know where they are?"

"I think they're away on holiday," said Morag. "The car has been gone a few days."

Cullen frowned. "It's a bit strange to be away late January, isn't it?"

"It's skiing season," said Morag, a knowing look on her face. "We usually go at this time of year but Andrew's been too busy to take leave."

Cullen racked his brain for anything they hadn't asked and came up blank. He thanked her for her time and handed her his card.

"If you hear of anything or recall anything that might help then please don't hesitate to give me a call."

6

They returned to the crime scene, looking for Bain and Lamb, Cullen wondering if they were any closer to discovering whether it was the scene of the murder or just where the body was dumped.

The young PC still stood guard at the cordon, shivering in the cold and rain. Cullen knew from bitter experience that he would likely be posted there for the rest of his shift, the promise of overtime being the only consolation. He chatted with him — his name was PC Johnny Watson — and found out the SOCO van had left, the body was removed and at least half of the officers had gone. He thanked him and they headed off.

They found Bain and Lamb stuck in a heated discussion, Murray listening in but keeping a distance from the two stags. Cullen shared a look of raised eyebrows with Murray as they approached. Law was looking bewildered — Cullen thought she had a certain look of cool detachment earlier, but having two senior officers at the point of battering each other had obviously fazed her.

"Let me be clear, DS Lamb, and remind you I have rank here," said Bain, his voice almost a hiss. "I'm the Senior Investigating Officer on this case and you're a Detective Sergeant."

Lamb didn't reply immediately, just held Bain's look.

Cullen imagined his thoughts were along the lines of city cops coming into his patch, stealing his case and any glory. The structure of Lothian & Borders CID was such that each division had its contingent of detectives. Edinburgh City — A Division — had by far the largest concentration but crucially had the higher ranks as well. Just about every regional station Cullen had been in had one DS with two or three DCs which was sufficient to cope with their usual caseload — burglary, drugs and the occasional assault.

The ranks of DI and above were administrative roles in the regional stations, rather than active investigating officers. Cullen knew cases like this were always a sore point with local police, when the likes of Bain were parachuted in to spearhead a high profile investigation. This case clearly looked like murder when they found the body, hence Edinburgh CID being called out so early on.

In Cullen's estimation, Lamb could be a useful foil for Bain. He knew the area, all the nooks and crannies of East Lothian. He also knew people — he had contacts from years of working in the community. He'd also got Bain's back up so soon which meant one more potential ally if Bain got into yet another vendetta.

"Fair enough," said Lamb, stepping back. He did so with a flounce, smiling to show there wasn't an issue to the junior officers present.

Bain looked like he wasn't finished with Lamb but his gaze settled on Cullen. "That was quick. Hope you two weren't arsin' about."

"Hardly," said Cullen.

He updated Bain and Lamb on the visit to Morag Tattersall and the news the couple who owned the gatehouse were probably away skiing. He passed on the names and address of Tattersall's neighbours who walked the Jack Russell every day — there was no answer on the way over.

Bain digested the information for a few seconds.

"I think we should interview all the residents," said Cullen. He'd hesitated in suggesting it, fearing he'd be asked to do it. "Something has clearly happened here between Mandy going to bed last night and Morag Tattersall finding her. Someone in those cottages might have seen something.

Bain nodded slowly.

Irvine appeared, his jaws pounding on the best part of a packet of chewing gum, DC McLaren trailing in his wake.

"You better be keeping my crime scene clean," said Bain. "Don't want any fuckin' nonsense, all right?"

"Aye, no bother, gaffer," said Irvine. "Got six people managing this place. Nobody's getting in or out without signing a form."

Cullen would be very surprised if the forms were legible by the time they were needed. Both he'd signed were already damp, despite the plastic covering.

Irvine looked at Cullen. "Pish result for your boys on Saturday."

Cullen's reaction to Irvine's comment about Miller's birthday meant he'd avoided the usual Monday morning football banter. "One all at Ibrox isn't that bad."

"Depends on who you support," said Bain. "Rangers are going to the wall. I thought all this shite with the Inland Revenue was enough, but drawing at home to Cullen's lot is the last straw."

While Bain supported Rangers, Cullen was an Aberdeen fan — the nearest to his hometown of Dalhousie were the two Dundee clubs, several lower league ones or Aberdeen. When he still lived at home, he used to make the drive up the A90 with his old man every second Saturday.

"I was at Tynecastle to watch us get turned over by Caley Thistle," said Irvine.

Bain shook his head. "I'm surprised you bring football up these days with the way Hearts are playing. How's the investigation going with those SOCOs?"

"Anderson said he'll fast track the forensic report," said Irvine, "but he's not confident he'll have anything decent to show due to the rain."

"Right," said Bain, shaking his head. "Never gets any fuckin' easier this, does it?"

Irvine took a tub of gum out of his pocket, shook it and threw another couple of pieces in his mouth. He pocketed it again without offering it around. Cullen reckoned he went through three or four tubs a week — one day he might start counting if he became particularly bored.

"So what do you want us to do then?" said Cullen.

"I want Lamb setting up an Incident Room locally," said Bain. "We've talked this through already — Haddington is too far, so we'll set up in the Garleton nick instead."

"I'm sure they'll love us coming in and trying to grab a room," said Lamb.

Bain glared at him. "They've no choice in the matter." He looked at Cullen and Angela. "Sundance, I want you and Batgirl to come with me. We're going to interview the deceased's family and friends. I want to know what happened from before she went to bed last night until they noticed she was gone. Somebody's seen something and they need to be giving a statement pronto."

"Fine," said Cullen with a nod.

Bain pointed at Murray and Law. "You two are with us."

They nodded.

Bain walked closer to Cullen. He took a deep breath then spoke in an undertone. "Sundance, we've got that Burns Supper tonight, so I want this wrapped up sharp-ish. I need a shit, shower, shag, shave before we head to Fettes."

"Understood," said Cullen.

Cullen had worked for Bain for close to a year now and knew he hated few things as much as being delayed going to the pub. DCI Turnbull had press-ganged his staff into attending the annual Lothian & Borders Burns Supper because, this year, he was to address the haggis. He wanted as many of his officers there as possible.

The only thing Cullen was looking forward to was that Sharon would be there, though he would much rather be spending the time alone with her.

"What about me?" said Irvine.

"You're supervising here," said Bain. "There are some cottages round the corner. At some point, somebody's brought Mandy here — dead or alive — and somebody must have seen whoever did it."

He rubbed at his moustache. "Batman and Robin here went to see this dog walker. I want her checked out further and visits made to the other cottages. One of the other neighbours goes round the ponds with their dogs every day, get them spoken to."

He thumbed back in the direction they'd come. "Also, that pain in the arse gatehouse at the end of the path, find out where the owners are. Sundance got a story that they're on holiday — get that confirmed."

"Fine," said Irvine. "I'll need some resource."

"You can have McLaren," said Bain.

Cullen noticed Lamb's eyes burn into the side of Bain's head.

"Won't be enough," said Irvine, chomping away.

"Right, come on, then," said Bain, letting out a sigh. "I'll get you some uniform." He led them off towards the largest concentration of idle officers looking for direction.

Lamb was smiling and shaking his head at the retreating figures. "He's quite something, isn't he?"

Cullen grinned. "The stories I could tell about him. I see you've already had your first encounter."

Lamb smiled. "He's a typical city cop. He's come out here, swinging his dick around. He'll come unstuck if he doesn't watch."

Cullen wanted to see that happen. "You been based out here long?"

"Eight years," said Lamb. "I was in Edinburgh before that."

"I was out in Livingston for six years so I kind of know where you're coming from," said Cullen.

"Don't get me wrong, this isn't the Wild West like you're used to. It's very different. A case like this, it's fine having an Edinburgh DI come in but Bain needs all the local co-operation he can get."

"Do you know the Gibson family?" said Cullen.

Lamb smiled again. "You know, you're the first to ask me." He rubbed his moustache again, stroking the triangle of beard downwards. "Charles and Elaine Gibson are pillars of the community in Garleton. Well connected and well off. He runs the Alba Bank branch in town. Two kids, big house, nice cars." He caught himself. "*Had* two kids."

"Do you mind us going to see them?" said Cullen. "What with us being big city cops."

"As long as you don't swing your dicks around," said Lamb, his face creasing into a wide smile.

"I don't have one," said Angela, "though it feels like I need one."

They laughed for a few moments.

"One last thing, though," said Lamb, his face stern. "There's something you should know about Mandy."

"What's that?" said Cullen.

Lamb looked into the middle distance. "She had learning disabilities."

7

Cullen drove them up Berwick Road, the main route from North Berwick into Garleton, his car again struggling with the steep incline. It was six and two threes whether they came that way, through Athelstaneford, or through Drem with its train station, though Angela insisted this was quicker.

They passed the glass and concrete high school, painted the orange that was so common in the older buildings of Musselburgh and Prestonpans.

Cullen stopped at the lights at the start of Garleton High Street, almost at the town's highest point. The engine idled as they waited, cars filtering through and heading towards North Berwick. The day was starting to clear, glimpses of pale blue appearing through the dark grey clouds.

The High Street was busy, mainly full of middle-aged women struggling with shopping baskets. Several bookies lined the road, each one with its very own punter smoking a cigarette outside. Cullen spotted the local Big Issue seller shoving his magazine in the faces of some women as they walked past.

"I'm surprised Bain was given this case," said Angela.

"I'm staggered," said Cullen. "He's lucky to still have a job. I'm just expecting him to go off on one. He's like a volcano — you're just waiting for the inevitable eruption."

She laughed. "Do you think Turnbull trusts him?"

"No idea," said Cullen. "Seems like he's got no other option just now."

DCI Turnbull had recently bolstered his team, bringing in a new DI alongside his existing two. The rumours Cullen heard generally suggested DI Alison Cargill was both a longer-term replacement for Turnbull himself as he moved further upstairs, and an insurance policy to keep Bain under control. Cullen figured Turnbull hadn't taken into account DI Cargill being in Tenerife for two weeks when a murder came up, leaving him the choice of Bain or Wilkinson, neither of whom were exactly covered in glory.

"I suppose we're stuck with him," she said. "Feels like we're in the special needs class."

"I know what you mean," he said, after he stopped laughing. "He's already on the wrong side of Lamb."

"Lamb was right about the big dicks swinging around," she said. "I've got a bad case of penis envy."

The lights finally changed and Cullen turned right down the High Street. Ancient vennels and closes led off, looking exactly like Edinburgh's Royal Mile. The town was perched on the Garleton Hills, cobbled streets stretching from Barnes Castle in the east to Garleton Castle in the west. They passed the modern triptych of a Subway, a McDonalds and a Starbucks alongside a couple of decent-looking old pubs and some upmarket cafés and delis.

One of the oldest buildings in the town, right next to the church, was a branch of Alba Bank. The building next door was painted bright yellow with a rainbow sign above the door — Cullen had no idea how it made it past planning as most of the street was full of listed buildings.

"Straight on at the end," she said.

Cullen turned off the High Street and drove down Dunpender Road. The old buildings gave way to more recent developments, all new builds. Since the eighties, Garleton had rapidly grown from a small village into the sprawling estates they drove past, covering the valley to the north and surrounding the Hopetoun monument.

"You know this area at all?" said Cullen.

"Aye, a bit," said Angela. "We thought of moving out here a

couple of years ago but never bothered."

"Bit of a change from Clermiston," he said.

Angela shrugged. "*He* could never be bothered."

Angela directed them to a new estate just at the edge of the town and they quickly found Dunpender Drive, a long, curving street. Cullen thought the houses were at the luxury end of the market — they weren't all rammed together and had lawns that would need a mid-range petrol mower.

The Gibson house was in the middle of the crescent and appeared to be the largest on the street. The front garden was largely bare — infant trees struggling to grow — and the only feature was a lawn bisected by a pebbled drive.

Two police cars took up the parking bay outside the house, with Bain's Mondeo a few doors down. He pulled in alongside it.

"Lamb sent some uniform round earlier, didn't he?" said Cullen.

"No idea," said Angela.

Cullen shrugged. "Important things first," he said, pointing to the house. "How much?"

"I'm thinking half a million," said Angela.

"I'll say six hundred," he said. "There's at least a hundred grand's worth of car as well."

A BMW X5 sat alongside a silver Audi A6 outside the double garage.

"Can't even get their cars away," she said. "I bet that garage is stuffed full of utter shite."

Cullen gave a chuckle as he unbuckled his seatbelt. "Let's see what our lord and master has been saying to them," he said, hearing a dog barking somewhere nearby.

8

The Gibsons' living room was a colossal space filling roughly a third of the ground floor. There were big feature windows overlooking the front lawn. From the inside, the garden looked minimalist rather than uncared for, as Cullen initially thought. At the rear of the room, the dining table and leather chairs looked out across the back garden, much smaller than the front and dominated by the biggest trampoline Cullen had ever seen. A shaggy-coated sheepdog stood barking at the patio doors, begging to come in.

Bain and Murray perched on the leather sofas opposite Charles and Elaine Gibson. Cullen pulled over two dining chairs for him and Angela.

A teenage boy sat on the other side on a leather armchair, rubbing his eyes with a hankie. He was wearing jeans and a hooded top with some logo Cullen was no longer cool enough to recognise.

PC Jennifer Wallace, the Family Liaison Officer Lamb had sent round, handed them cups of tea. Cullen set his down on a nested table beside Bain's end of the sofa, waiting for it to cool, while Angela cradled hers in her hands.

Bain had been waiting for Cullen to arrive, his leg jigging up and down. "Mr Gibson, I'm deeply sorry for your loss." He paused. "I've got a few questions I need to ask you."

Gibson nodded. He was short and looked mid-fifties, though Cullen wondered if he was younger and had pushed himself through a tough career. His hair was very thin but shaved short rather than off. His eyes were surrounded by dark rings, though Cullen couldn't tell if from crying or general fatigue. He clasped his wife's hand in his, stroking it gently.

"I know this will be hard for you," said Bain, "but can you retrace your steps this morning?"

"Okay," said Gibson, scratching his head. "We were getting the kids down for breakfast. We make sure they eat well before school and we sit down as a family." He pointed towards his son. "Thomas was up first. Mandy didn't appear so I went up to get her. She wasn't in her room."

"We searched the house for her," said Elaine, "but there was no sign. We checked absolutely everywhere."

She looked a lot younger than her husband, but Cullen wondered if she was closer to Charles' age than it initially appeared. She wore expensive casual clothing, Abercrombie & Fitch tracksuit bottoms which no doubt cost the best part of a hundred quid. She was plain looking, though Cullen imagined she hadn't the time or inclination to apply her make-up this morning.

"Who would have been the last person to see Mandy?" said Bain.

"My wife put her to bed at nine last night," said Gibson.

"Do you have any idea how she got out of the house?" said Bain.

Elaine furrowed her brow. "That's the thing. We've no idea how it could have happened again."

"Again?" said Cullen, frowning.

"Well, yes," said Elaine, turning to look at him. "She's run away many times before."

"How many times are we talking here?" said Bain.

Elaine shrugged. "Twenty? Maybe more?"

"Where would she go?" said Cullen.

Elaine sniffed. "Usually to Susan Russell's, her best friend."

Cullen scribbled the name in his notebook. "Does Susan live locally?"

"On Aberlady Lane, just round the corner," she said. "There's a path running down the back of the houses, she usually took that."

"I understand your daughter suffered from learning disabilities?" said Cullen.

Bain scowled at him — Lamb clearly hadn't divulged the information.

Elaine wiped her eye.

Gibson clutched her hand tight. "Yes, Mandy suffered from the condition of learning disability. She wasn't born like that." He swallowed. "We used to live in Edinburgh and... Well, she was a bright young girl, smarter than most at that age. She was run over by a bus. Lucky to survive. She was in hospital for months. The doctor said she'd had a 'brain trauma'. After she was discharged, we decided to make a new start."

"I'm sorry to hear that," said Cullen.

Gibson rubbed at his neck. "I worked at Alba Bank in the centre of Edinburgh, but transferred through to manage the branch here. I was away from home four nights a week and most weekends. I was burning out. After the accident, Elaine and I reappraised our lifestyle. Elaine left her job to look after Mandy."

"Excuse me," said Elaine, getting up, her hand clutched to her face as she left the room. The back door slammed soon after.

"This has hit my wife hard," said Gibson, pinching his brow.

"I'm sure it must be very difficult for you both," said Bain, no note of empathy in his voice, just the same even tone he normally used in situations like these.

"Believe me, it is," said Gibson.

Bain nodded. "What about your son?" he said, pointing towards Thomas. "Was he up late or anything? Could he have let someone in?"

Gibson violently shook his head. "Absolutely not. Thomas was early to bed last night, as with every Sunday." He looked over at the boy. "Tell them."

"I was in bed at half nine," said the teenager, in a deep voice. "I was reading my Kindle."

Bain nodded then paused for a few seconds. "Is it possible Mandy could have been abducted?"

Gibson's forehead creased. "I don't think so. I mean, I don't think anybody came in the house last night. I'm a light sleeper and I would have heard."

"Could it have been a kidnap attempt?" said Cullen. "You obviously have a lot of money — expensive house, expensive cars. You're a bank manager, which is a job that can lead to extortion. We need to consider the possibility your daughter was abducted due to your position."

Gibson sat back on the sofa, reclining it slightly. "Being a branch manager isn't like it used to be. It's a sales role these days. I manage product targets and some very junior staff. I don't have autonomy to give loans or mortgages on the golf course. That's all handled centrally. There's no big safe or bank vault only I can access."

Cullen noted it all down, the look on Bain's face not making him want to press it any further.

"After you noticed Mandy wasn't there, what did you do next?" said Bain.

"It's all a bit of a blur, really," said Gibson. "I remember looking around the house, in the attic, in the garden, in the garages. Elaine made me go up to the Russells' to see if she was there. But she wasn't. That's when we called the police."

"And the body turned up an hour or so later?" said Cullen.

"I'm afraid so, yes," said Gibson.

"And it definitely is Mandy?" said Cullen.

Gibson exhaled. "I was up at the ponds this morning. I saw her body. It's her."

"What did you do yesterday?" said Bain.

"In the afternoon, we went to East Links Country Park by Dunbar," said Gibson. "Mandy loved patting the animals." He looked at Thomas. "Her poor brother was bored to tears by this, of course, but we wanted to keep Mandy happy. He spent the afternoon playing *Angry Birds* on his phone. We then had our Sunday dinner, roast chicken with all the trimmings. Mandy's favourite but she could never manage to eat much."

"And before that?" said Bain, stroking his moustache.

"We went to church as a family," said Gibson.

"Is that the Church of Scotland on the High Street?" said Cullen.

Gibson smiled. "No, we're no longer members of the parish there. We attend the God's Rainbow group."

"Never heard of it," said Bain.

"I noticed a rainbow on a building on the High Street," said Cullen.

Gibson's eyes lit up. "It teaches us a way to live in the modern world. It takes elements of Christianity and Judaism and exposes the truth in all the Gospels."

"How big is this group?" said Cullen.

"It's just based in Garleton at present," said Gibson, "though we do have plans to expand."

Cullen frowned. "We?"

"I'm training to become a minister in the church," said Gibson. "I feel I have committed sins in my profession as a banker. I need to cleanse them more substantially than I do with my one-on-one sessions with Father Mulgrew. I want to help take our word to the wider world — Father Mulgrew intends to move away from this parish and set up in another town. East Linton is the current favourite."

"And Father Mulgrew is the minister at this God's Rainbow?" said Cullen.

Gibson paused for a second. "Father Seamus Mulgrew is the head of our church, if that's what you mean."

Gibson gave them an address for Mulgrew.

"And did anything unusual happen during the service?" said Cullen.

Gibson twitched. "No, it was perfectly normal, I'm afraid."

Elaine Gibson reappeared at that point, her face flushed. She was accompanied by the dog, wagging its tail furiously — it ran over to Cullen and started sniffing him. Elaine sat down next to her husband, cuddling in tight. "I'm sorry. This is proving a bit too much for me."

"Can I ask both of you if there is anyone you think wanted to harm your daughter?" said Bain.

Gibson screwed his face up and let out a sigh. "Define what you mean by harm," he said, almost in an undertone.

"Your daughter has turned up in a shallow grave three miles from her house," said Bain, "can you think of anyone who would wish to do that to her?"

"The only person I could even consider as being responsible for this would be Jamie Cook," said Gibson.

"Charles," said Elaine, her eyes wide. "Robert and Wilma are our friends, how could you consider accusing their son of this?"

"I could accuse that boy of bloody anything," said Gibson. He looked at Bain. "He is the local problem child."

"Is he capable of murder?" said Bain.

"Capable of anything," said Gibson.

"Anybody else?" said Bain.

Gibson shook his head slowly. "We make sure we don't wrong anyone. Jamie makes sure he wrongs everyone."

Elaine Gibson shrunk back into the sofa.

"Fine," said Bain, checking his watch. "I'm expecting Scene of Crime Officers here soon."

"Is that strictly necessary?" said Gibson.

Bain nodded. "We need to be extremely rigorous with this investigation. We can't rule anything out at this stage. I'm sure you want your daughter's killer brought to justice."

"But we're a family in mourning," said Gibson.

"There'll be plenty of time for that later," said Bain. "Right now, the priority is looking for any tell-tale signs of intrusion here. As it stands, we don't know how your daughter disappeared from her bedroom."

"She probably ran away," said Gibson.

"I'm not a man who takes probably for an answer," said Bain.

Cullen almost shook his head in disbelief. If ever there was a police officer who enacted entire vendettas on the flimsiest premise it was Bain.

Bain looked over at Elaine Gibson. "Would you be able to show DC Cullen around Mandy's bedroom?"

9

Cullen pulled the curtain aside and looked out at the garden. Mandy's room faced the back, looking south. The ground sloped up from the house to the Hopetoun monument, a local landmark visible all the way from Edinburgh.

The window was shut tight and locked with no sign of the key. He turned to focus on the room.

Elaine Gibson stood in the doorway, arms folded, looking like she was going to break down again at any moment.

Cullen didn't particularly want anyone with him at that point, but he had to follow Bain's instructions. "Do you know where the key to the window is?"

"It's in the safe in our room," she said. "It's still there, I have checked."

Mandy's room was bigger than any bedroom Cullen had ever been in. It was decorated in pink and looked more like it belonged to a six or seven year old, with rainbows and trees stencilled on the wall in thick paint. There were a few My Little Pony posters on the wall — he'd recently read about them becoming popular again, particularly with a weird faction of adult men.

The bed had clearly been slept in — the purple duvet pulled back, revealing the crumpled pink bed sheet and purple pillow. The rest of the duvet was covered in teddy bears — most of them Disney branded.

"You put her to bed last night?" said Cullen.

Elaine nodded. "She was like a five year old. She always needed a story to get to sleep. She could sleep through anything."

"When she gets out, is she sleepwalking?" said Cullen.

"No," she said. "She seems to be awake and fully aware of what's going on. I'm sure you can imagine how difficult it was with that happening in the middle of the night."

"How long has she been doing this?" said Cullen.

"It's going back a while now," she said. "Maybe eighteen months."

"It's not exactly normal behaviour," said Cullen.

"Mandy wasn't a normal girl," said Elaine.

"Do you have any idea why she was doing it?" said Cullen.

Elaine glared at him. "Since her accident, she's not exactly behaved herself." She exhaled. "We have been to behavioural psychologists. Nobody could get to the bottom of it."

"Could you give us the names of the people you spoke to?" he said.

She frowned. "Why?"

Cullen smiled. "You heard my boss downstairs. With a case like this, we can't rule anything out."

"I'll see what I can find," she said.

"What have you done to stop her getting out?" he said.

"What haven't we tried?" said Elaine with a sigh.

"Have you put a lock on her door?" said Cullen.

She closed her eyes. "My daughter wasn't some animal in the zoo."

"I still can't see how she escaped," said Cullen.

"She was very mischievous," she said. "She would steal a key and hide it from us."

Cullen noted it down.

"Is there anything else?" she said.

Cullen took a long look around the room. Her school uniform sat on a chair in front of a dressing table, her small leather satchel hanging off the back. "Let's get back downstairs."

～

IN THE COOL JANUARY AIR, Elaine Gibson opened the gate and led them down the path. She was wrapped up tight in a ski jacket, a thick scarf around her neck. It had been raining all day but just recently stopped, the grey clouds still ominously cruising overhead.

Bain had instructed Cullen to retrace Mandy's likely steps, taking Thomas, Law and Angela with him.

The small lane ran from the midway point in the arc of Dunpender Drive to the end of Aberlady Lane, six-foot-tall wooden fences lining both sides. The tarmac pavement underfoot was a mush of rotten leaves from the now bare oaks.

"Is this the only way?" said Cullen, as they slowly walked on, keeping eyes open for anything useful.

"It's the most direct," said Elaine. "You could go down the main road and double back, but it's a long way round. The other way is around the park, but this is the quickest route there."

"We usually walk Monkey this way," said Thomas, his expression unreadable.

"Is Monkey your dog?" said Law.

"He is," said Thomas. "Mandy named him." He turned away from them.

The path twisted to the right just ahead, with a gate straight in front of them.

"Does this path lead to the park?" said Cullen.

"It does," said Elaine. "We let Monkey off there for a run."

"And you caught Mandy running away down this path?" said Cullen.

Elaine nodded. "I was really worried she was sleepwalking and going down the main road. It was somehow reassuring that she took a safe route."

"I assume the doors to your house were all locked?" said Cullen.

"Yes," said Elaine. "Charles and I have a set of keys each and Thomas has a front door key. She still managed to get out."

"There weren't keys in the door last night, were there?" said Cullen.

"No."

"As far as I'm aware, we haven't found a set of keys on Mandy's person," said Cullen.

"I can only think the door must have been left open last night,"
said Elaine.

"But it was locked this morning?" said Cullen.

Elaine stopped in the path by the gate. "It was."

An elderly couple walked slowly down the path, heading away
from them.

Cullen hoped Bain was having more joy with Charles Gibson.
He pointed at the street beyond the gate, lined with houses that
were similarly sized — if not as grand — as those on the Gibsons'
road. "Is that where Susan lives?"

Elaine nodded. "Number seven."

"Would you mind introducing us?" said Cullen.

"Certainly," said Elaine, though she gave a sigh after her
answer.

Cullen opened the gate and let Elaine head through, holding it
open for Law to catch. She smiled warmly at Cullen — he let his
gaze linger a bit too long.

Thomas called out.

Cullen turned around to see Elaine running towards a small
continuation of path to the side. He followed. She was kneeling
about twenty feet from the gate, clutching something.

"What is it?" said Cullen.

Elaine's eyes were streaming, her body racked with sobs. She
rocked back and forth, holding something tight to her.

Thomas spoke up. "It's Mandy's favourite teddy bear."

10

———

Cullen eventually managed to prise the teddy bear from Elaine's clutches. He put on a pair of protective gloves, though he feared any forensic traces would be lost to the onslaught of rain.

It was a large brown bear, very classic looking, something from an earlier age unlike the many Disney tie-ins in Mandy's room. He turned it over looking for clues, but couldn't find anything. It was just a bear.

Elaine was on her feet now, still in floods of tears. Angela had her arm around her shoulder, slowly patting her back. Thomas stood beside them, unsure what to do. Cullen thought he was trying to look mature, but occasionally he caught glimpses of emotion tearing the boy's face apart.

"What shall we do?" said Law.

Cullen realised he was the most senior of the three officers present. While they were all constables, he was the only fully fledged detective, which only gave him a semblance of seniority. He looked back down the lane and tried to think.

A middle-aged woman opened the gate at the far end, struggling through with her dog. A million thoughts raced through his head — how had nobody seen the bear? The path looked like it was fairly well used and it led from a populous part of the town to a park.

How had nobody spotted anything?

How had nobody seen Mandy?

He took a deep breath and made a decision. "Can you take the Gibsons back home?" he said, looking at Law. "I want to speak to someone in the Russells' house."

Law raised an eyebrow. "Got a thing going with ADC Caldwell, have you?" she said, a grin on her face.

Cullen shook his head. "No, I don't. And don't listen to what Bain might say, either."

Law smiled. "Is she not your type?"

"Something like that," he said, smiling.

Law bit her lip. "So you know where they live?"

"Number seven, according to Elaine Gibson," said Cullen.

"I'll let you get on, then," said Law.

"You're okay doing this?" said Cullen.

Law patted his shoulder. "Used to be a Community Officer. Second nature to me."

THE RUSSELL HOUSE wasn't in the same league as the Gibsons' but it was still way out of the price bracket Cullen could ever afford, even if he made DCI.

"Awful business," said Cath Russell.

She was a big woman. Her rich voice had a strong Highland accent, reminding Cullen of an English teacher he had in school.

Cullen and Angela sat in her conservatory, located at the back of the house and looking across an immaculate, if small, garden — the lawn looked perfect even in winter. Cullen noticed another conservatory — he could barely understand one, but having two with such a small plot puzzled him. Even in January, the heat in the room was stifling and he noticed the radiators were on full blast.

Angela cleared her throat. "I believe you helped Charles and Elaine Gibson hunt for Mandy this morning."

"Indeed I did," said Cath. "My husband, Paul, had already left for work but I helped them search for her. Poor wee soul."

"They said Mandy has run away before and ended up here?" said Angela. "Is that true?"

Cath nodded. "Quite a few times," she said, sitting forward and clasping her hands together. "Mandy was friends with my Susan. I say friends, but poor Mandy wasn't particularly capable of the sort of friendship Susan requires. She's a very bright girl, you know, very advanced for her age."

"So what sort of friendship did they have?" said Angela.

"Well, because of the way Mandy *was*," said Cath, taking care with her wording, "it was less a friendship and more like Susan had a younger sister — much younger. Mandy really looked up to Susan."

"And they were in the same year at school?" said Angela.

"Well, yes," said Cath. "But you must remember Susan was in the top class for all her subjects and poor Mandy was in the special needs class. So really they were only in the same class for a few subjects. PE, religious education, that sort of thing."

"Can you explain why Mandy came here?" said Cullen.

"I've no idea," said Cath.

"No idea at all?"

"All I can think is she wanted to see Susan," said Cath, with a shrug. "My daughter is a very nurturing soul and Mandy must have been drawn to that. She's very much like me in that sense."

Cullen almost choked. "How many times has she come here during the night?"

"It was about once a month on average," said Cath.

"And when did it start?" said Cullen.

"Oh, now you're asking," said Cath. "I would say it was probably late summer twenty ten."

"So eighteen months ago?" said Cullen.

Cath nodded. "That would be about right."

Cullen felt his phone vibrate in his pocket but he let it ring out. "Was there any trouble at home, do you know?"

Cath scowled. "Heavens, no," she said, her voice high and lilting. "They were very loving towards Mandy. After what happened in Edinburgh, well, it would have driven most families apart, but it seemed to make Charles and Elaine even stronger."

"Does your daughter know what has happened to Mandy?" said Cullen.

"No, not yet," said Cath, biting her lip. "She's at school today.

I'll tell her after school but I don't want this harming her education."

Cullen glanced at Angela, who was virtually rolling her eyes. "I can understand that. Would I be able to see her after school?"

Cath nodded. "She usually gets home at the back of four."

"Would it be possible to speak to your husband?" said Angela.

Cath frowned. "As I said earlier, Paul had left for work by the time Charles came here."

"We'd still like to speak to him," said Cullen.

Cath turned her lip up. "I suggest I get him to turn up at whichever police station you're working from."

"We're based in Garleton while this case is ongoing," said Cullen.

"Then I'll send him there."

11

"Fat lot of good that was," said Angela, as they walked back along the lane to the Gibsons' house. "Can't believe how up herself she was. My daughter this, my daughter that. I'm a very nurturing soul."

Cullen nodded. "Other than getting corroboration of the Gibsons' story, it just made me glad not to live in a place like this."

"Yeah, but Portobello's not exactly amazing, is it?" she said.

"I'll hopefully not be there forever."

Angela winked at him. "Have you and Sharon been looking?"

This again, thought Cullen. "No, we haven't," he said. He'd been looking for a flat for two years, continually priced out of the market either by rising house prices or rising deposits. The market was finally stabilising just as he and Sharon were getting serious. He had so far managed to evade Angela's questions but that wouldn't stop the station gossip.

"Aren't things going well?" she said.

Cullen shrugged. "I wouldn't know. This is uncharted territory for me. I usually get up, wipe my cock on the curtains and float off into the night."

"What about a roller blind?"

"No way. A boy's got to have standards." They laughed. "In all seriousness, things are going well. I'm a bit surprised, to be honest."

"What, all that stuff with that girl you were supposed to be seeing?" she said.

Cullen closed his eyes. "We don't talk about that."

He had tried to forget about it. It continually staggered him how messy he could make his life, but there it was. He'd saved the life of a girl who shared a flat with his ex. In truth, his actions had put her in danger so saving her was the least he could do.

It made his early relationship with Sharon difficult and, even almost six months in, she still didn't quite trust him. He couldn't blame her, but he tried to gain her trust at every opportunity.

"So why are you surprised?" said Angela.

"Just the curtains thing, I suppose," said Cullen. "I mean I wanted to settle down, I just didn't see it being with Sharon, that's all."

"You mean you don't see yourself settling down with her?" said Angela.

Cullen wagged a finger at her. "That's not what I meant, so this goes nowhere near her. I didn't see myself going out with her. Nothing to do with her, more with me."

"But things are fine?" said Angela.

"Of course," said Cullen. "Better than I could have hoped." He opened the gate back onto Dunpender Drive, stepping aside to let a young mother with a buggy through. "Why are you asking?"

"Oh, no reason." Angela grinned. "It's just ADC Law hasn't taken her eyes off you."

Cullen halted. "Stop it right now. I'm not interested."

"Okay, just passing on what I noticed," said Angela, a smirk on her face.

"Well, if that's the game you're playing," said Cullen, "DS Lamb was taking an interest in you. Maybe he likes giants."

Angela shook her head. "Very funny. A lot of small men go in for tall girls like me."

"Yeah, I wonder what goes on in their heads," said Cullen. "How tall is your husband?"

"Six five," she said.

"Fair enough."

Cullen checked the missed call he received when they were speaking to Cath Russell — predictably, it was Bain. He dialled the number and held the phone away from his ear.

"If you see the caller display with my name on it," said Bain, "you fuckin' answer it, okay?"

"We were with someone," said Cullen.

"I don't care if you were with the fuckin' Queen, all right?" said Bain. "If you see my name, you answer."

"What did you want, sir?" said Cullen.

"Where are you?"

"Just about back at the Gibson house," said Cullen.

"Right, I'll see you outside then."

"Thanks," said Cullen to a dead phone line.

Angela looked over at him. "That sounded like it went well."

"Typical Bain," said Cullen.

They approached the house, noticing there were even more cars than when they left. He hoped Anderson and the other SOCOs were going through Mandy's room with a fine-tooth comb.

Cullen recognised PC Wallace, the Gibsons' FLO, chatting to ADC Law, standing on the gravel outside, far enough away from the house to avoid being overheard.

"Anything been happening here?" said Cullen.

Law smiled at him. "Scene of Crime have just turned up. I handed the teddy bear over to Anderson, Bain didn't seem interested."

Cullen was glad to avoid another interaction with Anderson. "What's Bain been up to?"

"Running around like a blue-arsed fly," said Law.

Cullen nodded. "That's what he does best."

"They've started going door-to-door," said Law. "Bain's got Murray out with a squadron of uniform."

"Why aren't you out with them?" said Cullen.

"I must have missed the opportunity when I was away with you," said Law. "What do you want me to do?"

Cullen clocked a grin on Angela's face, his glare only worsening it. "Bain should be here any minute." He looked at Wallace. "You got anything to report?"

"I was out with his wife just there and watched her tear through half a deck of fags," said Wallace, her voice coarse, as if she smoked forty a day herself. "She's torn to shreds."

"Well, you would be," said Angela, almost in an undertone but loud enough for Wallace to hear.

"You going to keep an eye on them?" said Cullen.

"Yeah, been told to by Lamb," said Wallace. "Cups of tea, bit of TLC here and there." She gave a conspiratorial grin. "I'll keep my eyes and ears open. I'll not take the piss either. They'll want shot of me at some point."

"Do you suspect them?" said Law, her blue eyes staring at Cullen.

"Not at the moment. Bain wants to make sure there's nothing funny going on here."

Wallace nodded. "He tried to convert me, you know. Asked if my sins were absolved."

Cullen checked his watch. 12.18. He shook his head in disbelief. "His daughter's body hasn't been found four hours and he's already trying to convert people to his religion."

Wallace raised her eyebrows. "You know what that lot are like. They get pretty funny about death."

"Anything else?" said Cullen.

Wallace shook her head.

Cullen handed her his card. "Okay, well, let me or Lamb know if anything happens, okay?"

Wallace nodded then trotted back along the path into the house.

Cullen looked down the street, still no sign of Bain. The clouds were already darkening again. He had half a mind to get his overcoat from his car.

"You religious, Scott?" said Angela.

"No."

"Thought you would be, what with you being a sheep shagger," said Angela. "It's all Calvinism and stuff up your way, isn't it?"

"Aye, but my old man was a punk," said Cullen, "no way was he taking his kids to church."

Angela and Law laughed. Cullen thought Law was laughing a bit too hard, trying to impress. Maybe Angela was right — he really needed to stop it, whatever it was he was doing.

"How about you?" he said. "Are you a bible basher?"

"*He* is," said Angela. "I had to convert to Catholicism to get married and everything, not that he bothers much, but his family's mental for it."

Cullen thought he would escape that with Sharon if it ever

went that far — her parents were religious only on a token basis, like an insurance policy for the afterlife.

"What about you?" said Angela.

Law frowned. "No, not at all."

"What do you know about this group?" said Cullen.

"God's Rainbow?" said Law, curling her hair behind her left ear, trying to hold it in place. "Don't really know much about them. Bill had to lift some wee ned from there on Saturday night for pissing against the wall." She caught Angela's look. "Unlike you city cops, we have to help out with rowdy Saturday nights sometimes. It was Port Seton for me on Saturday, but I'd much rather have been here."

Cullen nodded. "Charles Gibson mentioned a Jamie Cook earlier. You ever come across him?"

Law gave a mischievous wink. "Jamie Cook was the ned pissing against the side of the church."

Cullen heard Bain approach from behind.

"How come you've always got birds around you, Sundance?" said Bain. "I need to get some of that magic to rub off on me."

Angela raised an eyebrow.

"Well done for finding a cuddly toy," said Bain, shaking his head. "It's like the fuckin' *Generation Game* with you, Sundance."

"It looks like Mandy was abducted while she ran down the lane," said Cullen. "I'd say that's a result."

"Aye, looks like isn't good enough," said Bain. "While you've been trying to get a threesome with this pair, I've been out getting some proper police work done, the sort of shite a DC and a pair of ADCs should have been doing."

Cullen didn't know what to say in response.

Bain finally looked at Law and Angela. "Ladies, I think we've got a lead."

"What is it?" said Angela.

"DC Murray's been around a couple of the Gibsons' neighbours," said Bain. "Charles Gibson's car left the house at half past ten last night. I've just been putting the frighteners up this woman, making sure she's not trying to frame him for some neighbourly shite about falling asleep at a dinner party or chopping a tree down."

"Have you spoken to Gibson?" said Cullen.

"Just now, aye," said Bain. "He says he was off seeing this Father Mulgrew character."

"Do you want us to go round there?" said Cullen.

Bain grinned. "Can you check it out for me? Saves me a trip."

"Will do," said Cullen.

Law butted in. "Elaine Gibson gave me the name of a psychologist they took Mandy to. Do you want me to give her a call?"

"Good effort," said Bain. "Keep me up to date."

Cullen frowned — he'd dragged that out of them and here she was, taking the credit for it.

Bain spun around again to look at Cullen. "So what have you pair actually been up to?"

Cullen talked him through the notes he'd just taken at Cath Russell's.

"So nothing, then?" said Bain.

"She confirmed how long these midnight disappearances have been going on," said Cullen. "And Mandy didn't make it round there last night. From the teddy bear, it looks like she was intercepted on her way."

Bain nodded and scratched his head for a few seconds. "Right, Sundance, what does your genius brain say, then?"

Cullen bit his tongue. "I think there are a couple of things we need to look into. If we take Gibson at face value, Mandy was put to bed last night and somehow escaped. We've no idea how. The doors were all locked."

"Aye, that's a funny business," said Bain. "I think I need to chin Gibson about that one as well."

"I think we should go to the school," said Cullen. "I want to speak to Susan Russell and Mandy's teacher, maybe a few other kids."

"You know there are websites for schoolgirl fetishes, Sundance?" said Bain.

Cullen shook his head. "Can you stop? I want to see if there are any leads we can pick up there."

"Why, do you think there will be?" said Bain.

"There might," said Cullen.

Bain looked away. "No."

"What do you mean, 'no'?" said Cullen.

"I mean I don't want you going there," said Bain.

"But—"

"But nothing, Sundance," said Bain. "Speak to this Mulgrew character and do some digging there, then report back to me. You're on a tight leash."

"Fine," said Cullen, folding his arms.

"Anything else, genius?" said Bain.

"One other thing," said Cullen, trying to keep his voice level. "We need to think about whether Mandy was abducted because of Charles Gibson's job."

"Are you still going on about that?" said Bain.

"Yes," said Cullen, slowly and reluctantly.

"Cullen, this isn't *Die Hard*, you know," said Bain. "You're not John McClane and you're not looking at someone abducting bankers or their kids."

"Are you sure you want to exclude it?" said Cullen through gritted teeth.

Bain exhaled. "Fine, I'll get the most junior officer I can find to think about it and do nothing with it."

12

Cullen parked outside Mulgrew's house, a small cottage on the town's southern outskirts. He suspected the surrounding fields would be ripe for future development. The cottages must once have belonged to a farm, its land now subsumed into the rapidly expanding town. Mulgrew's house was the end cottage of a row lining Haddington Road. The cottage didn't look in great repair, in stark contrast to the gleaming new builds of the Gibsons and Russells. The lintel above the downstairs window was cracked and several of the stones on the house's corner were badly decaying.

The adjacent Bangley Road led into the middle of the town and was lined with grey-harled houses, the sort Cullen had seen all over Scotland. There were a few drives and avenues cutting off from the street. If a train line ran through the town, thought Cullen, this would definitely be the wrong side of the tracks.

Looking down the street, Cullen saw a few kids hanging around, a couple mucking about on BMX bikes. They should be in school. He had half a mind to go and cause some havoc to compensate for how pissed off he felt.

"Shall we go in?" said Angela.

Cullen looked at her. "Aye, I'll lead," he said, setting off down the path, the garden teetering on the brink of becoming overgrown. A decaying Volvo estate, which he guessed was older than him, sat on the drive.

Cullen had to knock four times before the door was pulled open with some force.

An old man stood on the threshold, short and stooped over, wearing red trousers and a plaid shirt.

"Yes?" he said, with a scowl.

"Seamus Mulgrew?" said Cullen.

"Father Seamus Mulgrew, if you will," he said in a thick Irish accent, as he offered a hand and a smile. "And you are?"

Cullen brandished his warrant card. "DC Scott Cullen, Lothian & Borders Police. This is ADC Angela Caldwell. We'd like to speak to you in connection with the death of an Amanda Gibson, known as Mandy."

"Mandy?" said Mulgrew, frowning.

"You know her?" said Cullen.

Mulgrew nodded quickly. "She's dead?"

"She was found this morning at Balgone Ponds," said Cullen.

Mulgrew stared at Cullen, his eyes not quite focusing on him. "I know the place."

"Can we come in?" said Cullen.

"Yes, yes," said Mulgrew, and led them in.

He ushered them through a narrow hall with an even tighter wooden staircase. The living room was a small dusty room containing a dark green three-piece suite, crammed in beside a battered old writing bureau.

There was a door to a kitchenette, a term Cullen's gran used and the only way he could describe the tiny space. Beige Formica units and wood-effect panelling surrounded a small stove and a porcelain sink, with a counter-top fridge that looked older than the house.

"From your accent, I take it you're not from around here?" said Cullen.

"No, you're right there," said Mulgrew. "I'm from the Emerald Isle, as they say."

"And you were in the church there?" said Cullen.

Mulgrew took a deep breath. "Yes, well, I was. Eventually, I chose a different path from a strict Papal one and I'm much happier for it. I'm doing the Lord's work now, rather than the Pope's. I thank him for the skills I learnt in the church but I had to do what was true to God."

"And you still choose to use the title of Father?" said Cullen.

"I've not renounced any of my vows to the Lord," said Mulgrew, "so I shall keep my title."

"Can you tell us about Mandy Gibson," said Cullen, "and your relationship with her?"

"Well, she was a nice, sweet girl," said Mulgrew, looking wistful. "She always seemed so happy and eager to please. Her parents are such dear people. Her father, Charles, is training as my protégé."

"So I gather," said Cullen.

"Mandy did have her problems, though," said Mulgrew.

"What sort of problems?" said Cullen.

"Well, there were demons in that girl," said Mulgrew, frowning.

"I thought she had a learning disability," said Cullen.

"No, no, no, she was weak," said Mulgrew, "and that weakness had let Satan enter her body, letting countless of his hordes of demons in."

Cullen struggled to listen to what he was saying but wrote it down verbatim nonetheless.

"Her family asked me to assist," said Mulgrew, "but it was pushing even my skills with the occult, I can assure you."

"Can you elaborate on these skills?" said Cullen.

"Certainly," said Mulgrew, briefly closing his eyes. "As a member of the Roman Catholic church, I was ordained in the ways of the occult — witchcraft, exorcisms, that sort of thing. There was a very select group of priests who were allowed access to this knowledge and given these skills, you know? I was among that group."

"Did you ever practice these skills on Mandy?" said Cullen.

"Just counselling," said Mulgrew. "It's a non-invasive therapy and all I practice these days."

Cullen flicked through his notebook, looking at the notes he'd taken at the Gibsons' house. "Can you tell me about this God's Rainbow group you're involved in?"

Mulgrew sat up in his chair. "I'm not merely involved, you

know," he said, his eyes glowing. "I run the group. I write the services, I wrote our own bible and I have a series of publications to educate our parish on the perils of modern life. I'm very proud of my work and I know the Lord is too."

"And do you make much money out of this?" said Angela.

"I'm a man of frugal means as you can see," said Mulgrew gesturing around the room. "It's how God wants us to live, you know?"

Cullen didn't say anything.

"The group is self-funding and not for profit," said Mulgrew. "We have plans for expansion, to bring our word to the wider world." He looked at Angela. "The group has more than just a Christian viewpoint. It takes God's word from multiple texts — Christian, Jewish, Islamic — and we spread it far and wide. We select everything where the true word of God is to be found."

"And how would you know what's true and what's not?" said Cullen.

Mulgrew grinned at him. "Not a religious man, are you?"

Cullen casually shrugged. "Not really, no."

"Well, let me tell you something," said Mulgrew, leaning forward on his armchair and putting the tips of his fingers together. "God made us in his own image. It follows that anything that is true to him should ring true in us. If you feel it's true in your heart then it's true."

"So why did you decide to branch out into your own sect?" said Cullen.

Mulgrew screwed his face up. "*Sect* is such an objectionable word."

"Okay," said Cullen, "why did you feel the need to set up your own group?"

Cullen caught Angela scowling and wondered if he was pushing things too far.

"Have you heard the term 'apostasy', Constable?" said Mulgrew, looking down his long, thick nose.

"Not really," said Cullen.

"And you?" said Mulgrew, looking at Angela.

"No."

"Okay." Mulgrew slowly rubbed his hands together. "Apostasy

is the idea that the mainstream Christian religions have lost touch with the teachings of Jesus Christ, and have incorporated many pagan ideas to subsume the masses."

"What would an example of that be?" said Cullen, interest piqued.

"Christmas."

"Christmas?" said Angela.

Mulgrew laughed. "Jesus, son of Joseph, was born in April, not December. The early Roman Catholic church, once the Emperor Constantine converted the Roman Empire to Christianity, used the December date to replace pre-existing pagan feasts in the wild lands of Northern Europe."

He gestured at Angela. "Another example would be the role of women in the church. The Roman Catholic church excised countless original Books of the Bible, most importantly the Gospels of Mary and Judas, which gave very different accounts of the life of our Lord and they edited those they kept, in order to indoctrinate the masses."

"So why include Jewish and Muslim texts?" said Cullen.

Mulgrew beamed again. "Jesus Christ was born and raised a Jewish man, so to exclude that from our work would be to reduce the context. It's also a little known fact that Jesus Christ was a prophet in the Koran. It gives further insight into the work of our Lord."

There was a period of silence in the room as Cullen and Angela digested what Mulgrew said. Cullen had encountered lots of strange schools of thought during his career but he had never come across anything like this. This was new, some unique mutation of mainstream religion thriving out in East Lothian, hidden from the rest of the world.

"I see," said Cullen. "How do you find the group is working out?"

"Well, this is a good place to start," said Mulgrew, looking at the filthy glass of the front window. "There are a lot of bad people in this area."

Cullen thought back to many conversations he'd had with Sharon's sister. "I'd heard Garleton was a good area. It's got the best school in East Lothian."

"Well, that's only one side of it," said Mulgrew, looking back. "There are some very bad kids here."

Cullen recalled a name from Charles Gibson. "Would Jamie Cook be one of these bad kids?"

Mulgrew held his breath for a few seconds. "Jamie Cook is the son of two of our parishioners," he said, looking down at the carpet. "Dear, dear people. I don't really want to speak ill of the boy." He paused. "I'm afraid to say he has the Devil in him."

"In the same way Mandy Gibson had?" said Cullen.

Mulgrew loudly exhaled through his nose. "No, I'm afraid you misunderstand me. Mandy had a demon in her. Jamie Cook is an entirely different matter. The boy has the Devil himself in him." As he spoke, his voice had risen, like he was in the pulpit.

"I'll have to take you at your word," said Cullen.

"Believe you me, I had to excise him from the group to avoid his poison spreading further," said Mulgrew.

"Could he have been involved in Mandy's death?" said Cullen, recalling Gibson's earlier suggestion.

Mulgrew nodded. "If you're looking for someone involved with wee Mandy's death then Jamie Cook would be a good place to start," he said, his voice a soft whisper.

Cullen noted it down. "Is there anything in particular about him?"

"There are no specifics, no," said Mulgrew, looking away.

Cullen jotted the name and address down. "Would he have had access to Mandy?"

"I'm not so sure," said Mulgrew. "You'd need to check with Mandy's poor, poor parents."

Cullen leaned forward in his chair. "One final thing I'd like to ask. We believe Charles Gibson visited here last night."

"That's correct," said Mulgrew.

"What time was this?" said Cullen.

"It would be roughly half past ten," said Mulgrew.

"And what was the purpose of the meeting?" said Cullen.

"As I told you earlier, Charles is my protégé," said Mulgrew. "We have ad hoc coaching and mentoring, as required by Charles' needs. He's on a very intensive programme and I hope to expand the group into another parish soon, with him taking over Garleton."

He cleared his throat. "Last night, his family went to bed and he came here to discuss some of the more technical points of the service that morning, to ensure he had as comprehensive an understanding as possible. After all, one day Garleton will be his."

Cullen noted it down — he had no idea what to make of it.

13

They stood by Cullen's car outside Mulgrew's cottage.

Cullen shook his head. "What did you think of that?"

"Interesting," said Angela. "All roads lead to Jamie Cook."

"They seem to," said Cullen.

He looked down the street. The kids were still there, the BMXers circling the others, all laughing and joking. Two of them got up from a play fight.

"Come on," he said, and marched down the street towards them.

The nearest one squared up to Cullen as he approached, even though he was about a foot shorter. He looked about fifteen, though his cheeks were already starting to sink down. There were seven of them sitting on the kerb. They wore hooded tops of various colours, hoods all up.

"Shouldn't you be in school?" said Cullen.

"What's it to do with you?" said the youth. He put his hand down his trousers, cupping his balls like some Harlem or South Central gangster. His trousers hung low, showing off the top of white trunks. The way Cullen was feeling after the encounters with Mulgrew and Bain, he had half a mind to pull them up.

"You should be in school," said Cullen.

"What are you going to do about it?" said the youth.

Cullen flashed his warrant card. "Detective Constable Scott Cullen. I can cause a lot of trouble for you."

"What do you want to know?" said the youth.

"Do you know who lives in the cottage at the end?"

The youth grunted and nodded his head. "Aye, it's Father Mulgrew. Freaky old radge. Can't stand us."

Cullen couldn't imagine why. "Do you ever have any run-ins with him?"

"Keep well away from that punter," said the youth.

"Why?" said Cullen.

The youth snorted. "My old boy told us to keep away from him."

"So you've never had any dealings with him?" said Cullen.

The youth grinned. "I'm not a dealer, pal."

Cullen smiled. "I meant have you ever spoken to him?"

"Only time was when he was out preaching his gospel at us a few weeks ago," said the youth.

"Why would he do that?" said Cullen.

The youth shrugged. "No idea why he picked on us." He snorted again then spat on the ground. "The cops were out here, somebody had their windows panned in."

"Was it you?" said Cullen.

"Was it fuck," said the youth, smiling towards his mates.

"But he thought it was you?" said Cullen.

"Must have done," said the youth.

"Do you know a Jamie Cook?" said Cullen.

"Aye," said the youth. "He's sound, like. A good lad."

"Do you know him well?" said Cullen.

"Pretty well."

"Any idea where he is?" said Cullen.

"Not doing your dirty work for you."

"Right," said Cullen. "I'll send a car round here this afternoon. I expect all of you to be in school by then."

The youth took a step back, looking Cullen up and down. "Aye, right."

"I mean it," said Cullen, pointing a finger at him. He turned away, leading Angela back to the car, his heart thudding from the encounter.

"Feel the big man now?" said Angela.

"Just checking out some background on Mulgrew," said Cullen. They stopped at the car, Cullen watching the group disperse.

"When will Bain be expecting another call?" said Angela.

Cullen smiled. "He'll get one when he gets one."

She laughed.

Cullen tried Bain just after they spoke to Mulgrew but there was no answer. He resorted to texting, partly satisfied it would seriously irritate Bain, text messages being yet another of his pet hates.

His phone rang. Bain. "Here he is." He leaned back against the car and watched the kids pass them on the opposite side. Cullen doubted they were going to put on their school uniforms and head in.

"Here, Sundance, you were supposed to give me a call," said Bain.

"You didn't answer," said Cullen. "I texted you."

"Don't start me on bloody text messages," said Bain. He paused for a few seconds. "Right, get yourself and Batgirl to the Garleton nick, I want to put my arms around this."

"Ten minutes," said Cullen. He ended the call and pocketed his phone before unlocking the car and climbing in the driver's side. He looked over at Angela. "He's 'putting his arms around this'."

Angela laughed. "That's one more for the bullshit bingo."

Cullen laughed as he turned the ignition and drove off. Before long, he was stuck at the traffic lights at the end of the High Street.

"Can you believe that Mulgrew guy?" said Angela.

"I'm trying to work out if it's our job to believe him," said Cullen. "That's some pretty far out stuff he's peddling. I'm astonished there's anyone interested in it these days."

"Tell me about it," said Angela.

Cullen tried to find a parking space in Garleton Police Station but found it didn't have a car park. The station sat on the High Street but there were no free spaces on that side of the road. He did a U-turn and pulled in across from the building, next to Starbucks and Subway. Cullen looked at the shops, his stomach starting to rumble.

"Don't suppose we've got time to find something to eat," said Cullen.

"Not without getting a severe bollocking over timekeeping," said Angela.

The station was an old building in the Scots Baronial style, turrets carved out of sandstone at either end of a front ten windows wide and three storeys tall. The station had been a major hub in the area until the mid-nineties — an old sergeant Cullen previously worked for was based there for a few years until a restructure demoted it, becoming a local station with at most four regular officers per shift. The building was big enough for an operation much larger than it currently held and it was only a matter of time before they sold parts off.

They entered the reception area, a cold, dark space with no natural light, painted a generic magnolia. At the far end was a security door and partition with a thin, wiry sergeant behind the desk, an elderly gentleman in tweeds and red trousers remonstrating with him.

"But I don't think you understand how much that piano score was worth."

The sergeant folded his arms. "Have you filled in your insurance form?"

"Of course I have."

"Well, then, it's an insurance matter now. Do you want me to check if it was in the report we made? If it wasn't, I could have a word with the insurance company for you."

The man frowned. "I don't know what you mean."

"A piano score worth ten thousand pounds was somehow omitted from the inventory on your burglary report. I'm not sure how they'd view that."

"I'm sorry?"

"Look, is there something you want me to do?"

"I want you to acknowledge my distress!"

"Fine, I will acknowledge it," said the sergeant. "But I must insist you stop shouting."

"I'm not shouting!"

The sergeant licked his lips. "As I explained, the matter is now with your insurance company. Other than providing them with a copy of the burglary report, which we've done, there's nothing further we can do."

"Fine," said the man, leaning against the desk. "David bloody

Cameron has the right idea, the police force in this country are next to useless." He stormed off out of the station.

Cullen approached the desk, holding out his warrant card. "Charming."

"Get that sort of shite all the time," said the sergeant. "Tweeds and red trousers don't cover up insurance fraud."

Cullen smiled. "I believe DI Bain has acquired a room."

"He can have the whole station if he fancies," said the sergeant, buzzing them in. "Through the door, turn left, go to the end, then up to the first floor, third room on the left."

Cullen nodded and headed through the security door, trying to remember the directions.

They came to a long corridor running to the left, again starved of natural light. The right-hand side seemed to be the extent of the active station, just a few officers sitting at desks.

Cullen strode down the corridor, noticing the walls hadn't been painted for several years. At the end was a door with safety glass, which Cullen was surprised was still intact. They went through and found a staircase, old stone steps worn down in the middle with a solid wood banister, the light flickering randomly. They climbed to their floor, Cullen having to push hard at the door and finding this corridor in an even worse state.

"Should have gone to Haddington," said Angela. "This is a total shitehole."

"I've been in worse," said Cullen.

"Shut up," she said.

"Seriously," he said. "Ravencraig in West Lothian is practically falling apart. This is at least still standing."

"Isn't that by Motherwell?" she said.

"You're thinking of Ravenscraig, the steelworks," he said. "There's a town called Ravencraig between Bathgate and Linlithgow. Worst place in Scotland."

"I'll take your word for it," said Angela.

The room Bain had acquired was full of stacks of toilet rolls, bin bags and dust, a young PC in the middle of clearing them to the side. Law sat at one of the few desks, typing on a laptop. Cullen and Lamb stood in the centre of the room, scratching their chins.

"I need a whiteboard," said Bain. "Can't work without one."

"You can barely manage with one," said Angela.

Lamb bellowed with laughter.

Law headed over, standing next to Cullen.

Bain scowled at Angela. "Less of that, Batgirl, or you'll be back to Queen Charlotte with a boot-shaped mark on your arse."

"Sorry, sir," said Angela.

Bain looked at Cullen. "Right, Sundance, did Mulgrew confirm that alibi?"

"He did," said Cullen.

Bain punched his fist into his hand. "Bastard. I had him marked as favourite."

Lamb frowned. "Killing his own daughter?"

Bain shrugged. "It would have been easy."

"I've only proved he had a valid reason to be out at that time," said Cullen. "We've no idea whether he did it or not."

"Let's keep an open mind on this one," said Bain. "What else did Mulgrew tell you?"

"He tried to recruit us into his cult," said Cullen, showing the pamphlet Mulgrew had given him. "Other than that, he backed up what Gibson said about Jamie Cook."

Bain raised an eyebrow. "That name rings a bell."

"Charles Gibson mentioned him," said Cullen, before reading out what Mulgrew had told them.

"The boy's got the *Devil* in him?" said Bain. "What sort of hick town is this?"

"This is an isolated incident," said Lamb. "This is just a little group in this one little town. It's a prosperous place, good school."

"It's not all prosperous," said Cullen, thinking back to the houses by Mulgrew's cottage.

"Every town has a downside," said Lamb. "This is no worse than North Berwick or Linlithgow, say."

"Right, so what about this Cook boy?" said Bain.

Lamb cleared his throat. "Charles Gibson said he's the local bad boy and he's right. We've picked him up over thirty times, charged him on ten occasions, never serious enough to put him away."

"What are we talking here?" said Bain.

"Mischief mainly," said Lamb. "Nothing too serious, bit of graffiti, vandalism, petty theft." He nodded at Law. "Eva will probably have already told you, I picked up Jamie Cook on Saturday night for urinating against God's Rainbow."

"And that's this Mulgrew boy's church?" said Bain.

"It is," said Lamb, nodding.

"Was there anything malicious going on, or was it just too much cider?" said Bain.

"He was absolutely out of his skull," said Lamb. "No idea what he'd been drinking, but he was as pissed as a tramp. We put him in one of the cells here, let him sleep it off."

"How old is he?" said Bain.

"Seventeen," said Lamb.

"So he's underage drinking then?" said Bain. He shook his head. "I wish you'd kept him in. We might not be investigating a murder here."

Lamb put his hands together in a 'T' shape. "Time out. Are you seriously thinking Jamie Cook is behind this, without a single piece of evidence?"

"I'll remind you I'm in charge here," said Bain. "He's our primary suspect now. When I get a fuckin' whiteboard or a flipchart I'll do some thinking on it." He looked at Cullen. "Sundance, can you take Batgirl here and try and find this Cook boy?"

14

The Cooks lived on Dunpender Drive, three doors down on the opposite side from the Gibsons. The house was in the same style but looked a few rooms smaller. The garden was extensively landscaped, a complex web of bushes, pebbles and decking making it look more of a family home than the Gibsons' show house.

"Is Bain at it again?" Angela parked on the road outside the house. A large ginger cat took the opportunity to rush across the street.

"Let's hope we find Jamie Cook before he does." Cullen marched up the drive.

Three cars were parked in the paved drive, a silver exec-class Lexus, a dark green Volvo SUV and a Renault Clio. The Lexus was a dead ringer for Charles Gibson's Audi, but Cullen couldn't decide who'd have the upper hand of the two. The Clio was modded — Cullen couldn't remember if that was the current in-phrase — its headlights replaced by tinted variants and a DayGlo strip along the top of the windscreen reading 'Clio Sport'.

Angela pressed the doorbell.

"I wonder which car belongs to the tearaway son?" said Cullen.

"Out this way, it'll be the Volvo," said Angela, with a raised eyebrow.

The front door was opened by a man in his mid-forties.

"We're looking for a Jamie Cook," said Cullen.

"I'm his father," said Robert Cook. He was tall and broad with a big belly, his hair receding at the front but shaved short, like Charles Gibson's. "Who might you be?"

Cullen held up his warrant card, allowing Robert to squint at it. "DC Cullen, Lothian & Borders Police. This is Acting DC Caldwell. We'd like to ask your son a few questions."

Robert frowned. "I'm afraid he's not in just now."

"Do you know where we could find him?" said Cullen.

"He's not been here since Sunday," said Robert.

Cullen exchanged a look with Angela. "Would we be able to speak to you instead?"

"Can I ask what it's about?" said Robert.

"It's regarding a serious matter," said Cullen, "so I'd rather discuss it inside."

"Certainly."

Robert showed them in to the living room, gesturing to a large sofa that filled three corners. He called upstairs for his wife then sat down opposite them on a leather reclining chair that looked as comfortable as it did expensive, though Cullen wondered how good it would be for his back.

"Aren't you at work today?" said Cullen.

"I work from home," said Robert. "I own a procurement business, buying, selling and leasing farm equipment. It's very lucrative these days."

At that moment, a woman entered the room. She was a virtual clone of Elaine Gibson in all but the face, round where Gibson's was pointed.

"This is my wife, Wilma," said Robert. "The police want to ask us a few questions about Jamie, love."

She sat on the sofa to the left of Cullen and Angela, close to Robert. "The twins are playing that stupid computer game in the playroom," she said to her husband.

Cullen thought they seemed unfazed by two detectives turning up looking for their son. "Aren't they at school?"

There was a nervous look between them. "We thought it wise to bring them home, given what's happened," said Wilma.

"Now can we help you?" said Robert, with a thin smile.

"We believe your son is acquainted with one Amanda Gibson," said Cullen.

Robert gave a pained expression. "Mandy?"

Cullen nodded. "Her body was found this morning. It would appear she's been murdered."

The Cooks exchanged a look, which Cullen considered might have been more concerned with what their son had done than anything else.

"Was this what you were referring to as 'what's happened'?" said Cullen.

Robert took a deep breath then nodded his head slightly. "It is."

Cullen noted that down. "Why did you bring your kids home from school?"

"Well, in case there's some madman around," said Robert.

Cullen frowned. "Is that what you suspect?"

"It could be anything," said Robert. "Better to be safe."

"Could you describe your family's relationship with Ms Gibson?" said Cullen.

"Well, we're all members of the God's Rainbow church," said Robert.

"Can you elaborate?" said Cullen, wanting to hear another take on it.

"It's a church group we attend as a family," said Robert. He paused. Cullen didn't fill the space. "We never socialised with the Gibsons much, just church activities."

"Do you know Charles Gibson well?" said Cullen.

"A little," said Robert. He glanced at his wife. "Look, can I ask what this is about?"

"We're just trying to obtain some background to the deceased," said Cullen, sitting back in the settee, in an attempt to relax the tense situation. "We want to paint a picture of what this town is like in general, and of Mandy's life. If we can understand her normal habits and behaviours then it will assist our investigation."

"I see," said Robert, biting a fingernail.

"Would Jamie have any contact with Mandy on a regular basis?" said Cullen.

"Only through the group," said Robert.

"What about Mandy's brother, Thomas?" said Cullen.

Robert slowly nodded. "Jamie was the best of friends with Thomas and Malcolm." He rubbed his forehead. "They used to have sleepovers."

Cullen frowned. "I'm sorry?"

"Jamie would sleep at Thomas's and occasionally at Malcolm's," said Robert.

Cullen realised this gave the boy opportunity at the Gibsons' house.

"How often would this be?" said Cullen.

"We're talking once a month," said Robert. "Maybe more."

"Who is Malcolm?" said Cullen.

"Malcolm Thornton," said Robert. "He's the son of another parishioner. They live round the corner, on Dunpender Loan."

"Did the boys ever stay here?" said Cullen.

"No," said Robert.

"What can you tell me about Father Seamus Mulgrew?" said Cullen.

Wilma answered this time. "Seamus is a very strong, God-fearing man," she said, eyes locking onto Cullen. "He has helped us out considerably." She smiled beatifically. "He's helped us repent our sins and live a life true to God's wishes."

Cullen sat forward, turning back a few pages in his notebook. "We have heard one or two things about your son."

"I imagine you did," said Robert, fists clenched. "Our boy has had a troubled life." He wore an earnest expression, his eyebrows raised, creasing his forehead. "Jamie is plagued by demons."

"He seems to have a bit of a reputation in this town," said Cullen.

Robert raised his voice. "What's Jamie got to do with Mandy Gibson?"

"As I said earlier, we're just trying to follow up on some information we have," said Cullen. "We need to identify whether Jamie is a potential suspect in this case."

Robert stared at the floor for a few moments. "As I say, our boy is troubled. He used to be such a good boy, very smart, very good at school. He went off the rails and there was nothing we could do to stop it."

"How did he go off the rails?" said Cullen.

"He's been in trouble with the police," said Robert. "It started out with him being disciplined at school, but quickly we just lost control of him. We tried locking him in his room but he'd escape somehow."

"How long ago did this start?" said Cullen.

"About two years," said Robert. "Jamie left school about a year and a half ago and he hasn't worked since. He just lies around the house watching television, or he's on the internet all day. He spends more time on that Schoolbook than he ever spent at school."

"Do you have any idea why this started?" said Cullen, looking for a trigger incident.

Robert slowly shook his head, as if in despair. "Believe me, we have asked ourselves many, many times. We've given Jamie everything he's ever asked for."

He rubbed his face and sat forward, the springs in the chair creaking. "Father Mulgrew said the boy has Satan in him, that it's not our fault. We're doing everything we can to make sure his brother and sister are not similarly afflicted. We asked Seamus to begin their counselling a lot earlier. They're good kids and we have high hopes for them."

"What counselling is this?" said Cullen.

"All members of the church receive counselling with Father Mulgrew," said Robert. "Some on a monthly basis, like our Sophie and Isaac. Most of the older kids on a weekly basis. Jamie did, until he left the group."

"What was he like before he went off the rails?" said Cullen.

"As I said, he was a kind, loving boy," said Robert. "He was a straight-A student and very diligent with it."

"In cases like your son's there's usually a rational explanation for such drastic changes in behaviour," said Cullen. "Can you think of any potential triggers?"

"The only trigger is Satan possessing my son," said Robert, tears welling in his eyes. "That's what started him getting involved with bad groups."

"Do you mean gangs?" said Cullen.

"Just undesirable elements in East Lothian," said Robert. "Prestonpans, Tranent, that sort of place." He said the names of the less salubrious towns with a curl to his lip.

"I noticed a Renault Clio out there," said Cullen. "I take it that's his?"

Robert looked up at the ceiling. "Yes, he passed his test just two weeks after his seventeenth. We bought the car as a desperate attempt to bring him back from the abyss. It's pretty much the only test he's passed in years."

"Do you know where he is?" said Cullen.

"We haven't seen him since yesterday," said Wilma.

"Have you any idea where he could be?" said Cullen.

Robert shrugged. "Your guess is as good as mine, I'm afraid. As I say, our son is a troubled boy. We don't know where he is from day to day."

"You said you saw him yesterday?" said Angela.

Wilma slowly exhaled. "Yes, at lunchtime. He grabbed one of those microwave hamburgers, muttered something to me then went up to his room. We went to see some friends in Haddington with Sophie and Isaac. When we got back, Jamie had already gone."

"What time was this?" said Cullen.

"It was late, back of eight, maybe?" said Robert. "One of the plates was out on the counter, so I presume he'd just left."

"And you have no idea where he might be?" said Cullen.

Robert scowled. "As I've explained, Jamie is a law unto himself."

Cullen looked to Angela. "Any more questions?"

"Not from me," she said.

Robert gave them Jamie's mobile number.

"Thanks for your time," said Cullen, rising to his feet.

Cullen pulled into a parking space directly in front of the station. Angela was on the phone, trying to obtain Jamie Cook's record.

He stared at the cars in front of them, the harsh winter sun appearing from behind the clouds, lurking low in the sky, almost touching the tips of the spires at the far end of the road. The High Street was at its widest point here, the ancient mercat cross in the middle splitting the traffic around its circular stone base, which Cullen imagined would be full of flowers in the summer but was now a patch of mud.

The rows of modern shops, intermingled with more traditional outlets, were in stark contrast to their upper floors' ancient Scottishness. It reminded Cullen of the Royal Mile in Edinburgh, but also the crow step gables of Culross in west Fife, an ancient town marooned in the Elizabethan era while the rest of Scotland moved on.

Cullen saw Angela jot information down about Jamie Cook. They desperately needed to speak to him, if only to silence the innuendo and hearsay already beginning to cloud the investigation.

Cullen couldn't get his head around the way these high-earning professionals were so rapidly converted to this faith. In his experience, religion was the province of three categories: older people frightened of death, people his age dealing with a tragedy — say the death of a parent — and the born again, alcoholics or just nasty bastards looking for absolution.

The Gibsons and Cooks didn't obviously fall into any category of born again. The world was pretty broken now, with austerity measures and a failing global economy — maybe the end of days scenario caused Mulgrew's group to thrive. Or maybe they were just looking to repent their many sins.

Cullen took his iPhone out of his jacket and dialled Jamie Cook's number. It rang a few times then went to voicemail. He left a short, curt message and hung up.

"No answer?" Angela snapped her phone shut.

"No answer," he said. "I love your old mobile. Don't they call them 'feature phones' now?"

"I've got a mortgage to pay," she said.

Cullen shut up. "Did you get anything?"

"His dad's story checked out," she said. "Ten minor crimes. Picked up thirty-one times. Nothing serious but ten is a lot."

"It is," said Cullen.

"So what do you reckon?" said Angela.

Cullen looked out of the window down the street, realising their leads were drying up. "We really need to speak to Jamie Cook."

"Seems like it," she said.

"I'm absolutely starving." Cullen checked his watch — it was just before two. "Christ, how did it get to that time?"

"That's called being busy."

"I don't think I can face Bain on an empty stomach," said Cullen. "I can't decide which of the three glories across the road I'm going to sample the delights of."

"Mickey D's for me," said Angela.

"Not a fan," said Cullen. "It'll have to be Subway."

They got out of the car and crossed the road. The local Big Issue salesman — a young guy with a hooded top — approached them as they reached the other side, Cullen finding it impossible to decline him.

"You're such a sucker for them," said Angela.

"Am I?" said Cullen.

"That's the fifth time I've seen them get you," said Angela. "Must have a target on your back."

Cullen shrugged. "Poor guy needs all the help he can get."

"I'll see you in the station." Angela walked off towards McDonald's.

Cullen checked his wallet — he was down to a fiver, which should be enough. He entered Subway and joined the three-strong queue. He inspected the display behind the counter and settled on a pastrami sub. He wasn't much of a fan of the chain, either, but he figured it was the least worst option. He took out his phone and tried Jamie Cook again while he waited. It went straight through to voicemail this time, no rings. Cullen frowned as he pocketed the phone.

The queue shuffled forward one place as the first customer headed off. It was Law. She smiled at Cullen then looked him up and down.

"How are you doing?" she said.

"Oh, you know, fine," he said.

"Your boss has been swearing his head off in there."

"You've not seen anything yet," he said.

She laughed loudly. "I can imagine."

"What did you go for?"

"Cajun chicken," she said.

"You like it hot?"

She nodded. "Oh, yes." She raised an eyebrow. "What are you going for?"

"Pastrami, I think," said Cullen.

His phone rang. He held it up to her, thinking it would be Jamie Cook. "Better take this."

She tapped his arm and grinned. "I'll see you back over the road."

Cullen felt himself blush as she walked off. He checked the display on his phone. It was Sharon. He reddened further. He needed to stop whatever Law was doing.

"Hey," he said.

"Hey. How's it going?"

"Flat out," he said. "I'm in East Lothian. Child murder."

"Oh magic, just what you want," said Sharon.

"What about you?" said Cullen.

"Stabbing in Wester Hailes."

"Trying to work out who's the luckier," said Cullen.

She laughed. "Listen, are you coming to mine before the Burns' Supper?"

"If you want me to," said Cullen.

"Is there any chance you can get some cat litter on your way home?" said Sharon.

"I'll try," he said, shuffling forward in the queue. "Can't promise anything, though. This isn't looking like it's going to wrap up any time this week."

"Fluffy peed in the bath again."

Cullen had a moment of clarity. In the past six months, his life had changed from talking about clubbing to cats pissing in baths. "I'll see what I can do."

"Thanks," she said. "Are you okay?"

"Aye, why wouldn't I be?" said Cullen.

"Scott, you're investigating a child murder, it's known as harrowing."

"I'm trying to be a seasoned detective, Sharon," he said, "this stuff has to just wash off me."

She laughed. "I'm serious."

"I know, I know. Look, it's okay. We'll get to the bottom of this and I'll be fine."

"Just make sure you are," she said. "I'd better go. Love you."

"See you later," he said.

He pocketed the phone, wondering why he couldn't say the 'L word' back.

16

Fifteen minutes later, Cullen sat at the back of the Incident Room, finishing off a foot-long sub, filling his stomach if not satisfying his taste buds. The Cajun chicken might have been the better option.

Bain had grabbed upwards of twenty officers, the majority of whom came from other East Lothian stations. Law, McLaren, Murray and Lamb sat on office chairs beside Bain, chatting amongst themselves as the great man stared at the newly-installed whiteboard, trying to conjure some leads from it.

Cullen was thankful Law hadn't come over and recommenced flirting. He needed to nip that in the bud — he'd done nothing and planned to do nothing, but Angela noticing meant it would be out in the open sooner rather than later.

Just as Cullen scrunched up his lunch bag, Irvine appeared carrying a Gregg's bag. He handed Bain a sandwich, sausage roll and coffee then sat down to tuck into his own lunch. He deposited his wad of gum into a receipt and put it on the table.

Cullen's phone rang — the display showed an unknown number. He knew people who never answered those calls but it could have been any number of contacts in West Lothian — snouts, busybodies, gossips — and, while he didn't work there any more, he could pass them onto someone who did.

He answered it.

Music blasted down the line — the rattle of a tambourine and a dirty throbbing bass guitar. He didn't recognise the song — it was the sort of indie rock Cullen had stood through at countless festivals over the years while his ex-girlfriend tossed her hair from side to side in time with it, usually before he had to hoist her onto his shoulders.

Guitar cut in, choppy chords played on a distorted electric, along with singing in a harsh and guttural Scottish accent, the sort that could have come from either Glasgow or Edinburgh or any of the myriad towns in between. The voice was singing a mantra — 'Where have you gone?' over and over as the music changed underneath.

He was cut off before the song went anywhere near a chorus.

Nobody appeared to have noticed.

Cullen was sweating — the room was only just warming up from its long-unused chill, but he was soaked through. He'd never received a crank call before. He didn't know what to do. He could think of a hundred people who would want to get at him but couldn't think of a single one who would have his number.

The only likely candidate he could think of was Jamie Cook — he'd phoned him half an hour previously. Why he would leave a message like that was beyond Cullen. Maybe Mulgrew and the boy's parents told the truth and Cook was so far off the rails that goading the police was a good idea to him.

Bain finally called the officers to order. Cullen fastened his suit jacket to hide the damp patches and headed over.

Bain was at home, poised beside the station's brand new whiteboard, a large screen mounted on a frame with metal legs ending in castors. He was pointing and prodding as he went over the case so far — Mandy's body, her parents, God's Rainbow, Seamus Mulgrew and Jamie Cook. He had a map of Garleton around the Gibsons' house and a larger scale one showing Garleton and Balgone Ponds, scribbles linking places of interest.

Cullen's investigation was augmented by bits and pieces gathered by Lamb and his team — witness statements from the streets had yielded little so far — as well as the information Murray discovered about Charles Gibson's car.

A printed photo of Mandy was stuck in the centre beside shots of her parents and brother. Cullen still wanted to speak to him one-on-one, away from his parents. Boxes on the board represented the Cooks, Russells and Seamus Mulgrew. A childish-looking drawing represented Mandy's teddy bear, an arrow connecting it to where it was found.

"Cullen found a teddy bear belonging to the deceased," said Bain. "James Anderson has taken the bear into the lab, but he's given us a health warning that we're unlikely to get anything from it other than a squad of dust mites."

He looked disappointed that nobody laughed. "It does confirm the likely chain of events. Mandy somehow got out of the house and was on her way to see her friend Susan Russell. It would appear Mandy was abducted during this trip." He stared at Cullen. "DC Cullen, you've been doing most of the door-to-door, so can you give us an update on any suspects?"

Cullen looked around at the strange faces and the few familiar ones. "We don't have a suspect just yet but there is someone we need to speak to. You've already mentioned him. Jamie Cook. His parents are members of the same religious group as the Gibsons. Nobody can say a good word about him, including his parents. Seamus Mulgrew said if there was a chief suspect in this case, it's Cook. We need to bring him in."

"Cheers," said Bain. He looked at Lamb. "DS Lamb, can you use your local colour and get your lot out looking for this boy?"

Lamb nodded. "Will do."

"I do have Jamie Cook's mobile number," said Cullen, leaving out the phone call he received. "We should get a trace on it."

"Fine," said Bain. "Think you can manage that?"

Cullen raised his eyebrows. "I'll get it done."

"We need background checks on Charles and Elaine Gibson," said Cullen, "and on Seamus Mulgrew."

"What sort of name is that, by the way?" said Bain.

"Irish," said Cullen.

"Aye, very good, Sundance," said Bain. "Don't you get too smart with me, all right?"

Time was that sort of comment from Bain wouldn't have rolled off Cullen so easily.

"What do we know about him?" said Bain.

"He's Irish, runs the religious group which most of the local community seem to have joined," said Cullen.

"What do we know about this group?" said Bain, looking at Lamb, McLaren and Murray.

"What we know is it's called God's Rainbow," said Lamb. "That's pretty much it. We've had some checks done. It's set up as a charity so the records should be public."

"I don't want us to go in two-footed on some group like this," said Bain. "We're investigating a murder, not a mass suicide. Keep focused on that." He took a deep breath. "I'd like you to dig up any further local gen you can."

"We're not going in too aggressively, Brian," said Lamb, his voice hard and forceful. "Us simple country hick officers are only used to investigating housebreakings, not infiltrating religious groups. I will defer to your authority."

There was a stifled laugh from Lamb's officers plus a few of the uniforms. Cullen himself had to look away.

"Okay," said Bain, trying to regain control. "Caldwell, can you do some digging into this Mulgrew's background while you're getting the trace done? Same with Mandy's folks."

Angela nodded. "Will do."

Bain looked at the wider group again. "We have interviewed the parents, though we didn't get much. Scene of Crime have been through Mandy's room, but haven't completed their investigation yet. We need a connection between Mandy and Jamie Cook, other than this religious group."

"Cook's parents told us he used to have sleepovers at his friends' houses," said Cullen. "Thomas Gibson and Malcolm Thornton."

"Wait, how old is this boy?" said Bain.

"Seventeen," said Cullen.

"And the other two?" said Bain.

"They're seventeen as well," said Lamb.

"So you're saying Jamie Cook had the opportunity to get at Mandy?" said Bain.

Cullen shrugged. "It's possible."

Bain shook his head and closed his eyes. "What are this lot up to at these sleepovers?"

"They're probably too pissed to go home so they crash out at the house with the most lenient parents," said Cullen.

"And you're saying that's Charles Gibson?" said Bain.

"Malcolm Thornton's parents, as well," said Cullen. "They don't seem to have stayed at Jamie Cook's house too often."

"Fine," said Bain. "Look into it."

"You said Mandy Gibson had an accident in Edinburgh a few years ago," said Cullen, "which instigated the family moving here."

"Aye, we've been over that, Sundance," said Bain, "if you'd actually bothered listening."

"What I mean is they might have run away from something," said Cullen.

Bain focused on Lamb and his team. "Bill, thoughts?"

Lamb screwed his face up. "I'd say this is more like running *to* than running *from*." He rubbed his moustache. "They came here to restart their lives in a nice small town with a good school. Do you live in Edinburgh yourself?"

"Bathgate," said Bain.

"You've escaped the city for a quieter life," said Lamb.

"Bathgate on a Saturday night is hardly quiet," said Bain. "Right, Cullen, anything else?"

"I'm not going to mention the possibility of abduction because of Charles Gibson's job," said Cullen, "but—"

"Good for you," said Bain, cutting him off.

"We need to spend some time working out how Mandy escaped from her house last night," said Cullen. "The Gibsons' statements have Elaine Gibson putting her daughter to bed at about nine. Charles Gibson went out in the evening to see Mulgrew. Could he have left the door open when he got back?"

Bain nodded slowly. "I see what you're saying. It's a bit of a blunder if he did, to say the least. I'll have a think about it." He stroked his moustache. "Right, are you done now?"

"For now," said Cullen.

"So what next for you and Batgirl, then?" said Bain.

"I'd like to speak to Malcolm Thornton and his parents about these sleepovers," said Cullen. "It would be useful if we could speak to someone at the school."

"Speak to the Thorntons and report back here," said Bain. He took a deep breath. "Right, DS Irvine, what's been going on up at the crime scene?"

Irvine snorted. "I'll be honest and say nothing much," he said, his jaws pounding and lips smacking together. "Of the four cottages, we've now spoken to all the residents. Two key things to note. The elderly couple DC Cullen told us about saw nothing. The wife has a cold so they didn't go out with the dog this morning."

Cullen took his scowl as blame for wasting his time speaking to them.

"The second thing is closing out whether the gatehouse owners saw anything — they didn't. We spoke to the couple in cottage number two — they're both teachers in Haddington — and they confirmed the owners are skiing in France. I can't even spell the name of the resort, so I won't try to pronounce it."

"That's fine," said Bain. "Tying up loose ends is good."

"Thanks," said Irvine.

"Time for actions for the rest of the afternoon," said Bain. "Bill, can you and your boys get on top of finding Jamie Cook?"

Lamb gave a reluctant nod.

"Take as many uniform as you need," said Bain. He looked at Cullen. "Sundance, you and Caldwell get over to speak to the Thorntons."

Cullen nodded.

"The rest of you, please speak to DS Irvine," said Bain. "And last but not least, Irvine and I will attend the post mortem." He checked his watch. "Anything else?"

Nobody said anything.

17

The Thornton family lived on Dunpender Loan, the street behind the Gibsons. From the relative positions of the houses, Cullen figured the gardens would pretty much border at the back.

They sat in the living room, Cullen and Angela across from Rebecca Thornton on matching leather settees. The room was full of generic neutral tones, equipped like a show home and spotless. It reminded Cullen of a Danish furniture showroom Sharon had dragged him to the last time they were in Glasgow for the day.

Rebecca wasn't a trophy wife like Elaine Gibson or Wilma Cook. She looked harassed and drawn, her skin red and blotchy, her dark hair grey at the roots and she seemed a good ten or twelve years older than them. She had an expression on her face as if the world was out to get her.

Cullen let Angela lead the conversation. She repeated the questions Cullen had put to the others, receiving similar responses. Rebecca trotted out the same junk about God's Rainbow. Cullen found himself wanting to jump in and ask about Jamie Cook and the sleepovers, but he held himself back hoping Angela would get around to it.

Cullen noticed a silver Mercedes parking outside the house.

"That'll be my husband," said Rebecca, getting to her feet.

"Were you expecting him?" said Angela.

"His lunchtime can be fairly sporadic," said Rebecca. She left the room and went into the hall.

"How am I doing?" said Angela.

"Fine," said Cullen. "Just focus on why we're here."

Angela nodded. "The sleepovers."

"Aye," said Cullen.

"I'm leading up to that," said Angela.

"Good."

William Thornton barrelled in, a blur of energy. He shook hands with Cullen and Angela then stood, hands on hips, waiting for a cue from the officers, his eyes jumping around like he was on amphetamines. Late fifties, maybe ten years older than his wife. Tall and lean, he was dressed in a three-piece pinstripe suit with shiny, patterned brogues on his feet.

"An advantage of being one of the big cheeses is I can come home for lunch every day," said Thornton.

As his wife had told them, he was the local Chartered Accountant, a partner in Thornton & McCulloch, a company with six offices spanning East Lothian. God's Rainbow certainly attracted the more affluent local residents — of the families they'd met all the husbands were successful professionals, sufficiently rich that their wives didn't have to work.

Thornton sat next to his wife on the sofa.

"I believe Malcolm is acquainted with a Thomas Gibson?" said Angela.

A brief flicker of surprise flew across Thornton's forehead. "Yes, he is. My son and Thomas are the best of friends. There's a real competitive streak runs through both boys."

"Is he also friends with Jamie Cook?" said Angela.

Thornton sighed and looked away. "I wondered if you'd heard of the local legend."

"Well, is he?" said Angela.

Thornton looked over at the window for a moment. "Malcolm hero-worships the boy." His tone dropped almost to a whisper. "He thinks Jamie is some sort of rock star."

Cullen felt a spear run through him — the phone call, the song. "Is Jamie Cook into music?"

Thornton gave a slight chuckle. "The boy's never played an instrument in his life or sung a note outside of church, but he certainly lives the lifestyle, that's for sure."

"What about DJing?" said Cullen.

"I'm not the right person to ask about that," said Thornton.

"Are you friendly with his parents?" said Cullen. "I notice you're all in the God's Rainbow group."

Thornton bit his lip. "Nice people," he said, almost reluctantly, "but I have to say the way they've brought that boy up is un-Christian."

"In what way?" said Cullen.

"Well..." He broke off, staring into space for a few moments before regaining his composure. "The way the boy has turned out shows they mustn't have done the right things."

"So you describe yourselves as Christian?" said Cullen.

Thornton frowned. "Well, maybe not strictly Christian now, but at some time in the past, yes."

"Does Malcolm see Jamie much?" said Cullen.

"More often than we'd like," said Thornton. "They're down at that bloody park most nights, though fortunately Malcolm doesn't partake in any substances."

"Substances?" said Cullen, sitting forward in the seat.

"Nothing too risky, I gather," said Thornton. "Marijuana, cider, that sort of thing."

"So Jamie Cook uses drugs?" said Cullen.

"Well, it's pretty much common knowledge," said Thornton. "He's been picked up by the police more times than I'd care to mention."

"I gather there have been times when Jamie Cook and Thomas Gibson stayed here," said Cullen.

"You're right, yes." Thornton straightened his tie. "They stayed at the Gibsons' far more frequently, though."

Cullen noted it down.

"It was generally at weekends," said Thornton. "They would usually go to the park. I think they were mucking about, watching films, playing games, that sort of thing. I don't imagine they did much sleeping." He took a deep breath. "Our view was it was better to let them do what they want here, under our supervision."

"Even with Jamie's reputation?" said Cullen.

"Even so," said Thornton. "He may have been a bad boy, but Malcolm looked up to him. He's at such a precocious age. We wanted to make sure he had an outlet while staying focused on his exams. Boys like Jamie will end up nowhere. Malcolm will take over my firm."

Cullen wondered what effect the pressures of a legacy would have on the boy. "When was the last time Jamie stayed here?"

Thornton exhaled. "Last weekend, I think."

"How long have you known Jamie?" said Cullen.

"A good few years," said Thornton. "Since he was a wee laddie."

"And has he always been like this?" said Cullen.

Thornton fiddled with his cufflinks. "Not really, no," he said, with a sad expression. "It was as he went into his Standard Grades, I think. Maybe the pressure was too much, maybe he didn't get enough parental or school support."

Cullen scribbled it down in his notebook. "Is there any chance we could speak to Malcolm?"

"The boy's at school just now," said Thornton. "We'd prefer there were no distractions."

"Mr Thornton, I'm investigating a murder," said Cullen, his voice stern. "I would like to reinforce how serious this is."

"Yes, yes," said Thornton, backing down.

"Perhaps you could visit him at school?" said Rebecca, the first time she'd opened her mouth since her husband returned.

"We just might," said Cullen.

OUTSIDE, in the car, Cullen tried to work out what to do next. Finding Jamie Cook felt like their highest priority but that was for Lamb and his boys now. He'd have to go back to Bain with his tail between his legs.

"Jamie Cook is like a bloody ghost," said Angela.

Cullen murmured agreement.

The sleepovers were worrying him — Jamie Cook had clear access to Mandy when he slept at the Gibsons' house. The fact that Mandy escaped with such frequency showed how careless the parents could be. They'd let Jamie Cook into their house, who knew what he was up to?

The more Cullen thought about it, the more he needed to

speak with the children — Thomas Gibson, Malcolm Thornton and Susan Russell — to get more background on Mandy and Jamie Cook. Christ knew how many secrets Cullen hid from his own parents as a teenager.

"It's too much *Stepford Wives*, not enough *Desperate Housewives*," said Angela. "There are all these fragile yummy mummies and professional husbands. There's just not enough juice. There are no rough surfaces or hard edges."

"Just like in their houses," said Cullen.

She grinned.

Cullen cleared his throat then tried to put a serious expression on. "One thing I wanted to say to you was about how quickly you handed the questioning over to me. You were doing well up to that point but as soon as Thornton appeared you passed it over. You need to stick to tasks like that. Bain won't be so forgiving."

"You took over," said Angela.

"You let me take over," said Cullen.

Angela looked out of the window. "Right."

"Come on," said Cullen. "It's just feedback. You were doing well."

Angela looked at him. "I'll do better next time," she said, in a cold, even tone.

"Don't be like that," said Cullen. "I'm sure that's not the worst feedback anyone's ever given you."

She laughed, and shook her head. "Is that because you think I'm shite?"

"No, it's not," said Cullen. "You're doing fine, but you're in a training role. It's very different to being on the beat."

Angela sighed. "So I'm not going to make the grade, right?"

"I think you will," said Cullen.

"You're hardly Mr Experienced, are you?" said Angela.

"What's that supposed to mean?" said Cullen. "I've been a DC for nine months, and was Acting DC for six months before that. I had two previous detachments for six months each in Livingston. I know what I'm doing."

Angela raised her eyebrows. "Well, as long as you're not annoyed I'll be the same rank as you in five months."

"You deserve it," said Cullen. "Just keep up the hard work."

His phone rang — Irvine.

"Just got a call through from Control," said Irvine. "No idea how it's come to me."

"Go on," said Cullen, expecting some admin to come his way.

"Jamie Cook's been spotted on Garleton High Street."

18

Cullen kicked down to second gear and flew through the red light, a horn blaring as a car narrowly missed them. He steered hard around the sharp left turn onto the High Street, pulling almost forty in a pedestrian area. The advanced driver training he'd received while in uniform — after writing off a police Volvo one frozen January morning — was finally paying off. He started to wonder if the old Golf would tear apart on the cobbles as they hurtled towards the police station.

"Got a hold of him yet?" said Cullen.

Angela had her mobile clasped tight to her face, her left hand gripping the grab handle, knuckles almost white. She was on the phone to Lamb who was tracking Cook on foot. A local uniform had called in the sighting and Lamb was at the station, ready to jump into action.

"Far end of the High Street," said Angela. A bump almost made them take off. "Jesus, Scott, slow down."

"He's not getting away," said Cullen.

They passed Alba Bank and God's Rainbow, then Starbucks and Subway, flashing blue lights in the distance.

Angela pointed to the right. "There."

Cullen slammed on the brakes and pulled in. A spotty uniformed officer stood by the police car, trying to look vigilant but failing.

They jumped out and sprinted off towards him. "Where's Lamb?" said Cullen.

The uniform pointed down a side street. "He just went off towards Crombie Place."

Cullen set off on foot, Angela following. The High Street forked just past the police station and they headed back the way they'd come.

"You still on the line with Lamb?" said Cullen, looking back at her.

Her face was almost purple already. "No, he hung up."

Cullen stopped and looked down the lane, a claustrophobic place full of bins, a flight of stone steps at the end leading back up to the High Street. If Cook was on foot then heading down there might be the logical way to shake off a pursuer.

"Which way?" said Angela.

"Quiet," said Cullen. He could make out heavy footfalls from the lane. "This way." He followed the sound.

A teenager in combat trousers and a hooded top came running towards them, pursued by Lamb, almost bouncing along the street, gazelle-like.

Cullen headed straight for Cook, who was looking over his shoulder. He didn't see Cullen until he slammed into him.

Cullen shoved him to the ground, holding him down despite the boy's wriggling. He had at least three days of stubble on his face and emitted a stench, like he hadn't washed for longer.

"Bastard!" said Cook, trying to shake Cullen off.

"Hold still," said Cullen, as he manoeuvred him around onto his front and dug his knee into his back.

Lamb stood away from them, bent double, gasping for breath. "Little bastard switched back on me. Thank God you were coming the other way."

Angela was leaning against the wall, breathing hard. "You could have warned me we'd be running," she said, between gasps. "I would have worn my sports bra."

"Nice day for a Wonderbra," said Lamb, grinning at Angela.

Cullen wondered if her face could go any redder. "Can either of you two help here? He's a wriggly little bastard."

Lamb came over and cuffed Cook's right hand. They both got to their feet.

Lamb looked down at the boy. "Ah, shite."

"What?" said Cullen.

"This isn't Jamie Cook."

19

"What sort of name is Whammy?" said Bain, his voice distorting in Cullen's iPhone speaker.

Cullen was in the Incident Room, walking around near the back, trying to avoid eye contact with anyone. He had drawn the short straw and called Bain to give him an update, the DI having returned to Leith Walk station for Mandy's post mortem.

"We think his name is William Hamilton," said Cullen. "He's the town's Big Issue seller."

"So how the buggery did we mistake him for Jamie Cook?" said Bain.

"He was wearing a big hoodie," said Cullen. "Same height and build. Lamb's guy only got a glimpse of him walking down the street and assumed it was him."

"I thought we had him," said Bain. "Useless bastards can't find a suspect in their own back yard." He muttered under his breath. "Is there anything else, Sundance, or are you trying to keep me out of the PM?"

"We found out Jamie Cook has been dabbling in drugs," said Cullen. "Hash, mainly."

"String him up then," said Bain. "This shite can all wait till I'm back."

"Fine," said Cullen. "That's all for now."

The line went dead.

Lamb was mooching around by the whiteboard chatting to Angela, though she had her mobile clamped to the side of her face. He spotted Cullen and wandered over, his eyebrows raised. "Well?"

"What do you expect?" said Cullen.

Lamb laughed. "I expect he was going on about me and the backwoods operation I run here."

"And you'd be right," said Cullen.

"Could have sworn it was him," said Lamb, for what felt like the hundredth time since they caught the youth.

"Those clothes are designed to make them all look the same," said Cullen. "Urban camouflage. Even Bain knows that."

"If we'd had something to keep that little sod in custody this weekend, that wee lassie would still be alive," said Lamb, two fingers rubbing the patch of beard.

"You think he killed Mandy?" said Cullen.

Lamb nodded slowly. "I'd put money on it," he said, his voice rough. He looked Cullen in the eye. "Jamie Cook is a nasty little bastard. There are very few things I would put past him."

Cullen's mobile rang again — the same number as before. He stroked across the screen to answer it.

The same song played, this time distorted. Cullen thought the mobile was held against a speaker. Just after the singing kicked in, someone started laughing and the line went dead.

Cullen checked his received calls menu and looked at the number — it wasn't Jamie Cook's but that wasn't to say he wasn't using a different phone. He copied the new number into his notebook then dialled it. No answer. He tried another couple of times but still nothing.

All the while, Lamb observed Cullen. "Who was that?"

"Crank call," said Cullen, pocketing his phone and notebook.

"You get them as well then?" said Lamb.

Cullen tried to play it cool but in truth he was worried. He had no idea who it could be, other than Jamie Cook. There was obviously a message behind the song, but the 'Where have you gone?' refrain mystified him.

Jamie Cook had disappeared and they didn't know where he had gone.

Was the bad boy of Garleton toying with him? Why Cullen? He'd left a message on Cook's voicemail earlier, saying he was from Lothian & Borders and he needed to speak to him. If Cook was behind the murder, as Charles Gibson, Mulgrew and now Lamb were insinuating, then he was arrogant with it and toying with the police.

"I get a crank call every couple of weeks or so," said Lamb. "I think I've got about three different callers, most likely people I've put away over the years."

"Aren't you doing anything about it?" said Cullen.

"Like what?" said Lamb, grinning. "Go to the police?"

"We can get checks done," said Cullen. "I've done it myself."

Cullen had used the Forensic Investigation Unit — the phone squad to most officers — to trace a mobile a few times in the past year or so.

"A bit of advice," said Lamb, leaning in close. "You're a DC, right? If you want to progress in this game, you need to develop a poker face for all this nonsense. If you're off getting Forensics to look into crank calls, that sort of chat spreads through the force. You've got to let it wash over you."

"Aye, I suppose so," said Cullen.

He didn't know what to do. He wasn't much of a fan of the 'just get on with it' mentality he'd seen so much in his youth, but then again he wasn't into the modern American-style care and share.

He needed to talk to Sharon about it. She always knew what to do, or at least could listen and help him work it out.

"What next, then?" said Cullen.

"Well, my boys are out hunting for Jamie Cook." Lamb stroked the beard triangle again. "And your Caldwell is looking into Seamus Mulgrew."

"She's not my Caldwell," said Cullen.

Lamb raised an eyebrow. "Is she anyone's?"

Cullen had noticed Lamb eyeing her up earlier. "Aye, she's married to a guy called Rod."

"She doesn't wear a ring," said Lamb, the glint in his eyes telling Cullen he was interested in the sport of chasing a married woman.

"Ten years in uniform meant she learned pretty quickly that she would lose it," said Cullen.

"Fair enough," said Lamb. He looked across the room. "You got any ideas?"

"I think we should go to the school and speak to Mandy's friends and some of Jamie Cook's," said Cullen. "There's stuff we're missing in the margins here. I can just feel it."

Lamb frowned. "You think Bain will be fine with this?"

Cullen shrugged. "Can't see why not," he said, thinking back to the bollocking he received for even suggesting it.

"Fine, let's go with your hunch then," said Lamb, tossing his car keys up and catching them.

20

G arleton High School sat on Berwick Road, just across from the public park at Garleton Castle grounds. It was a big seventies glass and concrete affair, typical of Scottish municipal buildings of the era, sprawling across a wide area. A six-storey tower section dominated one corner, set alongside playing fields with football, rugby and hockey pitches.

Cullen hoped these schools were a dying breed but not all had been replaced in the PFI boom of New Labour. He'd attended a similar-looking school in Dalhousie and remembered how much of a nightmare it had been trying to navigate the interior when every pupil was walking along the main corridors at class change.

As they crossed the car park, Cullen was reminded of Sharon's sister and his pseudo-niece, Rachel. She would most likely be going to Garleton High in the summer, the family tying into the Garleton community.

At the reception, Cullen completed visitor forms for both of them — it wasn't far off what he'd have to fill out for putting someone in a cell.

Mandy's teacher met them there and escorted them up the stairs to his classroom, his special needs pupils having joined a mainstream music lesson at half two.

Jonathan Hulse was a tall thin man with a beard and unkempt

greying hair. He sat behind an old lacquered wood-effect desk, Cullen and Lamb pulling two of the larger chairs over.

His classroom looked more like a primary school room. It had two large whiteboards on adjacent walls, scrawled with different words. One had 'Hello' written in big letters and the other had a few words with each individual letter underlined — 'cat', 'pigeon' and 'fireman' with the most prominent being 'sailor'.

Hulse gave a nervous laugh as Cullen checked out the content of the boards. "We had a new girl join the class today," he said, pointing to 'Hello'. His accent was Home Counties, not a hoarse Essex or Cockney but a more refined Oxbridge. "A young girl called Katie with Down's syndrome."

"And 'sailor'?" said Lamb.

Hulse smiled. "We were playing a game. They had to guess a letter at a time. It took them an hour to do all four."

Cullen smiled politely. "It must be quite challenging working with disabled kids."

Hulse gave a shrug. "I find it quite rewarding, actually. We're fortunate here with the kids being integrated into the school. It gives no end of benefit."

"Do the kids get bullied?" said Cullen.

Hulse looked away. "On occasion, yes. There have been instances over the years but nothing too severe, mostly just ignorant teasing. It might be the best high school in the Lothians but it does have some individuals who try to bring the rest down to their level."

"Care to name any names?" said Lamb.

"Fortunately, the worst of them is no longer a pupil," said Hulse. "Jamie Cook."

Cullen and Lamb exchanged a look.

"Could you give a few examples?" said Cullen.

"Making faces, chanting, name-calling, that sort of thing," said Hulse. "It became quite vindictive towards the end of his time here, that last six months. Of course, it's improved now he's gone but there are some children who take that as a shining example of how to behave."

"Any names?" said Lamb.

"I would give you them if I had them," said Hulse. "Unfortunately the children who receive the worst of the abuse tend to keep things to themselves. There are two with autism who find it very difficult to communicate and yet most of the communication they receive is abuse."

Cullen cleared his throat. "Thank you for the insight. The reason we're here, as I'm sure you can guess, is because of what happened to Mandy Gibson."

Hulse looked down at the desk and took a deep, long breath. "I heard," he said, his voice small and shrill. "I hope you catch the bastard." He looked up at them with fire in his eyes.

"We're trying to," said Cullen. "One thing that would help is to understand a bit more about Mandy, her classmates and any of the abuse you referred to, which may have been directed at her."

"Mandy was a very troubled girl," said Hulse. "She had severe disabilities. There were a few occasions I was close to recommending she be moved out of semi-mainstream education into more specialist treatment, but her parents and the head fiercely resisted it. What happened to her was horrible."

A tear slid down his face, getting lost in the depths of his beard. "Her parents once played me a video of her before the accident. She seemed like such a sweet girl — it's hard to reconcile. Most of the kids I deal with have been the way they are since birth or early infancy. With Mandy it was different."

"Did she have any close friends?" said Cullen.

"None in my class really," said Hulse. "She did seem to have an affinity with Susan Russell. Susan is very engaging — she used to spend some of her time helping in my class, which I massively appreciated."

"Did you know anything about Mandy's frequent disappearances?" said Lamb.

"You'd have to speak to the parents about that," said Hulse.

"Nothing at all?" said Lamb.

Hulse sighed. "I'm afraid I heard about it, but that's all. My pupils are very troubled and their home lives can often be disturbed. I try to give support to their parents but, really, I need to keep some sort of distance from it. I'm dealing with very problematic children and it is very easy to let it affect you badly."

"When you talk about the abuse your kids received, was there any directed at Mandy?" said Cullen.

Hulse screwed his eyes shut and gave a strange grimace, his

cheeks fleshing out and his chin moving up. "Not since Jamie
Cook left."

21

Cullen and Lamb waited in a meeting room just off the headteacher's office. The room was obviously used for family visits — it was decorated in a traditional manner with soft furnishings, rugs and drapes over the armchairs.

The door opened and the headteacher led Malcolm Thornton in. Malcolm was as tall as his father. He looked nervous, despite an air of aggression and rebellion. His hair was short and gelled back and he'd taken a few liberties with his school uniform — the top button of the white shirt undone, the black and red striped tie lazily hanging loose, sleeves rolled up and black jeans hanging off the hip.

"Malcolm," said the headteacher, "these are the police officers to see you." He sat him down at the table in front of them before leaving the room.

Lamb smiled at Malcolm who leaned back on his chair, trying to look casual and assured, his flushed face giving away his nerves. Cullen clocked a young man used to acting calm and in control in front of authority.

"Do you recognise me?" said Lamb.

"Vaguely," said Malcolm, his voice almost too deep as if it had only recently broken. "You picked Jamie up on Saturday, didn't you?"

"I did indeed," said Lamb. "Where is he?"

"I've no idea," said Malcolm, a cocky smile on his face.

"You sure about that?" said Lamb.

"Positive."

"You're aware Amanda Gibson's body turned up this morning?" said Lamb.

Cullen sat back and watched Malcolm recoil. Obviously, the school rumour mill wasn't as good as in Cullen's day. There would no doubt be an announcement to the media once the PM finished.

"You may know her as Mandy," said Lamb.

"I know who she is," said Malcolm, quietly. He was trying to stay cool but his voice betrayed him.

"And I'll ask you again, Malcolm," said Lamb, "where is Jamie Cook?"

"Why do you want to see him?" said Malcolm.

"Because we have some questions we want him to answer," said Lamb. "He's disappeared on the day an acquaintance of his has been found dead. That's a bit of a coincidence and if we find out he had people helping him hide they'll be in trouble as well."

Malcolm looked at Lamb with wide eyes. He cleared his throat. "I've honestly no idea," he said, speaking slowly and quietly. "Last I saw of Jamie was you arresting him on Saturday. I got a text from him yesterday saying he was out of the nick but that was it."

"He's a bad boy," said Lamb.

"You keep saying that," said Malcolm.

"I keep hearing it," said Lamb.

Malcolm shook his head. "People have it in for Jamie, but he's not that bad."

"Not that bad," said Lamb, making a show of scribbling it down in his notebook. "Were you at your church yesterday?"

Malcolm sighed. "Yes. I wish I could just leave like Jamie did."

"Do you indeed?" said Lamb.

"It's a total joke," said Malcolm. "Mulgrew has our folks under a spell."

"Was Mandy Gibson there?" said Cullen.

Malcolm looked away. "She was there, aye." He didn't say anything else.

"Malcolm," said Lamb, his voice hard.

Malcolm shot a look at him. "What?"

"Did anything happen to Mandy Gibson?" said Lamb, rising to his feet, staring at him.

"Well, aye..."

"What?" said Lamb.

"I don't know how to say this..."

Lamb shouted at him. "I don't care, Malcolm, this is a murder inquiry."

Malcolm's hands tightened around his thighs. "They performed an exorcism on her."

22

Malcolm Thornton went into the details quickly, his rebel cool disappearing and a confused young boy coming to the surface.

"She started screaming during the service. She was having some sort of fit, rolling around on the floor. She was screaming, just kept on shouting." He then spoke in a whisper. "She kept shouting out 'Fuck' and screaming 'No'. She was like that for at least a minute."

He started to speak louder again. "Her parents didn't know what to do. Mulgrew came over and grabbed her by the shoulders. He started shouting, something like 'Get thee out of her, Satan!' over and over. A couple of others joined in, Mandy's dad and Jamie's as well. My dad got up but my mum held him back."

He paused for breath. "The three of them were like that, shouting at the Devil, eyes closed, for a few minutes. A couple of others joined in. It was like in a film. It felt like there was electricity in the room. It felt like the Devil really was in her."

"Do you believe that?" said Cullen.

Malcolm shrugged. "You're told about it every day and you don't believe it but then you see something like that. It was really frightening."

"What happened next?" said Cullen.

"Nothing much," said Malcolm. "Mandy's dad took her away, out into their car."

"Did he say anything to anyone?" said Cullen.

Malcolm strained his face in concentration. "He said something to Father Mulgrew, something like she should be better by now."

Cullen frowned. "Do you know what he meant by that?"

"No idea," said Malcolm. "Father Mulgrew does counsel all of us, though. Maybe he'd been trying to sort Mandy out for a long time. I don't know."

"Was Jamie there?" said Cullen.

"He's not been there for a long time," said Malcolm. "Not since he left school. His parents kept threatening to chuck him out of the house unless he went back but it never got that far."

Lamb looked stunned. He obviously had no idea what went on behind the doors of God's Rainbow.

Cullen didn't know why none of the parents had mentioned this exorcism.

"What counselling is this?" said Lamb.

"It's sort of like a confession, you know, like you see in films," said Malcolm. "But Mulgrew's sitting in the room across from you, not in some box. And he doesn't tell you to do punishment for sins. He asks you what's been troubling you and stuff. He points out chapters of his bible that might help."

"Do you find it useful?" said Lamb.

"Not really," said Malcolm. "Actually, it's a load of nonsense. It feels like they're trying to indoctrinate us. Jamie used to do a funny impression of Mulgrew in the confession, used to crack me and Thomas up. That was the only good thing about the group, seeing Thomas and Jamie. It was never the same after Jamie left."

Cullen looked at Lamb, who just nodded. "Thank you, Malcolm, you've been very helpful."

23

"How come when I actually want to speak to Bain, he doesn't answer his phone?" said Cullen, as he pocketed his mobile.

Lamb laughed.

They were driving to Mulgrew's cottage having barely spoken since they left the school, other than to agree on their destination.

Cullen's phone rang as they pulled up in front of the cottage. He noticed a small scratch on the screen, no doubt a result of the skirmish earlier. It was Bain. He answered as Lamb got out of the car.

"Had a missed call from you, Sundance," said Bain. "I'm driving. You're on my hands free."

"Got some news for you," said Cullen, watching Lamb walk up the path to Mulgrew's cottage. "Mandy Gibson was exorcised at this church service yesterday."

Bain was silent for what felt like minutes. "What fuckin' year is it, Cullen? Nobody exorcises anyone any more."

"We're dealing with a pretty strange religious cult here," said Cullen. "Young Malcolm Thornton told us. She had some sort of fit and that's how it was dealt with. A few others joined in."

Lamb turned and shrugged his shoulders — no sign of Mulgrew.

"Hell's bloody bells," said Bain. "What are you doing about it?"

"We're trying to speak to Mulgrew again," said Cullen. "Doesn't look like he's at his cottage."

"Don't make a pest of yourself, Cullen, okay?" said Bain. "Christ knows I'm in enough hot water already."

"Don't worry, I won't," said Cullen.

"Sundance, I told you to stay away from that school," said Bain.

"DS Lamb approved it," said Cullen.

"Right, well, Irvine and I are just on our way out," said Bain. "Head over to Garleton nick and we'll see you there in ten minutes."

"What about speaking to Mulgrew?" said Cullen.

"I want to speak to you pair first," said Bain.

"Fine," said Cullen. He ended the call.

Lamb sat down. "Bain?"

"Aye," said Cullen, rubbing his forehead. "He wants us back at the station."

"Fine," said Lamb. "Mulgrew wasn't in."

"No surprises there," said Cullen, looking out of the window at a steady stream of children heading home from school. "The kids in these houses don't get dropped off in four by fours."

Lamb laughed. "Very true."

The group from earlier had moved on, no doubt bullying boys and chatting up girls despite not attending that day.

"I spoke to some playing truant earlier," said Cullen.

"Spoke to or threatened?" said Lamb.

"Bit of both," said Cullen, with a laugh. "They said Mulgrew was out trying to convert them."

Lamb shook his head. "Nothing like a zealot, is there?"

There were still two or three boys heading up the far end, most likely to the houses around Mulgrew's.

Cullen opened his door. "Let's do some more digging." He climbed out and marched down the street, stopping the first one, an overweight boy of about thirteen. He held out his warrant card.

"Are you police?" said the kid.

Cullen nodded. "Worse, we're detectives," he said, waiting for Lamb to catch up. "Detective Sergeant Lamb is local, I'm from Edinburgh."

"Cool," said the boy, his eyes wide.

"Do you know the man who lives in the cottage at the end there?" said Lamb.

The boy nodded his head. "Father Mulgrew. I live next door."

Cullen looked back down the street, seeing a row of four council houses, the last one almost touching Mulgrew's cottage. "Do you ever speak to him?"

The boy shook his head. "Mum told me not to. He's a weirdo."

"In what way?" said Cullen.

The boy shrugged. "She wouldn't say. I think it's all the bible stuff."

"What bible stuff is this?" said Lamb.

"He used to put things through our letter box," said the boy. "Books and papers and things like that. Mum shoved them straight in the bin."

"Does he ever speak to you?" said Lamb.

The boy shook his head more vigorously than before. "The only time I heard him speaking was when he was shouting at Dean and Kieron."

"Who are they?" said Lamb.

"They live round here," said the kid.

Cullen connected them to the youths he'd spoken to earlier. "Are they the ones who don't go to school?"

The boy nodded.

"Thanks," said Cullen. He doubted he'd do anything with it, but it was good to have their names.

The boy smiled. "Can I ride in a police car?"

Cullen laughed. "Even I don't get to ride in a police car. I have to use my own." He pointed to his Golf. "See, that's my car."

The boy frowned. "Is it a GTI?"

Cullen shook his head. "Just a standard one."

"Can't you afford a better car?" said the boy.

Lamb laughed. "Time to get on home to your mother."

The boy smiled and walked off, heading down the path to the last house before Mulgrew's.

"I feel positively enlightened," said Lamb. "Even a little ned from the worst bit of this town thinks your car is crap."

24

"Gather round," said Bain, standing at the front of the room, his shirt sleeves rolled up, tie loosened off and suit jacket casually hanging from a chair.

He waited until everyone was looking at him. Most leaned against walls or furniture. Lamb rocked slowly back and forth on a desk chair, his legs crossed.

Bain took a sip of his Red Bull clone. While he had lain off it of late, Cullen had experienced at first hand what happened when Bain was caffeinated out of his head.

"Right," said Bain, "I've just got the results of the PM now. It's not looking too good, I'm afraid." He held up a thick wad of paper, at least fifty sheets of A4 — some sections already highlighted in yellow.

"Jimmy Deeley's secretary gave me a copy of the transcript before we headed over."

He pulled cheap-looking reading glasses out of his top pocket and put them on, squinting at the paper as he read aloud. "The cause of death is asphyxiation. Several signs point to suffocation — there are petechiae on the victim's eyes. Additionally, there are minor contusions to the wrists but not to the throat or face, which could indicate a struggle."

He turned the page. "From the shape and size of the bruising, we can tell these contusions were inflicted perimortem, i.e. around the time of death. From this, I deduce the most likely method of suffocation is with a pillow, though I would look to forensic confirmation from the crime scene officers. Initial analysis points to white cotton being present in her gums, which supports the theory. We have not found any traces under the fingernails but samples will be analysed."

Bain took his glasses off and looked around the room. "For those of you who aren't as well versed in the arts of the post mortem as myself," he said, looking directly at Lamb, "that translates to suffocation with a pillow and it looks like she was held down."

He put the glasses on again. "Time of death is hard to pinpoint due to the environmental circumstances she was found in, but I would estimate between ten PM on Sunday and four AM this morning."

Bain leaned back against the desk and put his glasses down beside a yellow highlighter. "I will be up James Anderson's trouser leg like a ferret to get some of the forensic analysis accelerated. We may be able to get samples of the pillow used or trace evidence from the fingernails."

Bain took another deep breath. "One of the things we didn't expect Deeley to find, however, was the girl was not a virgin."

25

"She wasn't a virgin?" said Lamb, lurching forward in his seat.
"Her hymen wasn't intact," said Bain, "which isn't conclusive in and of itself. However, Deeley found several factors pointing to the fact she had been penetrated, most likely by a penis."

"That's a pretty bold statement for Deeley to make," said Lamb. "I've seen that sort of stuff before and it can fall apart in court."

Bain gave a sharp nod. "Believe me, I've given him a pretty thorough grilling on this. I dealt with an honour killing in Glasgow about fifteen years ago where an Indian lassie was murdered because she wasn't a virgin. Similar shite happened there as here. It turned out the lassie had burst it while riding a horse."

He fixed Lamb with a glare. "Deeley is pretty certain on this one. There are sufficient physical deformations to suggest she was sexually active."

"Are you saying she was sexually assaulted before she was killed?" said Cullen

Bain shook his head. "Deeley only found signs of sexual activity. There was no trace evidence pointing to her being raped last night, no pubic hairs, semen, blood, anything like that."

"What do you want us to do, gaffer?" said Irvine, pounding away on gum.

Bain stroked his moustache. "I want to speak to the parents again." He looked at Law. "What about that behavioural psychologist? Did you get anywhere?"

Law nodded. "Finally managed to speak to her. They didn't find anything conclusive to cause Mandy to run away. She put it down to a result of the trauma suffered in the accident. I've asked for a copy of the report."

"Sounds like you'll be wasting your time," said Bain.

The room sat in stunned silence.

Angela appeared through the door, nervously looking around at the faces. She clutched a wad of papers tightly to her chest. "Sir."

"Here she is," said Bain, looking at Cullen, "Batgirl coming in to save the day despite Batman telling her to stay in the Batmobile."

Angela rolled her eyes. "That's going to get you into trouble one of these days."

Normally, there would have been laughter at Bain being taken down a peg or two by an ADC but there was little or no reaction, given the circumstances.

"I've done some digging into police records like you asked," said Angela.

"Go on," said Bain. "You might as well tell half of East Lothian so I don't have to."

Angela read from the first sheet. "For the Gibsons, there's not much. There's a report about Mandy's accident in Edinburgh."

"This better be going somewhere," said Bain, slowly shaking his head.

"Seamus Mulgrew lived in Ireland before he came to Scotland nine years ago," said Angela. "Mulgrew said he was in the Roman Catholic Church and I tracked him down to a town just outside Cork. I asked the local Garda if they knew anything about the circumstances of his departure. I just got an email back."

"And?" said Bain.

Cullen was beginning to be impressed by Angela — Bain was being a cock but she was keeping professional, avoiding rising to the bait.

"The email says he was laicized," said Angela.

"What on earth's that?" said Irvine.

"I didn't know what it meant either, so I looked it up on the internet," said Angela. "It means he was chucked out of the church."

"What for?" said Bain.

"Gambling debts," said Angela.

"And that's it?" said Bain, his face like thunder.

Angela shrugged. "Thought you'd like to know."

"Something doesn't tie up with this boy," said Bain. "I've got some contacts in the Garda I'll tap up, see what I can find."

He pinched the bridge of his nose and stood there for a while.

"Right," he said, taking a deep breath. "There's two possibilities for Mandy's death I can think of. First, the parents are involved, so I don't want to go directly to them just yet, not until we have some more evidence. Second, Jamie Cook's been at her."

"Do you want me to raise any other possibilities?" said Cullen.

"No," said Bain, eyes aflame. "The rest of you, do some digging in the town, speak to people, see what we can dig up about Mulgrew. Cullen and Lamb, I want you to visit Mulgrew and get stuck into this exorcism business."

26

T he God's Rainbow building looked like it was once a shop. At some point, the entire front had been painted bright yellow except for a rainbow band the full width of the building. Up close, the rainbow looked cheap and badly done. There was no advertising outside — Cullen had never seen a religious organisation that didn't try to spread the word through aggressive street marketing.

Lamb hammered his fist against the door. They waited almost thirty seconds, Lamb thumping twice more before Mulgrew finally opened up, beaming at them. "Officers, how can I help you?"

Lamb pushed him aside and entered the building.

The main part of the church was obviously a chapel, a wooden pulpit at the far end, though it wasn't grand in any sense. Rather than oak, flagstones and gold, it was furnished with MDF, concrete and steel. Cullen figured there was space for about forty people at a push.

Lamb stopped in the middle of the room and turned around.

"It's not such a nice day out, is it?" said Mulgrew, catching up.

"We need to ask you some questions," said Cullen, before Lamb could start.

"Please, come into my office," said Mulgrew, gesturing them through a door to the side of the pulpit.

They followed him into a small, dark room, the walls a mixture of old wallpaper and bare plaster. A reasonably large desk sat in the middle, covered with copies of the Bible, Torah and Koran, all heavily read with place marks protruding. The wall was shelved, the left half crammed with old books, the right taken up with stacks of glossy pamphlets, titles such as 'Teenage Abortion' and 'Immigration'.

Mulgrew sat down at his desk. "Fire away, then."

"We believe you weren't entirely honest with us this morning," said Cullen, pulling up a chair.

Mulgrew's face was set in a serious frown. "Oh?"

"We have information suggesting you conducted an exorcism on Mandy Gibson yesterday at your religious ceremony," said Cullen.

Mulgrew rubbed his temples, not saying anything for a while.

"Did you?" said Cullen.

"Yes," said Mulgrew, finally. "Her parents asked me not to mention this to anyone. It's a private matter."

"Doesn't sound like a private matter if it happened in a public place and the victim of the exorcism then turns up dead," said Cullen.

Mulgrew squinted his eyes at Cullen. "She was not a victim of an exorcism, she was the *beneficiary*. She was the *victim* of demonic possession."

"She wasn't possessed," said Cullen. "She was hit by a bus and had a brain injury."

"We discussed this earlier," said Mulgrew.

"You said you could perform an exorcism," said Cullen. "Did it slip your mind that you performed one on Mandy?"

Mulgrew smiled as he got to his feet and retrieved a pamphlet. "Listen to me," he said in a patronising tone, "the Catholic Church shies away from it nowadays, but it is something that still needs to be done, especially in this day and age." He tossed the pamphlet on the table between them.

Cullen picked it up and looked at it. 'Demonic Possession & Exorcism: Cure All of Your Ills'. It looked shoddy, full of typos and poor layout, though the paper stock was high quality. "I believe you have one-on-one counselling sessions with your parishioners. Does this include exorcism?"

Mulgrew closed his eyes. "Only in exceptional circumstances, like with Mandy, and only with absolute agreement of any parents or guardians."

"So this counselling includes only the younger members?" said Lamb.

"No, it's the full parish," said Mulgrew.

"How many exorcisms have you carried out in your time here?" said Cullen.

"None until yesterday," said Mulgrew.

Cullen flicked through his notebook. "What about Jamie Cook? This morning you told me he had the Devil himself inside him. Isn't that enough for an exorcism?"

Mulgrew looked away. "I have a strong faith," he said, his voice a harsh whisper. "I know I have the good Lord on my side but I am just one man. I need my word to spread if I'm to be able to take on Lucifer himself."

Lamb was rolling his fingers on the table in a repeating pattern, growing increasingly frustrated with Mulgrew. "Mandy's post mortem showed signs of sexual activity."

Mulgrew almost spat. "Do you think it's abuse?"

"Almost certainly," said Lamb.

"What are you saying?" said Mulgrew.

"We're wondering if you knew anything about it," said Cullen.

Mulgrew leaned across the table, and roared. "Just because I'm a religious man, you can't come in accusing me of being a child molester." Spittle dribbled down the side of his mouth. "You've attacked my faith both times I've met you. I know your sort. You try to undermine that which we children of God hold dear, like that bus in London, or that infernal Dawkins man. Come judgment day, you will burn in Hell."

Cullen smiled. They were getting to him. "Father, I was asking if you knew anything about it, not whether you'd done it."

"There's not much more I can add," said Mulgrew.

"Nothing at all?" said Cullen.

Mulgrew rubbed his forehead. "Have you spoken to Jamie Cook yet?"

"Not yet," said Lamb, reluctant to admit they couldn't find him.

"Right you are," said Mulgrew. He scratched the back of his head for a few moments. "I really shouldn't be doing this but I suppose I have to." He took a deep breath and looked up to the ceiling, whispering something to himself or his God.

He looked back down again. "Earlier, you alluded to my counselling sessions. These sessions are supposed to be confidential, as you can imagine. However, in cases where I have information that might help, or assist, with something, and I suppose a murder investigation would fit, then I have to part with the information and deal with the sin in my personal discourse with the Lord."

"Spit it out, Seamus," said Lamb.

Mulgrew closed his eyes. "Jamie talked about the troubles that constantly plagued him. From the age of about fourteen, maybe fifteen, he had fantasies of molesting children."

27

Cullen didn't know what to think. "Jamie Cook told you this?"

Mulgrew hung his head heavily in his hands, his elbows on the desk. "Yes," he said, with a whimper.

"Did he mention Mandy Gibson?" said Cullen.

Mulgrew took a deep breath. "Just the once."

Lamb had a look of abject disgust on his face. "What did he say, Seamus?"

"He had a fantasy about taking her to a shack somewhere away from everyone," said Mulgrew, "and doing what he wanted to her."

"Have you any idea where this shack is?" said Cullen.

"No," said Mulgrew, his voice a croak.

"Does it exist?" said Cullen.

"I don't know," said Mulgrew.

"Did you suggest any action he might take?" said Lamb.

Mulgrew took a deep breath. "I suggested he refrain from masturbation and to avoid contact with children."

"Did he heed the advice, do you know?" said Lamb.

"As to the first, who knows?" said Mulgrew. "I would very much doubt it. The second, well, he flagrantly violated that. He has a brother and sister — the poor things are eleven. The Lord alone knows what he did to them."

"Have you done any counselling with them?" said Cullen.

"On a monthly basis for the moment," said Mulgrew. "Neither of them has mentioned anything, though, and they seem perfectly balanced. That's not to say it hasn't happened."

"When was the last time Jamie talked to you about any of this?" said Lamb.

"Our sessions became more and more tense right up to when he decided to leave my church," said Mulgrew. "That was eighteen months ago."

"Did you ever tell his parents?" said Cullen.

Mulgrew scowled. "There is no way I could have told them. Not directly, anyway."

"And you definitely didn't try and exorcise him?" said Cullen.

Mulgrew grimaced. "I would have needed parental approval," he said, quickly. "They knew the boy was troubled, just not how much. As I said, the boy has the Devil in him and dealing with Satan himself is completely out of my remit. You would need a bishop to even contemplate such an undertaking, if not the Pope himself, and even then... My little church doesn't have the resources or the number of believers. One day, maybe."

Cullen couldn't shake the image of Mulgrew's church as some sort of *Britain's Got Talent* show, aiming for a golden number of followers that would allow him to vote off the Devil.

"Didn't you feel you should have gone to them with this?" said Lamb. "Especially in light of what has just happened?"

"Perhaps," said Mulgrew. "Hindsight is a blessed thing, though. One can only atone for one's sins in hindsight. And besides, I've been trying to tell you to focus on Jamie Cook."

"Do you have any way of corroborating any of this?" said Cullen.

"Sergeant Lamb here will tell you how often he has to pick the boy up for some petty crime or other."

Cullen rolled his eyes. "I'm not sure how much of a correlation there is between youthful criminality and paedophilia."

"Listen, I suggest you speak to Jamie Cook," said Mulgrew.

28

C ullen and Lamb went next door to the Church of Scotland.

They stood in the cavernous hall, Lamb asking questions of the minister, Andrew Pask, their voices echoing around the space. As Lamb probed further and deeper, he unseated a welt of rage and Pask grew increasingly angry as he spoke about the neighbouring priest.

"The man is a fraud," said Pask. "He's telling a pack of lies, selling religion like a pastor in some Southern US state. I'm astonished he's not bought TV adverts yet."

"Why do you say he's a fraud?" said Lamb.

"Before he started, I'd have in the region of one hundred and thirty people on a Sunday," said Pask. "That may seem like a lot, but it barely half-filled this place. I still get seventy on a good week, but you need to look at the people who've left. He hasn't taken those most in need of salvation and redemption, you know. He's taken the bank managers, the accountants, the doctors, the lawyers."

He swallowed. "We don't charge a tithe in the Church of Scotland but I know he does. Seamus Mulgrew doesn't have a network of churches or a Vatican City to pay for. He's taking money for himself."

"What's he doing with it?" said Cullen. "I've seen where he lives and the car he drives."

"Fraudsters don't always wantonly display their gains," said Pask.

"So what do you think he's doing with the money?" said Cullen.

"I hear rumours of expansion," said Pask. "I fear my colleagues in the surrounding area may soon face the same battle I am now."

Cullen figured getting further into the debate wouldn't be of benefit. "Thanks for your time."

They left Pask behind and headed back to the station.

"You think Mulgrew's on the level?" said Cullen.

"Could be, I suppose," said Lamb. "The story sort of tallies. According to everyone we speak to, Jamie has been a bloody nightmare since he was about fifteen years old which is consistent with these supposed fantasies."

"I'm no psychologist, but it just seems a bit convenient to me," said Cullen.

"How come?" said Lamb.

"Well, Jamie Cook is the black sheep of the flock, isn't he?" said Cullen. "He turned his back on their little cult. It's a bit of a stretch accusing him of murdering Mandy."

"You could be right."

"What about Pask?" said Cullen.

Lamb shrugged. "Baseless accusations aren't a particular favourite of mine."

"You have to admit there's something funny going on here," said Cullen. "Focusing on the rich of the flock."

"This sort of thing isn't unprecedented in these parts," said Lamb. "You ever heard of the Unification Church?"

"No?" said Cullen.

"They were a South Korean Christian cult, I suppose," said Lamb. "They had a centre in Dunbar in the late eighties and early nineties. They were doing much the same thing."

Cullen exhaled. "That sort of thing terrifies the life out of me."

"Would you rather be dealing with a stabbing in Niddrie?" said Lamb.

Cullen nodded. "I could do with a comfort zone that isn't Bain going off on one."

Lamb bellowed with laughter.

Cullen's phone rang. He checked the number — the mystery caller again. Instead of stroking the red bar to answer it, he pressed cancel and bounced it to voicemail.

"Do you know anything about the expansion plans for God's Rainbow?" said Cullen, trying to keep his voice steady.

"They've got pretty much everyone in this town indoctrinated," said Lamb. "Everyone they want, at least. They're looking to buy the old church hall in East Linton and move in there."

Once again, Cullen imagined Mulgrew and Gibson pulling Sharon's sister and her family into the centre of their spider's web, ready to share their bible and counsel the children.

"How does Mulgrew do it?" said Cullen.

"Wish I knew," said Lamb. "The old bugger must be coining it in. As Pask said, they're all bank managers and lawyers."

"What did Pask mean by a tithe?" said Cullen.

"I think it's an old word for a tenth," said Lamb. "Landowners used to take a tenth of their tenants' incomes. The Catholic Church has the same but it's usually a higher percentage. I bet Mulgrew has applied it here. That will be a lot of income."

Cullen pulled one of the pamphlets from his pocket. He inspected the paper again - that quality of work would be expensive. His flatmate, Tom, had gone through a phase of doing club flyers. One club wanted a load of booklets as well, a gimmick explaining their ethos, but Tom didn't manage to wangle the deal for the paper any cheaper than a grand for two thousand sheets. Mulgrew's pamphlets were at the higher end of the market, in the territory of small printing presses.

"Law's good with stuff like that," said Lamb, "I'll get her to look into it."

They walked up to the front of the station, Lamb unlocking a Focus parked next to Cullen's Golf.

"I'd best get on, then," said Lamb.

Cullen opened his door. "Where are you off to?"

"Going to try and shake down some snouts," said Lamb, "see if I can't find Jamie Cook."

Cullen watched Lamb drive off as he called his voicemail, taking in the traffic on the street in the early evening darkness as he listened to the same bass line and mantra-like vocals. He stabbed his finger at the screen, ending the call.

He noticed the little phone icon had a red one beside it — a missed call from Tom Jameson, his flatmate. He rang back.

"All right, Scotty," said Tom. "That was quick."

"Sorry, I was on another call," said Cullen. "What's up?"

"Any danger you could be in tonight at half six?" said Tom.

"Not looking likely," said Cullen. "Why?"

"You know how the boiler's knackered?" said Tom.

"Of course I know," said Cullen. A broken boiler in a flat that faced the full onslaught of the North Sea wind as it attacked Portobello in late January was the sort of thing you noticed.

"It's just that I've got a bloke coming round tonight to have a look," said Tom. "I can't make it, got called into an incident at work."

"Can't Richard do it?" said Cullen.

Richard McAlpine was their newest flatmate, a school friend of Cullen's who'd moved back from London to a job on the *Edinburgh Argus*, working as a journalist.

"I don't want to ask," said Tom.

"Well, you'll have to," said Cullen. "I've got a work function tonight I need to be at."

"Fair enough," said Tom.

"You need to learn to trust him," said Cullen. "He's a good guy. Isn't he working from home today?"

"Aye, I suppose you're right," said Tom.

"I am," said Cullen. "I'd better go." He ended the call and headed back inside to update Bain.

He was nowhere to be found.

Cullen did locate Bain's copy of the post mortem on the edge of a desk. He picked it up and started leafing through. It sent a shiver up his spine. The cold, technical words in the document were in stark contrast to the photography. One shot showed Mandy's lifeless eyes looking at the camera, almost pleading with him to find her killer.

"Pretty sick," said DC Murray.

Cullen looked up. "That's not the half of it." He took a deep breath. "Stuart, isn't it?"

Murray nodded. "Heard a lot about you."

Cullen had no idea his reputation — good or bad — had passed into East Lothian. "Really?"

"One of the lads in Haddington station got called in to help with the Schoolbook case," said Murray.

"What's his name?" said Cullen, his interest piqued.

"Steven Wright."

It meant nothing to Cullen. "Doesn't ring a bell."

"Me and Ewan were trying to get on it but Bill was having none of it," said Murray. "Some smackhead in Tranent did his mum in and that was us." He raised his eyebrows. "Heard you cracked it."

"I found the killer," said Cullen, "not that it did me any favours."

"You knew the officer who died?" said Murray.

Cullen was wrenched back to the early August afternoon in Portobello, hearing that blood-curdling scream. "I was with him when he was stabbed."

"Us DCs have to stick together," said Murray. "Show the brass how it's done."

"Tell me about it," said Cullen, distracted.

Someone called his name. He spun around and saw Bain in the doorway, his finger pointing at him. "Sundance, you're coming with me," he said, ignoring Murray, before turning around and pacing off.

Cullen ran to keep up, only catching Bain outside the station.

"What's up?" said Cullen.

"Just off the phone to the Garda," said Bain, heading down the street to the crossroads. "Luckily, I dealt with some boys from Cork when I was in Glasgow, had some favours to call in. Got them to do some digging. Turns out Mulgrew did have gambling debts but that's not the real reason he was defrocked."

He stopped and took a deep breath.

"Mulgrew was caught shagging young girls."

29

Cullen had to run to catch up with Bain again.

"How young are we talking?" said Cullen

"Young enough not to be able to legally consent," said Bain, powering on, fists clenched.

"Do you have the details of his victims?" said Cullen.

"There's not a website of them," said Bain. "This was all hushed up. The last thing the Catholic Church wanted was another paedophile priest scandal."

Bain hammered at the door of God's Rainbow. No response. He tried the door. Locked.

"Doesn't look like he's here," said Cullen.

"I can bloody see that," said Bain. "Where is he?"

"We were just here with him," said Cullen. "Me and Lamb. We asked him about the exorcism."

Bain's face was red with anger. "And?"

"He pointed us towards Jamie Cook," said Cullen. "Said he'd told him he had fantasies about abusing children."

"Jesus Christ," said Bain. He kicked the door of the church. "Do you believe him?"

"I don't know what to believe," said Cullen. "What he said was quite detailed."

Bain shook his head. "You and Lamb should have put him in cuffs."

Cullen bit his tongue. "I'm going round the back," he said, his voice almost level. "He can't be gone. It was only ten minutes ago."

"Be quick," said Bain, going back to kicking the door.

Cullen headed down the narrow lane between God's Rainbow and Alba Bank. There was a barred window overlooking the lane. He stood on tiptoes and peered through. The building was dark inside.

He continued on to a small yard at the back of the church. He opened his phone and switched on the torch app, the continual glare lighting up the space. It was strewn with broken glass from vodka and beer bottles. Cullen crept across, careful not to slice open the soles of his shoes.

The blinds on the back windows were open — one was Mulgrew's office and the other the chapel. Cullen shone his light through both windows. He had a reasonable view of the whole building. It looked like nobody was there.

He returned to the front. "Nothing."

"I called Lamb and got the fucker over to Mulgrew's cottage," said Bain. "Radio silence since."

They stood looking at the door, thinking what to do.

The exorcism stuff was making Cullen suspicious about Mulgrew. They should have taken him into an interview room, but they'd let him go. Thinking about it, he had probably tipped him off — if he hadn't come here with Lamb, asking about the exorcism, Mulgrew would have been none the wiser.

Bain shook his head. "Right, Sundance, your notebook didn't see me do this."

He raised his foot and kicked the front door. It gave after three attempts. He stormed in and fumbled for a switch, calling for Mulgrew as the strip lights flickered to life. No answer.

Cullen went through to Mulgrew's office. It was empty.

"Bastard," said Bain, standing in the middle of the chapel. "Come on, we're going to his house."

They left the door hanging off its hinges, heading towards his car a block away. They'd only been inside for a minute at most but it was raining heavily again, the pavements starting to slick with water.

Cullen skidded to a stop beside the car.

Bain shook his head. "Get in, you clown."

The wheels spun as he took off, Cullen wrestling with the seatbelt.

Bain drove fast, up the tail of every car they encountered in the moderate traffic. He took a sharp left, taking the back way to Mulgrew's house. *Teenage Kicks* by the Undertones blared out of the stereo at deafening volume.

Cullen felt his ears would start bleeding any minute. "This is my dad's favourite song."

Bain turned round to glare at him. "Your dad?"

"Aye," said Cullen.

"What age are you, anyway, Sundance?" said Bain, as he swerved around two double-parked cars, almost hitting an oncoming van.

"Twenty-nine," said Cullen. "Thirty in March."

Bain shook his head. "Bloody hell."

"How old are you?" said Cullen.

"Forty-six in August."

"I take it you're a punk?"

Bain grinned. "Aye, I was. Mind, I was only eleven when *God Save The Queen* came out."

"My dad was into all those bands in the seventies," said Cullen. "Still is."

"What age is he?" said Bain.

"Fifty-two."

Bain laughed to himself. "And they say policemen are getting younger."

He screeched to a stop by Mulgrew's house. The rusting Volvo was conspicuous by its absence.

"He'd better be in," said Bain.

They raced up the path. Bain hammered at the door. No answer. He hammered again. Then scowled, pointing at the door. "Your turn, Sundance."

Cullen took a step back then launched himself shoulder first at the door. It cracked as he smashed through, tumbling to the floor of Mulgrew's hall.

Bain jumped over him. Cullen got up and followed him into the living room.

"Not looking too promising," said Bain. "You go upstairs, I'll have a butcher's in here."

Cullen took the stairs two at a time. The first door he tried was a small bathroom with an avocado suite and no shower. He quickly scanned the space, there was nowhere to hide.

He headed into the bedroom next door. The bed wasn't made, the bed linen almost grey from lack of washing. Cullen checked underneath, finding a dust-covered leather suitcase. He kicked it for good measure.

A big wardrobe dominated the wall opposite the bed. Cullen grabbed at the door half expecting to find Mulgrew cowering inside, but was confronted by clothes. He tossed them aside and searched the back of the wardrobe. Nothing, just piles of old shoes at the bottom.

The final door of the hall led to a tiny box room stuffed with large storage crates. He looked in them one by one, finding nothing. He gave up and went back downstairs.

Bain was standing at the back window, looking out, phone to his ear. "I expected you to be over here, Sergeant," he said into his mobile. "I don't care. I don't care."

He pointed at Cullen then through the back window. There was a shed at the end of the long, narrow garden.

Cullen found a switch by the back door, which turned on a light outside. He grabbed a key off a hook on the wall and beat a path toward the shed through the pouring rain. He turned the key and slowly pulled the door open. There was a lawnmower and some rusted garden tools — spade, fork, hoe — but no Mulgrew. Cullen locked up and headed back to the cottage.

"I will see you at the station in ten minutes, Sergeant." Bain slammed his phone shut. "Lamb is a useless bastard. Still can't find Jamie Cook from under his own nose. Provincial plods are the worst. The Leith lot don't know their arse from their elbow half the time but at least they've dealt with a crime worse than speeding."

"What now?" said Cullen.

"I really don't know," said Bain, rubbing his moustache. "Any bright ideas?"

Cullen exhaled. "The two things I'm thinking are either

Mulgrew's lying and he killed Mandy, or he's telling the truth and Jamie Cook killed her."

"Reckon Charles Gibson will know?" said Bain.

Cullen shrugged. "Worth a shot, I guess."

30

They were back with the Gibsons, Cullen having half a mind to drag them into the station for questioning. He scribbled the date and time in his notebook — 5.26pm.

"Why didn't you tell us about your daughter's exorcism?" said Cullen.

"I didn't think it was pertinent to your investigation," said Gibson. He looked drunk — Cullen had spotted an empty whisky glass on the table as they entered.

"I'd like to be the judge of that," said Cullen. "I prefer to exclude things, rather than not be presented with them in the first place."

Bain was keeping his counsel after Cullen suggested he calm himself down having already broken into buildings twice that evening.

"Is it pertinent?" said Gibson, his voice rising. "It's a *religious* treatment. Why do you focus on your prejudices and not think of the many *blessings* she received from our religious group? Why aren't you looking at her school, for instance?"

"We've been out there and spoken to her teacher and head-teacher," said Cullen. "There doesn't appear to be a link between the school and her murder. With this religious group, there are links all over the place. Jamie Cook, for instance. And now Seamus Mulgrew has disappeared."

"Disappeared?" said Gibson, scowling. "I spoke to him this afternoon, he—"

"We have visited both his church and home in the last twenty minutes," said Cullen. "Seamus Mulgrew was at neither. He's not answering his mobile. It seems a bit suspicious."

"Let me assure you there is absolutely nothing to suspect with Father Mulgrew," said Gibson, his mouth turning into the sort of smile Cullen thought only the very religious have.

"Do you know where he is?" said Cullen.

"I don't keep Seamus's diary," said Gibson, "but I would imagine he is either meeting our solicitor regarding the East Linton hall, or maybe taking some time out. It is a challenge being our figurehead, you know?"

He took a deep breath and looked at the ceiling. "He has been known to head off for a break on occasion. Having one of his closest parishioners murdered is a trying event for even a man of Seamus's stature. Not being contactable isn't a strange event in and of itself."

"Maybe," said Cullen, "but this isn't in and of itself. Father Mulgrew being missing the same day Mandy Gibson is found dead might be deemed a strange event."

"What do you expect me to do?" said Gibson. "I don't know where he is."

Cullen changed tack. "At the service on Sunday, I believe you said to Father Mulgrew something along the lines of 'she should be better by now'. Can you explain this?"

Gibson's forehead creased slightly. "Father Mulgrew was coun-selling Mandy and she didn't seem to be improving," he said, placing his hands in an open gesture. "That was all."

"Mandy had a fit, is that right?" said Cullen.

"She did," said Gibson.

"And did this happen often?" said Cullen.

"More than we would have liked," said Gibson, looking away. "It was most distressing seeing her lose control like that, convulsing on the floor, eyes rolling, her whole body shaking. We couldn't get through to her until it abated."

Elaine cleared her throat and wiped a tear from her cheek. "Can I ask why you're raising these questions now?"

"We're actively chasing leads, as you can imagine," said Cullen.

"Some of them relate to your family, and some to Father Mulgrew."

Cullen clocked Bain glance at him.

Elaine spotted it. "Look, can you just spit it out, please?"

"Okay," said Cullen. "I regret to inform you that your daughter's post mortem showed signs of sexual abuse."

"My God," said Elaine.

Gibson looked up, bleary-eyed, forehead creased in confusion. "What?"

"I understand this will be difficult to take in," said Cullen, leaning forward in his chair. He didn't continue, instead giving them space.

Gibson had tears in his eyes as he stared at the floor, his hand tightly gripping the arm of the sofa.

"Charles," said Elaine.

Gibson looked around at his wife. "I'm finding this incredibly hard to take in." He stared at Cullen. "My daughter was sexually abused?"

Cullen nodded.

"Had she been raped?" said Gibson.

"Rape is a legal term," said Cullen. "That said, given Mandy was only thirteen, she couldn't have consented. There were no signs she had intercourse around the time of her death. Do you have any idea who may have been responsible?"

"Well, it certainly wasn't me," said Gibson.

"We're not in any way suggesting that," said Cullen.

"Jamie Cook," said Gibson, looking away. "He was good friends with my son. He was in the house fairly often but I—" He briefly paused. "Perhaps he could've done something to Mandy."

"But you've never suspected anything?" said Cullen.

Gibson shrugged. "With a boy like that, you learn to suspect everything."

"Could he have abused your daughter?" said Cullen.

"I don't know," said Gibson. "Possibly." He took a deep breath. "We put a stop to him staying here about two months ago." He shook his head. "We just wanted to keep him away from Thomas. We were worried his grades might slip."

His eyes locked on Cullen. "Jamie may have taken a copy of

one of our keys. That could explain how he got Mandy out of the house on Sunday."

"Did you ever notice keys going missing?" said Cullen.

Gibson shook his head. "It's not something we paid particular attention to."

Cullen jotted it down. "What about Seamus Mulgrew? Could he have abused your daughter?"

Gibson scowled. "Father Mulgrew is a pillar of the community. He would never harm an innocent. Never."

"That's not what we've been told," said Cullen.

Gibson sat forward. "What's that supposed to mean? You come in here with your innuendo and your slurs against my religion. My daughter has been murdered. Can't you put yourself to good use by finding the animal who did this, rather than trying to take down a religion you don't agree with, but which has committed no crime?"

Cullen waited a moment before speaking again. "I've no interest in taking down your religion. I understand you're struggling to cope with your daughter's death, as most people would. However, we have done some investigation into Father Mulgrew's past. Do you know what he did before he came to this country?"

"He was in the Catholic Church," said Gibson.

"And do you know why he left?"

"I do," said Gibson, looking down. "Father Mulgrew was laicized."

"Any idea why?"

Gibson sighed. "Seamus told me he had a gambling habit that got out of hand. It was a confession I heard as part of my training. Of course, it's not strictly confidential in our faith, otherwise I could never tell you this."

Cullen nodded. "That's the official reason for the termination of his employment. Our sources in the Garda tell us a different story. Father Mulgrew was laicized by the Church for child molestation."

Gibson sat for a few moments, fist clenching and unclenching, before taking a deep breath. "I knew."

Elaine looked over at him. "Charles, is this true?"

"I'm afraid it is," said Gibson, closing his eyes for a few moments. "Seamus told me about it fairly early on in our sessions.

It was one of the key factors in him selecting me to take over from him."

"Can you please expand?" said Cullen.

Gibson coughed. "The gambling was used as a front. In truth, Seamus never gambled much, certainly nothing beyond the odd horse. He had a weakness for girls. It was ingrained in the Catholic Church, he said. Seamus poured his heart out into the wee small hours."

"Did he describe these girls?" said Cullen.

Gibson nodded. "He told me the girls in question were all fifteen, not far off sixteen. It was a grey area to him. He said they consented, that they were old beyond their years." He snorted back some tears. "He now acknowledges they couldn't have consented, but he believes he was a victim of their predation rather than the other way round."

"What did you do with this knowledge?" said Cullen.

"I suggested he received medical treatment," said Gibson. He looked at his wife. "You remember when I had to take over for a few weeks a while ago? That was when Seamus went to the Royal Ed."

Cullen knew the hospital — a great modern monstrosity that housed Edinburgh's mental health patients, stuck in the middle of Morningside.

"He stopped short of chemical castration," said Gibson. "It would have been the next step if he had the urges again. He hadn't had them in years."

Bain's eyes burned a hole into Charles Gibson's head. "You left both your children alone with a known sex offender?"

Gibson held Bain's gaze. "If we can't forgive then what are we? Seamus confessed his sins and was moving on with his life, spreading the word of God. Mandy and Thomas were perfectly safe with him."

He got to his feet, signalling the questioning was over.

"Given you obviously haven't yet managed to track down Jamie Cook, if I were you I would be focusing my efforts there rather than scurrilous innuendo against a great man."

31

Twenty minutes later Cullen sat in the Incident Room, wedged between Lamb and Angela along with more than thirty other officers, Bain having called the entire investigation team in.

"What we do know is there are two suspects here," said Bain. He pointed at the blown-up photograph pinned to the wall. "One is Seamus Mulgrew, the head of the God's Rainbow cult operating in this town. Maybe 'sect' is more accurate but I half expect this lot to burn themselves to death for the Lord."

Angela raised her eyebrows at Cullen while several other officers chuckled, with at least one face frowning.

Bain pointed to a photo of Cook taken at one of his frequent arrests. "The other suspect we've got is Jamie Cook. He's been a right menace to this town for the last couple of years and he's only seventeen." He looked at Lamb and grinned. "Pissing in public is the latest, right Sergeant?"

Lamb cleared his throat. "That's right," he said in an authoritative tone. "We picked him up on Saturday night for urinating against the side of God's Rainbow. We let him go without charge on Sunday morning and we believe he returned home. After that we have no idea where he went, or where he is now."

He paused, looking around the room. "We have numerous officers out searching for him. DC Cullen and myself responded to a reported sighting this afternoon but it was unfortunately mistaken identity. I appreciate the efforts you're all making in trying to find the boy and we just need to close the loop around him."

Bain cut Lamb off. "As for Mulgrew, he seems to have gone missing as well. We have received information he was a Roman Catholic Priest when he lived in Ireland. We have subsequently learned the reason for his defrocking was covered up at the time. We've just confirmed he was chucked out for child abuse."

The room exploded in a cacophony of noise, officers exchanging looks with each other as they mouthed disbelief.

Bain held his hand up and shouted over the hubbub. "If you tie that together with the post mortem showing clear signs Mandy had been sexually active then Mulgrew becomes a real suspect here."

He took a long drink from a can of Red Bull. "Trouble is, we have further information suggesting Jamie Cook might have liked a bit of fresh meat, if you know what I mean." He finished the can, crushing it in one hand. "Finding Jamie Cook remains our highest priority. I've asked Sergeant Lamb to do that by whatever means necessary."

Lamb nodded. "I've got another team coming in who will be put on this."

"The local CID officers have been out interviewing friends of Jamie Cook for further leads," said Bain, his passive voice insinuating they hadn't done a very good job of it.

Lamb looked around the room. "We've initially focused on his friends from school and in the town. We've not found anything additional so far."

Bain grumbled. "DS Irvine, can you give a précis of your activities?"

Irvine stood up, lips smacking together. He held up a few sheets of paper. "I've had a request in to trace his mobile. Early results look like he was in Haddington until just before two o'clock when the phone got switched off."

Cullen flicked through his notebook — that was when the crank phone calls had started.

"We checked the location, it turned out to be the Aldi," said Irvine. "There are no confirmed sightings of the boy from staff or shoppers." He folded the sheet of paper. "Obviously we'll get the nod if and when the mobile goes back on."

Cullen wondered what Irvine had been up to, where he'd spent his hours of activity.

"Good work," said Bain. He held up a sheet of paper and read out actions from it. "Finally, the Edinburgh-based officers have a meeting with DCI Turnbull at seven to update him on our progress out here. Dismissed."

Cullen thought it was probably best he didn't point out the real reason for the update was to head back into town for the Burns Supper.

He felt a tap on his shoulder. He turned around to see the desk sergeant from downstairs.

"Cullen is it?" said the man, his voice gravelly. "Got a Paul Russell downstairs for you."

32

Cullen appropriated Angela and an interview room on the ground floor.

Paul Russell was athletic looking, in stark contrast to his wife, and had already changed from his work suit into casual gear.

"My wife said you were interested in speaking to me," said Russell, his eyes darting between Cullen and Angela. "I work in Edinburgh, so apologies for not getting across earlier. I had to cycle up from the train station at Drem."

Cullen smiled. "Thank you for coming in. We wanted to ask you a few things about Mandy Gibson."

"I've heard the news," said Russell.

"We understand Mandy had a habit of turning up at your house in the middle of the night looking for your daughter, Susan," said Cullen. "Is that correct?"

"It is," said Russell, slouching back in the chair.

"How often did this happen?"

"Often," said Russell.

"Can you think of when it started?" said Cullen.

Russell looked around the room. "You're probably talking the summer of 2010."

Cullen scribbled it down, it tallied with everything he'd been told so far. "You and your wife are members of God's Rainbow, correct?"

Russell looked away from Cullen for the first time. "Yes, we are."

"And were you at the service yesterday?" said Cullen.

Russell scowled. "Yes, I was. I've been told about you, trying to persecute the entire town for its religious beliefs."

Cullen held out his hands to placate the man. "We're trying to piece together her movements before she turned up dead this morning."

"Right," said Russell.

"We have it on good authority that Mandy was exorcised at the ceremony," said Cullen.

Russell folded his arms. "That's true."

"Were you involved?" said Cullen.

"No," said Russell, decisively. "Father Mulgrew performed the exorcism. Mandy's father and Robert Cook assisted."

"What were you doing at that point?" said Cullen.

"I was sitting with my wife and daughter," said Russell, "trying not to get involved."

"Does this sort of thing happen often?"

"It's certainly the first time I've seen it," said Russell.

"Did you see or hear anything unusual before or after?"

"I'm afraid not," said Russell. "It was like any other Sunday morning."

"You didn't hear anything between Father Mulgrew and Charles Gibson, for instance?" said Cullen.

"No."

Cullen knew he wasn't getting anything more out of him on the exorcism. "When was the last time you spoke to Father Mulgrew?"

"Just before the ceremony yesterday," said Russell. "Can I ask why you want to know?"

"We're just checking up on a few things, that's all," said Cullen. "What can you tell us about the counselling Father Mulgrew gives the children?"

"I would say it is one of the best things that has ever happened to the community," said Russell. "In all honesty, it has greatly assisted my daughter in achieving top grades."

"What particular trauma is Susan overcoming?"

Russell didn't respond.

"Is there one?" said Cullen, starting to lose patience.

"No."

Cullen shared a look with Angela, who raised an eyebrow. He stared at Russell again. "We're looking to verify a few statements about Father Mulgrew."

The fire disappeared from Russell's eyes. "Seamus is a strong and kind man. He has taken a broken community and turned it right around. It is no coincidence this town now has the top performing school in the Lothians."

"Are you sure?" said Cullen.

"Absolutely."

Cullen leaned across the desk. "What if I told you Seamus was defrocked as a priest in Ireland?"

"I know he was," said Russell, his eyes screwed up. "He was an outspoken critic of the Catholic Church. He quite rightly thought they'd lost their way, much like the other mainstream Christian religions."

"Did he tell you the real reason?"

"The real reason is because of his words," said Russell.

"Not his gambling debts?" said Cullen.

Russell looked tired and irritated. "I'd say that was a good cover story."

"For who?" said Cullen. "The Church or Mulgrew?"

Amusement danced over Russell's face. "The Church."

Cullen turned over a piece of paper on the table. "The real reason was he had been abusing children."

Russell's Adam's apple bobbed up and down quickly. He slowly licked his lips. "I'm sorry?"

Cullen pointed at the highlighted marks on the sheet. "This piece of paper contains the results of Operation Stingray, an investigation into Seamus Mulgrew and other priests. The Garda presented their findings to the bishop in Cork."

"That seems like a slur on a perfectly good man," said Russell. "My faith in Seamus is resolute. I believe him and his word more than I do the Irish police or the Catholic Church. You think he's a paedophile just so you can get a result. It's deplorable."

"He told Charles Gibson about it," said Cullen.

Russell leaned back in his chair and yawned. "Did he now?"

Cullen nodded slowly, trying to appear in control. His shirt was damp from sweat, having only just dried. He had been pushing these people on their religious views all day, trying to find out what the hell was going on, but no-one pushed back as strongly as Paul Russell, not even Charles Gibson.

"Do you know where Father Mulgrew is?" said Cullen.

"No," said Russell. "I work in Edinburgh. I was on the half seven train this morning and I've just got back home. I'm hungry and I wouldn't mind seeing my family."

"Did Father Mulgrew speak to you about Jamie Cook?" said Cullen.

Russell sighed. "The whole town speaks of Jamie Cook. The boy is a bad influence on the other kids. He's pure evil. I was glad he left the group. I didn't want his poison affecting Susan." He tapped at the desk. "Have you considered Mandy's disappearances started up because of Jamie Cook?"

"What are you suggesting?" said Angela, becoming animated.

Russell's eyes bored into Cullen's. "You do know he used to stay over at the Gibsons' house, don't you?"

Cullen nodded slowly. "We're aware of it."

Russell shrugged. "Something Jamie did might have triggered Mandy's night wanders."

"We'll consider that," said Cullen.

"Can I go?" said Russell.

Cullen checked his notebook — nothing else presented itself. "For now."

Russell got to his feet and pulled his jacket on. "If I were you, Jamie Cook would be my prime suspect."

Cullen had never been inside DCI Jim Turnbull's office before, their few encounters were mainly at the front door, around Bain's desk or in one of the Incident Rooms. Turnbull had a corner office on their floor in Leith Walk police station, the gleaming new building which regularly attracted strong criticism from the local press in these straitened times. It looked down on the flow of red and white lights on Leith Walk, now slicked with rain in the early evening gloom.

Turnbull sat behind his large desk, already in full Highland dress ahead of the Burns Supper

Bain sat immediately opposite, flanked by Irvine and Cullen, with Angela sitting off to the side.

"Brian, Brian, Brian," said Turnbull, weary of Bain's continual excuses.

Cullen didn't know why Turnbull had them all there, but he enjoyed watching Bain squirm at every answer Turnbull forced out of him.

"We've been here before with you," said Turnbull. "You need to start squaring the circle with DS Lamb. He has a central role to play in this investigation. He knows the lay of the land out there."

"The circle is square enough," said Bain.

Turnbull screwed his eyes up. "Brian, that doesn't mean anything. You need to be able to work with officers like DS Lamb."

"I can work with him," said Bain. "He's got a problem with authority."

"Maybe it's *your* authority he has the problem with," said Turnbull.

"Having a loose cannon running around doing what he wants doesn't help either of us," said Bain.

"Brian, you're fishing in the wrong pond here," said Turnbull. "I'm warning you now."

"I'm just saying," said Bain.

"I've been given operational command of DS Lamb and his officers for as long as it takes you to secure an arrest in this case," said Turnbull. "I hope it's soon."

"I'm warning you now, if it's not it'll be because of Lamb," said Bain.

Turnbull shut his eyes and took a long breath. "Brian, in lieu of you being able to obtain the buy-in of the local CID," he said, his voice recovering the smooth calm, "can we do a deep dive on the case, in particular your two suspects?"

Bain gave him detailed outlines of Seamus Mulgrew and Jamie Cook, Cullen tuning them out and using the time to make some notes. He couldn't decide on the most likely suspect, stuck between Mulgrew's child abuse and Cook's access to Mandy.

Cook's continued absence was seriously hampering the investigation. If you've nothing to hide, why hide?

He didn't want to jump to conclusions about Mulgrew either, having seen what could happen when Bain latched onto a suspect with insufficient evidence.

Cullen looked up as Bain concluded his summary.

"Thanks," said Turnbull. "Okay, let's turn the hothouse around here. Which of the two suspects is your favourite?"

Cullen had never heard 'hothouse' and 'deep dive' before. He scribbled them down, making sure he added them to the office bullshit bingo later.

"I'm currently edging towards Jamie Cook," said Bain. "For the main part, Mulgrew has five or six character witnesses we'd need to navigate."

"You do have the information from the Garda in your locker, Brian," said Turnbull. "If we have to mount a rearguard action then I'm prepared to, you know that."

"I'll bear it in mind," said Bain.

"What do you have on the Cook boy, then?" said Turnbull.

"A police record longer than your arm before he's eighteen for starters," said Bain. "Very few charges, mind. Mulgrew told us Cook had child abuse fantasies."

"I'm not sure offsetting one suspect against the other is a particular path we want to tread," said Turnbull.

"Charles Gibson could back them up if pushed, I would suspect," said Bain.

"Brian, he's a grieving father."

"Cook had sleepovers with Mandy's brother, Thomas," said Bain. "That gave him access to her. He might have copied the keys for the house, we don't know."

"And Mulgrew?"

"We're working on it," said Bain.

"Have you got them in custody?" said Turnbull.

Bain closed his eyes. "They've both gone to ground."

"Both?" said Turnbull. "Jesus Christ. Are you seriously telling me you've lost both of your suspects already?"

"Well, to be fair," said Bain, sitting forward in his chair, "we've had a call out all day on Jamie Cook and Mulgrew disappeared after we learnt about his defrocking."

Turnbull shook his head slowly. "This is going south, isn't it?" He looked at Cullen and Irvine for confirmation.

"We've only been at it since this morning," said Irvine. "Can't expect us to work miracles."

"Sergeant Irvine, the general public *does* expect us to, I'm afraid," said Turnbull. "I'm not sure the press would deem tracing two people in a small town as particularly miraculous." He looked at Cullen, leaning back in his chair. "Any thoughts, Constable?"

"Finding Jamie Cook is a priority," said Cullen. "Whether he did it or not, I would say he's the key to this case."

Turnbull locked eyes on Bain again. "Why haven't we found him? Garleton is a small town. I'm sure Lamb and his boys can shake down their black books at the drop of a hat and rustle him up."

"That's what you'd think," said Bain. "Trouble is, they've not been able to." He chuckled. "They did find a *Big Issue* seller who looks a wee bit like Cook, mind. Cullen had to assault him before they realised it wasn't him."

Cullen raised his hands in defence. "I was apprehending a potential suspect."

"Fair enough," said Turnbull.

"Aren't there other local CID officers I could use?" said Bain. "With Lamb and his boys, it feels like we're scraping the bottom of the barrel."

Turnbull smacked his hand on the desk. "Enough. I've worked with Bill Lamb for almost fifteen years. He is a good officer, out of the top drawer. If you're looking for insight, passion and leadership, he's your man."

"He's still not turned up a wee ned on his back doorstep," said Bain, leaning back and crossing his legs. "We did a phone trace — the boy's been in Haddington. That's where Lamb's based, right?"

Turnbull leaned forward and pointed at Bain. "I've told you that's enough. DI Cargill is back from leave on Thursday. If this isn't resolved by close of play on Wednesday, she's taking over the case."

Bain rubbed furiously at his moustache but said nothing.

"I'm serious," said Turnbull. "You don't want me out in Garleton drilling into the detail here."

"Are you wanting us to head back out there to assist Lamb?" said Bain.

Turnbull sat back in his chair. "You know full bloody well I need you at this Burns Supper tonight. I've got precious few of my men in attendance as it is."

He pointed a finger at Bain.

"Maybe keeping you out of DS Lamb's hair will do the case good."

34

H alf an hour later, Cullen sat in the corridor outside the function suite at Fettes, sipping from a pint of lager, leaving the others to the pre-dinner drinks so he could meet Sharon. She was late, as ever.

He looked across the wet car park, lit up by sodium lights as the January wind blew rain about in wild swirls, thinking through the chaos of the day and struggling to keep an open mind on who had killed Mandy Gibson.

It was now over twenty-eight hours since anyone had seen Jamie Cook. The longer he was missing, the worse it looked for him. The information they had so far pointed to a lonely soul disowned by his community and tormented by unknown demons, figurative or psychological.

In his mind's eye, Cullen pictured him on the run, hiding from the police, his parents and Mulgrew. It reminded him of another of his dad's favourite tunes, *Police On My Back* by The Clash, about some guy on the run, wondering what he'd done.

Maybe that was Jamie Cook.

Seamus Mulgrew was an enigma to Cullen.

The many stupid sectarian attacks he'd seen after Old Firm games in West Lothian meant he didn't have a positive view of religion, but he was trying to make sure any prejudice didn't cloud his judgment.

He still wanted to explore Mulgrew's past further.

He took another sip of his pint — gassy and tasteless, unlike the German or Czech lagers he was so fond of — and checked his watch. He took a deep breath.

Cullen and Sharon had been an item for nearly six months. Although he wasn't drinking any less, he was behaving differently, the twelve pints of lager with his flatmates replaced by bottles of red wine at her flat.

Sharon still had doubts about him, mainly with his notoriety for sleeping around, but she was beginning to trust him more and more. She was surprisingly territorial and possessive, making sure they ended up at her flat after work or nights out.

He checked the football news on his phone, rubbing at the new scratch on the screen. It didn't look like Aberdeen would do any strengthening in the January transfer window.

Looking down his received calls list, the unknown-number hoax calls stood out. Other than Jamie Cook, he couldn't think who it was. Sharon might have some insight on it.

"Little boy lost."

He looked up at Sharon, his heart surging, feeling something close to love. He stood and she put her arms around him. He held her in a long kiss, his hand caressing her back and hips.

She whispered into his ear as she nibbled it. "I could take you into the toilets and have you there."

The twitch in his groin suggested he could, too. "Don't tempt me."

She kissed him on the lips. "We'd better wait until later. I don't want to get caught at it inside HQ." She sat down on the chair next to his.

"Do you want a drink?" said Cullen.

"I'm fine just now," said Sharon.

"I was looking for your car."

"Chantal gave me a lift," she said. "She had to drop some evidence off."

"Isn't she coming?" said Cullen.

She shook her head. "Got a date." She looked around. "Is the big bad wolf here?"

Cullen nodded. "He just got a carpeting from Turnbull. He threatened to pass the case onto Cargill."

"Oh?" said Sharon, eyebrows raised.

Cullen knew Sharon and Cargill had previous, having fallen out five years ago when they were DC and DS respectively, but she hadn't expanded on it further.

"That's all you need," she said. "Bain will be going loopy."

"Tell me about it," said Cullen.

"How is it going?" she said. "There's a lot of attention on it."

Cullen gave her a download of the case, save for the phone calls.

"I can see why Turnbull is talking about Cargill," she said. "This is classic Bain territory. He's like an unexploded bomb at times."

"He's had a few explosions today already."

She laughed. "How are you coping? Child murder is hard to deal with. I've been on courses about it, Scott. You haven't."

"You know me. I'm fine."

"I do know you," she said, "and that's why I'm worried."

"I'll be fine," said Cullen. "Really."

"Okay," she said with a bright smile.

"How's your day been?"

Her face quickly turned sour. "Kenny Falconer is back on the scene."

Cullen knew him well, a nasty little ned with a penchant for knives. "What's he done now?"

"Stabbed a mate's mother," said Sharon.

"Jesus Christ," said Cullen. "He continually manages to sink to new depths."

"I've had him in for questioning all day and of course he denies it. He's got a solid alibi. We've been all over this guy and it seems sound. There's nothing we can find to discredit him."

"Bastard," said Cullen

"You're telling me," said Sharon.

She took a long, deep breath and looked into his eyes. Cullen could have sat like that forever.

"Time for that drink," she said, getting to her feet.

35

"'*Ye pow'rs wha mak mankind your care*','" said Turnbull, raising a knife in the air, his voice rising to a crescendo, "'*An' dish them out their bill o' fare, auld Scotland wants nae skinkin' ware, that jaups in luggies, but, if ye wish her gratefu' prayer, gie her a haggis!*'"

He shouted the last line, finishing Burns' famous *Address to a Haggis*, before plunging the blade deep into the pudding, slicing the gut wide open, the steaming contents spilling out onto the serving dish. Cullen knew from attending many such events that Turnbull had missed the correct cue, the haggis usually being stabbed much earlier in the poem. The quantity of single malt swilling around the DCI's guts no doubt had something to do with it.

Turnbull beamed, glowing in the attention from the assembled officers.

ACC Bill Duffin — Turnbull's boss — stood beside him, also dressed in full Highland garb, having acted as the Master of Ceremonies and reading the Selkirk Grace before the first course.

The canteen serving staff now started handing round plates of haggis, neeps and tatties. Turnbull served the first few plates until he lost interest and sat down next to Duffin and DCS Whitehead at the top table.

Cullen sat between Sharon and Angela, opposite Bain and

Irvine, their window table overlooking the car park, two away from the senior officers.

"Thought you'd be up with the big knobs," said Sharon, looking at Bain.

"I'd rather lose a bollock," said Bain, his face already flushed from the whisky. "Their chat's rancid."

"Not that ours is much better," said Irvine, putting his wad of gum into a receipt.

"Speaking of rancid chat," said Bain, "where is your boss, Butch?"

Sharon bristled at the nickname. "He muttered something about not attending Scottish rubbish."

Bain shook his head. "Turnbull gave me a rocket up my arse to attend. No idea how Wilko gets off with it."

"Can't see why he went to so much trouble to get you here," said Cullen.

Bain grinned. "Can I get you another whisky, Constable?"

"Go on," said Cullen, pushing his empty glass over.

During the soup course, Bain had produced a bottle of Dunpender single malt, a light Lowland whisky from East Lothian, not far from Garleton. Cullen had already drunk three nips and Bain gave out generous measures, a good couple of fingers in each. He was beginning to regret going onto the grain so early, especially after Bain's insistence on a seven AM briefing out at Garleton the following morning.

Bain pushed the glass back to Cullen. The bottle was halfway down, only Cullen, Bain and Irvine having dabbled.

Bain's eyes froze as he looked over Cullen's shoulder. "Oh for fuck's sake."

Cullen turned round.

Bain tugged at Cullen's arm. "Don't do that, you daft shite."

Cullen spotted the problem. DI Alison Cargill. She sat between Turnbull and Whitehead at the top table, both making a fuss of her.

"What's she doing here?" said Bain. "Supposed to be in the bloody Canaries."

"Maybe she got back early, gaffer," said Irvine.

"I can see that, Irvine," said Bain. "Christ."

Sharon leaned low across the table. "What's the ice queen doing here?"

"Seems like guest of honour at the big boy's table," said Bain. "Maybe she'll do a dance for them, see if she can get a DCI post out of it."

"There are very few things we agree on," said Sharon, "but she's one of them."

"You lucked out going to Wilko instead of her," said Bain.

"Wouldn't call that luck," she said. "Least worst."

"I hope that doesn't include me," said Bain.

"No comment," said Sharon, smiling.

Bain laughed.

A white-haired officer came over, grinning from ear to ear, offering a bottle of Likely Laddie round the table. They all politely refused the cheap supermarket blend, Cullen preferring to stick to single malt. The way Bain was pouring, there wouldn't be many drams left. The man was clearly drunk. He smiled before sauntering off to another table.

Cullen leaned over to Bain and Irvine. "Who was that?"

Bain grinned wide. "That's your mate Tommy Smith," he said, revelling in winding Cullen up. "Phone Squad. You spunked a few grand on getting a cell search done last summer."

Cullen remembered now. Smith did some checks on a mystery mobile for him. "That's him?" he said, having only spoken to him on the phone. "Forensic Investigation Unit, right?"

Bain nodded.

"Doesn't look like he'll be doing many forensic investigations tomorrow," said Angela.

Bain bellowed with laughter.

36

An hour or so later, the ceilidh was in full flight. Cullen managed a Gay Gordons with Sharon before his long held antipathy to Scottish country dancing took root.

Sitting down again, he watched Turnbull and Bain lead Angela and Sharon through the Dashing White Sergeant. Bain's whisky had run dry so Cullen and Irvine naturally gravitated towards Tommy Smith and his bottle of Likely Laddie, the three of them sitting at one of the few tables not cleared away for the dance.

"You're not a fan of Burns then, boys?" said Smith, slurring, his cheeks deep red as he poured more Likely Laddie into their glasses.

Cullen sank half of the measure, enduring the acrid burn. "I can't say I am. He's like the Scottish version of Shakespeare. No relevance in modern society and yet he's forced down our throats at school."

"Oh aye?" said Smith.

"I did English Literature at uni," said Cullen.

"Did you?" said Irvine, jaws chomping on a fresh wad of gum. "Never knew you were a poof."

Cullen took a deep breath, realising his loose lips had let slip another gem for Irvine. "What I studied has nothing to do with my sexuality."

"Wait till I tell the gaffer," said Irvine.

"Tell him what you like," said Cullen, arms folded, dreading another Bain nickname.

"I need some new curtains in my flat," said Irvine, "any danger you could help me pick some out?"

"I told you," said Cullen, glowering at him. "Piss off."

"Boys, boys, boys," said Smith. "I studied Scottish Literature for a bit in my youth. Christ knows how I got into the phone squad with that on my CV, mind."

He took another big gulp of whisky. "What you boys are missing about Burns is he was a bit of a deviant. There's a long line of Scots deviants from Burns right through to Billy Connolly and I suppose that Frankie Boyle. Sick bastards but funny with it."

"How?" said Irvine.

"Okay, buddy," said Smith, "I shall recant thee some verse. *Auld Lang Syne* is a great example. You probably know the first line — *should old acquaintance be forgot da dum da dum da dum* — arms linked in with each other, Maggie bloody Thatcher outside Big Ben, crowds in New York and Tokyo. Well, the joke's on them." He took another drink. "It's about an old prostitute, Jo, thinking back on all the cock she's had in her life."

"Is it hell," said Irvine.

Smith laughed. "Do you know *Comin' through the rye?*"

"Aye, who doesn't?" said Irvine.

Smith sat forward, rubbing his hands together. "That's a classic example. The whore in *Auld Lang Syne* is mentioned in it." He closed his eyes. "*'Oh, Jenny's all weet, poor body, Jenny's seldom dry. She draigled all her petticoatie, comin thro' the rye!'*"

"And what's deviant about that?" said Irvine.

Smith ignored him. "The chorus goes *'Gin a body meet a body, comin thro' the grain, gin a body kiss a body, the thing's a body's ain.'*"

"And your point is, caller?" said Irvine.

"That's the version you'll read in Burns collections," said Smith. "The original is different." Again his eyes closed. "*'O gin a body meet a body, comin' thro' the rye. Gin a body fuck a body, need a body cry. Comin' thro' the rye, my Jo, an' coming' thro' the rye, she fand a staun o' staunin' graith.'*"

"Shut up," said Irvine, laughing.

"I'm not joking," said Smith. "It's about the same Jo as *Auld*

Lang Syne but she's young and shagging guys in a field. And you know what a *'staun o' staunin' graith'* is?"

"No," said Irvine.

"It's a big cock," said Smith, laughing.

"Is there any more?" said Cullen.

"Aye," said Smith, then broke off laughing. "The thing that's *'a body's ain'* is the C-word in the original. I'm too polite to say it aloud here."

"So, you're saying Burns used fuck and sang songs about whores and their fannies?" said Irvine, eyes screwed up.

"You've got to think back to the times," said Smith. "Burns didn't make his money from books. Hardly anybody could read. He went around whisky bars and gin palaces in Ayrshire and Glasgow, singing his songs. He had a version for the day time when the wives were there, and one for the evening when he had a room full of pissed up lads."

Irvine finished his whisky. "I'm off for a slash. Good story, by the way."

"Cheers, buddy."

Irvine staggered off in the direction of the toilet.

"How is the Phone Squad?" said Cullen.

"Comme ci, comme ça," said Smith, laughing.

"That search you did for me got me into a load of trouble," said Cullen.

"Aye?"

"The cost," said Cullen. "Still, we got some good evidence from the second one, so cheers." He tipped his glass.

"Well, buddy, it's pretty quiet just now," said Smith. "No gangs trying to kill each other, no serial killers, nothing juicy."

Other than stealing Smith's whisky, Cullen had an ulterior motive. "I was wondering if you could do me another check?"

"Sure thing," said Smith, "what's it for?"

"Suspect in a child murder has gone missing," said Cullen. "He's made a few calls to me. I think it's another mobile."

"Invoice to the usual place?" said Smith.

Cullen nodded. "Bain's already had a trace done on the suspect's mobile. If this turns out to be his as well, it could lead to us finding him."

He wrote the number on the back of one of his business cards.

"Should have something for you tomorrow," said Smith, pocketing the card and refilling his glass in one smooth movement.

"Are you telling me you're working tomorrow?" said Cullen, feeling about a quarter as pissed as Smith looked.

"In at nine," said Smith. "Should just about be sober by then. I'll get onto your request first thing."

There was nothing as pure in the world as the science of hangovers as practised by Scottish piss artists.

"So you don't like Shakespeare either?" said Smith.

Cullen felt a hand on his shoulder. Sharon. "Time for you to head home."

He looked up. She had beads of sweat on her forehead. Cullen sometimes regretted being a drinker rather than a dancer. For one thing, it would lessen the hangover.

"Really?" said Cullen.

"Bain's heading off," said Sharon, "says it's my fault if you're not in Garleton at seven."

37

Cullen tied up the condom, wrapped it in a tissue and put it on the bedside table. The alarm clock read 10.58. He lay down again as Sharon snuggled up to him, her hand across his chest.

"You're getting better," she said, eyes closed, looking blissful.

"Must be all the practice. What is it they say about woman reaching their sexual peak in their mid-thirties?"

She smacked him lightly and bit his nipple, much harder than he expected.

"Ow." He sat up.

"Grow up," she said, hugging him close.

Cullen switched off the light, lay down again and closed his eyes. The room was spinning from the whisky. He couldn't remember being that pissed for a long time. He tried to sleep but his mind had other ideas, wandering through the case, images of Mandy, chasing who they thought was Jamie Cook, the faces of the family, Mulgrew.

Sharon's cat, Fluffy, jumped onto the end of the bed and lay on top of his feet.

"What are you thinking about?" said Sharon, sounding irritated as she switched her light on.

"Who says I'm thinking about anything?"

"You've been on the coffee again."

"I have, aye," he said, "but that's not the problem. This bloody case is."

She propped herself up on his chest and looked into his eyes. "Anything in particular?"

"Not really," he said, looking up at the ceiling. "Okay, there's something."

"I knew it," she said. "Spill."

"There's this religious group in the town," he said.

"You mentioned it earlier."

"Aye, but what I didn't say was they're talking of moving into East Linton," he said. "I can't help but think of Deborah and Rachel getting dragged into it."

"Deborah's not going to get involved," said Sharon. "She's too strong. What is there to worry about? Having some pamphlets thrust at you when Rachel's favourite uncle makes a visit?"

He laughed. "I suppose."

"There's something else, isn't there?"

"Would you stop with that psychic stuff?" he said. "It's freaking me out."

"I'm hardly psychic, Scott," she said. "Just promise me something."

"What?"

"If you ever play poker, don't bet the house."

He nibbled at a fingernail. "I've been getting these phone calls today. Hoax calls. There's music playing, some song I don't know. The words are something like '*Where have you gone?*' over and over."

"I know that song. I think it's called *Where Has He Gone?*, funnily enough. Can't remember who it's by. "

Cullen sat up against the headboard. "It's a Scottish band," he said, reaching out to gently stroke her hair.

"Aye, it's on the radio all the time."

He retrieved his phone from the bedside table, searching for the name of the song. "Expect Delays?"

"That's them," she said.

"It sounds like Glasvegas."

"I like Glasvegas," said Sharon.

He laughed. "I just can't get past the accent. Expect Delays at least have a slightly nicer voice."

"So anyway," she said, sitting up alongside him, "how many calls have you had?"

"Three," said Cullen.

"Have you mentioned it to Bain?"

"Hardly," he said.

"Who do you think it is?" she said.

He gave a long sigh. "It could be anyone, really. I've pissed off so many people over the years."

"And what about civilians," she said.

"Aye, very good," said Cullen.

"Is there anyone on the case you're working on?"

He thought it through, still coming up with the same suspect. "The only one I can think of is this lad called Jamie Cook. He's Bain's main suspect. We haven't been able to speak to him, but we've heard an awful lot about him. A lot of people think he did it."

"And did he?"

"He could have, I suppose," said Cullen. "We're struggling on the old evidence front."

"Doesn't usually stop Bain."

"No, he's like a force of nature," said Cullen.

She snuggled up close to him, taking his hand in hers. "Have you any idea why he's phoning you?"

"I can't think of anything concrete. Hoax calls are usually meant to irritate or tease someone. Jamie Cook is the only one I can think of. I phoned him this morning, not long before these calls started up."

"I can think of someone," she said, biting her lip as she moved away slightly.

"Who?" said Cullen, drawing a complete blank.

"Alison."

Cullen closed his eyes. The girl he saved from the Schoolbook Killer at the expense of Keith Miller. "She stopped calling me ages ago."

"She might have started again," said Sharon.

"Look, it's not her," he said. "She was phoning me and speaking to me, leaving voicemails before I got her number blocked. It's not her."

"So, what are you going to do?" said Sharon.

Cullen blushed. "I've started a cell trace with Tommy Smith."

"That's what you were talking to him about earlier?" she said, before exhaling.

"It's for the case," he said, defensive.

"It's *maybe* for the case," she said. "There's a difference. Bain will stop at nothing to cover his own arse. If this is unconnected, he'll be down on you like a ton of bricks."

"I'd better save his arse from public embarrassment again then, hadn't I?" said Cullen.

She laughed, before cuddling closer. "Speaking of public embarrassment, I think I'm due another for not getting caught in the toilets at Fettes."

DAY 2

Tuesday
24th January

38

"Scott."

Cullen tried to open his eyes. His head stung.

Sharon put a cup of tea down on his side of the bed. "You need to get up."

He pulled himself over and grabbed the cup. Something ginger sprang from his feet. "What time is it?"

"It's quarter to six." She sat on the edge of the bed and drank her cup of tea, wet from her shower, wearing just a towel.

"Don't get any ideas about morning action," he said.

She laughed. "You've not got the time even if you wanted some."

He drank half the stewed tea in one go, feeling slightly better. "Did you wash my shirt?" he said, referring to one he'd left there at the weekend.

"Yes," she said. "That's the last time, Scott. I'm not your mother."

"Pants and socks?"

"Them as well," she said. "Last time."

"Fine."

"You're in late tomorrow," she said. "You can sleep your hangover off then." She stood up and dried herself before putting her bra on.

Cullen started to feel something stir. "I'm getting ideas now."

"The only thing you're getting is the train," said Sharon.

"Eh?"

"All that whisky you drank last night," she said. "You're well over the limit."

"But my car's just at the station," said Cullen.

"Then it'll be there when you finish," she said with a smile. "You don't want to get caught drink-driving."

"When's the train?" he said.

"Ten past six."

He downed the rest of the tea and shot off in the direction of the shower.

CULLEN GOT off the train at quarter to seven and crossed the bridge, blinking through the driving rain.

He'd left Sharon's flat at six, just catching the first North Berwick train from Waverley. It didn't stop on the way, so he'd had to wait as it doubled back to Drem, wasting twenty-odd minutes.

He stood in the car park, taking cover beside the ticket machine, shivering through his hangover and drinking from a litre bottle of water.

Lamb's car pulled up, headlights flashing.

Cullen got in. "Thanks for this."

"Not a problem," said Lamb. "You don't quite look yourself this morning."

"A few too many drams of Likely Laddie last night," said Cullen.

"So, this is what Bain's got you doing while I'm out looking for his main suspect?"

"It was political," said Cullen. "It was Jim Turnbull's big night. He was addressing the haggis and he wanted his squad there to show off to the big boys."

Lamb laughed. "A likely tale," he said, pulling out of the car park and heading left onto the main road back to Edinburgh. "Well, I was in till midnight."

"Did you catch Jamie Cook?" said Cullen.

Lamb grimaced. "Did we hell."

They crossed the railway bridge then turned left towards Garleton.

"Did you get any further forward?" said Cullen.

"Not really, no," said Lamb. "Complete waste of time. Don't want your boss showing me up."

"You just know he'll try, don't you?" said Cullen.

"I've no doubt of it," said Lamb.

BAIN'S seven o'clock briefing descended into chaos after only four minutes, Cullen's hangover telling him it was far too early for shouting.

"How can you not find him?" said Bain.

"We've had officers out all over East Lothian and parts of Midlothian looking for Jamie Cook," said Lamb, calmly. "It's a big area. If he doesn't want to be found, he won't be."

"This is your own back yard, Sergeant," said Bain, drinking his favourite hangover cure, a mix of Red Bull and Lucozade.

"I appreciate that, Brian," said Lamb. "How easy is it to find someone in Edinburgh?"

"It's not the same thing," said Bain. "Edinburgh has half a million people, there's probably only about a hundred thousand on your patch and most of them are in Musselburgh."

"It's a lot of space," said Lamb, remaining calm. "Takes a lot of time to cover."

"You've had a lot of time," said Bain. He took a deep breath. "Right, I want you to get back out there and find him."

"I will endeavour to," said Lamb, leaning back in his chair.

Bain looked down his nose at him. "Have we had anyone go through his stuff at his parents' house yet?"

"We were over there last night when you went back into the city," said Lamb. "DC McLaren has a couple of new leads."

"What about the boy's computer?" said Bain.

"What about it?" said Lamb.

"I want Technical Investigations all over it." Bain looked at Angela. "Can you take his laptop straight to Charlie Kidd?"

"I've got to head back to Edinburgh?" said Angela.

"Is that a problem?" said Bain.

"Fine." Caldwell folded her arms.

"Are you just focusing on Jamie Cook?" said Cullen, his voice almost an octave deeper, betraying his hangover.

"Come again?" said Bain.

Cullen cleared his throat. "You've been giving DS Lamb a doing for not finding Jamie Cook, but he's not the only suspect. Seamus Mulgrew still hasn't turned up either."

"Right," said Bain, looking over at Murray. "Can you look into Seamus Mulgrew, please?" He looked back at Cullen. "Cullen and Irvine, I want you two speaking to all of Jamie Cook's contacts. There must be someone who knows something."

"Fine," said Cullen.

"Dismissed."

39

"You're not a fan of Starbucks?" said Lamb.

Cullen sipped at the Americano. "Can't say I am. I'm more of a Caffe Nero kind of guy. Costa at a push."

They were sitting in Starbucks just across from Garleton nick, looking out of the window at the early morning traffic. Lamb had ordered a bucket of the sort of syrupy, milky coffee it specialised in and which Cullen detested.

"I've no idea why Bain got us in at seven," said Cullen. "I could have done with an extra hour in bed."

"It's called a murder investigation," said Lamb. He laughed. "I learnt a long time ago not to go to events Jim Turnbull insisted I attend. They usually involve a raging hangover."

"You know him well, then?" said Cullen.

"Aye," said Lamb, taking a bite of his croissant, the sight of it making Cullen feel ill. The wasabi peas he ate on the train were repeating, his stomach warning him food wouldn't be tolerated yet.

"We worked together in Galashiels about fifteen years ago, then I was a DS for him in Edinburgh for a good while, just after he got his DI. Still go golfing with him a couple of times a year."

"Are you a Borders boy?" said Cullen.

"Aye, Hawick."

"You've not got the accent."

Lamb grinned. "Got shot of it pretty early on."

"Why did you move out here?" said Cullen.

Lamb gave a shrug. "Looking for the easy life as much as anything. I didn't get on with the city. I'm a country boy at heart."

"You could have commuted," said Cullen.

"I couldn't be arsed with it," said Lamb. "I sold my flat in Edinburgh and bought a cottage out here."

"Is there a Mrs Lamb?"

Lamb held his left hand up, no rings. "For a detective, Cullen, you're not very observant."

Cullen laughed. "It pays not to make assumptions."

"True," said Lamb, taking another bite of the croissant, covering his moustache with flakes of pastry. "No, there's no Mrs Lamb any more. We got divorced last year. She moved back to Edinburgh."

"Couldn't handle the pace of country life?" said Cullen.

"Something like that," said Lamb. "She's off shagging guys half her age. And good luck to her."

"Must be hard for you," said Cullen.

"It was more of a relief when she went," said Lamb. "I've kept the house and the dog, she's got her flat."

"No kids?"

"No bloody way," said Lamb. "Not with her, anyway."

"Was she in the force?"

"She works for Standard Life," said Lamb. "What about you?"

"Got a girlfriend," said Cullen. "She keeps talking about moving in together."

Lamb nodded. "But you're scared?"

Cullen wondered whether Sharon had picked up on the signs. "Aye."

"She in the force?" said Lamb.

"Aye, she's a DS," said Cullen. "Used to work for Bain."

"And with you?" said Lamb.

Cullen paused. "Aye."

Lamb grinned. "Bad boy." He forced the rest of the croissant in his mouth.

"What did you think of Bain's briefing this morning?" said Cullen.

Lamb violently stabbed his pen into the hole in the coffee lid then drank from the slot at the front. "This helps the air flow. Stops a vacuum getting built up."

"And I asked what you thought of the briefing."

"Aye, all right, Cullen," said Lamb, before taking a deep breath. "Is he always like this?"

"Pretty much," said Cullen, shrugging.

"He was out of order," said Lamb. "It's fine to raise his thoughts with me personally, but not in front of my officers and half of East Lothian."

"I've had run-ins with him before," said Cullen.

"Surprised Turnbull tolerates him," said Lamb.

"He doesn't really," said Cullen. "Last night, Turnbull gave Bain a doing roughly equivalent to the one you got just now."

"I see," said Lamb, nodding.

"He said if it's not solved by Thursday, he's getting replaced."

"I suspected as much," said Lamb, fingering at the crumbs on his plate. "Who by?"

"DI Cargill," said Cullen.

Lamb screwed his face up. "Alison Cargill?"

"Aye, why?"

Lamb pushed his plate to the side. "I didn't think this case could get any worse."

"Is she that bad?" said Cullen.

Lamb laughed. "She reported to me when she was a DC, that's all. Must be about ten years ago now. She's since climbed the greasy pole and now she's a DI. I couldn't face her being my boss. She's always had a nasty way with her."

Cullen finished his coffee and took a long drink of water. "Is she worse than Bain, though?"

"No. No, she's not. I might have a word with Jim about Bain's conduct. See if I can't expedite things."

40

Cullen had to endure a Blur live album as Irvine drove them back to the Gibsons' house in his black Astra.

"They're all the same these provincial coppers," said Irvine, jaw chewing away. He seemed quite fresh considering the amount of whisky he'd consumed. "Lamb, Murray, McLaren, all useless bastards."

"You think so?" said Cullen.

"There's a reason they're out here in the sticks and not in the city where the action is," said Irvine.

Cullen ranked Irvine as the second most useless officer he'd worked with. He had reported to him for the four months since he and Sharon were kept apart, feeling more like Irvine was the junior officer. He was sloppy and lazy, living off tales of his previous achievements rather than creating any new ones.

"You've never fancied working out here?" said Cullen, as Irvine turned onto their street.

"Not really, no," said Irvine.

Cullen was no longer surprised at how often Irvine missed the odd snide remark he made. "You'd fit in."

"Would take me an age to get out here in the morning," said Irvine.

"What, compared with getting to Leith Walk from Dalkeith?"

Irvine pulled up in front of the Gibsons' house. "I'm not travelling at rush hour, though. Takes forever to get anywhere out here."

"You're not Lamb's biggest fan then?" said Cullen.

"He's a wanker," said Irvine. "The gaffer had it spot on this morning. How can that bloody tube not find the Cook boy in his own back yard? It beggars belief."

It looked like the Gibsons were up. Cullen wondered how they were coping, whether the true magnitude had sunk in yet.

"How are we going to play this, then?" said Irvine.

Cullen glared at Irvine — he should be telling not asking. "How about we ask about Jamie Cook then you keep Charles Gibson out of my hair while I speak to the son?"

Irvine nodded. "I like it. Let's do it. You know, you might get to DS one of these days."

Cullen refrained from replying.

GIBSON LOOKED as though he was suffering in a similar way to Cullen, the skin around his eyes red and puffy. "My wife isn't up yet, I'm afraid. How can I help?"

"It's about Jamie Cook," said Irvine.

"Tell me you've caught him," said Gibson.

"I'm afraid not," said Irvine. "We're still actively pursuing him."

Gibson nodded. "I hope you've given up hunting down Seamus."

"Has he been in contact?" said Cullen.

"No," said Gibson. "As I said before, I'll start to get concerned after a few days. I've got other things on my mind just now, as I'm sure you can imagine."

"I understand," said Irvine. "Yesterday, you said Jamie Cook may have had an opportunity to abuse Mandy."

"He *may* have done," said Gibson.

"Is there anything to back this up?" said Irvine.

"I've been thinking about this," said Gibson, before taking a drink of tea. "We looked over the family calendar from the last couple of years. We keep them, you know. Jamie hasn't stayed here for a few weeks, as I said." He set the mug down on the coffee table. "One thing we noticed, though, was Mandy's disappearances started up roughly the same time he began staying over."

"Are you sure?" said Cullen.

"Absolutely," said Gibson. "August 2010 was Mandy's first night wander and Jamie had been here for the previous six months, once or twice per month on average."

"How do you think he could have abused your daughter?" said Cullen.

"He must have crept into her room," said Gibson. "He was a strong boy and my daughter was a frail girl." He took a deep breath. "It would explain a few things. We could never understand why Mandy ran away but the timelines fit, don't they?"

"Would you mind if I spoke to your son?" said Cullen.

"Be my guest," said Gibson, looking reluctant.

41

C ullen sat on the desk chair in Thomas Gibson's bedroom, facing into the room. The boy was hunched on his bed, back against the wall, knees raised, shrouded in a duvet.

Cullen pointed at the wall, covered in football posters — Fernando Torres, Andrey Arshavin, Didier Drogba, Robin van Persie. "Not settled on a team?"

"Arsenal," said Thomas.

"Good side," said Cullen. "They play good football. Surprised you'd have Drogba and Torres up as well."

"Great players. Torres is incredible but he's injury-prone. He's been rubbish since he went to Chelsea."

"Do you think Arsenal will finish in the top four this season?"

"I hope so," said Thomas, sitting forward and pushing the duvet off. "We need to keep Van Persie fit. We're pretty weak at the back." He pointed at the Arshavin poster, shushing the crowd in his famous goal celebration. "Arshavin is really inconsistent. If only we had someone like Torres."

Cullen smiled. "Thomas, I know you've had some bad news, worse than you could have imagined, but I need you to help me if we're to find who killed your sister."

Thomas swallowed. "Okay."

"I believe you're good friends with Jamie Cook."

Thomas nodded. "He's a Man U fan."

When Cullen was growing up, everyone had an English team — Man United or Liverpool, usually — but they had a Scottish team first and foremost, Aberdeen and then Everton in Cullen's case. With these boys — the Sky generation — there was no Celtic or Rangers, Hearts or Hibs. He wondered if Thomas had been to a live football match.

"What's Jamie like?"

"He's cool," said Thomas. "Really cool."

"In what way?" said Cullen.

The boy shrugged. "Jamie just does what he wants."

"Did he have a good relationship with Mandy?"

Thomas frowned. "Mandy?"

"Yes, your sister," said Cullen, nodding.

"Why are you asking about Mandy and Jamie?"

Cullen looked to the bedroom door, spotting Charles Gibson listening in on their conversation, out of his son's sight line. Irvine was supposed to be keeping him occupied. Gibson spotted Cullen and walked back downstairs.

"Was there anything between them?" said Cullen.

"How could there be?" said Thomas, a scowl on his face. "Mandy was a *spacker*."

Cullen was stunned at the boy describing his own sister that way. "Did Jamie call Mandy that?"

"Once or twice, just as a joke," said Thomas. "If we were talking about girls he'd tease Malky about going out with her. They both said they wouldn't touch her because she was a *spacker*."

"And how did that make you feel?" said Cullen.

"They were just joking," said Thomas. "Malky doesn't have any brothers or sisters, so he didn't understand. Jamie's twins are loads younger than him."

"Were you protective of Mandy?"

"I was," said Thomas. "Some boys at school would take the piss out of her."

Cullen recalled Jonathan Hulse saying Cook was one of the worst culprits. "What did you do to them?"

"They were in Mandy's year and we were a lot bigger than them. Jamie helped me sort them out."

"Jamie helped you?" said Cullen, frowning.

"He did, aye," said Thomas, scratching the back of his head. "What you'll hear about Jamie is the bad stuff. You won't hear about him sticking up for me or Malky."

"I gather Jamie shouted abuse at Mandy," said Cullen. "Is that correct?"

Thomas scowled. "He did a couple of times, aye. He stopped after the other kids started."

"And this was when Jamie sorted them out?"

"Yes," said Thomas.

"Was Jamie ever violent to these boys?" said Cullen.

Thomas shook his head. "Jamie wasn't a fighter, really. He could make a good threat, though."

"Okay," said Cullen. "What happened after Jamie left school?"

Thomas sighed. "I told you already. He just does what he wants."

"Did he keep going to God's Rainbow?"

"No way," said Thomas. "He left the same time he left school."

"How did his parents take this?" said Cullen.

"Not well," said Thomas. "They shouted at him. He started coming over here or to Malky's and hanging out in the park. Just avoided them, really."

"Did he ever stay over?"

"Yeah, quite a lot," said Thomas. "Used to sleep on the floor on Dad's old inflatable mattress from when we used to go camping. Malky stayed sometimes, too."

"When was this?" said Cullen.

Thomas stared at his football posters. "A few times while Jamie was still at school, I think. Since then it was usually after he'd had a row with his parents, which was most weekends."

Cullen noted it down — he needed to check whether the timelines stacked up. "How did your parents and his get on?"

"Dad reckoned Jamie's dad was a bit simple," said Thomas.

"When Jamie and Malky stayed over, did either of them say anything or do anything to Mandy?" said Cullen

Thomas screwed his eyes up. "What are you saying?"

Cullen leaned forward. "Thomas, I'm trying to put together a picture of your sister's life. One of the things we need to know more about is Jamie's relationship with Mandy."

"There was *no* relationship with Mandy," said Thomas, his

voice rising. "I told you before, he wouldn't touch Mandy. She was a *spacker*."

Cullen was wary of pushing the boy too far, so changed tack. "Were you out with Jamie on Saturday night?"

Thomas paused for a few moments. "Is Dad still there?"

Cullen glanced over. "No."

"Can I tell you this in secret?" said the boy.

"This is inadmissible as evidence anyway," said Cullen. "I need corroboration from another officer, so you're speaking off the record."

Thomas breathed a sigh of relief. "I had a bottle of cider. Malky did, too. We got pretty pissed then came home at about ten. I heard from Malky that Jamie got nicked."

"Who bought the alcohol?" said Cullen.

"Jamie did," said Thomas.

Cullen realised Lamb could have done him for buying alcohol underage. "When was the last time you heard from Jamie?"

"On Saturday, just before we came home," said Thomas.

"No phone calls or texts since?" said Cullen.

"Nothing," said Thomas. "That's the truth. Malky told me they kept him in all night. You can check my mobile if you want."

Cullen smiled. "That's not necessary. Did Jamie have other friends? Out of town, maybe?"

"He's quite a drifter," said Thomas, slowly nodding. "He always gets on well with people he's just met. There's a load of people in Haddington and Tranent he knows. There was a girl in Dunbar he was seeing."

Cullen frowned. "What's her name?"

"Can't remember," said Thomas. "Don't know much about her. Jamie kept that side of himself quiet. Malky might know."

Cullen scribbled a note in giant letters, ready to pass to Lamb. "These friends in Haddington and Tranent, do you have any names or phone numbers?"

"Never met them," said Thomas. "Sorry."

"What did Jamie have to say about Father Mulgrew?"

"Jamie blamed him for ruining his life," said Thomas.

"How?"

Thomas took a deep breath. "He never said, but—"

Gibson burst into the room. "That is *enough*," he said, voice raised. "My boy's been to hell and back and you've had your questions."

Irvine entered the room, going forehead-to-forehead with Gibson. "Back off," he said in a strong but measured tone.

"My son needs space and time to grieve," said Gibson.

"And we need to find your daughter's killer," said Irvine. "Now, we can speak to your son here off the record, or we can put him on the record at the station."

Gibson flared his nostrils.

Cullen stood up. "I'm asking questions which may help to bring your daughter's killer to justice. Your son has a lot of useful information."

Gibson stared at his son who looked away, pulling the duvet back over his legs.

"Fine," said Gibson. "Finding out Jamie Cook was abusing Mandy has clearly upset us. Thomas in particular."

"Thomas," said Cullen, "do you have any idea why Jamie thought Mulgrew had ruined his life?"

"No," said Thomas.

"Father Mulgrew kicked Jamie out of the group," said Gibson. "That's what ruined his life."

"Is that true, Thomas?" said Cullen.

The boy shrugged, avoiding eye contact with anyone.

Cullen glared at Gibson then left the room.

42

Cullen stood outside the house, fists clenched, heart pounding. The rain teemed down on his head, still thick with a hangover.

Gibson had frightened the boy, not letting him finish, shutting him up when Cullen asked about Mulgrew.

Irvine was on the front lawn with PC Wallace, chatting her up as she smoked. Irvine drank in each puff, the chewing gum clearly the crutch of an ex-smoker.

"Did you get anything?" said Irvine.

"Nothing much," said Cullen. "Got a couple of vague leads on Jamie Cook."

"Well, that's good," said Irvine.

"I would thank you for keeping Gibson away from his son," said Cullen, "but you just didn't bother."

Irvine frowned.

Cullen walked up to him and stabbed his finger in the air in front of his face. "You were supposed to keep him out of my way. He shut Thomas up when I was asking him about Mulgrew."

"I had to go to the bog," said Irvine.

"This is important," said Cullen. "We may have missed something."

"Just have to take your word for it," said Irvine, grinning. "Pull the boy into the station and get a statement out of him."

Cullen looked Irvine up and down before deciding he wasn't worth the effort. He took a step back as Irvine turned his attentions to Wallace.

Cullen wondered if Irvine might have a point — they were pussyfooting around the family, maybe they needed to start getting harder with them. He turned to Wallace. "Have you just turned up?"

"Aye," she said, before inhaling deeply.

"What happened yesterday?" said Cullen. "Any visitors or phone calls?"

"Nobody's been in," said Wallace. "The phone was going constantly while I was there. I didn't get to answer them all. It was mostly family members, friends, work colleagues."

"Is that the house phone?" said Cullen.

"Aye," said Wallace, nodding.

"What about mobiles?" said Cullen.

Wallace took another drag, holding it in her lungs for a few seconds. "Mostly the husband. He's taken a few calls on his mobile. Work, I think. There have been a couple I haven't heard, mind."

Cullen took a deep breath, trying to avoid inhaling any smoke. A thought struck him. Could Charles Gibson have been abusing his daughter, killing her to hide his crime? "Do you have any reason to suspect Gibson might have been abusing Mandy?"

Wallace paused again. "I don't think so. I've been doing this for years and I've seen my fair share of that sort of thing in the Pans or Mussie. Gibson just doesn't seem the type, you know? Good job, got a fit young wife."

Cullen didn't see what his affluence had to do with his sexual urges. "Isn't it the quiet ones you've got to watch?"

"I'll keep my eyes and ears open," she said with a smile, "but really I just can't see it."

"You should suggest it to the gaffer," said Irvine.

Cullen looked sideways at Irvine. "Maybe," he said, expecting a tirade of abuse.

"What do you want me to do?" said Wallace.

"Stay here as long as they'll let you," said Cullen.

She looked at her watch. "I'm not sure they need me much longer. Only so many cups of tea a family can drink."

"Just make sure there's a point in you being here, okay?" said Cullen.

Wallace smiled. "I do know how to do my job."

Cullen looked at Irvine. "Let's get back."

CULLEN WATCHED the rain thunder down on the yard behind the station.

He downed his second mug of tap water, feeling a slight pang of conscience about being idle even for a minute.

The only other person in the Incident Room was ADC Law, typing on a laptop. He thought she was pretty, figuring he must still be pissed. Their eyes met and he smiled. He nodded and looked away, back out of the window.

Out of the corner of his eye, he spotted her walking over.

"How's it going?" she said.

"I feel like shite," he said, knowing he wasn't at his most beautiful. He'd caught sight of his blotchy skin in the bathroom mirror earlier, the bags under his bloodshot eyes adding to the ultra-sexy image he portrayed that morning.

"You were at that thing last night, then?" said Law.

"The Burns Supper," said Cullen.

Law sat on the table beside him and crossed her legs. She was wearing a skirt with no tights. "Was it fun?"

"It wasn't bad," said Cullen, blushing. "Got arseholed on free whisky."

Law laughed, throwing her head back. "I love a good night like that."

Cullen nodded, remaining silent to avoid encouraging her.

"What time do you reckon we'll be finished tonight?"

Cullen shrugged. "No idea. You know how it is with these cases, they can drag on and on in the early days."

"Never been on a murder before," said Law.

Cullen nodded.

Law looked up at him, biting her lip. "I was wondering if you maybe wanted to go for a drink after?"

Cullen scrunched his eyes up. "Sorry," he said, looking her right in the eye. "I'm just not looking for that sort of thing."

She stared at him for a few seconds, before standing up. "I was just asking."

"I don't want to lead you on," said Cullen. "I'm spoken for."

"Fine," said Law, rubbing at her forehead.

Cullen started to feel bad. "You're a nice girl and—"

"Don't," she said. "Just don't."

She rushed out of the room.

Cullen leaned back and felt even worse, if that was possible.

"What have you done now?"

He looked up. Caldwell. "What?" he said, playing innocent.

"I just saw Eva Law run down the corridor in tears," said Angela. "Did you show her your willy?"

"Very good," said Cullen. "She asked to go for a drink and I knocked her back."

"Good work," said Angela. "Exactly what we need on a case like this."

"You can talk," said Cullen. "You and Lamb."

Angela raised her eyebrows. "Nothing going on there. I suggest you drop it."

"Fine," said Cullen, realising he was definitely on to something.

"I need to get Jamie Cook's computer out to Charlie Kidd," said Angela. "Any cars?"

"Not got yours?" said Cullen.

"Got a lift in from Bain this morning," said Angela.

"Go downstairs and get a squad car," said Cullen. "Not sure they'll have many here."

Angela nodded. "That's what I was thinking," she said, before leaving.

Cullen felt bad for Law, but these things happened, at least to him anyway. He hadn't handled it with tact and grace. He checked his watch and dialled a number on his phone.

"Tommy Smith."

"Tommy, it's Scott Cullen."

"Christ, buddy," said Smith, "I'm only just in. I've barely had a chance to sit down."

"I'm not chasing you," said Cullen. "I need another search done." He gave him Charles Gibson's mobile and house numbers.

"What's the priority here?" said Smith.

"This request first, then my other one," said Cullen. "Did DS Irvine submit one for the phone records of Seamus Mulgrew?"

"Aye, he did," said Smith. "I've got the young lad on it now."

Cullen ended the call. He spotted the pamphlet Mulgrew had given him on the philosophy of God's Rainbow. He picked it up and leafed through it.

The overriding theme, as far as he could tell, was redemption of sin. He now knew Mulgrew had serious sins to atone for.

He struggled to see the sect's appeal for the likes of the Gibsons and the Cooks. They had 'problem' children, Cullen supposed, but Mulgrew's little group thrived in Garleton, looking to expand into other towns, while the Kirk on the high street died on its arse.

Gibson was training to take over the Garleton faithful. Perhaps the promise of power appealed to someone like him, having previously occupied a senior position at the bank. He couldn't see how Mulgrew could offer a package to compete with Alba Bank, a famously generous employer.

Cullen tossed the pamphlet aside before stretching and looking out of the window. The rain had just stopped and the sun was threatening to break from the ceiling of grey cloud.

He went over and checked the whiteboard, noting a few additions in the two hours since the briefing, the most prominent being a satellite photo of Balgone Ponds.

Cullen thought the area nearest the road was a strange place to hide a body. They still had no idea how she'd been transferred there. There were no annotations indicating whether the wider area had been searched.

He examined Irvine's notes from the previous day, interviewing the residents of the cottages but covering very little of the ponds. The forensic report was very scarce on that detail.

It was a long shot, but Cullen thought heading back to the area might be worthwhile, or at least keep him occupied until Bain stopped playing games and came up with some proper direction. Besides, it would put him far enough away from Eva Law.

Cullen headed for the door, hoping Angela hadn't taken the last squad car.

43

Cullen stood by the locus, the police tape still flapping in the light breeze. He stopped at the outer cordon, taking in the scenery.

How did Mandy get here?

Her teddy bear was found in the lane outside her house. She had most likely escaped from her room and gone to see Susan Russell.

Then what? She had somehow been suffocated.

Deeley's post mortem pointed to a white pillowcase, which they still hadn't found. Mandy's own bed had a purple pillow, making it unlikely she'd been killed at home.

Someone must have met her and abducted her. Mulgrew or Cook were their entire focus so far but was there anyone else?

Could Charles Gibson have abused and killed his own daughter? The man was destroyed by her death, falling apart and drinking heavily. Was it bereavement or guilt? They certainly had no direct evidence to accuse him. Yet. Wallace might come up with something.

His phone rang. Irvine. He let it go to voicemail then screened it.

"Cullen, I need you to interview another two families with me. Bain will get told if you don't call me back right now."

Cullen couldn't be arsed with him. They had more than

enough officers to ask run-of-the-mill questions — Angela or Law, any number of local plod. Repeating yesterday's actions wouldn't push them further forward.

Irvine was a total joke, he'd just never stepped out of line badly enough to be caught. It pissed Cullen off that Irvine was a sergeant and he was never likely to be, the way things were going. When they worked together, Cullen acted the lead officer despite being Irvine's subordinate. That he earned significantly more bit into Cullen.

Irvine's notes confirmed the focus of the forensic analysis was the spot surrounding Mandy's body. There could be undiscovered evidence in the rest of the area. He wrapped his overcoat tight as he walked into the freezing winter wind, away from Mandy's grave.

He passed the first pond on his left, surrounded by reeds. Trees on the far shore partially hid a cliff and he could make out some fallen boulders on the far side, not all of them covered in moss.

Mud and giant brown puddles blocked his way at several points. His boots were absolutely caked by the time the path split, forking left between the ponds. Another path went around the second pond, through a coniferous wood. He went right, figuring he could eventually double back and check the other path later.

As he walked, the rain started up again, lighter than before.

The second pond was much larger, less reedy and looked deeper. He could see a badly damaged boat alongside a broken jetty on the far shore.

At the end of the pond, he drew closer to another fork, the left hand looping back to the other side of the pond, the right crossing some sheep-filled fields.

He took the left path, figuring it would probably join up with the other pond. After a few minutes of walking, he spotted a swing, just a length of rope tied to a tall old tree, a small seat improvised from a stick — they'd called it a *Tarzie* when he was growing up.

He came to a large shed nestled in the trees, almost hidden from sight, roughly five metres by four. On closer inspection, it appeared to be a summerhouse with glass doors and a veranda out front. A barbecue sat to the side, a rotting shell of brick and charred, fat-encrusted steel. It appeared to be uninhabited, the local farmer probably only using it a couple of times a year. He pulled the doors open and entered.

A man lay on a mattress in the middle of the room, face down, his feet pointing towards the door.

"Hello?" said Cullen.

No response.

There was no breathing or other movement. He tugged a glove from his pocket and put it on. Kneeling down by the head, he felt for a pulse, almost recoiling from the cold skin. He reached down and turned the head over.

It was Seamus Mulgrew.

44

A fter Bain, Lamb and the other officers arrived, Cullen kept a low profile, spending twenty minutes in the squad car writing down his movements in copious detail.

His decision to recheck Irvine's work had led to finding the body. He knew better than to admit his motives for taking a wander around the ponds, so he made up a story about verifying the exit points on the crime scene log.

He went back to find Bain, the puddles worse since he'd last crossed.

Irvine was Crime Scene Manager again, arranging the two standard cordons around the shack. PC Watson stood at the top of the hill marking out a possible exit point. Cullen didn't envy him — the Arctic gale would be cutting right through him up there.

The inner cordon was tight around the shack itself, Law standing guard in the entrance.

Irvine was garbed in the full Scene of Crime suit, managing access at the left-hand side. "DC Murray's got the far end," he said to the approaching Cullen.

"Has Deeley turned up?"

"Stuck in traffic," said Irvine. "Accident on the bypass." He checked his clipboard. "The SOCO boys were already attending an incident in Dalkeith so they diverted one of their vans here."

"Where's Bain?" said Cullen.

Irvine pointed at a figure beside Law, glaring into the cabin.

"You wanting to suit up?" said Irvine.

"I'll see if I can get the mountain to come to Mohammed," said Cullen, preferring to avoid Law after their earlier incident. He called to Bain, who scowled, nodded at Cullen and wandered over.

"What in the name of the wee man happened in there, Sundance?" said Bain, shaking his head.

"Got an MO yet?" said Cullen.

"Aye, and I don't like it," said Bain, before taking a deep breath. "Looks the same as Mandy."

"Suffocation?" said Cullen.

"Aye," said Bain, with a slow, resigned nod. "I know one when I see it. Need Deeley to confirm it, obviously, but I'm thinking it's the same killer."

Cullen could imagine Bain hectoring Deeley while he sat stuck in the late morning gloom.

"We've lost a suspect here. A bloody paedo and our Plan B. I don't like his body just turning up like this. Not one bit."

"It's not looking good," said Cullen.

"What were you doing out here?" said Bain.

Cullen shrugged, trying to look cool. "The board in the Incident Room said nobody had been around the pond. I wanted to find how Mandy was transported here and make sure the crime scene log stacked up. I've been done over for it before. We've got loads of exit points here, at least twenty I can think of."

"It's very lucky you're a nosey bastard," said Bain.

"Not for Mulgrew," said Cullen.

Bain grunted. "What is this place anyway? A fuck shack in the middle of nowhere is what it is."

Cullen winced. "Shite. Mulgrew mentioned something about a shack." He flicked through his notebook. "Here. Mulgrew told us Jamie Cook had sexual fantasies about abusing children, talking about taking Mandy to a shack."

"Reckon this is it?" said Bain.

"Or Mulgrew's messing with us," said Cullen.

Bain spat on the ground. "Could Jamie Cook have met him here and done him in?"

"I don't know," said Cullen.

"Fuckin' mess this is," said Bain, shaking his head again.

"What do you want me to do?" said Cullen.

"I want you to come with me," said Bain. "I'm going to speak to Charles Gibson, see what he's got to say about this. His daughter and the head of the church turning up dead two days apart is too weird for me. We're doing it at the station, as well."

"Fine," said Cullen.

Irvine waddled over, mask off, chewing away. "Just had a call on the old Airwave. Jimmy Deeley's on his way through this bloody mud right now."

"Sundance, give me ten minutes then we're off," said Bain. "Wait by my car."

"Anything you want me to do?" said Cullen.

"Just keep out of my hair."

Bain and Irvine went off to meet Deeley half way.

Cullen spotted Angela and Lamb standing apart from the group. From a distance, it looked like he was showing off to her, making big hand gestures as though he was talking about fishing.

Angela turned away as she clocked Cullen's approach. "You're under Bain's wing again."

Cullen raised an eyebrow. "Sadly."

"Heard you found the body," said Lamb. "That's some good work, Cullen."

"It was pure chance. I just came upon it."

"Strange place to be wandering about, though," said Lamb, raising an eyebrow.

Cullen shrugged. "Irvine led the search here."

Lamb laughed, almost too loud. "I see your point."

"How's the hunt for Jamie Cook going?" said Cullen.

Angela took her notebook out. "We spoke to Malcolm Thornton about the girlfriend in Dunbar. He's heard of her, but never seen her."

"This isn't looking good for Cook," said Cullen.

"We've got guys in Haddington and Tranent out looking," said Lamb. "Shouldn't be too long now."

"I guess not," said Cullen, but he didn't see their luck changing any time soon.

"I had Eva Law in floods of tears earlier," said Lamb.

Cullen checked his watch. "I'd best go wait for Bain."

45

Charles Gibson shook his head again. "I can't believe it."
They were in an interview room in Garleton station, in the section still inhabited. The tape machine whirred on the chipped tabletop. Gibson sat across from Cullen and Bain, one of the local uniforms stood by the door.

"You're not under arrest or suspicion, merely giving a statement about your friend's death," said Bain.

Gibson nodded.

Cullen knew Bain would be on shaky ground if Gibson came under suspicion later. The recent Cadder case in the new UK Supreme Court ensured all Scottish suspects had a lawyer present during interviews, and everybody seemed to know it.

"You can see why it seems strange to me," said Bain. "Two unexplained deaths so close together is a funny business."

"I can see that," said Gibson.

"Is there any possibility Father Mulgrew has taken his own life?" said Bain.

Cullen couldn't work out why Bain was asking that question — Mulgrew had been suffocated and they'd found nothing near the body to suggest he'd done it himself.

"There is absolutely no way Seamus took his own life," said Gibson, shaking his head. "Suicide is one of the biggest sins in our faith. If you'd read any of our literature, you would know this."

"You don't think he did himself in?" said Bain.

Gibson scowled. "No, Inspector, I don't think he 'did himself in'."

There was an awkward silence in the room, with Gibson evading their gaze.

"Did Father Mulgrew have any enemies who might have done this?" said Cullen.

"Jamie Cook," said Gibson.

"You think the boy's capable of murder?" said Bain.

Gibson's eyes squinted. "I do. I think he's responsible for my daughter's death and I think he's responsible for Seamus's. That boy is capable of absolutely anything."

"Have you thought any more about whether Jamie could have abused your daughter during those sleepovers?" said Bain.

Gibson took a drink of tea. "Jamie could have been abusing her under our noses. We could have been entirely negligent as parents."

Bain nodded. "See, what I don't understand is how the lassie got out of her house the other night. She's run away and wound up dead. Nobody saw anything."

Gibson rubbed his ear. "I'm probably not the most reliable man in the world with that sort of thing. I checked on her after I came home from Father Mulgrew's. It's just possible I didn't lock the door." He sighed. "Jamie must have met her outside."

"How would he have known?" said Cullen.

"I've no idea," said Gibson. "The teddy bear proves she left the house and went down the lane. She was repeating an established pattern. It's not exactly a secret that Mandy went to Susan's."

"How was the front door locked in the morning when you checked?" said Bain.

"All I can think of is Jamie made a copy of the key," said Gibson. He screwed his eyes up. "I'm going to have to live with this for the rest of my life."

"Why would she run away?" said Bain.

"We've been over this many times," said Gibson. "Mandy was a troubled girl, plagued by demonic possession."

Bain looked like he was ready to jump in with both feet. "We need something a bit more concrete here."

"Please respect our opinions," said Gibson. "We've suffered two losses in twenty-four hours."

"In a normal week, would Mandy and Jamie have any contact?" said Cullen.

"Even though we put a stop to the sleepovers, the boy was usually around the house when I wasn't," said Gibson. "I work locally, but I'm not here that often. Recently, I've been somewhat busy with church matters."

Cullen looked at Gibson, still avoiding eye contact. "Why do you assume it was him that killed your daughter?"

Gibson shrugged. "Most likely explanation."

"But you've no evidence?" said Cullen.

"Nothing concrete, anyway," said Gibson, rubbing his hand across his forehead.

"And you can't think of anyone who would want to harm Seamus Mulgrew?" said Cullen.

"Just Jamie Cook," said Gibson.

46

Back in the Incident Room, Bain went to the whiteboard to sulk in peace.

Cullen kept his distance while the cogs clicked round, reading through the statements taken from the Gibson family, looking for contradictions but not finding any.

"Gibson asked me to leave."

Cullen looked up. PC Wallace.

"That figures," said Cullen. "We were really taking the piss having you there that long. Anything happen today?"

Wallace shook her head. "Not that I've seen. They've been keeping me away from most of it. Until you phoned me to bring him in, I've not really had anything to do."

"Thanks for your help," said Cullen.

"You still need me on this case?" said Wallace.

Cullen shook his head. "I'll give you a call if we have to go over anything."

Wallace looked relieved as she left the room.

Cullen walked towards Bain and his precious whiteboard. "PC Wallace got nothing today. I let her go."

Bain grunted.

"What are you doing?" said Cullen.

Bain stabbed a finger against the board, setting it rocking on its feet. "We've got no leads other than finding Jamie Cook, and Lamb is making a royal mess of that. Our second suspect has just turned up dead, same MO as the first victim."

"You think it's Jamie Cook?" said Cullen.

Bain closed his eyes, pausing for a few seconds. "Yes, I do."

"How certain are you?"

Bain shrugged. "Sundance, there comes a time when even the greatest men begin to doubt themselves."

Cullen had to resist laughing.

"I'm struggling to figure this one out," said Bain. "Everything points to Jamie Cook but we've no hard evidence." He shook his head at the whiteboard. "Help me, here, Sundance. What actual facts do we have?"

Cullen thought for a few moments. "The only thing we know is it *looks like* the same killer for both."

"Looks like?" said Bain.

"Aye," said Cullen, clearing a space on the whiteboard. "It could be one person, right?"

Bain nodded.

Cullen scribbled a few boxes and joined them together. "It might be two in collaboration. The trouble is, these people must be connected in some way because the MO's are similar. If there are two people involved, then they were either responsible for one each or both were present but only one committed the act at each murder."

"Could they be unconnected and the second killer knew about the first one and copied?" said Bain.

"I was just about to say that," said Cullen.

"Assume it's two different killers," said Bain. "Unconnected. What does that tell us?"

Cullen thought about it. "They'd have to be close to the case to know the MO."

"So the person who killed Mulgrew knew Mandy was suffocated?"

"It looks that way," said Cullen.

"How could they?" said Bain. "How many people on this case know exactly how Mandy was killed? It's a handful at most. Not even the family knows. It's hardly likely to be a copper, so who could have found out?"

"You briefed roughly twenty officers yesterday," said Cullen.

"It's not likely," said Bain.

"What I'm saying is it's not a handful," said Cullen. "You read the PM report to a lot of officers."

"Are you saying someone on this case is leaking information?"

"If so, it's most likely inadvertent," said Cullen. "A slip of the tongue. Careless talk costs lives and all that. Someone tells his wife who tells her friend, she tells her friend and so on."

"That sort of shite takes time," said Bain. "There's roughly twenty-four hours between the deaths. I could accept it if the gap was longer and they had time to plan all this through. These crimes seem pretty hot-blooded."

"What if the opportunity was present because someone has been a little bit careless?" said Cullen.

"Sundance, would you quit it with this?" said Bain. "I gave my briefing at half four yesterday. That's five or six hours for the information to seep out, for our killer to hear it then go and kill Mulgrew."

He looked at Cullen with a sour expression. "Tell me you've not been blabbing, Sundance."

"No, I haven't," said Cullen, holding his hands up. "You're right — as far as I'm aware, nobody else knows Mandy was suffocated."

"Right, so what next?" said Bain.

Before Cullen could answer, Bain's mobile rang. "Irvine, you better have solved it." He started wandering around the room listening to the update.

As Bain belittled Irvine, Cullen put his mind to the case. Two separate deaths by suffocation was an extremely improbable chain of events.

Bain snapped his clamshell phone shut.

"What did Irvine want?" said Cullen.

Bain looked over with a grin. "They've found Mulgrew's car."

47

B ain drove down the lane by the cottages, away from Balgone Ponds. "You got any more than your two options to my little puzzler earlier, Sundance?"

"Still the two," said Cullen.

"It's always two with you, isn't it?" said Bain, grinning. "Maybe I should call you Two Face rather than Batman. Magic film that *Dark Knight* was, by the way."

"I learned pretty early on to keep an open mind," said Cullen.

"We're in the results business, though," said Bain. "We've no time for idealism, just for putting the bad guys away."

After a mile Bain pulled up past an entrance to the left, just as the tarmac turned into a farm track, full of potholes and puddles.

They got out of the car and started down the lane.

"On the left up ahead," said Bain, pointing at a row of beech trees spreading their branches across the path. There was a gap and a trail leading off.

PC Johnny Watson stood guard, clutching a clipboard to his chest.

"Through here?" said Bain.

"Yes, sir," said Watson, his voice almost too loud. "DS Irvine is leading the investigation, sir."

Bain shook his head. "He's supposed to be over at the ponds."

"He said it was the same case, sir," said Watson.

"Right," said Bain.

They hurried up the overgrown path. After a few hundred metres, they saw the luminous yellow jackets guarding the locus. As they walked, Cullen felt the puddles splash up his trouser leg.

Irvine met them halfway, clutching an Airwave handset and chomping away on gum. "Just over there," he said, pointing to a gap in the hedge.

The old Volvo was almost hidden from sight, wedged between two trees, the doors open and two SOCOs crawling around inside.

"That looks like it," said Cullen, recalling the car parked outside Mulgrew's cottage the previous morning.

"Aye," said Irvine. "The plates match."

"Anything from inside?" said Bain.

"Not yet, gaffer," said Irvine.

"I want to know if he was killed inside that car," said Bain.

"According to our friendly neighbourhood SOCO, it doesn't look that way," said Irvine.

"It's at least a mile to where the body was found," said Cullen. "I'd say it's unlikely he was killed in the car."

"How come?" said Bain, scowling.

"Mulgrew was a heavy man," said Cullen. "That's over a mile he'd have been carried, across a main road and through a bastard of a hedge. Someone would surely have seen that."

"What about dumping the car here?" said Bain.

"Mulgrew's key was in his trouser pocket," said Irvine. "It looks like he parked here himself."

Bain took a deep breath. "Any sign of a murder weapon yet?"

"Deeley confirmed suffocation," said Irvine.

"So a pillow, right?" said Bain.

Irvine nodded. "Aye, so he thinks."

"And I take it we've not found one out here?" said Bain.

"No." Irvine held up his Airwave. "Just had a call through from DC Murray. He's doing another door-to-door at the cottages. Morag Tattersall saw a car leaving last night."

"Did she, indeed?" said Bain. "She found Mandy, right?"

"Aye," said Irvine.

Bain looked at Cullen. "Right, Sundance, let's speak to her."

48

C ullen and Bain stood while DC Murray read back Tattersall's statement.

"You were taking the dogs out to the front garden last thing at night, just before the News at Ten. You think the clock read nine fifty-seven."

Morag nodded. "That's right."

Cullen saw Bain crosscheck his wristwatch with the antique clock on the wall.

"You saw a car drive down the lane at speed," said Murray. "It turned right at the end towards North Berwick."

Morag nodded again.

"The description you gave is of a large, silver saloon," said Murray. "An expensive marque, a Mercedes or a BMW, but you couldn't tell which. The car then sped off towards town."

"Yes."

Murray pointed to the uniform sat next to him. "You mentioned this to PC Barnes when he came to your door at ten fifty this morning."

"Well, I didn't think anything of it at the time," said Morag, "so I didn't call you. We get cars down the lane all the time."

"What sort?" said Murray.

"Small ones, you know, the sort that kids have done up and made noisy," said Morag.

Bain looked like he was about to explode.

"Sir, can we have a word outside?" said Cullen.

"Fine," said Bain.

Bain, Cullen and Murray stepped outside the cottage and stood in the front garden.

"Why didn't she call this in?" said Bain.

"It's a fairly standard occurrence around here, I'd have thought," said Cullen. "Fast car emerging from a country lane."

"Aye, it's fine if it's some neds, not some punter in a Merc," said Bain.

"What about dogging?" said Murray.

Bain scowled. "Eh?"

"It must be a pretty good spot for it," said Murray.

"Is it fuck," said Bain. "They do it in car parks so they can be watched, you tube."

"Expert, are you?" Murray smirked.

"Watch it, Constable." Bain pointed a finger at him. "I'll let you have one point, though. It could be someone having an illicit rendezvous down there."

"Do you want to add this to our assumptions?" said Cullen. "This car is connected to Mulgrew's murder."

"You reckon?" said Bain.

"It could be," said Cullen. He took out his notebook. "Just looking at the people we've interviewed, Charles Gibson has an Audi A6, William Thornton has a Mercedes and Robert Cook has a Lexus, all silver."

Bain slapped his hand to his forehead. "This is getting worse."

49

"I don't have to tell you where I was at any given time of day," said Gibson, looking furious.

"You just said you weren't in the house all night," said Bain, perching on the side of the sofa. "You need to tell us where you were."

Gibson took a deep breath and closed his eyes. "Okay," he said, after a pause. "I was meeting Seamus Mulgrew. I went to his cottage and he wasn't there."

"How long did you wait?" said Bain.

Gibson shrugged. "Half an hour or so. I gave up eventually." Tears welled in his eyes. "Now I know why he didn't turn up."

"What was the purpose of this meeting?" said Bain.

"My daughter was *murdered*," said Gibson. "In case you haven't noticed, I'm deep in grief. I needed to speak to someone about it. I can't unload this on my wife, not the way she's feeling. Seamus is my counsellor and I needed to share with him. Being alone with my thoughts while I waited was the loneliest I've ever felt in my life."

"What time would this be, then?" said Bain.

"I left here about quarter to nine," said Gibson. "I must have got back about half nine or so."

Cullen jotted it down — it tied in perfectly with the sighting at Balgone Ponds.

"Was this pre-arranged?" said Bain.

"I'm sorry?" said Gibson.

"Had you arranged to see Father Mulgrew or did you just turn up on spec?" said Bain.

Gibson nodded slowly. "We arranged it in the afternoon. He offered to counsel me."

"Why didn't you mention it when we spoke this morning?" said Bain.

"Am I under suspicion here?" said Gibson. "You told me I wasn't earlier."

"Why didn't you tell us about this arrangement when we were looking for Father Mulgrew last night?" said Bain.

Gibson loosened his collar. "I thought he would reappear when he decided the time was right."

"Father Mulgrew was a suspect in a murder inquiry," said Bain. "I could have you done for withholding information."

"I'm sorry," said Gibson, looking down at his shoes.

"We'll be in touch," said Bain.

Bain led Cullen outside, marching quickly and muttering to himself.

"What do you reckon?" said Bain once they were in his car.

"The timeline works," said Cullen. "His alibi is unverifiable."

"Not quite," said Bain, pulling out his mobile and placing a call. "Irvine? It's Bain. Can you get Murray or the other one to go door-to-door round Mulgrew's house, see if there was a silver Audi parked outside last night? McLaren, is it? Couldn't remember. Right, cheers. Let me know how he gets on. Bye."

"Good idea," said Cullen.

"I'm full of them," said Bain, turning the key in the ignition. "Follow me and you'll start picking them up, Sundance."

50

William Thornton's office was on Barnes Castle Road, an extension of the High Street.

"We're investigating a sighting of a silver executive class saloon late last night near to where Seamus Mulgrew's body was found," said Cullen. "We need you to detail your movements last night."

"Are you considering me a suspect?" said Thornton.

"If we were, you'd be in the station sitting next to your lawyer," said Bain.

"We have to keep an open mind," said Cullen. "You're acquainted with Seamus Mulgrew and you have a silver exec-class saloon. Where were you last night?"

Thornton took a long, deep breath. "I was at home all night with my wife and son, Malcolm. We watched a film."

"Which one?" said Bain.

"*Up in the Air* with George Clooney, if you must know," said Thornton.

"And you've got a receipt for this?" said Bain.

"It was on Sky," said Thornton.

"What time?" said Bain.

Thornton looked long at Bain, his eyes narrowed. "It started at about half past eight, I think, but we missed the first ten minutes or so."

208

"So you started watching it at quarter to nine?" said Cullen.

"That would be correct, yes," said Thornton.

"What about before that?" said Cullen.

Thornton frowned. "Is this really necessary?"

"Yes," said Cullen.

"We had dinner as a family," said Thornton. "I was meeting a client till the back of seven, so we didn't get a chance to sit down until half past."

"What was the name of the client?" said Cullen.

"It's a farmer just by Drem," said Thornton. "Name of William Millar."

"Okay, thanks for that, Mr Thornton," said Bain, in a condescending tone. "We may have to be in touch again about this."

"By all means," said Thornton.

Cullen and Bain left the office, heading back to Bain's car.

"Where to next then, Sundance?" said Bain.

"Robert Cook," said Cullen.

"Right," said Bain. "Where's that?"

"Next to the Gibsons'."

"You're kidding me," said Bain. "You've made us travel across town for no reason?"

"You chose to come here," said Cullen.

"Did I?" said Bain. "Well, now we're here, I could do with something to eat."

Bain crossed the road, heading towards Gregg's.

51

B ain wiped the sausage roll crumbs from his moustache then took a big gulp of stewed coffee. "Feel a bit more human now. Too much whisky last night."

They sat outside the Cook's house, facing the Gibsons', Cullen watching intently for movement while he ate a floury white roll. He got flashbacks to a surveillance operation just before Christmas, two weeks of twelve-hour shifts stuck with Irvine in the freezing cold.

"Tell me about this Robert Cook," said Bain.

Cullen gave him a potted history — managing director of his own local procurement business, member of God's Rainbow and father of Jamie Cook. "He drives a silver Lexus."

"One of the hybrid ones?" said Bain.

"I didn't notice," said Cullen.

"Cullen, it's the details you've got to focus on in a case like this," said Bain.

"I'll try to be more attentive in future," said Cullen, looking out of the window.

"Just been thinking," said Bain. "This Cook guy, right, what if he is covering up for his son?"

"How do you mean?" said Cullen, turning to face Bain.

"Well, there's a silver saloon spotted by the murder scene last night, right? Gibson and Thornton seem to have alibis leaving us with Cook. Assuming we don't have a mole inside the squad, we know someone was involved with both killings, right?"

"Okay," said Cullen, slowly.

"Jamie Cook seems to be up to his conkers in this case," said Bain, finishing his coffee. "What if Jamie is involved in both deaths, but his old man helped him to kill Mulgrew?"

Cullen was reluctant to admit Bain might be right. "You could have something there."

"Course I do," said Bain.

Cullen finished his own coffee, his hangover now a distant memory. "Shall we go inside?"

"Aye, give us a minute," said Bain. He let out a long burp. "Been waiting for that all morning."

They got out of the Mondeo and walked up the drive to the front door. Bain rang the bell, holding it down for longer than may have been appropriate.

Wilma Cook eventually opened up, scowling at Cullen as she stood on the top step, hand on hip, pulling the door to behind her. "We've been helping your colleague try to find our son. What else do you want?"

"This is a separate matter," said Cullen. "We're looking for your husband."

"My husband?" said Wilma, frowning. "Why?"

"It's related to the death of Seamus Mulgrew," said Cullen.

Wilma Cook nodded slowly.

"Can we speak to him or not?" said Bain.

"We're struggling to come to terms with the loss," said Wilma.

"I'm sure you are," said Bain. "Can we speak to your husband?"

Wilma glared at him. "My husband is in Edinburgh today on business."

"Can you give me a mobile number?" said Cullen, regretting not obtaining it before.

"Robert will be in meetings all day."

"I'm sure he can make time for the police," said Bain.

"Very well." She gave them the number. "Now, is there anything else?"

"Just let us know when your son turns up," said Bain.

Wilma didn't say anything as she went back inside, the door slamming behind her.

"Pleasant woman," said Bain, as they walked down the drive, past the Volvo SUV Cullen noticed the other day.

Bain pulled out his mobile and started dialling. "Mr Cook, this is DI Brian Bain of Lothian & Borders Police Service. I appreciate you may be busy, but this is an important matter. No, I understand. No, this isn't in relation to your son."

Cullen stopped and frowned. Looking back up the drive, something wasn't right. He flicked through his notebook to the previous afternoon's notes. He'd jotted down both the brown Volvo and the now absent silver Lexus. He'd also noted a Renault Clio, Jamie Cook's car.

It was missing.

"Are you one hundred per cent sure?" said Cullen, standing on the Cooks' drive, phone cradled to his ear.

"Aye, I definitely saw it," said Angela. "A Clio. You made a snarky comment about it."

"I did," said Cullen, noticing Bain wrapping up his call to Robert Cook. "I'd better go."

They put their phones away at the same time.

"Shite," said Bain. "Says he was at home last night. I'll get Lamb and his laddies to check it."

"I've got something for you," said Cullen. He pointed at the drive. "Jamie Cook's car has disappeared since yesterday."

Bain's ears pricked up. "You fuckin' what?"

"Aside from the Volvo and Robert Cook's Lexus, there was a Renault Clio here yesterday."

Bain stared at Cullen for a few seconds. "Right, you check with his wife, I'm calling him back."

Cullen walked up the drive towards the house, checking the flagstones for glass or any other sign suggesting the car had been broken into. Nothing. He hammered on the door.

Wilma Cook answered again, her expression even more distasteful. "What is it now?"

"If you recall, I was here yesterday with ADC Caldwell," said

Cullen. "There was a Renault Clio parked in the drive. Is that your son's?"

She gave a slight nod. "It is."

"Do you know where it is now?" said Cullen.

"I'm sorry, I don't know what you mean," said Wilma. "It's still there."

"It's not," said Cullen. "Have a look."

Wilma came down the steps. "Oh my God. You're right."

"When was the last time you saw it?" said Cullen.

"I've no idea. It's not something I particularly notice."

Cullen didn't believe it for one second. His own mother would have known exactly where the teenage Cullen was at any moment and would definitely have spotted his purple Fiesta disappearing. He couldn't accept for one minute that Jamie Cook's battleaxe of a mother didn't precisely know the Clio's movements.

"You don't notice whether your son is at home?" said Cullen. "Even when the police are looking for him?"

"Well—"

"You didn't notice it disappearing during the night?" said Cullen.

"No," said Wilma. "I haven't been out today, what with all the business with Father Mulgrew."

"I take it Jamie has his own car keys?" said Cullen.

"He does," she said. "I've got a spare set just inside the door."

"Could you check they're still there?" said Cullen.

Wilma went back inside, rummaging around in the porch. "They're still here."

"Could it be in the garage?" said Cullen.

"I'll check," said Wilma. She grabbed a key fob and walked over to the double garage, pressing a button and starting the doors sliding up. Inside was the usual assortment of surplus furniture, sports equipment, bikes and garden tools. No Clio.

Cullen scribbled some notes and tried to clear his head, struggling to think of any more questions. "Okay, thank you. We'll be in touch."

She went back inside, slamming the door.

Cullen walked back to Bain's Mondeo.

"Slipping her a length were you, Sundance?" said Bain, his face sour.

"Hardly," said Cullen. "She hadn't noticed the car for days. It's not in the garage, either."

"Fuck's sake," said Bain. "She's probably out of her fuckin' head on Prozac or something."

"Did you get through to Robert Cook?" said Cullen.

"Aye," said Bain. "He saw it had gone when he left this morning in a tearing hurry to get into Edinburgh for his meeting."

"He didn't think to tell us Jamie's car disappeared overnight?" said Cullen.

"He thought his wife had put it away," said Bain. "Reckons it might have been gone last night. Sergeant Lamb is going to have some questions to answer about why no-one was watching this place."

Cullen took a deep breath. "Are they trying to cover something up?"

"Could well be," said Bain. "Their son is murder suspect number one and they don't want us to find him."

"He could be innocent," said Cullen.

"It's not looking likely," said Bain. "And I think they know it." He paused for a minute. "I want someone taking a statement off the pair of them."

53

Half an hour later, Bain was running a briefing in the Incident Room, making sure every officer attached to the case was pulled back, reassigning priorities in light of recent developments.

"Jamie Cook's car has disappeared," said Bain, "most likely some time yesterday afternoon."

A shockwave went round the room.

"DC Cullen noticed the car has gone missing since he and ADC Caldwell visited the property yesterday morning."

He took a sip from a fresh can of Red Bull. "Jimmy Deeley still hasn't performed the post mortem on Father Mulgrew but he gave an indicative time of death at some point yesterday evening. This mystery car fits right into the window and it's likely it's our killer. Robert Cook's Lexus could be that car."

He paused before opening his notebook, putting his glasses on and reading. "I want to talk about suspects for a bit. Jamie Cook is now the main suspect in this case. We have a means that allowed him to carry out the murder. DS Lamb still hasn't managed to find him."

"Any idea why Jamie would do it?" said Lamb, leaning against the wall at the back of the room, one hand stroking his beard.

"We have a few likely motives," said Bain.

"Why would Robert Cook help his son?" said Lamb.

Bain held his gaze for a few moments. "I'm sorry?"

"Robert Cook is one of the key members of God's Rainbow," said Lamb. "I find it a bit strange to think he'd murder the leader."

"What about protecting his son?" said Bain.

"But why?" said Lamb. "They'd largely disowned him. I don't get it."

"Fine," said Bain, "let's discuss this later." He finished the can of Red Bull and crushed it with some force. "Of the car suspects, we have alibis from Gibson, Thornton and Cook."

"It could be someone else," said Lamb. "You've focused on those three to tie it to Jamie Cook, haven't you?"

"Drop it, Sergeant," said Bain.

Lamb shrugged. "Fine."

"As I mentioned earlier," said Bain, entirely focused on Lamb, "Jamie Cook now has the means with which to commit the crimes. Balgone Ponds is roughly four miles from Garleton."

Lamb started to speak but Bain cut him off. "Sergeant, you and I will have a conversation after this."

Cullen could guess what Lamb was going to say. There were means and motive for the Mulgrew murder but they couldn't pin Mandy on Cook. They only had Bain's assumptions and the matching MO.

"Now, I'm going to set some actions and I want hourly updates from all officers to be passed through DS Irvine," said Bain. "I will contact each lead officer every three hours for personal updates. Expect some difficult questions."

Bain looked at Angela. "ADC Caldwell, I want you to go into Edinburgh and go through the CCTV network from the A1 into the city. I want you to find Jamie Cook's car." His focus switched to Lamb. "DS Lamb, I want you to perform a similar exercise locally. Search all the CCTV on the A1 and all other main roads leading from Garleton."

Lamb screwed his eyes shut. "Will do."

Bain dished out further instructions to the uniformed officers, mainly door-to-door in the Dunpender estate and the streets around Seamus Mulgrew's cottage, to confirm the nocturnal movements of Charles Gibson and Robert Cook.

"Finally," said Bain, "I want DS Irvine and DC Cullen to take over the search for Jamie Cook. For over twenty-four hours now, DS Lamb has been leading the investigation but we need to freshen things up and actually find the boy. Dismissed."

Cullen felt himself deflate as the group dispersed.

"DS Lamb," said Bain, "a word."

THEY WERE BACK in the Starbucks, sitting by the window looking across to the police station. Bain had ordered Cullen to obtain all Lamb's information about Jamie Cook, with Lamb suggesting they discuss the matter away from the Incident Room.

The rain had eased off and the day was brightening up again, though there were the first hints of a bitter wind coming in, the early afternoon shoppers struggling against it as they made their way up the High Street.

"You're looking better than you did this morning," said Lamb. "It's fair to say you can hide a hangover."

"You look like you survived Bain's one-on-one mauling pretty well," said Cullen.

Lamb snorted. "He's a pussycat when you get him alone. All mouth and no trousers."

"Is he?" said Cullen, raising an eyebrow.

Lamb laughed again. "Not really." He took a drink of his latte. "What's all this Batman shite with him?"

"I've no idea where he's picked it up from," said Cullen. "You'll have noticed he likes to have nicknames for people. He calls me Sundance. It's a cheap joke at my girlfriend's expense. He calls her Butch."

"Is she a lesbian?" said Lamb.

"Hardly."

"Wonder what he calls me," said Lamb.

"If he calls you by your real name, you know it's bad," said Cullen. "What happened, then?"

"He tore into me," said Lamb. "Usual stuff about not questioning him in front of the officers."

"You raised some valid points," said Cullen.

"I think your DI isn't someone who appreciates valid points," said Lamb. "He's lucky my own DI is excluded from this case."

Cullen had wondered why the local DI, based in Musselburgh, hadn't been consulted. "Why have they been?"

"What, other than the fact Bain operates a divide and conquer strategy?" said Lamb.

"You don't know the half of it," said Cullen. He finished his Americano — the only coffee in the place he could stomach.

"I think I'm going to report DI Bain's conduct to DCI Turnbull," said Lamb.

Cullen was puzzled by the use of formal titles and language. "It's your battle."

"I never lose," said Lamb.

Cullen took out his notebook. "Okay, onto the reason we're here. Can you give me the list of all leads on Jamie Cook?"

Lamb retrieved a stapled document from the pile of papers in front of him and handed it to Cullen. "This is the detailed list of all lines of investigation we've followed. I had Murray type it up at lunchtime. Funnily enough, I suspected something like this might happen."

Glancing through the many pages, Cullen saw they'd spoken to more than eighty witnesses so far. "That's a lot of people."

"I'm nothing if not thorough," said Lamb.

"Where should I be focusing my efforts?" said Cullen.

Lamb grabbed the paper and turned to the last page. He pointed to a line of text halfway down. "That would have been my next line of inquiry. It came from you."

The name meant nothing to Cullen. "Keith Green?"

"One of Jamie's friends in Tranent," said Lamb. "You unearthed the link but it still took a hell of a lot of asking around to get a name. For a young lad, Jamie Cook sure doesn't like to leave a trail behind."

"Thanks," said Cullen.

Lamb grabbed hold of the paper before Cullen could take it. "If any of this turns out to be useful in finding Jamie, make sure I'm given some credit."

"You're not afraid of the big bad Bain are you?"

Lamb laughed, a little too loud for Cullen to think it was

genuine. "No, I'm not, but I recognise a game player when I see one and I don't want to be on the losing side."

"I'll make sure you get all the credit you're due," said Cullen.

"You mean it?" said Lamb, his face betraying his insecurity.

"Of course."

54

I rvine indicated off the dual carriageway, the sporty Astra heading inland away from Prestonpans and the Forth coastline. Tranent hid behind new housing estates lining the A1, a sprawl of white boxes leading up from the valley floor to the town.

Cullen looked up, pretending to review his notes being the best way to avoid conversation with Irvine.

Irvine pulled in just past a large Co-op. "What did you say this boy's name was?" he said, as they got out of the car.

"Keith Green."

They quickly found the block of ex-council flats, Irvine pressing the buzzer and waiting. "Bet he's not in," he said, before pressing it again.

The intercom burst into life. "Aye?"

"Mr Green, it's the police," said Irvine. "We need to speak to you."

"Fine."

The buzzer didn't sound and the door didn't click open.

Irvine closed his eyes. "Can you let us up, please?"

There was another delay. "Aye." The door clicked open.

"Prick," said Irvine, as they entered the building.

Green lived on the second floor. His door was open and Irvine gestured for Cullen to go first.

The flat was in a state, the paint flecking off the door

surrounds and skirting, the walls mostly bare and the carpet worn down to the underlay in places.

Cullen got out his warrant card and walked down the hall towards the din of television. "Mr Green, it's DC Cullen and DS Irvine of Lothian & Borders CID."

The voice came from a door at the other end of the hall. "I'm on the bog."

"We'll just wait for you here," said Cullen.

Irvine shut the flat door behind them, before whispering in Cullen's ear. "I'm beginning to think this is Lamb messing us about."

"What makes you think that?" said Cullen.

"This feels like amateur hour," said Irvine.

"We can't all aspire to your levels of professionalism," said Cullen.

Irvine clearly didn't know how to take the remark.

The toilet flushed and Keith Green appeared. Cullen noticed his hands were dry and made a mental note not to shake if offered. He was tall and skinny with short dark hair, and wore grey track-suit bottoms and a branded t-shirt that had seen better days.

"Come on through," said Green, leading them into the kitchen, doubling as a living room.

The cabinets were yellowing melamine, the strips coming unstuck, with an old bottle green three-piece suite at one end in front of a cheap LCD TV on a unit covered in stacks of copied DVDs. A large bong took pride of place on the mantelpiece.

Green spread himself out on the armchair in front of the TV. Cullen and Irvine remained standing.

"What do you want?" said Green.

"Is this your home, Mr Green?" said Cullen.

"It is, aye," said Green. "*I* pay the rent. I'm a joiner. It's my day off so you're lucky to get us."

"I believe you're acquainted with a Jamie Cook," said Cullen

"I know Jamie," said Green, grinning.

"Do you know where he is?" said Cullen.

"Are you looking for him, likes?" said Green.

"Yes," said Cullen, losing patience with him.

Green gave a little chuckle. "He's a daft wee bastard. I haven't seen the boy in weeks."

Irvine rolled his eyes. "Do you know anyone who might have?"

"Big Alan McArthur would," said Green.

"And do you know where big Alan McArthur is?" said Cullen.

Green gave them an address a few streets over.

Irvine handed him a card. "Give us a bell if he pitches up."

Green showed them to the door.

Once they were outside, Irvine stopped by his car and looked back up. "Did you see his DVDs?"

"We could get Lamb's lot to bust him if we wanted," said Cullen.

"Give that useless bastard something to do, you mean?" said Irvine.

Cullen was beyond fed up with Irvine's attitude to the local CID. "I didn't say that."

They drove towards Alan McArthur's parents' house in the middle of an estate halfway out of town, filled with post-war houses, none particularly well presented.

All Cullen knew about Tranent was its focus had been coal mining before the industry was killed off in the eighties. Scotland struggled to generate money at the best of times leaving a huge vacuum during the worst. From years of working in West Lothian, Cullen knew what social cleansing had done to local communities, the redundant workers siring generations of lost kids with no future, prospects or hope. The social structures of strong patriarchs disappeared along with the men's self-respect, replaced with cheap alcohol, heroin and crime.

Irvine pulled up in front of a rundown semi-detached house, the front lawn mostly bare and filled with puddles of water, a battered Vauxhall Cavalier sitting on bricks.

"Help me out with something here," said Cullen.

"What?"

Cullen pointed at the house. "This doesn't exactly look like the best house in East Lothian."

Irvine looked out of the side window. "What's your point, caller?"

"Jamie Cook is from a well-off family," said Cullen. "His dad runs his own business and he lives in a big house in Garleton."

Irvine looked around. "I'm still not getting you."

"Why's he mucking about with guys from Tranent in places like this?" said Cullen.

Irvine shrugged. "Cultural slumming."

"I've never seen it like this, though," said Cullen.

Irvine stretched out. "Let's just see what this boy has to say."

They walked up to the house, the blinds and curtains drawn.

"Bloody hell," said Irvine. "Nobody's in."

"You've not even tried yet," said Cullen.

He reached over and pressed the doorbell, quickly answered by a woman in her mid-forties, her ginger hair full of grey streaks. She was wearing a dressing gown, though it was just after three.

"Mrs McArthur?" said Cullen.

She nodded. "Who's asking?"

"We're police officers," said Cullen, holding up his warrant card and introducing them.

She folded her arms. "And?"

"We're looking for your son," said Cullen.

"Which one? I've got four."

"Alan," said Cullen.

She tutted. "Right."

"Is he in?" said Cullen.

"No."

"Do you know where he is?"

She nodded across the road. "He's at his pal's."

Cullen took a deep breath. "Mrs McArthur, can you please tell me exactly where your son is."

She scowled at him. "Across the road, number fifteen. His pal's called Paul."

"Thank you," said Cullen, with a disingenuous smile.

She went back inside.

"Charming," said Irvine, looking across the road.

"Your turn next," said Cullen.

"Come on, then," said Irvine, "show you how it's done."

He crossed the road, reaching into his pocket and retrieving a green drum of chewing gum, throwing a handful of pieces into his mouth.

"Aren't you going to offer it around?" said Cullen.

Irvine stared at him. "You want some?"

"Not really, but you never ask."

224   ED JAMES

"Did you get me a sausage roll earlier?" said Irvine.

"That isn't the same thing," said Cullen.

Irvine scowled. "How not?"

"It just isn't," said Cullen.

Irvine stopped outside the front gate. "Keeps me off the fags."

"Fair enough," said Cullen, losing interest in winding Irvine up. He looked up at the grey concrete building, part of a terrace of six, which looked barely one room wide.

"Time to do this properly," said Irvine, before hammering on the front door.

They heard a muffled voice through the door. "Get that will you?"

Cullen shared a look with Irvine while they waited, the door opening to reveal a tall, heavyset man in a saggy grey jumper and faded blue jeans. "What?"

"We're looking for Alan McArthur," said Irvine.

"You've found him."

"Mr McArthur," said Irvine, showing his warrant card and introducing them. "We're looking to track down an acquaintance of yours, a Jamie Cook."

McArthur's face was blank. "Who?"

"Jamie Cook," said Irvine. "Lives in Garleton."

Cullen held up the photo they had of Jamie, taken at a party a few weeks before, the boy smiling in a fug of smoke. McArthur's face continued to look blank for a few moments, before he clicked his fingers. "You mean Biscuit, right?"

"Biscuit?" said Irvine.

"Aye, that's the boy," said McArthur. "Skinny wee bastard. Curtains haircut. Gets called Biscuit or Cookie." He tapped the photo. "That's him."

"Well, have you seen him recently?" said Irvine.

"Not since last weekend," said McArthur. "We were at a party on the Saturday."

"And you haven't heard from him since?" said Irvine.

"No."

"No texts or emails?" said Irvine. "Nothing on Facebook, Twitter or Schoolbook?"

"Do I look like I tweet?" said McArthur.

"Mind if we have a look inside?" said Cullen.

A wave of panic crept across McArthur's face. "Have you got a warrant?"

"No," said Cullen, "we're just looking for Jamie Cook."

"He's not here," said McArthur. "This isn't my place."

"Then you won't mind me having a look inside," said Cullen.

He pushed past McArthur into a flat as sparsely furnished as Keith Green's. Three people sat round a large TV and an Xbox in the living room playing a shooting game.

"Have any of you seen Jamie Cook?" said Cullen, holding up the photo.

They looked up from the game long enough to glance at the photo and shake their heads.

Cullen went upstairs, finding a bedroom and bathroom. Jamie Cook was in neither. He sighed and headed back outside.

"You satisfied now?" said McArthur.

Cullen looked at Irvine. "He's not here and none of the three people present recognise him."

"Do you know anyone who might know where Jamie is?" said Irvine.

"Have you checked with his bird?" said McArthur. "Works in the Asda in Dunbar. Think her name is Kirsty."

55

Cullen waited at the customer service desk while Irvine went to the toilet, having jigged his leg all the way from Tranent. The assistant put out a call on the PA system for a Kirsty-Jane Platt. Cullen took out his notebook, scribbling down the full name.

"Excuse me, officer?"

Cullen turned back to see the attendant pointing away from him. "That's Kirsty there."

"Thanks."

Irvine was walking over, tugging at his belt, drying his hands on his trousers. The girl in front of him wore a green Asda jacket. She looked at the service desk attendant then at Cullen.

"Kirsty?" said Cullen.

She nodded. "What is it?" Up close she looked really young, barely over sixteen.

Cullen showed her his warrant card and introduced them as Irvine caught up. "I believe you're acquainted with a Jamie Cook of Garleton."

Kirsty looked at him for what felt like minutes. "Jamie?"

"Yes, do you know him?"

"I do," said Kirsty, pulling her fleece tighter around her. "I've told the police to drop the charges."

Cullen's heart fluttered. "What charges?"

"The rape."

56

Kirsty's revelation left Cullen on the back foot. He struggled to understand how Lamb or his officers knew nothing about Jamie Cook allegedly raping someone.

"I suggest we go somewhere private," said Irvine.

"The only place that'll be free is the canteen," said Kirsty. "There's no breaks due for another hour."

They went upstairs and found a plastic table in the corner of the empty canteen. Kirsty fiddled with a sugar container. Her mobile sat next to it, a flash Samsung with a large screen. Cullen wondered how much of her wages the contract took up.

"What did you mean by the rape?" said Cullen.

"I don't have to say anything, right?" said Kirsty.

Cullen decided to leave it for a bit. "Can you tell me about your relationship with Jamie?"

"Why?"

"We're looking to interview him in connection with a case," said Cullen.

Kirsty closed her eyes. "What's he done now?"

"I'm not at liberty to divulge that information," said Cullen. "Can you please describe your relationship with him?"

"I'd rather not," she said, tugging her fleece tight again.

"When was the last time you saw Jamie?" said Cullen.

"A couple of weeks ago."

"Do you know precisely when?" said Cullen.

She fiddled with her phone. "Last Monday night."

"Was this when he raped you?" said Cullen.

Tears welled in her eyes. "Aye."

"Was Jamie your boyfriend?" said Cullen.

Kirsty nodded, tears now streaking down her face. Cullen reached over to a box of tissues on the next table and handed some to her. "Thanks."

"How long have you been seeing Jamie?" said Cullen.

"About eight months," she said. "It was great at first. He used to take me driving in his car."

"What happened?" said Cullen.

She blew her nose. "He started talking about sex."

Cullen left a pause, waited for her to fill it.

"We used to, you know." She gave a 'wanker' gesture with her hand — the dying art of mutual masturbation. "It wasn't enough for him. He wanted to *do it*."

"And did you want to?" said Cullen.

She closed her eyes. "I don't know," she said, her voice tiny.

Irvine's jaw was tightly clenched for once. "Did Jamie put pressure on you?"

"He did, aye," she said. "He became a bit of a pest about it."

"Did you talk to anyone about it?" said Cullen.

Kirsty scowled. "No."

"What happened last Monday?" said Cullen.

Kirsty blew her nose again then rubbed at her eyes with another tissue. "We were in his car. We'd parked at Tyninghame beach, halfway between here and Garleton, sitting in the back seat and we were, you know, doing it. Jamie said he wanted to do it properly. He had a condom and everything. He put it on, then—"

She burst into tears, huddling forward and rocking.

Cullen rested a hand on her shoulder. "It's okay."

She pushed his hand away then looked at him, her eyes red raw. "It's not okay," she said, her voice loud. "I didn't stop him."

"Did you say yes at any point?" said Cullen.

Her eyes closed briefly. "No."

"And did you want him to have sex with you?" said Cullen.

"No."

"Okay, so he raped you," said Cullen.

Kirsty closed her eyes again. "I didn't say no either. I just let him do it. It didn't last very long."

"What happened after?" said Cullen.

She took a fresh tissue and dabbed at her eyes. "We just lay there. He pulled me close to him and we lay on the back seat for a while. That bit was quite nice." She blew her nose. "Then he dropped me at home. I was late and my dad was shouting at me." She clenched the tissue tight in her fist. "I panicked and told him what happened. He freaked out and called the police."

"What did they do?" said Cullen.

"They came out and took my statement," she said. "They took me to the hospital in Edinburgh, got some tests done then took me back home."

"Did they pick Jamie up?" said Cullen.

She rubbed her nose. "Aye."

"And what happened?" said Cullen.

She said nothing.

"Ms Platt, what happened next?" said Irvine.

Kirsty took a deep breath. "My dad's a policeman in Dunbar."

It was Cullen's turn to close his eyes. He could just picture it. A local old-school officer disenchanted with life in the police after years on the beat, battering seven shades of shite out of the animal that raped his daughter.

"What did your dad do?" said Cullen.

She looked scared. "I wasn't there."

"Was it something other than questioning him?" said Cullen.

"I think so," she said, almost a whisper.

"But you dropped the charges?" said Cullen.

She nodded, almost imperceptibly.

"Did your dad tell you to?" said Cullen.

"I'm not saying anything else."

Cullen slumped back in his chair, rubbing his forehead. "Can you think of anyone who could help us track Jamie down? We've already spoken to Alan McArthur and Keith Green. Is there anyone else?"

"I can only think of Stevie Young," said Kirsty. "He's a friend of my brother's. That's how we met. We were at a party at his flat about a year ago, when I was still at school. Jamie used to be round there at Stevie's all the time, when he wasn't seeing me that is."

"How old were you?" said Cullen.

"Fifteen."

"Are you sixteen now?" said Cullen.

"Turned sixteen in July," she said. "Left school and got a job here. Mum works on the checkouts."

"Was Jamie pressuring you to have sex before you were sixteen?" said Cullen.

She fiddled with her phone for a few moments. "Aye."

"And did you do anything with Jamie?" said Cullen.

"I'm not answering that here."

Cullen scribbled in his notebook. "Could you give us the address of this Stevie, please?"

Kirsty picked up her mobile again. "The invite was on School-book. I'm sure it's on here." She fiddled with the phone. "There."

She handed Cullen the phone and he took down the address in Haddington.

57

Rather than run the risk of spooking Jamie Cook with the arrival of a strange car, Bain decided to send DC Murray and two uniformed officers to help with the arrest, instructing them to wait at Aldi just around the corner. Assuming Cook was actually at Steven Young's flat.

The day was still dry, but the wind was even colder and it was getting dark, the sun having disappeared behind the hills surrounding Haddington.

"But isn't Aldi for poor people?" said Irvine.

"No," said Cullen, "I used to do all of my shopping at the one in Musselburgh."

"Thought you lived off takeaways?" said Irvine.

"Okay, when I occasionally put something in the oven."

"Can't beat Tesco for me, man," said Irvine.

"Look at the people and cars," said Cullen, gesturing across the car park, filled with Audis, Range Rovers and a selection of Volkswagens, Saabs and Volvos.

"Never noticed that before," said Irvine. "That's bizarre."

"Look after the pennies and the pounds look after themselves."

Irvine nodded.

"On the subject of supermarkets," said Cullen, "what are we going to do about Kirsty?"

They hadn't informed Bain of the rape charge yet, deciding face-to-face would be better.

Irvine shrugged. "That's something Bain can get Lamb lost in. If a suspect rapes a young girl, it's got to be part of this case, hasn't it?"

"He was going out with her before she was sixteen," said Cullen.

"I'm not sure I believe her about no action before she was legal," said Irvine. "He could have done anything. Silly little bastard shouldn't have been doing it with an officer's daughter."

"What will happen to him?" said Cullen.

"He's going to get Professional Standards having a word with him as soon as Bain finds out about this," said Irvine. "Can understand where he's coming from, though. Some wee toerag is noncing up his daughter, stands to reason he'd want to boot the shite out of him."

Cullen spoke in slow, measured tones. "Giving him a shoeing while on duty in a police station isn't a smart move. If it gets out, someone senior will get a doing. He's obviously got other officers involved, as well."

"Don't tell me you of all people are into all that checks and balances shite, Cullen."

"Of course I am," said Cullen, his voice rising.

Irvine laughed. "No, you're not. You take the piss all the time. You're a cowboy, man."

Cullen shook his head. "Where do you get that from?"

"You're the biggest game player I know," said Irvine.

"What do you mean, *Sarge*?" said Cullen, staring at him.

"That case last summer," said Irvine, "you were always going behind the gaffer's back."

"Bain was *wrong*."

"You've got to support him, though," said Irvine. "He's the Senior Investigating Officer on the case. It's his arse on the line. It's his call."

"He was wrong," said Cullen.

"You should have presented your case to him and let him make the decision."

"Have you lost your mind?" said Cullen. "You were on that case. Bain wasn't listening to reason."

Irvine leaned over and whispered, his voice low and harsh. "You were playing games, Cullen. You were up to your own little investigation, keeping the rest of us in the dark. You and your dyke bird."

Cullen grabbed Irvine by the collar, pulling him close, faces almost touching. "Don't you dare bring Sharon into this. And don't forget who was wrong and who was right in that case. I wasn't playing games. I was doing my job." He let go.

Irvine cowered back against the door.

"I don't play games," said Cullen. "Are we clear?"

Irvine said nothing.

"I said, are we clear?"

"Aye," said Irvine.

Cullen got out of the car, slamming the door and leaning against it, his pulse racing. He was already regretting it, but Irvine was out of order.

This shite about Sharon being a dyke or butch, he needed to make sure Bain got a doing for it. His stupid acolytes like Irvine just followed along, looking for a lead from the pack's alpha dog. Keeping in with Bain gave them protection.

Cullen had to watch his step. While things had been okay with Bain recently, he was only ever a second away from snapping.

Cullen spotted a squad car pulling into the car park. He tapped the window and opened the door. "Back up's here," he said to Irvine. He hurried over to Murray, the first one out. "That was quick."

"Aye, anything to get away from CCTV," said Murray, smiling. "Bain's stitched Bill up good and proper with that."

Irvine wandered over, throwing more gum into his mouth as he walked. Two uniforms got out, PC Watson and one Cullen didn't recognise.

"Come on," said Cullen, avoiding eye contact with Irvine. He led them out of the car park towards the houses, the vein in his neck still throbbing from the encounter.

Stevie Young's street was lined with the sort of two-storey buildings so common in Edinburgh and its surrounding towns, white harling turned yellow and brown from the weather.

The building was split into four flats, two on each floor. Cullen studied the intercom — *S. Young* was second floor on the right.

Cullen took a few steps back and looked up — the curtains were drawn in Young's flat. He pointed at Watson and Irvine. "You two stay here." He gestured for Murray and the uniform to follow him up.

The front door was open to the street. Grey, untreated concrete festered in the stairwell, the only light was from a small rectangle of glass on the front door and a flickering stair light. There was no back door.

"Stay here," said Cullen, getting a nod from the uniform in response. He walked up to the green front door, 'Stevie's Place' inscribed in black marker, before knocking and waiting. No reply. He knocked again. Nothing.

He pushed open the letterbox and called inside. "Mr Young, it's the police."

He banged the door again after a few seconds then peered through the letterbox. It was pitch black inside.

Cullen looked at Murray. "Doesn't look like he's in."

"What do you want to do?" said Murray.

Cullen pointed at the other flat. "Let's try next door."

He marched over and knocked, eventually answered by an old man peering out from behind a security chain. "Who is it?"

"It's the police," said Cullen, showing his warrant card through the gap. "We're looking for your neighbour."

The door opened. The man was clearly over seventy and hunched over on his walking stick. "Alec Nicholson," he said, offering his hand. "Thank God you lot have finally come out."

"I'm sorry?" said Cullen.

"I called up about the noise from next door," said Nicholson. "Please tell me it's about that."

"I'm afraid not," said Cullen. "We're looking to speak to your neighbour in relation to another inquiry."

Nicholson looked deflated. "I see."

"Has Mr Young been in today?" said Cullen.

Nicholson looked up. "Aye, he has."

"Is he likely to come back?"

Nicholson shrugged his shoulders. "You're asking the wrong man, I'm afraid."

"Did you say you'd put in a complaint?"

Nicholson nodded. "They had a party on Sunday night. It can

get awfully wild with Steven and his pals. The little buggers were at it again last night. I didn't bother phoning you lot."

"When did they leave?" said Cullen.

"They cleared off this afternoon, just after *Neighbours*," said Nicholson. "I saw a car shoot off down the street."

Cullen held up the photo of Jamie Cook. "Do you recognise him?"

Nicholson screwed his eyes up, before nodding. "Seen him a few times. Couldn't tell you if he was here last night, though."

Cullen didn't know if that was good or bad. "Do you have any idea where they might have gone?"

Nicholson shook his head. "No. I'm just glad the little bastards aren't here today."

58

"This is getting beyond a fuckin' joke," said Bain. He punched the whiteboard sending it rolling back against the wall, the aluminium frame tumbling over and cracking.

Cullen stared at it for a few seconds, before looking at Bain.

"How's he managing to avoid us?" said Bain.

"Jamie Cook doesn't want to be found," said Cullen, trying to remain calm despite his racing pulse. "We've checked out countless known acquaintances. DS Irvine and I interviewed two of his friends and his ex-girlfriend."

"Cullen might have a point about the lad, gaffer," said Irvine. "We're trying hard to find him and he's nowhere. Nobody knows where he's gone. He could be dead."

"What?" said Bain.

Irvine sniffed. "Mulgrew was found dead. What's to say Jamie Cook hasn't been killed?"

Bain glared at him, clearly lost for words. "This is all I need."

Cullen took a deep breath. "The only other thing I can think of is chaos—"

"*Chaos?*" said Bain. "Cullen, this isn't *Jurassic fuckin' Park*. You don't come in here going on about chaos theory, all right? "

"If you'd let me finish?" said Cullen. "Jamie isn't someone who follows patterns, therefore it's difficult to get a hold of him."

Bain stared hard at him. "That's an interesting way of looking at it, Cullen," he said, his voice almost a hiss. "The other possibility, something not from science fiction, is the little bastard is on the run having killed two people."

Cullen shrugged. "If that's the case, he'll most likely be lying low somewhere."

"The boy is out there, believe you me," said Bain. "We'll find him!"

Cullen swallowed hard, realising he was developing a thick skin when it came to the constant verbal barrage from Bain. He held firm, knowing he had a point. "Everything in his life indicates he's a drifter."

He knew the type from school, reasonably bright guys who bought into the whole slacker thing, preferring to sit around people's bedrooms and garages smoking joints and listening to music, rather than making any effort to do well.

Cullen wasn't the most academic of people but he had pushed himself towards university. Although he dropped out, he achieved his goal of joining the police by taking on a shite office job and using his spare time to train for the physical exams.

"Guess we'd better tell you about the rape, gaffer," said Irvine.

"Rape?" Bain's eyes bulged. "What fuckin' rape?"

"Cook was charged with raping some lassie in Dunbar," said Irvine.

Bain turned to stare at Murray. "Why don't we have this on record?"

"First I've heard of it," said Murray, with a shrug.

Cullen jumped in, trying to distract Bain. "It was never on the record. We don't even know if she was technically raped. The girl herself was beating herself up about consent."

He cleared his throat. "Her dad is a cop, based in Dunbar. He got her to accuse Cook. They brought Cook in, beat the shit out of him then let him go. She dropped the charges and it looks like they haven't filed the paperwork. It might have been lost."

Bain stared at Irvine. "This right?"

"More or less," said Irvine.

"So, I've got to point the Complaints at Dunbar as well as everything else?" said Bain.

Cullen considered suggesting Bain might get some brownie

points from reporting it, but he didn't want to be a whiteboard substitute.

Bain rubbed his hand across his face. "Right, I'll get someone looking into this."

"How's Angela getting on?" said Cullen.

Bain scowled at Cullen's curve ball. "Eh?"

"Well, we've been looking for Jamie Cook locally," said Cullen. "Now we know he has his car, have we managed to track it down?"

Bain closed his eyes, trying to focus himself. He reopened them and stared at Cullen. "Yes, she called in. Turns out the car got on the A1 at Haddington and left at the exit for Tranent."

"Has it appeared anywhere since?" said Cullen.

"No, it hasn't," said Bain.

"When?" said Cullen.

"Eleven fifty-eight this morning," said Bain. He looked at Irvine. "You were out at Tranent, weren't you?"

"We were, gaffer, aye."

"And there was no sign of him?" said Bain.

"None," said Irvine. "We spoke to six people, none of them had seen him."

Cullen winced. "We missed him by four hours."

"Good one boys," said Bain, looking around the room, lingering on Murray in Lamb's absence. "Jesus fuckin' Christ. Did you check the houses yourselves?"

"Of course we did," said Cullen. "I went through every room."

"You obviously weren't thorough enough." Bain pinched the bridge of his nose then exhaled deeply. "Irvine, I want you back in Tranent going through those leads you had. Somebody must know where the little toerag is."

"Sure thing," said Irvine.

"I want someone staking out Steven Young's flat," said Bain, looking at Cullen. "Can you do it?"

Cullen thought fast, desperate to avoid the task. "I could, but there are a few other leads I should be following up. There are a few kids from school I'd like to speak to, see if they know anything. I get the distinct impression Jamie Cook is a bit of a bragger. It stands to reason he might have let slip a bit too much. I could do with DC Murray's local knowledge."

"If it keeps you out of my hair then fill your boots." Bain looked at Murray. "Any idea where your buddy is?"

"Lamb?" said Murray, arms folded.

"No, you fuckin' tube," said Bain. "McLean, McLaren, whatever his name is."

"DC Ewan McLaren is with Lamb, sir," said Murray.

Cullen suppressed a smile.

"I'll get him to do the stakeout." Bain looked at PC Watson. "Can you go and fetch him?"

Watson nodded. "Will do, sir."

Bain rubbed at his moustache. "Right, let's get out there and find this little bastard."

59

As Cullen reassembled the damaged whiteboard he tried to expand on his diversion of speaking to Cook's friends, searching for loose threads. He got one. Mandy's friend Susan Russell hadn't been interviewed. He probably should have spoken to her, but had been diverted.

Cullen grabbed Murray and headed to the Russells' house.

"You managed to handle Bain well," said Cullen.

Murray shrugged as he turned a corner. "I've seen his sort before. Had a murder out here two years ago, some big shot from Edinburgh came out swinging his dick around. DI Davenport. Bill Lamb caught the guy in the end."

"I worked for Davenport at St Leonard's," said Cullen.

"Lucky you," said Murray. "Same shit happening here."

"What do you mean?" said Cullen.

"You're not exactly succeeding where we failed, are you? Bain's got his big city dream team, you and Irvine, out looking for Jamie Cook. He's split you up already."

Cullen didn't want to labour the point too much. When they travelled back to Garleton separately, he suspected Irvine was grassing him up to Bain or Turnbull. The only thing in Cullen's favour was the absence of any witnesses.

"Have you ever had any dealings with Jamie Cook?" said Cullen.

"Just when he left school," said Murray. "The headteacher had a Mercedes. On the last day of term, someone bent the logo thing off the front. We thought it was a drunk sixth year, turned out it was Jamie Cook."

"A right little tearaway," said Cullen, wondering how many other stories of petty vandalism there were involving the boy.

"Tell me about it," said Murray.

They sat in silence as Murray drove, passing the turning for the Cooks' and Gibsons', before pulling up in front of the Russells' house.

Murray knocked on the door. No answer.

Cullen peered in the living room window. "Doesn't look like there's anyone in." He flipped the letterbox open. "Susan, it's the police."

No answer.

Murray knelt down and looked through the letterbox. "There's movement. Slow and steady but definitely someone moving about." He peered back through and called in. "I can see you."

"Who is it?" said a girl's high-pitched voice.

Cullen now saw a figure in the gloom.

"It's the police," said Murray.

The body came closer, an overweight teenager with pigtails.

"How do I know it's the police?" she said, her face right by the letterbox.

Murray held up his warrant card to the hole. "DC Stuart Murray of Lothian & Borders CID."

"What's CID?" she said.

"Criminal Investigation Department," said Murray.

"Okay."

"Can you let us in?" said Murray.

"No."

Murray laughed. "Is your name Susan?"

"Yes."

"Where are your parents, Susan?"

"They've gone out," she said. "I think they're planning tomorrow's vigil for Father Mulgrew."

"Why aren't you with them?" said Cullen.

"I've got homework to do."

"Okay," said Murray, his eyes warning Cullen to back off. "Can you let us in?"

"My parents told me not to let anyone in," she said.

"Susan, they would be very angry if they found out you hadn't let the police in," said Murray.

"They'll get angry anyway," said Susan.

"We've got a couple of questions to ask about Mandy," said Murray. "I'd rather not do it through the letterbox."

Susan's face dropped at the mention of her friend. "Okay," she said, opening the door.

She led them to the kitchen where they sat around the breakfast table. She offered them tea or coffee, quite the little lady, though both refused.

Cullen saw why Susan's mother had taken them to the conservatory — the kitchen was in a state, dirty dishes on the counter, piles of recycling by the back door.

Susan frowned at Cullen. "Who are you?"

Cullen smiled as he produced his own warrant card. "DC Scott Cullen."

She smiled. "Are you CID too?"

"Yes," said Cullen, "though I'm based in Edinburgh. DC Murray here is based in Haddington."

Susan nodded. "Do you like it?"

Cullen smiled. "It's fine."

"I want to be a policewoman," she said, "but my dad says I should be a lawyer."

"I can see why," said Murray.

"How?"

"You're very good at asking questions," said Murray.

Susan smiled.

"Was Mandy Gibson your pal?" said Murray.

"Yes," said Susan, her smile turning sour. "She was."

"When were you told about what happened to her?" said Murray.

"I'd already guessed," she said. "Her parents were over this morning before school. They said Mandy had got out again."

"How many times had she 'got out' before?" said Murray.

"Quite a lot," she said. "She used to run over here in the middle of the night. She made it all the way a few times. I got woken up by the noise when her parents came to take her home."

"Did Mandy ever speak to Jamie Cook?" said Murray.

She looked away. "Jamie is a bad boy." She sniffed. "He used to call Mandy a spacker. It wasn't nice."

"Did he do anything else to Mandy?" said Murray.

"No," said Susan, her tone brimming with confidence. "He was Thomas's pal. Thomas didn't like it when Jamie did that but he never did anything about it."

"That's Thomas Gibson, yes?" said Murray.

Susan nodded.

"Did Jamie ever bully Mandy at school?" said Cullen.

"He wasn't very nice to her," said Susan.

Cullen frowned, recalling Thomas Gibson tell them Cook had stuck up for Mandy. "Did he ever help her?"

"Just before he left school," she said. "Mr Hulse's class used to get a lot of mickey-taking. Jamie and Thomas sorted a couple of boys out."

"What do you mean by sort out?" said Murray.

"There was a big fight at the bike shed," she said. "The head-teacher came out and broke it up."

"Did anything happen to the boys?" said Murray.

"I think they got detention," she said. "Thomas and Jamie didn't get into trouble. It was because it was Mr Hulse's class."

"And this was just before Jamie left school?" said Cullen.

"Yes."

"Do you know Father Mulgrew?" said Murray.

Susan looked away. "I heard about what happened to him. It's a shame but I didn't like him."

"Why not?" said Cullen.

She paused for a few seconds. "The counselling."

"Can you elaborate?" said Murray.

"What does elaborate mean?"

Murray laughed. "Expand further. Explain more."

Susan sighed. "I didn't like it," she said, after a while. "He used to ask really difficult questions. He used to make me say stuff I hadn't thought, just to make him stop."

"What sort of thing?" said Cullen.

"About how I felt about boys," she said. "It was difficult, I didn't like it."

"Which boys?" said Murray.

She blushed. "Thomas," she said, her voice small. "He doesn't seem to like me, though."

"Isn't he four years older than you?" said Murray.

"Doesn't mean anything," she said. "My parents are four years apart."

"It's quite important at your age," said Murray. "Thomas could get into a lot of trouble."

Cullen butted in. "Did Father Mulgrew ask you about which boys you liked?"

She bit her lip. "Yes."

"How did he ask the question?" said Cullen.

"It was sort of like 'which boys do you like, Susan?' and I said I didn't know and he said I must as I wasn't such a little girl any more and things were happening to my body he could see and if I wasn't careful then I could let the Devil in just like with Jamie and Mandy."

"Did the other kids have these counselling sessions?" said Cullen.

"I think so."

"Did you just go once a week?" said Cullen.

"We all did," she said.

"Did Father Mulgrew have extra sessions with some children?" said Cullen.

"Jamie Cook," she said. "Father Mulgrew said Jamie was possessed by the Devil, that's why he was so evil."

"Did people believe him?" said Cullen.

She nodded her head vigorously. "Definitely. All of the parents didn't like Jamie. They tried to stop Malky and Thomas seeing him, so they didn't get possessed too."

"How often did Mulgrew have these sessions with him?" said Cullen.

"It was at least a couple of extra ones a week," she said.

"Did anyone else get this special treatment?" said Cullen.

Susan nodded. "Mandy."

60

C ullen and Murray returned to the station, desperate to track Bain down, finding him cornering Lamb in the Incident Room.

"Say that again," said Bain, eyes blazing at Lamb.

"I've decided to narrow down the search," said Lamb. "We're burning through manpower and Caldwell already found he turned off at Tranent. I've left McCulloch in Haddington going through the tapes in case he's gone to Musselburgh or anywhere else. We've not got a great CCTV coverage in East Lothian, nothing like Edinburgh."

Bain stared at Lamb. "How do you solve crimes out here?"

"We don't generally have a lot of big crimes," said Lamb. "Those we do get usually come with a DI who wants to run the show."

"Don't get smart with me," said Bain.

Lamb smiled. "You wouldn't know smart if I showed it to you."

Bain glared at him for a few moments then turned to face Cullen. "What have you pair got for me?"

"We've been speaking to Susan Russell," said Cullen.

"Thought you'd seen her yesterday?" said Bain.

"Her mother didn't let us," said Cullen. "She was pretty useful, though." He took a deep breath. "Some kids had extra counselling with Mulgrew every week. Jamie Cook and Mandy Gibson."

"We knew this, Cullen," said Bain. "For crying out loud."

"We knew Mandy was getting counselling related to this possession," said Cullen. "We didn't know exactly what it was."

"You didn't ask?" said Bain.

"No," said Cullen.

"Jesus Christ," said Bain. "This is basic stuff."

"Listen to me," said Cullen. "I knew the counselling was like a classic Catholic confession. It turns out Mulgrew had selected Mandy and Jamie for special attention."

"So what are you saying?" said Bain.

"Mulgrew gave Mandy special counselling twice a week," said Cullen. "Trying to get the demon out."

Bain scowled. "Sounds like he was trying to get his todger in." He pulled his arm back, ready to punch the whiteboard again, but managing to find the self-control from somewhere to resist it. "Fuckin' fuck."

"What do you want us to do?" said Cullen.

"I don't know, do I?" said Bain.

Cullen went over to the whiteboard. "Do you think Mulgrew killed Mandy?"

"Looks like it," said Bain.

"What evidence do we have?" said Cullen. "The post mortem said she was abused." He pointed at the board. "We've got two suspects and both of them had opportunity. Jamie Cook stayed with the Gibsons on a few occasions, that was his opportunity. His child abuse fantasies are according to Mulgrew, not exactly a reliable witness."

"Or even a witness any more," said Bain.

"What about this Kirsty girl he was supposed to have raped?" said Lamb. "Wasn't she underage?"

"She wasn't when he was supposed to have raped her," said Cullen.

"Okay, but he likes fresh meat," said Lamb. "He was seeing her when she was fifteen."

Cullen threw his hands up in the air. "He's seventeen. Unless he's out getting snared by cougars in nightclubs, I would say he's looking for girls roughly his own age."

"But he's fitting the profile," said Bain.

"Fine," said Cullen, shaking his head.

"Right, go on then, Sherlock," said Bain, stroking his moustache. "You're in the drawing room and you're away to point the finger at Professor Plum."

Cullen bit his tongue. "Mulgrew's history of paedophilia was why he was kicked out of the Catholic Church. He had access to Mandy at these one-on-one counselling sessions."

Bain scratched the back of his neck. "So?"

"One possibility is Jamie Cook killed them both," said Cullen.

"That fits," said Bain.

"How about Mulgrew killed Mandy then Jamie Cook killed Mulgrew?" said Lamb.

Cullen frowned. "Why would he do it? How did he know what's happened? From everything we've heard, he doesn't sound like some sort of vigilante who's bumping off paedophile priests."

"True," said Lamb. "Is there anyone we still need to speak to?"

"Jamie Cook," said Cullen.

"Don't go there, Sundance," said Bain. "Cullen, Murray, Lamb, let's put our heads together. We've got ten minutes to find something out before I'm phoning Jimmy Deeley and making a nuisance of myself about Mulgrew's PM."

"Could anyone else have done this?" said Cullen.

"Charles Gibson?" said Bain.

Lamb bit his bottom lip. "What's his motive?"

"It's difficult having a disabled child?" said Cullen. "He's a religious nut, could be shame at having a demonic possession in the family."

"Murder is a sin, though," said Bain. "No way a training minister is going to do something like that. Doesn't tally."

They stood in silence for a few moments, trying to think things through.

Lamb spoke up first. "If Gibson was abusing Mandy, could have told Mulgrew about it and Mulgrew said he was going to grass? He killed him to shut him up?"

"Seems quite far-fetched," said Bain. "He's not a suspect at present."

"Shouldn't he be?" said Lamb. "It's much easier for him to abuse his own daughter and murder Mulgrew than it is for Jamie Cook."

"The gaffer's got a point," said Murray.

Bain looked at Cullen. "Does Gibson have alibis for both murders?"

"Not really," said Cullen. "Both were with Mulgrew. The second one we couldn't even check."

"Interesting," said Bain, stroking his moustache. "This is pretty messy. If we had some evidence pointing towards Gibson then we might have a case. It'll be thrown out of court if we went with it now. I'd like to have something more than a vague possibility."

Cullen was going to suggest he didn't even have that, when Lamb's Airwave radio crackled.

He held it to his ear. "You're kidding me."

"What is it?" said Bain.

"They've found Jamie Cook's car."

61

Bain's car powered along the A1 heading towards the city, Cullen in the passenger seat tightly gripping the grab handle as Bain swerved between both lanes of traffic, throwing Lamb around in the back.

Uniformed officers from Queen Charlotte Street traced Jamie Cook's car to an address in Edinburgh, a row of decrepit Victorian flats beside the dying docks at Seafield.

"This isn't a registered pursuit vehicle," said Lamb.

Had they been following protocol, the squad car carrying Murray, Law and Watson should have led the way, blue sirens blazing, but Bain's Mondeo was a good half a mile ahead by the time they reached Musselburgh.

"Shove your health and safety up your arse," said Bain. "I'm not pursuing anybody, I'm just trying to drive into town and speak to a suspect."

"Then slow down," said Lamb, almost shouting.

"I'm not slowing down for anyone," said Bain. "We need to speak to this little bastard."

Lamb let out a loud sigh. "We still don't know where he is."

"You got hold of that Buxton boy yet?" said Bain, looking over at Cullen.

Cullen shook his head. "Tried his phone and the Airwave. He's not answering either."

His phone rang. He half expected another crank call, at the worst possible time. He answered it.

"Cullen, it's Buxton."

Cullen had dealt with PC Simon Buxton on a few cases during the previous six months and, while he was young and English, Cullen thought he showed promise.

"Finally," said Cullen.

"Sorry, we've been busy running an obbo," said Buxton.

"Have you got Cook?" said Cullen.

"I think so," said Buxton, "based on that photo you sent."

"That was quick," said Cullen. "You just had his car the last I heard."

"Two undercover officers were checking the local pubs," said Buxton. "They were doing the rounds anyway, so don't let Bain go off the deep end about the cost. We found Cook in the Dock. We've just detained him."

Cullen knew it, an old docker's pub famous for opening at five in the morning now remodelled as a slacker bar in trendy Leith. "What's he up to in there?"

"Drinking heavily by the looks of things," said Buxton. "He's with a Steven Young and some locals."

"We'll be there in five minutes," said Cullen, ending the call. He looked at Bain. "Head to Leith. They've got him in a pub on Seafield Road."

Bain cut across the lanes to the sound of blaring horns.

"He's in Leith?" said Lamb, shaking his head slowly.

"Aye, Leith," said Cullen. "He might be pissed."

"That's all we need." Bain stopped at a set of traffic lights.

"I'm still waiting for an apology," said Lamb.

Bain turned around. "You what?"

Lamb folded his arms. "I notice you haven't mentioned Jamie Cook turned up in *your* back yard, not mine. That deserves an apology."

Bain stabbed his finger in the air. "If you'd actually found this little toerag when you were supposed to, before the wee bastard got his car, this wouldn't have happened, would it?"

"Keep telling yourself that," said Lamb, looking away.

Bain started forward, driving onto Harry Lauder Road towards Leith. "This isn't the end of the matter, Sergeant."

"I don't imagine it is," said Lamb, taking a deep breath. "I think we should both let this one drop."

"If you think for one minute I'm not having your bollocks on a plate, then you're very much mistaken," said Bain.

"You're not exactly covering yourself in glory here," said Lamb. "Just be mindful of that."

They drove in silence for a few minutes as Bain ploughed down the long straight of Seafield Road, past the car showrooms and the cat and dog home, past where Cook's car was found. Horns blared as Bain overtook where he shouldn't. The Dock pub was surrounded by police cars with flashing lights. They parked on a side street and walked over.

Cullen shivered from the icy North Sea blast, puddles from the earlier rain close to freezing.

The Dock was the ground floor of a tenement on the boundary between revamped Leith and the still-industrial Seafield.

Buxton appeared from inside, dressed in uniform.

"What's going on?" said Bain.

"Cook's in there with a geezer from Haddington," said Buxton. "They're with a bloke who lives just up the road and a couple of Granton boys."

"I want statements off the Edinburgh three," said Bain. "The other two I want up at Leith Walk."

Buxton nodded. "Sure thing. Just one thing, though, guv. Cook is absolutely shit-faced."

62

B ain sped into the car park underneath Leith Walk station, parking across two spaces. He was first out, jogging to the stairs, Cullen and Lamb following.

They'd stayed behind to speak to Cook's drinking buddies while Buxton brought Cook and Young to the station in a meat wagon. The companions were mates of Steven Young who'd just met Cook that day so they let them go.

"I want you two in that room with me," said Bain, pointing at Cullen and Lamb.

Cullen couldn't understand Bain's thinking at times, starting to suspect he would blame them if it all went wrong. Conversely, he'd no doubt find technicalities to ensure they didn't share his glory.

Bain headed to the reception desk on the ground floor, manned by Jim Mullen, the red-faced desk sergeant. "Where is he?"

"Who?"

"Jamie Cook, where is he?" said Bain, shoving his warrant card in Mullen's face.

"I know who you bloody are, Brian," said Mullen. "What do you want?"

"I need to see Jamie Cook," said Bain.

"Please calm down, sir," said Mullen, his tone betraying many years of dealing with difficult members of the public.

"I am calm," said Bain.

Mullen shook his head. "PC Buxton brought him in ten minutes ago. He's in three."

"That's all I wanted to know." Bain marched off behind the desk and swiped his ID card through, before yanking it over his neck.

"Here, you," said Mullen, pointing at Lamb. "You need to sign in. Fire regulations and all that."

"I'll do it," said Cullen.

"Catch me up," said Bain.

Cullen pulled his own ID card out and filled out a visitor's form for Lamb.

"Lucky there were no members of the public around," said Mullen, slowly printing a guest card and copying a few details from Lamb's warrant card.

They followed Bain through the security door, walking down the long corridor that ran the length of the station, heading for the interview rooms.

"He's a loose cannon," said Lamb.

Cullen almost laughed, recalling Bain using the same description for Lamb. "Tell me about it."

They turned the corner to see Bain arguing with Buxton outside interview room three, eyes bulging as his hand scratched the stubble on his head. He marched over.

"You wouldn't believe it," said Bain. "Campbell bloody McLintock is his lawyer."

Buxton walked over, shaking his head. "Cook is definitely too drunk to be interviewed."

JAMIE COOK WAS CLEARLY out of it, struggling to stay upright in the seat and focus on what was going on. It had been a while since Cullen had seen someone so bad just on drink.

Cook was only seventeen but he looked older. He had several days' worth of stubble, though his beard was patchy. His bloodshot eyes looked vacantly at the wall, a spaced-out grin on his face. A cup of machine coffee sat in front of him, steam rising in a swirl.

Campbell McLintock sat next to him, wearing a turquoise shirt and yellow tie under a dark green suit.

Lamb and Bain sat opposite Cook with Cullen standing. PC Buxton stood by the door, guarding the exit.

"Jamie," said Bain.

Cook didn't respond.

"My client is not in a fit state to answer questions," said McLintock. "I would suggest you defer this until such time as my client is sufficiently recovered."

"I'll be the judge of that," said Bain. "Jamie."

Cook looked round at them.

"Do you know why you're here?" said Bain.

"Police brutality?" said Cook, a smirk on his face.

"This is unacceptable," said McLintock. "You're breaking several laws here. This is harming your case more than my client's defence."

Bain ignored McLintock, instead focusing on Cook. "Listen, sonny, I've sat for ten minutes watching you dribble onto the table after spending two days trying to find you. You need to speak to us now."

Cook had an impudent look on his face. "Aren't you listening to my lawyer?" he said, his voice slurring badly.

"We're going to ask you some questions and you're going to answer them," said Bain. "Now, are you going to co-operate?"

"Aye, whatever," said Cook, looking bored.

Lamb cleared his throat. "Can you take us through your movements from when you left the police station in Garleton on Sunday morning, right through to now."

"What day is it?" said Cook.

"It's Tuesday," said Bain.

"Inspector," said McLintock, "I really insist you close this interview down now and we reconvene once my client has had the opportunity to take some rest."

The boy sat there silent, staring into space, still smirking. Bain stared at McLintock, silently fuming.

"Sir," said Cullen, gesturing to the door.

Bain paused the interview and left the room, Cullen and Lamb following, leaving Buxton with Cook and McLintock.

Bain was pacing back and forwards in the hall outside.

"There's something fishy going on and Cook is stinking. He's going down for this."

"You need to listen to McLintock," said Cullen. "Jamie Cook isn't in a fit state to be answering these questions. He's off his face."

"We can get a formal statement later," said Bain.

"Not with his lawyer present," said Cullen. "He'll tear you apart in court."

"He's right," said Lamb. "This is harming us more than it is him. If he confesses now, it'll be on record how out of it the boy is. We need to wait until he is sober enough to know what day it is."

Bain punched his fist into the wall, leaving a slight dent in the plasterboard. "We've not got the time. We need to get a collar and quick."

Cullen felt rage boil, realising Turnbull's deadline was pressuring Bain into arresting someone, regardless of guilt. "*You* need to get a collar quick, you mean."

"You cheeky little bastard," said Bain.

"Cullen's right," said Lamb, getting in the way. "Interviewing him while he's out of his head isn't the right way to do this."

"What do you suggest then, Sergeant?" said Bain.

"He's not going anywhere," said Lamb. "We wait it out."

"You know what McLintock is playing at here, don't you?" said Bain.

"Enlighten me," said Lamb, folding his arms.

"He's playing for a release without charge," said Bain. "The boy isn't likely to be sober any time this week, let alone in the next eleven hours."

"You know yourself there are a few ways we can play that game," said Lamb. "If we get him full of coffee, we'll stand a fighting chance."

Bain nodded his head slowly. "I've got a few cans of Red Bull up in my desk drawer."

"What's the operational procedure here?" said Lamb. "Do you have to get Turnbull's approval if you want to extend the detention period?"

Bain snorted. "Aye, I have to ask him."

"Do you think he'll extend it?" said Lamb.

"Doubt it," said Bain.

"You need to get on top of this," said Lamb.

"Are you suggesting I'm not?" said Bain.

"Speak to Jim," said Lamb.

Bain nodded. "Should we interview this Young boy?"

"Let's see Turnbull first," said Lamb.

"We need to go back in and let McLintock know," said Cullen.

Bain stroked his moustache, before throwing the door open and terminating the interview.

63

C ullen sat in the canteen drinking his umpteenth coffee of the day. He looked up and saw Bain and Lamb marching across the room, heading straight for him.

"Turnbull gave us another twelve hours," said Bain.

Cullen glanced at his watch. "Right, so we've got him until four PM tomorrow, now?"

"Well done, Sundance," said Bain. "You can add."

Cullen finished his coffee. "Is Cook sober yet?"

Bain shook his head. "Gave him two cans of Red Bull. See what happens."

"We've got Robert and Wilma Cook downstairs in an interview room," said Lamb.

Cullen frowned. "What for?"

"Not happy their pride and joy has been found," said Bain. "Come on."

He led them downstairs, Cullen wondering if Bain's success in getting an extension would give him a stay of execution with Cargill taking over the case.

The Cooks sat in the interview room, looking like they hadn't spoken to each other in months.

"How can I help?" said Bain, sitting down opposite, Cullen and Lamb finding seats.

"You're holding our son without charge," said Robert Cook.

"Don't worry, Mr Cook," said Bain, "once your son has sobered up, we'll continue the questioning and look to charge him forthwith."

"I see," said Robert.

"Your lawyer will be present," said Bain.

"Of course," said Robert.

"It's somewhat unusual for Mr McLintock to have clients out your way," said Bain. "He's usually Edinburgh only."

"I have many business dealings in the city," said Robert. "He comes highly recommended and we only want the best for our son."

Bain grinned. "If that's the case, can I ask again why you were unaware of your son's movements over the last two days?"

Robert looked at Lamb, eyes pleading. "Bill, can't you do something to stop this?"

"I'm afraid I can't," said Lamb. "Your son is the main suspect in a double murder."

"You can't think Jamie killed Mandy and Seamus, can you?" said Wilma.

"Mrs Cook," said Bain, "we have sufficient evidence to suggest your son is responsible for these murders."

"But why?" said Wilma.

"We're not at liberty to divulge that at present," said Bain.

"Come on, Bill," said Robert. "Can't you do anything here? This is totally preposterous. You know Jamie. He's not a bad boy."

"His criminal record would suggest he is," said Bain.

Robert closed his eyes. "Jamie has got himself involved in some mischief, that's all."

"He's got a record longer than my arm," said Bain.

"It's a big difference between underage drinking and murder," said Robert, still looking at Lamb. "I'm begging you to reconsider this."

"Can I request you direct all questions to me rather than my subordinate officers, please?" said Bain. "I'm the Senior Investigating Officer, not Sergeant Lamb."

"Very well," said Robert.

"Now, I will repeat the question, and this time I expect you to give me an answer," said Bain. "Why were you unable to assist

Sergeant Lamb in tracing your son's movements over the last couple of days?"

"We did all we could," said Robert. "Tell him, Bill."

Bain looked at Lamb. "Is this correct?"

Lamb nodded. "I don't have any reason to think they knew where Jamie has been, including whether he'd gone into Edinburgh."

Bain ground his teeth. "Thank you. And neither of you noticed your son's car disappearing from your front drive at some point yesterday?"

Wilma gave a sigh. "No, we didn't."

"I already told you I noticed it last night," said Robert. "I didn't really think anything of it at the time."

Bain shook his head. "Noted."

"You're based in Edinburgh, aren't you?" said Robert, eyes flicking between Bain and Lamb.

"I am," said Bain.

"Why did you expend so much effort in East Lothian when our son was through here?" said Robert.

"That's not what we're here to discuss," said Bain.

Robert's hands gripped the edges of the table. "Then what is? Sergeant Lamb asked if we knew where Jamie was. We didn't. The so-called evidence you're using to prove Jamie murdered two people, as far as I can tell, is the fact we find it very difficult to know where he is from moment to moment."

"We should close this now," said Lamb. "They didn't know where Jamie was, let's move on."

"Fine," said Bain, his glare lingering on Lamb. "Mr Cook, can you confirm your whereabouts last night."

"We went over this on the phone earlier, didn't we?" said Robert.

"Strangely enough, one of your neighbours spotted your car last night," said Bain.

Robert's eyes bulged. "What?"

This was news to Cullen.

"We have a witness statement from one of your neighbours suggesting you drove off at the back of eight, not returning for another hour," said Bain.

He paused but Robert didn't fill the space. "As I explained this morning, we have another witness statement placing a car similar to yours near where Seamus Mulgrew was killed."

"I was at home all evening," said Robert, sweat dripping from his brow. He looked at his wife. "Tell them."

Wilma nodded slowly. "He was at home all night. We watched *Wall-E* with the twins."

"Supplying a false alibi is a serious crime, you're aware of that, aren't you?" said Bain.

"I am," she said. "I'm not supplying a false alibi. I'm telling the God's honest truth."

Bain sat back in his chair and folded his arms. "What can you tell us about Jamie's friends?"

"We know next to nothing about the people he hangs about with," said Robert.

"Shouldn't you?" said Bain.

"If you've spoken to Father Mulgrew, God rest his soul, then you will have confirmation of Jamie's possession by the Devil," said Robert. "There's nothing we can do."

"That's inadmissible as evidence," said Bain, his voice calm and level.

"Why?" said Robert.

"We would need proof," said Bain. He shrugged. "Maybe something like horns growing out of the top of his skull or a big red tail."

"Are you discriminating against me on the grounds of my religion?" said Robert.

"Perish the thought," said Bain. "I just can't substantiate your claim that a supernatural being is responsible for two murders."

"Perhaps we should change the line of questioning," said Lamb.

"If the boy has the Devil inside him," said Bain, "then surely he's capable of murder, isn't he?"

Robert moved to speak but didn't.

"Can we discuss this outside?" said Lamb, nodding to the door.

Bain stared at him. "DS Lamb, I've not finished questioning Mr and Mrs Cook."

"All the same, I would like to discuss this in private," said Lamb, getting to his feet and leaving the room.

Bain sat back in his chair. "I will return in two minutes. Your story had better change."

Lamb was halfway down the corridor, leaning against the wall, one foot resting on the wallpaper. "What the hell are you up to in there?"

"What do you mean?" said Bain.

"I've absolutely no idea what you're trying to achieve with this," said Lamb.

"I'm trying to get to the bottom of what their son has been doing," said Bain, "and who he's been killing."

"They clearly don't know where he's been or what he's been up to," said Lamb.

"All this shite about the Devil..." Bain rested a hand against the wall. "They're talking utter bollocks."

"That's as maybe, but I don't think it's a good idea for a Detective Inspector to be criticising their religion," said Lamb. "If this gets out into the press, you'll know all about it."

Bain took a deep breath. "All I'm trying to do is work out why they didn't know where their son was."

"You've openly accused me of not doing my job properly," said Lamb.

Bain started laughing. "That's a classic."

"Where did the stuff about the car come from?" said Lamb.

Bain shrugged his shoulders. "A little bit of creative policing," he said, grinning.

"You've had my men out trying to ascertain Jamie's whereabouts," said Lamb. "The last thing we need is you putting yourself on the record stating we have non-existent evidence."

Bain laughed. "It's not on tape. Besides, there are many ways to cover it up. Your wee ADC, Law I think her name is, she could have written something down wrong and we didn't realise until later."

Lamb held his gaze. "What are you trying to achieve here?"

Bain folded his arms, tilting his head to the side. "I'm trying to glean information from the suspect's parents."

"Okay, so what have you learned from them?" said Lamb.

"They don't know what their son is up to half the time," said Bain. "They can't give him an alibi when I finally get to speak to him."

"Fair enough," said Lamb, slouching back against the wall, shaking his head.

"I want to ask you something," said Bain. "What's all this 'Please, Bill' shite coming from Robert Cook? Pretty close to him, are you?"

"He's played golf with my brother a couple of times," said Lamb. "I met him once in the clubhouse at Archerfield. That's it. I've spoken to him more in the last day than I have in the rest of my life."

"For crying out loud," said Bain. "That sort of nonsense can get this thrown out of court."

"There's no need to register it," said Lamb, his voice shaking.

"I'll let the Procurator Fiscal be the judge of that," said Bain.

"I barely know the guy," said Lamb. "I've nothing to hide."

"I'm beginning to wonder if you aren't trying to protect your mate here," said Bain.

Lamb stood upright. "I'm sorry?"

Bain looked over at Cullen. "Here, Sundance, how does this sound? Bill here is keeping me away from his mate's son."

"Leave me out of this," said Cullen.

"Oh come on, Sundance," said Bain. "It looks exactly like incompetence to anyone else but it's just good, old-fashioned corruption."

"You twat." Lamb pushed Bain against the opposite wall, grabbing his throat.

They struggled for a few seconds, before Bain wriggled free of Lamb's grip. He got behind Lamb, pulling his forearm around his throat.

Cullen tried to squeeze in, receiving a kick in the knee from Lamb as he elbowed Bain in the stomach. Bain loosened his grip and Lamb pushed back, sending Bain bouncing off the wall.

Cullen finally managed to get between them, arms coming in from front and back. "Stop it!" He pushed Lamb against the opposite wall, but he ploughed forward, trying to punch Bain.

"What is going on here?"

They turned around to see DCI Turnbull marching towards them.

"You three, my office, now."

64

Turnbull bounced his fountain pen on his desk, staring at the closed door. He looked at the three officers in front of him. "What the hell was going on down there?" he said, his voice loud.

No one answered.

"I don't expect to see that sort of behaviour in this station from criminals, let alone from three of my supposedly better officers."

Cullen felt his career slide into the toilet, Turnbull's hand poised over the handle, ready to flush.

Turnbull reached into his desk drawer and retrieved a form, three or four sheets stapled together. "This won't have passed your desk yet, Brian, but DS Lamb has lodged a formal complaint against you."

Bain glowered at Lamb. "I wasn't aware of this."

"From what I can see from my vantage point, you three are continually at each other's throats over God knows what," said Turnbull.

"Don't include me in this, sir," said Cullen. "I was trying to keep them apart."

"If you're not trying to solve this, then you're part of the problem," said Turnbull.

"Cullen's right," said Lamb. "This is between DI Bain and me. He shouldn't be dragged into it."

"Your actions *have* dragged him into it, Sergeant," said Turnbull. "I shouldn't see a DC pulling apart a DS and a DI. This isn't in the game plan."

"With all due respect, DS Lamb has proven incapable of doing his job on this case," said Bain. "He has singularly failed to track down a suspect on his own patch."

"That particular suspect turned up in Leith, which is on your patch the last time I checked," said Lamb.

"He wouldn't have got to Leith if you'd done your job properly, Sergeant," said Bain.

"Gentlemen," said Turnbull, his voice booming. "This is precisely the sort of pettiness I wish to avoid."

"It's a serious point," said Lamb. "DI Bain has castigated me and my team for failing to track Jamie Cook down. He acted completely unprofessionally, berating me in front of junior staff in a briefing. When the suspect turns up in Edinburgh, well out of my jurisdiction, I don't hear Bain hauling DS Irvine over the coals."

"My boys actually found him, though," said Bain.

"Enough," said Turnbull. "I shouldn't have to tell you this, but it is notoriously difficult tracking down people who don't want to be found."

He focused on Bain and Lamb, maintaining silence for a few seconds. "I want a drains-up on what's going on out in Garleton. I get mixed messages from both of you every few minutes. Brian's doing this. Bill's doing that. You're both coming to me with problems and I need solutions. I want a helicopter view on this. I need to be able to drill down through the noise and understand which agenda points I need to pull into a meeting with the pair of you, once we've achieved closure on this case."

He took a deep breath, leaning back in his office chair, his shirt buttons straining and revealing the spider legs of his hairy chest. "You were both in here not half an hour ago. I thought things had improved, but clearly not. McLintock will have us for breakfast with the way you pair are acting. We'll look like idiots."

"What do you want us to do, sir?" said Bain.

Turnbull leaned forward, adjusting his tie. "First things first, I need to know if you two can be trusted to work together."

"I believe we can," said Bain.

"Bill?"

Lamb sighed. "I'm prepared to give it another shot, sir."

"DI Cargill is managing this case as of fourteen hundred hours tomorrow," said Turnbull.

Bain swallowed. "What does that mean?"

"It means she'll be Senior Investigating Officer," said Turnbull. "Both of you will report to her. You'll be her deputy, Brian."

"But—"

"But *nothing*," said Turnbull, stabbing his finger in the air. "We have to try out new engagement strategies with the public. As you well know, DI Cargill has been leading the thinking across the three largest forces in Scotland and this is the perfect opportunity to roll it out. As soon as we go out to the press with it, the profile of this case will explode."

"That isn't what we need here," said Bain.

"I'll be the judge of what we need here," said Turnbull. "Your cavalier attitude to policing isn't what could be described as being on the front foot, Brian, you know that. We need a different slant and a different approach."

"I thought she wasn't back till Thursday?" said Bain.

"I've asked her to come in a day early," said Turnbull. "If I hear of anything remotely like what happened downstairs then she'll be in even sooner. Am I making myself clear?"

"Crystal," said Bain.

"I want an hourly update from you, Brian. And I want this nonsense to absolutely, resolutely cease. You've got the rest of the evening to document everything and formulate a plan, while this suspect sobers up. Dismissed."

They got up to leave, Cullen thinking he'd got off lightly.

"Can you stay behind, Constable?" said Turnbull.

Cullen sat back down again, butterflies flapping in his stomach.

Turnbull waited for the door to shut. "You know you're highly thought of among my team, Cullen. Your name is not unfamiliar to those of the upper echelons of this particular police service. I want to make sure you're not tarnishing yourself with the actions of your current superiors."

Cullen rubbed his hand across his face. "I try to make sure I don't get too involved with it, sir. It can be challenging when I'm working directly for DI Bain."

"I understand," said Turnbull, looking out of his office window. "I inherited DI Bain when I took over this role from DCS White-head. With Bain and Wilkinson, I'm continually astonished we solve *any* crimes in this city."

He looked back at Cullen. "I've tried to move them on, but it's increasingly difficult in this environment. I've fought hard to bring another DI in, and that's DI Cargill. Things should change, Cullen, but I need to know you're part of my glorious new future and not clinging on to Bain's coat tails."

"I wouldn't say I'm clinging on to anything relating to DI Bain," said Cullen. "I like to think I carry myself in a professional manner and bring methods to the table which Bain and Wilkinson don't necessarily appreciate."

"I see," said Turnbull. "And how would you say you get on with the rest of my team?"

Cullen couldn't figure out what Turnbull was getting at. "You know about my relationship with DS McNeill. I'm okay with DC Jain. I don't have many problems with DS Holdsworth. ADC Caldwell is a good friend."

Turnbull nodded. "And DS Irvine?"

Cullen's pulse raced. "Alan and I have a mutual respect," he said, his mouth dry.

Turnbull reached into his desk drawer, producing another sheet of paper and placing it on the desk in front of Cullen. "Unfortunately, I received another formal complaint today. DS Irvine made this against you."

Cullen felt the colour drain from his face. "What about?"

"He alleges you grabbed him by the throat in a car park in Haddington earlier this afternoon," said Turnbull. "Is that true?"

Cullen felt cold sweat trickle down his spine. "That's not what happened."

Turnbull raised an eyebrow. "So, *something* happened then?"

Cullen closed his eyes. "We had an argument, that's all."

"Was it on the scale of what I witnessed downstairs?" said Turnbull.

Cullen shook his head. "What you saw downstairs was a fight.

We had an exchange of words, as a football commentator would say. Not even handbags."

"I see," said Turnbull. "Was there anyone else in the car at the time?"

"No," said Cullen, reaching for assertive but not quite managing. "We were parked at the Aldi in Haddington, waiting on uniform support. We had a lead on Jamie Cook's whereabouts."

"What instigated the incident?" said Turnbull.

Cullen looked away. "I'd rather not, if it's all the same."

"Constable, I've got a complaint lodged by one of my more experienced officers," said Turnbull. "I'm afraid I have to know."

"Fine," said Cullen, folding his arms. "If you must know, DS Irvine called my girlfriend a 'dyke'."

"This is more Bain nonsense, isn't it?" said Turnbull.

"It could be attributed to him, yes," said Cullen.

Turnbull looked out of his window again for a few moments, before switching back to Cullen, eyes boring through him. "Cullen, I need to know if you attacked DS Irvine."

"I can categorically state I did not attack him, sir," said Cullen.

"Are you accusing DS Irvine of lying then?" said Turnbull.

"I don't wish to stoop to his level," said Cullen. "Given the investigation we're working on, I'm astonished he's managed to find time to complete this paperwork."

"I see," said Turnbull, picking up the complaint form. "I'll have a word with the officer in question and see if I can persuade him to rescind his complaint. Lack of evidence is the grounds I'd formally suggest but there are informal measures I may revert to."

"Thank you, sir," said Cullen, his shirt now damp with sweat.

"You don't have to thank me," said Turnbull. "But if you do feel indebted to me, you could perhaps keep an eye on DI Bain and DS Lamb."

"I have been," said Cullen. "But yes, I will."

"Thank you," said Turnbull. "I may be in your debt one day."

"I'll keep you informed."

Turnbull looked him up and down then checked his heavy wristwatch. "It's half past six now, Constable. Given your exertions last night and the impasse we've currently reached with our suspect, I'd suggest you get yourself off home."

65

Cullen met Sharon across from the station, just by the Oddbins. He kissed her deeply.

"Scott, you absolutely stink."

"Don't suppose there was another shirt in the closet?" said Cullen.

"You'll have to wash that one and hope it's dry by tomorrow."

"Right."

She held up a bag from the off-license. "Got a nice Rioja."

Cullen winced. "After the amount of booze I had last night..."

"Wimp," said Sharon. "You sure you won't join me?"

Cullen took the bag and inspected the bottle. "Maybe a glass," he said, handing it back.

"That's my boy," she said. She grabbed his hand and led him up Leith Walk towards her flat. "How's that case going?"

He couldn't help himself — he started unloading all the grisly details. "And to cap it all off, Turnbull has cut Bain's time limit. Cargill's taking over if he's not charged this boy by two o'clock tomorrow."

"Oh."

"Oh, indeed," said Cullen. "That'll give her two hours with him after Turnbull extended the custody."

"I'm glad I'm not in your shoes," said Sharon.

"And I had to tear him and DS Lamb apart. Turnbull caught us."

"How has Bain still got a job?"

"Hopefully he won't after tomorrow." Cullen exhaled. "How's your day been?"

"Uneventful," said Sharon. "Just been processing the Kenny Falconer stuff. Making sure everybody's notebooks are up to scratch. The PF isn't too hopeful of it."

"Nightmare," said Cullen.

"How are you feeling?"

"About what?"

She raised her eyebrows. "Maybe about the child murder you're working on?"

Cullen pressed the button for the pedestrian crossing. His hands were shaking.

Sharon noticed. "Are you okay?"

"I don't know."

"You can get counselling for this stuff," she said. "You sound like you need it."

"I always thought I was hardened to this," said Cullen.

"Why?"

"Because I'm a police officer? I don't know."

"Scott, you're a human being, okay?"

Cullen nodded and they crossed the road. "This is infinitely worse than two scumbags in Oxgangs glassing each other."

"Of course it is," said Sharon. "You've been through a lot in the last six months. It's okay to get help."

"I know. I just don't want to be some basket case who's traumatised by all this shite that's happened to me."

"This will *stop* you being a basket case," she said.

"Yeah, you're right," he said, wiping at his eyes and feeling a small amount of relief. "I'm shattered."

"Make sure you're not too tired," said Sharon. "I don't want you getting a cold."

"Aye well, I've had more coffee than Bain has Red Bull."

"Scott..."

"I know, I know."

"What do you want to do tonight?" said Sharon.

"Forget about all this shite," said Cullen.

DAY 3

Wednesday
25th January

66

Cullen entered the canteen at quarter past six, desperate for coffee and to get stuck into Jamie Cook. He hadn't quite managed to sleep the hangover off but he felt better, the two glasses of Rioja sending him off early.

He spotted Lamb and Bain at the table known as bollocking corner, sufficiently far from the nearest tables that conversation didn't carry should a private office or meeting room not be available at the time of need.

Cullen left them to their heated conversation, instead joining the queue behind what felt like half of the day shift dropping in for a break. When he reached the front, he felt the familiar vibration of his phone. He answered it.

The same caller. The same song.

He closed his eyes. He'd hoped the calls would end with Jamie Cook's arrest. Cullen knew of apps to pre-program phone calls, but Cook's phone sat in evidence, switched off.

Tommy Smith hadn't been in touch yet. Maybe it was time to check.

"Can I help, love?"

Cullen looked up. Barbara, the oldest and friendliest of the canteen staff, was smiling at him. "The usual," he said, pocketing his phone.

"We've run out of lettuce."

"Just bacon and tomato then," he said. "Brown sauce, as well."

"And the coffee?" said Barbara.

"Oh aye," said Cullen. "Black, cheers."

Cullen paid, then waited to one side while his roll was thrown together. Looking over at Bain and Lamb, he saw the case file open on the table and Lamb pointing at a page, his finger stabbing the paper amicably enough.

"Here you are, love."

Cullen took his roll and coffee over to the table, sitting opposite them. "Just wondering which of you is getting the bollocking."

"Neither," said Bain without looking up from the file. "We're trying to frame this little bastard." He looked at Cullen's tray. "You could have got me something."

"You could have got yourself something," said Cullen. He took a bite of the roll, only then realising how hungry he was.

Bain stood up and cracked his spine. "Right, bugger it, I'm getting one. Plays merry hell with my bowels but I'm starving. That sausage roll yesterday had me doubled over on the pan but beggars can't be choosers." He walked over to the queue, counting change from his pocket as he went.

"How was Turnbull last night?" said Lamb.

"You know how he is," said Cullen.

"Better than most. Was he fishing on me and Bain?"

"Irvine's put a complaint in against me," said Cullen.

Lamb raised an eyebrow. "Are you serious?"

"I am," said Cullen, wiping brown sauce from his chin. "He says I assaulted him."

"Did you?" said Lamb.

"What do you think?" said Cullen.

Lamb rubbed his beard. "I've worked with him for a couple of days now and I would swing for him myself." He looked at Cullen for a few moments. "I would suspect he's lying, though."

"You saying I couldn't do it?" said Cullen.

Lamb laughed. "I'm not saying that."

Cullen took another bite of the roll. "You seem relaxed."

Lamb nodded his head slowly. "I'm not the one who had a rocket up his arse."

"You think?" said Cullen, frowning.

Lamb grinned. "Last night was classic Turnbull. Bain got a

toasting there but Jim will get a few hours of focus from him, long enough for Cargill to get her feet under the table."

Cullen wouldn't be surprised. "How has he been?"

"Focused," said Lamb, smiling. "He's got a few decent ideas for once."

Cullen took a big drink of coffee. "I wouldn't be so sure you're in the clear. Turnbull caught you fighting with Bain."

"I would've battered him if you hadn't stepped in," said Lamb.

"This isn't a playground," said Cullen. "Turnbull was right, I shouldn't be the one pulling you two apart."

"Aye, whatever," said Lamb. "Let's just see what happens, okay?"

"So you've kissed and made up?" said Cullen.

Lamb raised his hands in the air. "What can I say? We're both quick to anger and we've calmed down since."

Cullen doubted they would stay that way. He dipped the last of his roll in the spillage of brown sauce. "Why didn't you mention the fabricated evidence?"

Lamb rubbed his moustache. "I like to keep something in my back pocket."

Bain put his tray on the table, before sitting down and tucking into his roll. "Bacon, haggis and tattie scone," he said, through a mouthful. "Thank the fuckin' Lord for the breakfast roll."

"What's our plan of attack?" said Cullen.

"I got a call from Buxton when I was in the queue," said Bain, out of the side of his mouth as he chewed. "McLintock reckons his client is ready to speak to us."

"Okay, so who do you want in there?" said Cullen.

"Both of you, at least initially," said Bain. "I want to go through his movements since Sunday morning. There must be huge holes there, not least because of the state the wee toerag was in. Once we've got his statement, I want you pair to tear it to shreds."

67

"Interview commenced at six fifty-four AM on Wednesday the twenty-fifth of January," said Bain. "Leading this interview is myself, Detective Inspector Brian Bain. Also present are Detective Sergeant William Lamb, Detective Constable Scott Cullen and Police Constable Simon Buxton. Finally, we have Jamie Cook and his solicitor, Campbell McLintock, both present."

He cracked his knuckles, fixing a stare on Cook who looked exhausted from a night in the cells.

"Mr Cook, I want you to give me your movements between being released from Garleton police station on Sunday morning right through to when you were picked up by PC Buxton yesterday afternoon."

Cook grinned idiotically. "When I was let out, I went back to my folks' house. They started nipping my head the moment I got in."

"Can you please explain what you mean by 'nipping your head'?" said Bain.

"My client means his parents were asking where he had been," said McLintock. "They were concerned about his wellbeing."

"Please can you tell us specifically what they were asking?" said Bain.

"Usual shite," said Cook.

"And what would that be?" said Bain.

"What I'm doing with my life, why I wasn't at church, where I'd been all night," said Cook.

"And where had you been?" said Bain.

Cook laughed. "In the cells, as you said."

"Noted," said Bain.

"Getting quite used to them now after last night," said Cook.

"What else did you do at your parents' house?" said Bain.

"Had something to eat," said Cook. "Then I got some kip. I hadn't slept all night. I woke up later and went out."

"What time did you wake up?" said Bain.

Cook rubbed his nose. "Half six?"

Bain frowned. "Are you sure?"

"As sure as I can be," said Cook. "I'm not someone who lives their life by the clock."

"Haven't you got an alarm clock by your bed?" said Bain.

"Do you think I need one?" said Cook. "I don't have a job."

Bain scowled at Cook. "Where did you go when you left the house?"

"I just hung out," said Cook. "Went to the park. Wasn't anyone there, though."

"Is this John Knox Park in Garleton?" said Bain.

"It is," said Cook.

"And what did you do there?" said Bain.

"I just sat on the swings and thought about stuff," said Cook.

"You're a deep thinker, are you?" said Bain.

"I don't like the tone of the question," said McLintock. "Trying to intimidate my client is not what this interview is about."

"Okay," said Bain, smiling at the lawyer. "What did you think about in the park?"

Cook slouched back in his seat. "I know you'll probably have heard a load of things about me, mainly from that bastard Mulgrew, but I do think about stuff a lot."

"I'm sure you do," said Bain. "What did you think about, then?"

Cook rubbed his ear. "I don't remember."

"You don't remember?" said Bain, eyebrows raised.

"No," said Cook, with a smile. "It might come back, you never know."

"Where did you go after the park?" said Cullen, before Bain could start asking any more inappropriate questions.

"It was about half ten," said Cook. "It had been dark for ages."

"That's a lot of thinking," said Bain, before sifting through his notebook. "You said you went to the park at the back of half six and were there till half past ten. It's January, it would have been dark and cold. You've managed to lose four hours to *thinking*."

"There are CCTV cameras all over the park, if you don't believe me," said Cook.

Bain looked round at Lamb. "Stephen Hawking here managed to lose a couple of hours to thinking about quantum mechanics. Can you check it out?"

Lamb coughed. "None of the CCTV cameras are recorded in Garleton."

Bain closed his eyes in disbelief. Lamb shouldn't have let that slip. He shook his head then pointed at Cook. "Right, so what did you do next? Did you go into Edinburgh to look at the telescopes in the observatory?"

Cook rolled his eyes. "No, I called on Malky."

"Would that be Malcolm Thornton?" said Bain.

"Aye," said Cook. "Nobody answered the door."

"I'm not surprised," said Bain. "Half ten on a Sunday night, I doubt many people are going to let the town's bad boy in."

"My client's reputation is irrelevant to this discussion," said McLintock. "I would appreciate if you stuck to the facts and did not resort to slander."

Bain stared at McLintock for a few seconds without saying anything.

"Where did you go after Malcolm Thornton's house?" said Cullen.

"I got the bus from Garleton to Haddington," said Cook.

Bain scribbled down in his notebook. "Thank you."

Cullen hoped he wasn't going to land a game of hunt-the-bus-driver.

"Where were you going in Haddington?" said Bain.

"I was off to my pal Stevie's," said Cook.

"And who's he?" said Bain.

"Steven Young," said Cook. "He stays in the houses behind Aldi."

"Anyone else there?" said Bain.

"It was just me and him," said Cook.

"Very romantic," said Bain.

"I will not tolerate that sort of innuendo," said McLintock.

"What did you get up to at this Stevie's flat?" said Bain.

"Just drinking and listening to music," said Cook. "He had some new tunes on. He does some DJing on a Saturday night at a pub in the Pans. He was trying to find some stuff to play next week."

"I see," said Bain. "I bet his neighbour was thrilled. And you stayed there overnight?"

"Sort of," said Cook. "We were up most of the night drinking."

"Then what?" said Bain.

"Crashed out at about six," said Cook. "We'd run out of Jack. The stuff Stevie gets out of Aldi that's just like it."

"Okay, so what happened on Monday?" said Bain.

"I got woken up at about two in the afternoon by a phone call," said Cook.

"Who was it from?" said Bain.

Cook shrugged. "No idea. Never answer an unknown number."

Cullen reddened, figuring his phone call woke Cook up. "Did you call the number back?"

"What do you think?" said Cook, with a wink.

Cook staying up all night listening to music connected to the current hit single being played to him during the calls. Cullen still hadn't told Bain about them.

"Okay, so you were woken up," said Bain. "What did you do next on Monday?"

"Stevie and I got the bus back to Garleton and picked up my car," said Cook. "Stevie's not got his own motor."

"Did you speak to anyone when you collected your car?" said Bain.

"No," said Cook. "Dad must have been at work and Mum out with the twins."

Cullen noted a sense of jealousy or resentment from the boy towards his siblings by the way he drawled 'twins'.

"So nobody saw you?" said Bain.

"I didn't see anyone," said Cook. "I can't say if anybody saw me."

"But as far as you're aware," said Bain, "nobody saw you."

"What has this got to do with the alleged offences?" said McLintock.

"I'm trying to establish a clear timeline from your client's perspective," said Bain. "If there are witness statements I haven't yet obtained, it's my duty to get them."

"Continue," said McLintock.

"Okay," said Bain, focusing again on Cook. "So, you've got your car but you don't think anyone has seen you going back home."

"That's right," said Cook.

"Where did you go?" said Bain.

Cook grinned. "We just went back to Stevie's flat."

"Why did you take the car?" said Bain.

"Just because," said Cook. "Knew my parents would be out, so I went and nabbed it."

"How would you describe your relationship with your parents?" said Cullen.

"Distant," said Cook.

"Through your actions or theirs?" said Cullen.

"They disowned me," said Cook. "Soon as I left school and that freaky group of theirs, they wanted nothing to do with me."

"Right, this has got us to Monday afternoon," said Bain. "What did you do in Haddington next?"

"We popped into Aldi and got more booze," said Cook. "Beer, wine, vodka, whisky."

"Did you buy it?" said Bain.

Cook smiled at Bain. "Hardly. I'm underage so I kept outside in the motor. We went back to Stevie's and had a few drinks. One of his mates, Spider, asked if we wanted to go for a few at The Pheasant so we went and joined him."

"The Pheasant is a pub in Haddington?" said Cullen.

"Aye," said Cook.

"Does Spider have a name?" said Cullen.

"Aye, Spider," said Cook.

"A real name," said Cullen.

"Never met him before, sorry," said Cook, shrugging. "It might be Simon or Steven, something like that."

"Was it just the three of you in The Pheasant?" said Bain.

"It was," said Cook.

"How long were you in there?" said Bain.

"Until closing time," said Cook. "We went back to Stevie's afterwards for more drinking. We were up until about three then I crashed out again."

"And you were in The Pheasant all that time?" said Cullen.

"We got there about four, half four," said Cook. "Must have been chucked out about midnight."

"Fine," said Bain. "What happened yesterday morning?"

"Me and Stevie got up and drove into Edinburgh," said Cook.

"Where in Edinburgh?" said Bain. "It's a big city."

"Stevie's got a mate called Simmo," said Cook. "We met up with him and Nicky at Simmo's flat in Leith, just off Seafield."

"Can you give us full names for Simmo and Nicky, please?" said Bain.

"Aye, Tommy Simpson and Graeme Nicholas," said Cook.

"Tommy Simpson lives in Leith, is that right?" said Bain.

"Aye," said Cook.

"What about Graeme Nicholas?" said Bain.

"First time I'd met the punter," said Cook. "Seems pretty sound, like."

"Was there anyone else there?" said Bain.

Cook shook his head. "Not at Simmo's flat, no."

"When was this?" said Bain.

"Lunchtime, maybe," said Cook. "I don't know."

"Twelve? Two?"

"Nearer twelve," said Cook.

Bain scribbled in his notebook. "So what did you do after your rendezvous at Mr Simpson's flat?"

"We had a couple of drinks there," said Cook, "then headed out to the pub and met one of Nicky's mates, a boy called Dean."

After Biscuit, Spider, Simmo and Nicky, Cullen was relieved someone Cook knew didn't have a nickname.

"Please confirm the name of the pub," said Bain.

"The Dock," said Cook. "It's on Seafield Road or Salamander Street. I think it changes somewhere round there."

"And it was still the five of you?" said Bain.

"Aye, it was," said Cook.

"And you were there until we apprehended you last night?" said Bain.

"That's right."

"Did you do anything else between going to the pub and then?" said Bain.

"Not that I can recall," said Cook.

"I see," said Bain. "You were in some state when you were brought in. I'm glad you've sobered up to your lawyer's satisfaction."

Cook looked up at the ceiling. "Why are you bothering to check so much stuff out about me for pissing against a church?"

Bain smirked at McLintock. "Your solicitor clearly hasn't briefed you adequately."

McLintock glared at Bain.

Bain winked back. "The reason we've detained you is you're the main suspect in two murders."

Cook looked from Bain to Cullen, swallowing hard. "What?"

"You heard," said Bain.

The room was quiet for a while, Cook biting his lip, sweating and breathing heavily.

"Mr McLintock, I'd like to point out I didn't need to tell him which murders," said Bain. He smiled at Cook. "He knows already."

Cook's eyes shot up.

"That was over a minute," said Bain, tapping his watch. "You haven't asked who."

"Who's dead?" said Cook.

"Right, this is nonsense," said Bain. "You know full well."

"I don't," said Cook, glaring at Bain. "I've genuinely got no idea. Unless you tell me, I can't help you."

"The record will show my client has co-operated fully with your investigation thus far," said McLintock.

"Point noted," said Bain. "It's interesting your client pretends he doesn't know who the victims are."

Cook was close to shouting. "I don't know."

"Jamie, please keep your voice down," said McLintock.

"You need to tell me who they are," said Cook. "Who's died?"

"Have a guess," said Bain.

McLintock closed his eyes and shook his head lightly.

"I can't," said Cook.

"Why?" said Bain. "Too many enemies? Too many victims?"

"Just tell me," said Cook, his eyes filling with tears.

Cullen saw the little boy in there, separate from the man about town talking about bottles of Jack and meeting boys from Leith in pubs.

"Right, okay, then," said Bain, shuffling his notebook. "The first is Mandy Gibson."

Cook looked at Cullen and Lamb. "Mandy?"

"We believe she is a victim of your depravity," said Bain.

"How is Mandy a victim of mine?" said Cook, banging the table with his fist. "Who told you that?"

"We believe you stayed with the Gibsons a fair few times," said Bain.

"For Christ sake, I was smoking dope with Thomas," said Cook. "Has someone told you I was at it with his *sister*?"

"We can't divulge that," said Bain.

"Was it Thomas?" said Cook.

"It wasn't him," said Bain.

"She's *thirteen*," said Cook. "I'd *never* touch her." He looked around the room, biting his fingernail. "It'll be Mulgrew, I bet. Bastard."

"As I say, I cannot divulge that information," said Bain.

"What did Thomas's old man say about this?" said Cook.

"He seemed to agree, suggested it could have been you," said Bain. "But it wasn't him, he merely agreed with the suggestion."

"There is no way," said Cook, pulling at his hair, stretching it almost to breaking. "No way."

"We believe you've had sexual intercourse with another underage girl," said Bain. "We have a witness statement from the victim."

McLintock's eyes bulged in his head. "What is this?"

"A rape allegation was made against Jamie Cook," said Bain, producing the charge sheet recently retrieved from Dunbar.

"That was dropped," said Cook.

"That's as maybe," said Bain. "It still shows a certain predilection of yours. When you started seeing the girl in question, she was fifteen."

Tears filled Cook's eyes. "I didn't do anything with Kirsty until she was sixteen," he said, his voice at breaking point. "I'm not as old as you lot. She's my age. There's nothing wrong with it."

"I'm not sure they would see it that way in court," said Bain.

"These rape allegations against my client were dropped," said McLintock. "Please desist."

Cook screwed his eyes up. "I think you lot will want to make sure it doesn't go to court either." He rolled up his sleeves, showing yellowing bruises on both arms. "I'll give you three guesses where I got these from."

"You deny having sexual relations with a Kirsty-Jane Platt before she was of the age of consent?" said Bain.

Cook rolled his sleeves down. "Nothing happened," he said, rubbing at his eyes, clearing the tears away. "When was Mandy killed?"

"You still haven't asked who the second victim is, you know?" said Bain, a smile on his face.

Cook hit the table again. "Would you stop playing games with me?"

McLintock placed a hand on Jamie's arm. "Inspector, this withholding of information is trying my patience."

Bain grinned. "Jamie, the second victim is Seamus Mulgrew. He was murdered some time on Monday evening."

Cook sat there with his mouth open.

Bain cleared his throat. "Mandy's time of death was approximately eleven PM on Sunday night."

Cook's eyes flicked from Bain to Cullen and back again. "They weren't killed at the same time?"

"Very good," said Bain. "Keep trying."

Cook looked at Cullen. "Was Mandy killed on Sunday night?"

"That's right," said Cullen, nodding.

Cook sat there, silent and unmoving.

Cullen took the initiative. "Jamie," he said. Cook looked over to him. "By your own admission, you were in Garleton at approximately the time of Mandy's death. Is that the case?"

"I was still in the town but, as I said, I got the last bus to Haddington," said Cook.

"And what time was that?" said Cullen.

"I've told you this," said Cook. "It's at eleven on the dot. Leaves North Berwick at quarter to, I think. Gets to Haddington at ten past."

"Aside from the driver, was there anyone else on the bus?" said Cullen.

"Just me," said Cook.

"Could anyone else have seen you?" said Cullen.

"No," said Cook, rubbing his temple.

"Nobody else?" said Cullen.

"No."

"Very convenient, son," said Bain.

Cook burst into tears, looking every inch the little boy he was. "I didn't kill them."

Tears slicked Cook's face. He pushed his hair back making it stand up, held in position by the sweat.

Bain leaned forward. "You're in a lot of trouble here. You've got a motive and no alibi."

Cook gasped. "Where was she? In her house?"

"Balgone Ponds," said Bain.

Cook frowned. "But that's miles from Garleton."

"Aye," said Bain. "They were both found there."

"And you think I killed them?" said Cook.

"Didn't you?" said Bain.

"Of course I didn't," said Cook. "My car was at the house all day on Sunday."

"Have you got any witnesses who can confirm your car was there all the time?" said Bain.

Cook's eyes lit up. "You've got nothing on me, have you?"

"We've got something," said Bain.

"What?" said Cook.

"Motives for killing both victims," said Bain. "Most judges and juries just love that."

"I was in Haddington when Mulgrew was killed," said Cook. "How could I have done it?"

"You were in Garleton when Mandy was killed, before you left in something of a hurry," said Bain, his lip curled up. "I'll settle for your conviction on that one."

Cook sat in silence for a while, his skin a few shades whiter than when they started. "I just remembered something. My brain's frazzled with all the drink. I saw someone when I got on the bus on Sunday night."

"Right," said Bain, folding his arms and leaning back. "Who?"

"I saw Mandy's dad take her to Mulgrew's house."

68

They sat in the corner of the busy Incident Room. Bain still hadn't held a briefing that morning.

"What was that all about?" said Bain.

"He's playing us," said Lamb. "The little bastard is always up to tricks like this. The way I see it, he's desperate and clutching at straws."

Cullen thought through the new development, deciding it was shades of grey rather than the black or white Bain preferred. "I don't think we should immediately assume he is trying to throw us off. He might be telling the truth."

"We should give him the benefit of the doubt?" said Bain, scowling.

"I think we should investigate his claims," said Cullen. "If it's true then it blows all of our assumptions. You've got something like forty officers on this case, right?"

"Thirty seven," said Bain.

"I'd suggest you put five or six on checking his story out," said Cullen.

Bain looked at Lamb. "Thoughts?"

Lamb shrugged. "It's your case."

"Too right it is," said Bain. "Fine, let's do it." He took a deep breath. "Did Cook kill them both?"

"It fits," said Lamb.

"I agree it fits," said Cullen, "but we've not got enough to charge him just yet."

"What else do we need to cover, then, genius?" said Bain.

"The car at the crime scene on Monday night for starters," said Cullen.

"We've still got two suspects for that," said Bain. "Charles Gibson and Robert Cook. My money is on Robert Cook helping his son out."

"Didn't cover his tracks very well," said Cullen.

"These aren't cold-blooded killings," said Bain.

"You're certain of that?" said Cullen.

"As certain as anything," said Bain.

"Don't forget you've got your eyewitness saying Robert Cook left his house at the right time," said Lamb, with a wink.

Bain glowered. "That could still pay off, Sergeant."

"What about Charles Gibson's alibi?" said Cullen, trying to keep them from each other's throats. "He was supposed to be waiting outside Mulgrew's cottage at the time of his death three miles away."

"McLaren's been round the houses in that street," said Lamb. "Nobody saw anything but he needs another two or three passes before he's got complete coverage."

Bain ran his hand through the stubble on his head. "I want a team round every house on that street, three times over. I want everyone who lives there or was there on Monday night found, even if they're in Timbuktu. If one punter has spotted him, it clears Gibson, right?"

"Fair enough," said Lamb.

"North Berwick is where all the business executives live," said Cullen. "There are thousands of silver exec-class saloons across East Lothian. The car could be unrelated. It could be some banker taking his secretary down a country lane, or a couple from a golf club meeting up so their respective husbands and wives don't find out."

"Might be one we lose from the file when we hand it to the PF," said Bain.

"What else do we need to focus on?" said Lamb.

"Before we hit Cook again," said Bain, "I want this Stevie Young boy interviewed. Cullen?"

"Fine," said Cullen.

"What about me?" said Lamb.

"This bus driver," said Bain. "I want him in here giving a statement."

"I get all the great jobs," said Lamb, smiling.

"Don't push it," said Bain.

"What about these other mates of Jamie's?" said Cullen.

"Spider, Simmo, Dean and Nicky, right?" said Bain, stroking his moustache. "I'll put Irvine on it."

"Can I have Angela?" said Lamb.

"You'll need to get one of your wee laddies across, I'm afraid," said Bain. "She's with Cullen. Isn't Law here, anyway?"

"Fine," said Lamb, stroking the triangle of beard, looking disappointed.

"You heard Turnbull last night," said Bain. "I'm on hourly updates to him, so I need half-hourly from you boys, right? I will pull you out of interview rooms for an update as well, so consider yourselves warned."

69

S teven Young had a face full of metal, hoops and studs in his nose, ears and eyebrows, a metal spike protruding from his jawbone, the earlobes rings cutting at least two centimetres out of the flesh. Cullen didn't want to think about what might be pierced beneath his clothes.

He was a big guy, Cullen estimated at least eighteen stone, with his head shaved and a thick beard from the sideburns down. He was wearing all black, a fiery logo on his t-shirt of a metal band Cullen had never heard of.

"Thanks for helping us with inquiries," said Cullen.

"Don't I get a lawyer?" said Young.

"You're not under arrest," said Cullen. "We're taking a witness statement, and you don't need a solicitor."

"Can I just leave?" said Young.

Cullen paused. "Not yet. If you leave, there are some nice charges we could throw at you." He shuffled some papers on the table. "Can you confirm you're acquainted with one Jamie Cook of Garleton?"

"Aye, I know Jamie," said Young, looking bored.

"We understand Jamie came to your flat in Haddington on Sunday night," said Cullen.

"He did, aye."

"When did he arrive?" said Cullen.

"About quarter past eleven."

"And what were you doing at the time?" said Cullen.

"I was on my decks," said Young.

"Decks?"

"Record decks," said Young. "For music. DJing."

"Are you a DJ?" said Cullen.

"Aye," said Young.

Angela wasn't getting much to write down. Cullen left a gap, trying to force Young to fill it.

"I play in Prestonpans," said Young. "At the Goth Tavern. Every Saturday."

"What did you and Mr Cook do once he arrived?" said Cullen.

"I had some bottles of the Jack Daniels clone from Aldi," said Young, with a shrug. "We just started firing into that."

Cullen decided raising the fact Cook was underage might hinder Young's limited co-operation. "Did you go to sleep at any point?"

"We did, aye," said Young. "I stayed up later than Jamie. Got to my scratcher at about eight in the morning."

"When did you get up on Monday?" said Cullen.

"We got up at the back of two," said Young. "I was shattered but we went to pick up Jamie's car. We got back to mine and met up with my pal, Spider."

"Does Spider have a name?" said Cullen.

"Aye, Simon Spink," said Young.

"Does he live in Haddington?" said Cullen.

"He does, aye," said Young, before giving them an address on the west side of the town.

"And what time did you meet up with him?" said Cullen.

"Just after half four," said Young.

"And you were there all night?" said Cullen.

Young rubbed his eyes. "Aye, we were. Right till we got chucked out."

"Was anyone else with you?" said Cullen.

"Just the three of us," said Young.

"Did Mr Cook leave at any point?" said Cullen.

Young played with the spike through his chin. "He did, aye."

Cullen's heart started hammering. "When?"

"It was late on," said Young, "back of eight, maybe. I can't remember. I was pretty trashed. I was playing darts with some old boy."

"And he came back?" said Cullen.

"He did, aye," said Young.

"When?"

"No idea," said Young. "Could have been an hour, could have been ten minutes. Sorry."

Cullen flicked through his notebook.

Mulgrew died between seven PM and midnight, according to the interim post mortem.

Cook had a window of opportunity of maybe an hour to drive to Balgone Ponds, kill Mulgrew and return to the pub.

It was possible.

He wasn't pulled over for drink-driving but then those roads weren't heavily policed.

"Do you know where he went?" said Cullen.

"Some food, maybe," said Young. "We'd just had crisps all day."

"When did you leave the pub?" said Cullen.

"Back of midnight," said Young. "They were chucking everyone out. We got fired into some more drink at my flat but we crashed out not long after, maybe the back of three."

"Was Spider with you back at your flat?" said Cullen.

"He was, aye," said Young. "He got up at six for his work."

"Do you know where he works?" said Cullen.

"A call centre in Granton," said Young. "That's all I know."

Cullen knew of at least five. "What did you and Mr Cook do when you got up yesterday morning?"

"We drove into Edinburgh to meet up with my mate Simmo," said Young.

"This is Tommy Simpson, correct?" said Cullen.

"It is," said Young, taking a deep breath. "His mate Nicky was there. We went to the pub round the corner and bumped into Dean."

"And you drank in there all day?" said Cullen.

Young snorted. "We did, aye."

"Can you give me the names and addresses of Dean, Nicky and Simmo, please?" said Cullen.

"I only know where Tommy lives," said Young, before giving the address on Seafield Road where Cook's car was found.

"What about Nicky or Dean?" said Cullen.

Young shrugged his shoulders. "No idea."

"Do you know anything about them?" said Cullen.

Young shook his head. "Maybe Simmo can help."

"What time did you go to the pub yesterday?" said Cullen.

"Back of twelve," said Young.

"And you were there all day?" said Cullen.

"Aye, until that copper came and grabbed us," said Young.

"Okay," said Cullen, rubbing his temple, trying to think through the fatigue, focusing on the chain of events.

Cook left the pub around the time Mulgrew was killed. He must have been pretty coherent if he carried it out.

"How was Mr Cook both days?" said Cullen.

"How do you mean?" said Young.

"How did he seem when he got to yours on Sunday night?" said Cullen.

"Typical Jamie," said Young. "Always looks a bit haunted."

"Was he keeping up with the drinking on Monday?" said Cullen.

Young paused long enough for Cullen to worry he was clamming up again. "Didn't really notice," he finally said, toying with the spike. "Now you mention it, he wasn't putting them away as much as I was."

"What about yesterday afternoon?" said Cullen.

Young laughed. "You saw the state he was in, didn't you?"

Cullen thought it through.

Cook could have been holding back on Monday before getting away reasonably sober and meeting Mulgrew.

He was absolutely wasted when they found him the previous evening. Cullen wondered if it was a sign of trying to escape something he'd just done, or celebrating his achievement.

"Mr Young, thanks for your help," said Cullen. "I'll need you to sign a statement with ADC Caldwell here. And we may need further information."

Cullen sat in the mercifully empty Incident Room, needing some space to himself. He found a laptop and typed up the notes from the Steven Young interview. When he finished, he tried Lamb.

Getting no answer he called Murray, hearing a blast of wind down the line. "All right?"

"You got Lamb with you?" said Cullen.

"No, sorry," said Murray.

"Where are you?" said Cullen.

"Doing door-to-door in Garleton," said Murray.

"I need someone out that way to speak to a Simon Spink," said Cullen.

"Spider, right?" said Murray.

"You know him?" said Cullen.

Murray laughed down the phone. "Who doesn't? He's the Haddington version of Jamie Cook, older and maybe not quite as bad."

"Can you get a hold of him?" said Cullen. "It's urgent."

"I'll see what I can do," said Murray. "I've been round his house a few times over the years and I think I know where he works."

Cullen ended the call then leaned back on the chair, wondering what else he could do other than searching the station for Bain. It was supposed to be Bain getting updates from Cullen, not the other way round.

The Incident Room had a kitchen annexe, just a sink and a tap. He went over and put the kettle on. Twelve dirty mugs sat in the sink, most of them with a drop of curdling coffee inside. Cullen washed the least disgusting.

PC Johnny Watson bumbled into the room clutching three mugs in one hand.

"Have you seen Bain or Lamb?" said Cullen.

"Weren't you at the briefing?" said Watson.

Cullen shook his head. "I was interviewing someone."

"They're in with a bus driver," said Watson.

Cullen nodded — that explained his difficulty. "Where have you been?" he said, pouring hot water over the tea bag then mashing it against the side of the mug.

Watson rinsed the mugs in the sink. "Stuck at that pub in Haddington all morning."

"And you're back out here?" said Cullen.

"DI Bain's orders," said Watson. "We interviewed every person who was there."

"Did anyone say whether Jamie Cook stayed all day on Monday?" said Cullen.

Watson opened his notebook. "He went out for a bit just after eight, according to the barman. He'd half a mind not to let him back in."

Cullen ran his hand through his hair. "Anybody else confirm that?"

"Most of them were totally out of it or didn't notice," said Watson.

"And the barman didn't think Jamie Cook might be underage?" said Cullen.

Watson shrugged. "Guess not."

"Did you speak to Simon Spink?" said Cullen.

Watson frowned. "Doesn't ring a bell."

"Do you know if anyone else has?" said Cullen.

"No idea," said Watson.

"Could you find out?" said Cullen.

Watson held up the mugs. "I've got to make the coffees."

Cullen pointed his finger at him. "Forget the coffee. Find out about Simon Spink."

Watson put the mugs down and scurried off.

Cullen took the teabag out and checked the milk. It was starting to smell but hadn't gone lumpy yet.

"Learning from the master, obviously."

Bain stood in the doorway, eyes locked on Cullen.

"How much did you hear?" said Cullen.

"Enough," said Bain, grinning. "You know, you're technically the same grade so you shouldn't be giving him orders."

"Promote me, then," said Cullen.

Bain laughed, rubbing his hands together. "Come on, Sundance. Jamie Cook, take two."

Cullen looked at his cup of tea, lumps of milk floating to the top. He left it and followed Bain down the corridor.

"How did it go with Stevie Young?" said Bain.

"We could have something here," said Cullen. "Jamie disappeared from the pub around about eight o'clock on Monday."

Bain stopped in the corridor. "You're kidding me."

"No, I'm not," said Cullen. "The barman told Watson he noticed Cook leaving."

"We've got him," said Bain, punching his fist into his hand. "The little shite definitely did Mulgrew."

"Has his PM come back?" said Cullen.

"Time of death was seven PM to nine PM," said Bain, grinning. "Tallies *perfectly* with the time Cook left the boozer." He set off towards the interview room. "We've nailed the wee tosser."

"How did he do it, then?" said Cullen.

Bain shrugged his shoulders. "He must have met Mulgrew there."

"So he drove there?" said Cullen.

"Aye," said Bain. "Met him, killed him, pissed off. End of story."

"That's a lot of organisation for someone who'd been out on the lash all day," said Cullen.

"Sundance, it is possible do an all-dayer and not get totally blootered," said Bain. "Lager tops every couple of hours, pint of water at the bar with every round. Easy. I infiltrated a gang when I was in Strathclyde. Took me eighteen months but I got my DS position out of it. I learnt how to drink sensibly, not like you with Tommy Smith's cheap whisky the other night."

"Don't remind me," said Cullen.

"Has anyone asked how pissed Cook was on Monday night?" said Bain.

Cullen nodded his head. "I did, aye. Stevie Young couldn't confirm how much he'd had."

"Was anyone else with them?" said Bain.

"Some boy called Spider," said Cullen. "Real name Simon Spink. DC Murray is trying to bring him in for questioning. I'll make sure he asks."

"Let me know how it goes," said Bain.

Cook killing Mulgrew was becoming more plausible.

"How did it go with the bus driver?" said Cullen.

"We gave him a proper going over," said Bain. "It checks out, but only at a 'fits the description of' level. He confirmed he saw a man carrying a girl into a cottage at the same time Jamie got on the bus. That's it."

"So, Cook didn't kill Mandy?" said Cullen.

"We can nail Cook with both murders," said Bain, stopping outside the interview room.

"You just told me Cook has an alibi for Mandy's death," said Cullen.

"Deeley said it looks like the same MO as Mandy," said Bain. "We can get him with that."

"The bus driver picked up Jamie Cook and saw Mandy Gibson going into Mulgrew's cottage, *alive*," said Cullen. "We've got statements covering Cook's movements from that point on. Gibson seems to have been involved in Mandy's death. We need to speak to *him*, don't you think? "

"Hold your horses, Sundance," said Bain. "All the bus driver said was he saw someone matching Gibson's description carrying Mandy inside. She could already have been dead. Cook could have killed her beforehand."

"Are you serious?" said Cullen.

"Come on, Sundance," said Bain, shaking his head. "She leaves home in the middle of the night, meets Cook outside. He kills her, dumps the body in that lane. Her old man finds her, rushes her to Mulgrew's to see if his exorcism skills stretch to resurrection."

He rubbed at his moustache. "Meanwhile, Cook gets the bus to Haddington to lie low. That's the nearest stop to their houses. He sees Gibson take his daughter in, points it out to the bus driver so he's got an alibi. Misdirection at its finest."

Cullen shook his head. "And not a single piece of evidence."

"We'll get some," said Bain. "This is only day three. We can be looking for evidence for months. We've got time."

"*You* haven't," said Cullen. It was just past eleven — three hours to go.

"Cargill can take a running jump," said Bain. "We'll see what Jim has to say when I give him a collar." He checked his watch. "Do you want to lead this?"

Cullen could see himself being sucked into Bain's vortex.

71

C ook looked like he was asleep, his head resting on the desk. McLintock sat beside him, legs crossed, scribbling on a notepad. Buxton stood by the door.

"Are you okay, Jamie?" said Cullen, sitting down.

"Course he is," said Bain.

"My client is ready," said McLintock.

"Get on with it," said Cook, sitting up.

Cullen started recording. "Interview with Jamie Colin Cook commenced at eleven oh six on Wednesday the twenty-fifth of January 2012." He listed the attendees.

"Jamie," said Cullen, "can you tell me about your relationship with Seamus Mulgrew?"

Cook bit his lip. "I don't want to."

"I understand there may be personal reasons for not wishing to, but you're the chief suspect in his murder," said Cullen. "Can you detail your relationship with Father Mulgrew, please?"

"No."

"My client does not have to answer that question," said McLintock, looking up from his notepad, eyes peering over his chunky glasses.

Bain just gestured for Cullen to continue.

Cullen took a deep breath then looked at Cook for a few seconds. "Okay, Jamie, let's try again, shall we? I just met Steven

Young. He told me you left the pub at around eight o'clock on Monday night."

"What?" said Cook, his eyes lighting up.

"The bar staff at The Pheasant in Haddington have backed it up," said Cullen.

Cook shared a look with McLintock.

"Well, did you or didn't you?" said Cullen.

"No comment," said McLintock, tearing his glasses off and staring at Cullen.

"Jamie, where did you go?" said Cullen.

"Who else have you spoken to?" said Cook. "Spider?"

"Not yet, but we will," said Cullen.

"What I'll tell you is me and Spider went out to get some dope from his mate," said Cook.

Cullen glanced at Bain, grinding his teeth. "When you say dope, you mean cannabis?"

Cook sat in silence for a while. "Yes. Marijuana. Dope. Ganja."

"I appreciate your honesty," said Cullen.

"We were only gone half an hour, maybe three quarters at the very most," said Cook.

Bain tapped the table, making Cullen look over. He gestured to the door. Cullen paused the recording and left the room.

Out in the corridor, Bain was rubbing his moustache. "Think this is right?"

"No idea," said Cullen. "Sounds plausible."

"I think it's shite," said Bain.

Lamb appeared behind him. "What's going on?"

"We have a gap in Jamie Cook's statement," said Bain. "Funnily enough, it's when he could have killed Mulgrew."

"Jesus Christ," said Lamb.

"We need to speak to some mate of Steven Young's called Spider," said Cullen.

"Simon Spink?" said Lamb.

"That's the one," said Cullen. "Cook claims he and Spider went off to score some dope."

Lamb nodded. "Murray's just found him."

72

DC Murray followed up a tip from a contact in Haddington and found Spider at his work, the Scottish Gas call centre in Granton, before driving him to Leith Walk.

Cullen could see how he got the nickname. He had incredibly long arms and legs and a comparatively short torso. He was almost skeletally thin, with a shaved head and a silver hoop in one ear. He spoke eloquently despite his appearance, years of call centre training reprogramming the guttural Haddington accent.

"I believe you're acquainted with one Steven Young of Haddington," said Cullen. "Is that right?"

"That's correct," said Spink.

"And a Jamie Cook of Garleton," said Cullen.

"We're acquainted," said Spink, "but I wouldn't say we know each other, if you catch my drift."

"We have reason to believe you were drinking with Mr Young and Mr Cook in Haddington on Monday night," said Cullen.

"Aye, in The Pheasant," said Spink. "It's not my favourite in the town but it's one of the few that will let those two over the threshold."

"We're investigating a double murder," said Cullen. "Jamie Cook is the primary suspect. I'd like to point out the seriousness of this matter.

"Noted," said Spink.

"We'd like you to recount your movements on Monday night, from meeting up with Mr Young and Mr Cook onwards," said Cullen.

"Can I have my lawyer in here, please?" said Spink.

"You're not under police caution and therefore you don't need a lawyer present," said Cullen. "Can I ask why you want one?"

Spink looked away. "No reason."

"Can you go through your movements, please?" said Cullen.

"Fine," said Spink, sitting forward and cradling his fingers on the tabletop. "I'd arranged to meet Stevie at the back of four for a couple of pints. I don't work Mondays. It was the end of my weekend and I wanted a few beers to get through the night. I usually don't sleep well after the weekend. I got to the pub at the back of four and had a pint on my own while I waited. They pitched up at about twenty past."

"And how did they appear?" said Cullen.

"They didn't look too good," said Spink. "It was like they'd been out all day."

"Had they?" said Cullen.

"I think they'd been out the night before," said Spink.

"You think?" said Cullen.

Spink laughed. "Aye, well, they said they'd been up till stupid o'clock drinking, if that's what you mean."

"Thank you," said Cullen. "Please continue."

"After they turned up, we got into some pretty crazy drinking," said Spink. "Stevie was firing into the pints at a rate of knots."

"What about Jamie?" said Cullen.

"Jamie was drinking a fair amount," said Spink. "We had a kitty going. Started off with a tenner each, think I spent thirty in total."

"Who was going to the bar most often?" said Cullen.

Spink played with his earring for a few seconds. "We all were. Jamie was going the most, if anyone."

Bain's pet theory about lager tops and pints of water was looking more promising.

"We understand Jamie left the pub at about eight o'clock," said Cullen. "Can you confirm or deny that?"

"No comment," said Spink.

Cullen frowned. "I'm sorry?"

"No comment."

"Mr Spink," said Cullen, his voice rising, "can I remind you we're investigating a double murder here and Mr Cook's whereabouts are of the utmost importance."

"And I said no comment," said Spink, avoiding eye contact.

"Mr Cook said he went to procure cannabis," said Cullen. "Is that correct?"

"If you want anything out of me," said Spink, "I want a lawyer here."

Cullen leaned over to the tape recorder. "Interview terminated at eleven fifty-two."

CULLEN BRIEFED BAIN, Lamb, Irvine and Angela on the interview with Spink.

"You beauty," said Bain.

"Steady," said Cullen. "He's refused to co-operate. Don't think he's told us Cook's alibi was a pack of lies."

"It's not that bit I'm worried about," said Bain. "Cook could have been buying soft drinks."

"Spink told us Cook was buying some of their rounds, that's all," said Cullen. "We don't know if he drank soft drinks."

Bain had a look Cullen knew too well, eyes flicking around and nostrils flared out wide. He took a deep breath. "We've interviewed the bar staff, right?"

"My boys did it this morning," said Lamb.

"Christ, that's all we need," said Bain. "They'll have made a total arse of it."

Lamb got up and squared up to Bain for a few seconds, before shaking his head and taking a few steps back.

Cullen looked around the room, spotting Watson by the sink, staring into space and mashing a teabag. He called him over.

"What is it, sir?" said Watson.

"You interviewed the bar staff at The Pheasant, right?" said Lamb.

Watson nodded.

"Did you ask the bar staff what Jamie Cook was drinking?" said Bain.

"Don't think we did," said Watson. "The barman didn't mention anything. We found out he wasn't there for about an hour. Isn't that enough?"

Bain repeated the earlier look. "Right, Constable, can you get your arse back out there and speak to them again. I want confirmation of what Jamie Cook bought at each and every round. We suspect it was soft drinks, and I count lager tops in that."

"What's lager tops?" said Watson.

"A shandy," said Bain.

Bain's mobile rang. He swore when he checked the display. "Just on my way up, Jim," he said, marching out of the room. "Think we've just about got Cook for Mulgrew."

73

C ullen sat with Charlie Kidd at his desk in the Technical Investigation Unit, responsible for all IT-related analysis.

"I hear Bain's up to his usual tricks," said Kidd. "Word travels fast in this place, especially if everyone's favourite DI is involved."

"What have you heard, then?" said Cullen.

Kidd played with his ponytail for a few seconds. "Heard he's supposed to be losing the case today."

"Bad news travels faster than the speed of light," said Cullen.

"Tell me about it," said Kidd. "I'm just getting used to how Bain operates. Christ knows we don't need another one running around with a different set of stupid questions."

"I'm with you there," said Cullen. "You've not had any dealings with Cargill, then?"

Kidd shook his head. "Not had the pleasure yet. She usually sends one of her cronies up." He looked hard at Cullen. "If you're here chasing me up about Mulgrew's computer, I told Bain it's so old it won't even connect to the internet and it doesn't have any pictures on it."

Cullen raised his eyebrows. "I didn't know Mulgrew's computer had been taken in."

"Aye, doesn't even have Windows XP on it," said Kidd. "Can't believe it still turns on."

Cullen nodded. "Fine." He gestured at a Dell desktop connected up to Kidd's own PC. "Is that Jamie Cook's?"

"It is, aye," said Kidd. "Been a bloody nightmare."

"We could have done with some leads while we were still looking for him," said Cullen.

"Aye, funny," said Kidd. "The problem is he just doesn't seem to do much on the computer."

"How do you mean?" said Cullen.

"The only emails I found were pretty uninteresting," said Kidd. "Updates to Schoolbook and Twitter, feedback requests from Amazon or eBay."

"Nothing more interesting than my own account," said Cullen.

Kidd laughed. "Trouble is, though, this is a teenager in the middle of nowhere. He must be bored out of his head."

"Have you been in his Schoolbook account?" said Cullen.

Kidd didn't reply for a few seconds. "I'm not going back in there without Bain and the PF sitting next to me." He handed Cullen a printout. "I've managed to get some leads for you by trawling his emails. Here."

Cullen read the list of ten or so names. It would have been useful earlier, but they'd already spoken to everyone. He leaned back in the chair, folding up the sheet. "If nothing else it means there aren't any last minute surprises."

"Aye, your speciality," said Kidd.

Cullen stood up. "Better head back down and see what sort of arse-kicking Bain got off Turnbull."

BAIN RETURNED to the Incident Room wearing a smile, the last thing Cullen expected given the circumstances. He grabbed Cullen and Lamb and led them towards the interview room. "Jim is impressed with our progress."

"You did give him the warnings I gave you twenty minutes ago, right?" said Cullen.

Bain glared at him as they walked down the stairs. "Jim's not a detail man. When you get to my position, you'll appreciate how to manage upwards."

"What are we doing now, then?" said Cullen.

"We need to find out what happened here, Sundance," said Bain. "This is a pigsty. Can you probe him on Mulgrew?"

"He totally blocked us off last time," said Cullen.

"I know he did," said Bain. "This is your big chance to shine. You make a passable 'good cop'."

"Cheers," said Cullen, hoping Bain caught the sarcasm in his voice.

They entered the room and sat down, Cullen and Bain across from Cook and McLintock, Lamb to the side and Buxton standing by the door. Cullen started the interview.

"I need to ask you about Seamus Mulgrew," said Cullen.

Cook kept his eyes on the table. "He's better off dead."

"What my client means," said McLintock, "is there was no love lost between him and the deceased and the antagonism was all from the deceased's perspective."

"How would pissing against the wall of the deceased's church fit into that?" said Bain.

"If I can please continue the line of questioning?" said Cullen.

Bain raised his hands in mock defeat. "Fire away, Constable."

Cullen smiled at Cook, trying to buy into his favour. "You seem to have an interesting history with Father Mulgrew. He told me you had the Devil in you."

Cook said nothing.

"No comment from my client," said McLintock. "I would like that to be formally recorded."

"Jamie, you need to speak here," said Cullen. "DI Bain is quite keen on charging you with the murder of Father Mulgrew. I think it's in your best interests to talk to us right now and clear up any ambiguity."

"No comment," said Cook.

Cullen lay his hands palms up on the table. "You do realise how much trouble you're in here, don't you? If you're convicted of murder, you're looking at a minimum of twelve years' imprisonment with good behaviour. You'll be eighteen by the time this gets to court. You won't go to a young offenders'. Your full sentence will be served in mainstream prisons. I've been inside them. These are not nice places. A boy like you from a well-off background will be *popular* in there."

"Can you please stop with the clichés?" said McLintock. "You are threatening my client with a sentence when you have not presented us with one shred of credible evidence so far."

Cullen ignored McLintock. "Jamie, you're taking a big risk here with your future and your life. Mr McLintock's only risk is financial."

"I don't appreciate the insinuation I am a 'No Win, No Fee' lawyer," said McLintock. "The terms and conditions of my engagement are confidential to myself, my client and his parents."

"The point still stands," said Cullen. "You're assuming you'll be let off."

"I didn't kill him," said Cook, in a small voice.

"We have evidence," said Cullen.

"No comment," said Cook.

"Jamie, you'll be sexually abused in prison," said Cullen. "There's very little anyone can do to fully police a prison. All it needs is a small window of opportunity — a moment in the showers or maybe in the kitchens — and they will pounce on you."

A tear slicked down Cook's cheek. "You don't know what I've been through," he said, his voice cracked.

"Tell me," said Cullen.

Cook looked up at Cullen, eyes blazing. "I've had a devil in me, that much is true." He took a deep breath, blinking back tears. "That devil was called Mulgrew. He used to fuck me."

74

The light on the recorder blinked in the silence of the room.

Lamb swore under his breath.

McLintock's bulging eyes betrayed the shock as he wrote on his pad.

"Can you elaborate on that, Jamie?" said Cullen.

A drinks can was still on the table. Cook fiddled with the ring pull, bending it back and forth. "He fucked me every week for two and a half years."

Tears were coming thick and fast. Cullen thought Cook looked defenceless, innocent and younger, closer to his actual age.

"He fucked me during his counselling," said Cook. "He'd sometimes take me to this hut by the ponds. It had a mattress. I tried to blot it out but it's impossible."

"Father Mulgrew said you told him about fantasies of abusing children in a shack," said Cullen.

"Did he?" said Cook, shaking his head. "Sick bastard. He took my virginity there, took my future away as well."

"Did you not not say anything to your parents?" said Cullen.

"How the hell could I?" said Cook. "Mulgrew was like *Jesus* to the pair of them. They'd never believe me."

"There would be evidence," said Cullen.

Cook looked at him, eyes hard. "The police wouldn't have believed me," he said out of the corner of his mouth, glancing at Lamb. "Who would you lot have listened to between a pillar of the community and a tearaway rebel like me? It would be his word against mine."

"What did he do to you?" said Lamb.

"He fucked me up the arse," said Cook.

Lamb spoke in a quiet, soft voice. "Jamie, there would have been evidence. You'd be surprised what can be done."

Cook shook his head, but said nothing.

"You weren't always a tearaway," said Lamb.

"I was fourteen when he started this," said Cook. "I couldn't say anything. He just destroyed my life. All those rumours. Jamie is a bad boy. Jamie is possessed by the Devil. He was a master at it."

"You didn't exactly help your case," said Bain. "Underage drinking, fighting, drugs, pissing against churches, God knows what else."

Cook shrugged. "It was a reaction to it. It played into his hands, though, didn't it?"

"I believe you," said Cullen, "but I need you to confirm something for me."

Cook looked up, a glimpse of hope in his eye. "What?"

"What happened with Kirsty-Jane?" said Cullen.

Cook slammed the can down on the table. "Nothing."

"Jamie, you were charged with rape," said Cullen.

"She consented," said Cook.

"Did she?" said Cullen.

Cook pinched his temple. "She did, aye."

"That's not what her father thought," said Cullen.

Cook clenched his fists. "Don't mention him."

"Jamie, what happened when you were taken in for questioning?" said Cullen.

Cook looked over at McLintock, the solicitor having quietly listened for the last few minutes, Cullen unable to decipher whether he felt Cook's statement would help his case, or if he was merely shocked. Cook leaned over and whispered into the lawyer's ear. McLintock tapped his pen against the paper for a few seconds, before whispering something back.

"He beat me up," said Cook.

"Who beat you up?" said Cullen.

"Kirsty's dad," said Cook. "There were a couple of others who watched and held me down."

"Thanks, Jamie," said Cullen. "Did you at any point pressure her into having sex with you?"

Cook took a long deep breath. "I wanted to prove I was normal. I wanted to have sex with a girl, try to show I could. I didn't want to be a *poof*."

"There's nothing wrong with being homosexual," said Cullen.

Cook glared at him. "Aye, but I'm not."

"Did you feel you weren't normal?" said Cullen.

"No, I didn't," said Cook.

"You can get counselling, you know?" said Cullen.

"That's no use," said Cook. "My life is over. I've got no future." Spit flecked his mouth as he glared at Bain. "You want to know what I was thinking about in the park on Sunday night? I was thinking about killing myself."

Bain swallowed, his Adam's apple rising and falling. "You're only seventeen. If this is all true, you've got a chance to rebuild your life."

Cook stared at the table.

"You didn't rape Kirsty?" said Cullen.

"As my client said, Kirsty-Jane Platt gave consent for penetrative intercourse," said McLintock. "There is no question of rape."

"You know something?" said Cook, leaning forward. "If I'd topped myself on Sunday, you'd have three deaths to investigate. I hope you'd have found out what Mulgrew was doing to me." He laughed. "You'd have nailed Mulgrew for killing Mandy earlier. He would've had no-one to pin Mandy's death on if I was gone."

Cullen leaned across the desk, inches away from the boy's face. "Why would Mulgrew kill Mandy?"

Cook wiped his eyes. "Once I left the group he pounced on her. She had a devil inside her as well, didn't she? Thomas told me she was away twice a week with him after I left." He crushed the can in his hand. "Me leaving meant he picked on her. I feel *sick*."

Cullen looked at Bain for guidance. He got nothing.

"You know what else I was thinking?" said Cook. "The thought of Mulgrew moving on to my brother and sister when he got fed up with Mandy. He liked boys and girls, didn't he? He could have no end of twisted games with them."

"Interview terminated at twelve thirty-three," said Bain.

They sat in silence.

Cullen didn't know what to say.

Lamb spoke up. "Jamie, you need serious counselling."

75

"So do you believe him?" said Lamb, back in the Incident Room.

"Not sure," said Bain.

"I believe him," said Cullen. "It's whether you think this puts him in the clear for killing Mulgrew or it puts him in the frame."

Bain screwed his face up. "Give me strength."

"I believe Mulgrew was abusing him," said Cullen. "We've got statements pointing to Mulgrew being a paedophile and, it would appear, was abusing Mandy Gibson as well." He paused, letting his brain catch up with his mouth. "This means one of two things — either Jamie Cook had nothing to do with Mulgrew's murder or it was revenge."

"You keep changing your tune, Cullen," said Bain. "One minute, he's innocent, the next he's guilty. Which is it?"

"We have very little in the way of hard evidence," said Cullen. "We'll need a confession to secure this one. All I'm doing is keeping an open mind and letting the facts speak for themselves."

Bain scowled at Cullen. "I've warned you before about you and your games."

Cullen shrugged his shoulders. "I'm not playing any games, sir. It's possible Jamie Cook killed Mulgrew."

"How's the alibi checking out with Spink?" said Bain.

"We're still waiting on his solicitor coming in," said Cullen.

"That Cadder has really buggered everything up. Every little toerag we bring in thinks they're on *NYPD Blue* and they get a phone call and a fuckin' lawyer." Bain pinched the bridge of his nose. "Let me know when he's in, right?"

"Will do," said Cullen.

Bain looked at Lamb. "What do you think, Sergeant?"

Lamb took a deep breath, all the time looking at Cullen. "I think DC Cullen is right. We need to keep an open mind on this."

"Have you brought Charles Gibson in yet?" said Cullen.

Bain paused. "No."

"No?" said Cullen. "We've got two statements implying his direct involvement in the death of his daughter. We really need to speak to him."

"Cullen, this is the last warning," said Bain. "Shut it. Until you're the SIO on a case you don't get to call the shots, all right?"

Cullen shook his head. "You're making a mistake."

Bain stroked his moustache for a few seconds. "We can't find Gibson."

Lamb laughed hard. "This just gets better, doesn't it?"

"I'm not going to tolerate any more of your nonsense," said Bain.

"You need to bring Charles Gibson in," said Lamb.

Bain took a deep breath. "I will, once we find him."

"Shouldn't we get out to Garleton and look for him?" said Cullen.

"Lamb's boys can do that," said Bain, rubbing the stubble on his head. "It feels like we're grasping at things. I want us to get hard evidence against someone."

"Chance would be a fine thing," said Lamb.

Bain glared at him. "It's time we visited the lair of Jimmy Deeley."

76

The mortuary was located in the basement of the station. In the dim light of his office Deeley still wore his medical gown, looking like something out of one of those weird seventies horror films Cullen's dad liked, cutting up bodies, dead or alive, before unleashing a barrage of camp jokes.

"You've seen the report, Brian," said Deeley, rocking back on his chair. "What else do you need me to spell out for you?"

"Aye, very funny, Jimmy," said Bain. "Let me know if you ever get good at catching criminals."

"You, too," said Deeley, a cheeky glint in his eyes.

"If we both stick to our jobs we might get there with this case," said Bain. "Spell it out for us."

"Fine." Deeley tore open the report, leafing through the pages until he found the summary. "It's very similar to your other body. Again, the bruising was perimortem, as with Mandy Gibson. There are, however, more contusions to the wrists, pointing to a great deal of struggling."

"Is it homicide?" said Bain.

"Most definitely," said Deeley.

"Suffocation?" said Bain.

"Absolutely," said Deeley.

"With a pillow, right?" said Bain.

Deeley scanned along a line in the paperwork with his finger.

"Not so sure. With Mandy, we found small traces of white cotton in her gums."

He took a large A4 photographic print from the folder and picked up a magnifying glass from his desk. He inspected the photo then gave up. "It's got so much bloody harder since they made us go digital," he said, putting the file down and leading them into the morgue itself.

The icy cold room contained stacked lockers holding the bodies waiting for autopsy or, like Mulgrew and Mandy Gibson, waiting while investigation into their deaths concluded.

Deeley pulled two racks out, one after the other, first Mulgrew then Mandy. "Here we go. You boys have a look at Mandy. I need to have another check on Mulgrew."

Cullen could feel his stomach churn. Mandy lay there, her skin ice white, looking younger than her thirteen years. He focused, determined not to lose the contents of his stomach as he'd so infamously done the previous summer.

"Gentlemen," said Deeley, clearing his throat.

They looked across. Deeley was on tiptoes, leaning over Mulgrew's body, using some metal medical tool to prise open his mouth.

"There are no traces of cotton, synthetic fibre, duck down or anything of the sort," said Deeley. "No traces of anything at all, other than some bread, consistent with the victim's last meal." He fiddled around with Mulgrew's lips and paused, frowning. "Oh, bloody hell."

"What is it?" said Bain.

Deeley pointed at Mulgrew's top lip. "Look at that."

"You must think I'm younger than I actually am, Jimmy," said Bain, "but my eyesight isn't as good as it used to be."

Cullen leaned in close, just about making out small blotches. "Bruises."

"Five points to Gryffindor," said Deeley. "There are small contusions on the victim's lips."

"And?" said Bain, clearly growing tired of Deeley's showboating.

Deeley rolled his eyes. "It's a tell-tale sign of manual strangulation."

"What's that supposed to mean?" said Bain.

"This," said Deeley, walking over and grabbing Bain in a chokehold, his free hand clasped tight over Bain's mouth and nose.

Bain struggled manically, arms flapping, trying to grab hold of something.

Deeley eventually let go, a bit later than was strictly necessary.

Bain dusted himself off. "Don't try that again."

"The killer didn't use a pillow," said Deeley, "he used his hands."

"Thought this was the same MO?" said Cullen.

Bain shrugged. "Based on a draft report. They were superficially similar." He looked at Mulgrew for a few seconds while Deeley put Mandy away.

"Where does this leave us, then?" said Lamb.

"We think the killer knew the MO of Mandy's death," said Cullen. "He tried to make them look the same."

"You could be right," said Bain. "What about the fact one was done with a pillow and the other with hands?"

"So, Mulgrew's killer wasn't there when Mandy died?" said Lamb.

Cullen nodded. "He found out some other way."

"How did Jamie Cook find out how Mandy was killed?" said Bain.

"Eh?" said Cullen.

"Keep up," said Bain. "Cook killed Mulgrew and tried to make it look the same."

"We don't know it was Cook," said Cullen.

"The boy's got a point," said Deeley.

"Keep out of this, Jimmy," said Bain, still rubbing his throat.

Deeley shrugged. "I'll leave the holy trinity to it, then. If you need me, you know where I'll be."

Bain turned back to Cullen. "Go on."

"We know the Mulgrew killer tried to make it look the same as Mandy," said Cullen. "Given the differing MOs, it's probably not the same person who did both."

"I'm still putting money on Jamie Cook," said Bain.

"Then we need evidence which hasn't come from the mouths of either Seamus Mulgrew or Charles Gibson," said Cullen.

Bain nodded. "Can you get that Spider boy to refute the alibi?"

"Once his lawyer shows up," said Cullen.

Bain stared at Lamb. "Sergeant, if you'd accompany me up the stairs to brief Turnbull on this."

77

C ullen and Angela sat on one side of the table, Spink and his lawyer opposite. Cullen didn't recognise the solicitor, a young man named Douglas Stewart.

Cullen started the interview. "Mr Spink, when we last spoke, you didn't answer the question relating to what Jamie Cook was doing between the hours of eight PM and nine PM on Monday the twenty-third of January 2012. Mr Cook says he was buying cannabis, can you confirm or deny that?"

"My client would prefer not to comment on the matter," said Stewart.

"Can I ask why?" said Cullen.

"Mr Spink will not comment on the matter," said Stewart.

Cullen fixed a stare on Spink. "Can I remind you we're investigating a serious crime here? Mr Cook is the prime suspect in a murder."

"Is it just the one now?" said Spink, a smile on his face. "You said this was a double murder earlier, you seem to have lost one."

"This isn't a laughing matter," said Cullen. "Jamie Cook has provided an alibi which hasn't been confirmed. The only statement we have is Jamie not being in The Pheasant between those hours. You have confirmed you were there. If Mr Cook wasn't there, then that's all you need to say. However, if you know where he went and it didn't involve killing someone then I really need to know."

"No comment," said Spink.

"Fine, if that's how you want to play it," said Cullen. "This is a murder case. You have confirmed you were with the prime suspect at the time of the murder. If it turns out Jamie Cook did murder Father Seamus Mulgrew, then you'll be an accessory. I hope I don't need to remind your solicitor of the prison sentence."

Spink swallowed. "No comment," he said, his voice shaky.

Cullen leaned across the table, covering the microphone with his hand. "I would suggest you consult your lawyer about this."

Spink looked over at Stewart, before whispering in his ear. They talked back and forth for a few seconds. Finally, the lawyer nodded his head slowly.

"It was grass," said Spink, slouching back. "Jamie and I went to get some skunk. It was for personal use, I assure you."

Cullen knew there was an influx of super-strength marijuana in the Lothians, the dope equivalent of Special Brew lager.

"Can you provide the name of your supplier?" said Cullen.

Spink shook his head. "No chance. I've given you what you wanted. Jamie and I went to a house in Haddington to buy some skunk. Half an ounce, well within the realms of personal use."

"Thank you, Mr Spink," said Cullen. "Can I get you to sign a statement with ADC Caldwell, please?"

78

Cullen got upstairs to find Bain and Lamb still in with Turnbull.

He sat at a vacant desk and phoned Murray.

"Stuart, it's Cullen. How's it going out there?"

"Brilliant," said Murray, wind blowing against the microphone. "I just know we're going to get our arses kicked for not finding Gibson now."

"Have you lost him?" said Cullen.

"Not exactly," said Murray. "I've just got here. Feeling pulled from pillar to post, I tell you. Just outside his house now. He's not in."

"I'll speak later," said Cullen.

He stabbed a finger against the screen and ended the call, before leaning back in his chair. He looked over at Turnbull's office and saw Bain standing by the window, his arms gesticulating. There was no sign of them getting out soon.

"Just about done, isn't it?"

Cullen's heart jumped. Angela.

"You scared the shit out of me," he said.

She laughed. "You big wimp," she said, sitting down next to him. "What's happening?"

"Just waiting on Bain and Lamb getting out of Turnbull's office to see what further fun's in store for today," he said. He showed her his watch. "Bain's got an hour left."

Angela nodded. "I saw Cargill's car in the car park."

"Surprised she's not in there with them," said Cullen.

"Do you believe Jamie Cook?" said Angela.

"I do," said Cullen. "It all makes sense."

"Do you think he killed Mulgrew?" said Angela.

Cullen blinked. "No. I think Spider is telling the truth. One thing I don't get, though, is they went to see some guy over the other side of town and nobody spotted them? We had an APB out on Cook and he just walked through the town centre."

Angela tapped at her nose.

"Spill."

"I'm just up from the Incident Room," said Angela. "PC Watson said they've got a confirmed sighting of Spink at the time we're interested in, walking past the RBS on Haddington High Street just after half eight."

Cullen sat up. "Was Cook with him?"

"Someone matching the description was," said Angela, nodding.

Cullen leaned back in the chair and closed his eyes. "Thanks for checking it out."

"No problem," she said. "What now?"

"I don't know," he said. "Speak to Gibson, I suppose."

"Assuming Bain's still in charge?" she said.

Cullen nodded slowly, trying to think. "Did Watson say anything about what Jamie Cook was drinking?"

She frowned. "He mentioned something, aye. Something like the barman couldn't remember if he was ordering soft drinks or not."

"Fine," said Cullen, realising it was irrelevant now.

Angela bit her lip.

"What's up?" he said.

"Eh?" she said, her eyes darting up too quickly for there to be nothing.

"I can tell something's up," he said.

"Nothing," she said, shaking her head.

Cullen thought of Lamb looking her up and down the other

morning, the comment about a Wonderbra and asking Cullen if she was single. "It's Lamb, isn't it?"

She rubbed her face. "How did you know?"

Cullen smiled. "Despite what Bain might say, I am actually a detective. I can tell when someone's lying most of the time and I'm good at picking up on signs, especially when they're as unsubtle as Lamb's."

Angela nodded slowly. "He asked me out for a drink."

"Thought there was nothing going on?" he said. "So?"

"So, I'm married, Scott," she said.

"So was Lamb," he said. "Aren't you tempted?"

"He seems like a nice guy," she said, nibbling her lip again. "Things haven't been great with Rod, recently. He's pressuring me to have kids."

"Don't you want them?" said Cullen.

She shook her head violently. "No way. He knew this when we got together. I've just got this job, the last thing I want to do is drop it for some kids."

"Have you told him?" said Cullen.

She looked at the floor. "Not in so many words, no."

"Maybe you should," he said. "What are you going to say to Lamb?"

"Let him down gently, I suppose," said Angela.

"Probably for the best," said Cullen.

She nodded back. "Got your little infatuation sorted out?"

He rolled his eyes. "She hasn't spoken to me for over a day. I'm leaving it like that."

"Sounds like you broke her poor wee heart," she said.

Cullen shook his head. "How do I keep attracting them?"

"I've no idea," she said. "You're a twat when it comes to girls. I've no idea why Sharon puts up with you."

"Thanks for the vote of confidence," said Cullen.

Cullen spotted Bain and Lamb leaving Turnbull's office, neither of them looking happy. Cargill stood in the doorway, still talking to Turnbull.

Cullen marched over, Angela following. Lamb winked at her.

"Have you found Gibson yet?" said Bain.

"No we haven't," said Cullen. "He's not at home, Murray can't find him."

"Jesus Christ," said Bain. "How come every little twat in East Lothian has a habit of disappearing when I need to speak to them?"

"Turnbull and Cargill want us to focus on Gibson as a priority," said Lamb.

"It looks like Cook is in the clear," said Cullen. "His alibi is confirmed by two sources, one of them police."

"We're heading back to Garleton," said Bain. "See if we can find the wee shite."

Cullen remembered speaking through the letterbox to Susan Russell.

"I think I know where he might be."

79

Cullen banged on the door of God's Rainbow, patched up since Bain's forced entry. Bain and Lamb were alongside him, with Angela, Watson and Law down the lane at the back. Irvine and Murray remained in separate cars, ready to pounce if necessary.

William Thornton answered the door, frowning immediately. "Can I help you?"

"We need to speak to Charles Gibson," said Cullen.

Thornton smiled. "I'm afraid that's impossible just now. We're in the middle of a service. And this is a private religious building."

"Bollocks it is," said Bain, squaring up to him. "We're grabbing him now for questioning."

Thornton tried to spread himself across the door. "I'm afraid you'll just have to wait. Charles is delivering an important service. His daughter has died and our spiritual leader has been murdered. Our congregation needs to heal."

Bain grabbed him by the shirt collar. "Listen, pal, I'm speaking to him now, okay?"

Cath Russell appeared behind the door. "What's going on here?"

"Where's Charles Gibson?" said Lamb.

She frowned at him. "I'm afraid you can't just—"

"Shut it," said Bain, brushing her to the side and barging inside the church.

Gibson stood in the pulpit, a ceremonial robe over his clothes, his voice booming out in the packed church.

Bain marched up the middle of the room, heading straight for Gibson, Cullen following. Lamb stayed at the door, guarding the exit.

"What do you want?" said Gibson.

Bain stopped in front of him. "I need to speak to you."

"You'll have to wait," said Gibson. "We have suffered two great losses to our flock."

People were on their feet now, crowding round them.

"Aye and you're responsible for both deaths," said Bain, as he approached the front.

"I beg your pardon?" said Gibson.

"Just stop it, Gibson," said Bain. "Come and speak to me at the station."

Jamie Cook's parents advanced on them. Cullen was surprised to see them there, with their son still in an interview room in Leith Walk.

"Charles has done nothing," said Robert Cook.

"How can you be here when your son is sitting in a police cell in Edinburgh accused of murder?" said Bain.

"We spoke to you yesterday," said Robert Cook. "We gave Jamie our solicitor."

"That's very Christian of you," said Bain.

"It's probably the most Jamie deserves," said Robert.

Gibson looked around the room at the bedlam. "Will you please leave?"

"Do you want me to tell your friends here what you hid from them about Father Mulgrew?" said Bain.

Gibson hung his head, his hand gripping the lectern. "Okay, I'll come and speak to you."

"Charles," said Robert. "You can't let them do this."

Gibson stood up straight. "I know I'm innocent, as does the Lord."

80

"You need to start answering my questions," said Cullen, sitting in the interview room in Leith Walk station an hour later. "You're facing serious accusations here."

Charles Gibson sat opposite. His solicitor was an associate of McLintock, Williams & Partners, the recommendation no doubt coming from Robert Cook.

"Can you confirm your daughter had two sessions a week with Father Mulgrew?" said Cullen.

"No comment."

All through the interview, Gibson's tactics had been denial and refusal to co-operate, every single question met with the same response.

"If you want to play like that," said Cullen, "I can certainly speak to your son or your wife, who I'm sure—"

"All right," said Gibson. He snorted. "Mandy had two sessions a week with Father Mulgrew."

"And you know Mandy bore signs of sexual activity," said Cullen.

"Not until you—" He shut up immediately.

It hit Cullen like a hammer. He searched through his notebook. Gibson wasn't aware of the abuse, or of Mulgrew's history, until Cullen told him on Monday. In one instant, he cracked the case and screwed it up.

"Can you confirm the first you knew about Father Mulgrew's history was when I informed you at half five on Monday afternoon?" said Cullen.

"No comment," said Gibson.

"You have to confirm this," said Cullen, his voice loud.

"Constable, my client has already given an answer," said the lawyer. "I refer you back to that."

Cullen felt Gibson slipping between his fingers. The more he grabbed, the less he had.

Cullen thought hard, searching for anything he could use, finding something Gibson had said at the back of his head, which hadn't registered fully at the time. He struggled to find it in his notebook, lost in the four times they spoke to him.

He found it. The alibi for the car.

Gibson had been waiting for Mulgrew, which nobody in his street had confirmed. Cullen had written some of it down verbatim and one sentence stuck out.

'Now I know why he didn't turn up'

Gibson was there just after nine.

They had interviewed him about Mulgrew's death at ten thirty the previous day, but hadn't told him when Mulgrew was killed.

Cullen looked across the table, Gibson's eyes focused on the desk, his lawyer tapping a propelling pencil off his own notebook.

The lawyer cleared his throat and looked at Bain. "My client is being detained here for absolutely no purpose I can determine. Your underling is doing some admin while we sit and wait. This is not effective use of mine or my client's time."

Cullen looked at Bain. "I need a word," he said in a low tone.

Bain leaned over, pausing the interview and pointing a finger at Lamb. "You stay."

Bain marched into the corridor. He stood, arms folded, glaring at Cullen. "This better be good."

"I think I've got him," said Cullen.

"How?"

Cullen showed Bain his notebook. "He's slipped up. When I spoke to him yesterday morning, he shouldn't have known Mulgrew died at around nine o'clock on Monday night." He read out the quote. "I think I can get him."

"Fill your boots, Sundance," said Bain.

They went back in and Bain resumed the interview.

"Mr Gibson," said Cullen, "I'll give you a quote from your statement from yesterday morning relating to an alibi for your whereabouts on Monday night. You said 'Now I know why he didn't turn up'. Can you confirm that?"

"If that's what you wrote, then that's what I said," said Gibson.

"We'd asked for your whereabouts on Monday night, but we hadn't told you why we were looking," said Cullen.

Gibson swallowed, but remained silent.

"How did you know Father Mulgrew was killed on Monday night before you were due to meet him?" said Cullen.

"He was killed on Monday, *you* found the body," said Gibson.

"You didn't know the time of death," said Cullen. "In fact, you shouldn't even know it now."

Gibson's breathing quickened.

"Why did you say you knew the real reason Mulgrew hadn't turned up?" said Cullen.

"I don't know," said Gibson, rubbing his ear.

"You made it clear it related to the death of Father Mulgrew," said Cullen. "Yet, you didn't know when he died."

"I'm not sure how you get that from my statement," said Gibson, visibly rattled, his hands shaking, sweat pouring down his brow.

"I will refer to my previous question," said Cullen. "The first you knew about Father Mulgrew's child abuse was when I informed you at half five on Monday afternoon, wasn't it?"

"Seamus had told me before," said Gibson, looking away.

"That's not true, is it?" said Cullen. "You would really entrust your daughter's care to a known sex offender?"

"We had no secrets between us," said Gibson.

"I'll ask again, was the first you knew of Father Mulgrew's history when I told you?" said Cullen.

Gibson looked around the room, before closing his eyes. "Yes."

"Did you take any further action?" said Cullen.

Gibson started crying. "I didn't know... I..."

"Can you confirm what happened at Balgone Ponds?" said Cullen.

"Seamus called me on Monday afternoon," said Gibson. "He was frightened. He thought the police would be after him."

Cullen recalled the FLO, PC Wallace, telling him about some calls Gibson had taken on his mobile, no doubt from Mulgrew.

"Were you in regular contact with Father Mulgrew throughout the day?" said Cullen.

"I was," said Gibson.

"What about?" said Cullen.

"Church matters," said Gibson.

"Are you sure that's the answer you want to give?" said Cullen.

"No comment," said Gibson.

"What did you do when Father Mulgrew phoned you?" said Cullen.

"I arranged to meet him," said Gibson. "I didn't know what he'd been doing to Mandy. It was only when you told me I began to put two and two together. Jesus."

"Did Seamus attack you when you got there?" said Cullen.

"No comment."

"Are you sure?" said Cullen.

"I'm sure," said Gibson, nodding.

"Did you attack him?" said Cullen.

"No comment."

Cullen sighed, before sitting back and looking hard at Gibson. "Does any of this have anything to do with the exorcism?"

"Which one?" said Gibson.

Cullen was thrown. "What do you mean 'which one'?"

Gibson grimaced. "Well, of course, you mean at the service. That's the only exorcism."

"Your daughter screamed 'Fuck! No!' over and over, I believe," said Cullen. "It was a cry for help, wasn't it?"

Gibson swallowed, wiping away at tears. "I know that now."

"We have two witness reports placing you and Mandy at Father Mulgrew's cottage at exactly eleven PM on Sunday night," said Cullen. "This is the approximate time of death for your daughter."

"What?" said Gibson, eyes wide.

"You heard," said Bain.

Gibson put his head on the table. "I didn't mean for any of this to happen," he said, slumping back on his chair.

"Mr Gibson may later retract this statement," said the lawyer.

"What happened?" said Cullen, ignoring him.

"I took Mandy around to Father Mulgrew's house," said Gibson, taking a deep breath. "He was going to exorcise her again. He told me he could get rid of the demon once and for all." A tear slicked down his face. "Seamus took Mandy upstairs for the ritual."

"And she died?" said Cullen.

Gibson nodded. "She just stopped breathing."

"Just stopped breathing?" said Bain, his face screwed up.

Gibson massaged his temples. "Father Mulgrew said the demon had taken her life when he left her body."

"And you believed him?" said Cullen.

Gibson nodded again. "At the time, yes."

"Did you see this happen?" said Cullen.

"I was downstairs," said Gibson, shaking his head.

Bain cleared his throat. "The post mortem report said she was suffocated with a pillow."

Gibson screwed his eyes shut.

"Did you try to make it look like Jamie Cook was responsible?" said Cullen.

"We did," said Gibson. "It was Seamus's idea. He said it would leave fewer questions and the town would be free of its biggest blight."

"So, you tried to frame an innocent boy for murder?" said Cullen.

"Yes," said Gibson.

"What happened when you met up with Father Mulgrew at Balgone Ponds that night?" said Cullen.

Gibson looked away. "He was desperate. His eyes were red raw. His hands were shaking." He swallowed. "I asked him about the abuse in Ireland. He denied it. I asked him about Mandy's abuse. He blamed it on Jamie. I asked him how Mandy died, he said it was my fault."

He exhaled through his nose. "I grabbed hold of him. I asked him again what happened with Mandy. He told me he suffocated her, said she might tell people about what he'd been doing. It would all come out, him and Jamie Cook, him and Mandy. He pleaded with me, said it would ruin our mission. He said our faith had to be strong. It was God trying us."

"What did you do?" said Cullen.

Gibson fiddled with the cufflink on his left sleeve, his eyes filling with tears. "I strangled him."

"Why?" said Cullen.

"To make it look like Jamie Cook had done it," said Gibson.

Cullen shook his head. "What about the teddy bear?"

"I planted it," said Gibson. "I wish I hadn't."

Cullen looked at Bain, who shrugged his shoulders. Cullen checked his watch. "Interview terminated at fourteen eighteen," he said into the recorder, then turned it off.

Bain stood up. "Get to your feet."

Gibson slowly rose.

"Charles Gibson, I'm charging you with the murder of Seamus Mulgrew."

81

Cullen tapped away at his computer back at Leith Walk, having charged and processed Gibson. He didn't think the case would go to a full trial, hoping Gibson stuck to his confession.

Cullen checked his watch. Just after half two. He reckoned he needed another twenty minutes to finish his section of the case report, then he would head back to his flat and get some washing done. Bain had given him tomorrow off, but he suspected he might be called at some point.

For once, they hadn't gone to the pub to celebrate the arrest, everyone involved politely declining Bain's offer, which Cullen took to be an indication of how badly affected they all were.

He was pleased with the day's work, managing to solve the case, astonished by what was festering below the surface in Garleton, tiny details known only to a select few. He wondered what would happen to God's Rainbow, their leader murdered and outed as a child molester, the second-in-command awaiting trial. Some might re-join the Church of Scotland, others would likely give up on religion.

The Gibson family would never recover. Daughter dead, husband a murderer. A single moment of madness was all it had taken.

Cullen confessed to Bain he'd given Gibson the two pieces of information that tipped him over the edge. Bain doubted there would be any repercussions, but Cullen would wait and see.

He stood up and stretched, needing a break from writing. He had a rummage through his pigeonhole, finding several newsletters he'd never get round to reading and an approved holiday request form. The last item was a brown A4 envelope. He frowned as he opened it, no idea what it was.

It was from Tommy Smith, the phone traces he'd requested. The first sheet referred to the two Gibson numbers, which would have been helpful earlier, but it would be useful background material for the report.

The second sheet had the results of the trace on Cullen's mystery caller.

82

Cullen sat in the car and waited, listening to the early evening January rain thunder down on the roof, watching it pour down the windscreen. He looked at the house, the warm glow of lights from behind curtains, deciding to wait another few minutes until the rain quietened down. He'd been procrastinating for the last twenty minutes, reluctant to move.

He picked up the envelope from the passenger seat and opened it again. He read the memo for the umpteenth time that day, before putting it in his jacket pocket. He went through all the things he wanted to say.

The rain slowed enough for him to consider going to the door. He locked his car and ran across the path to the house, sheltering under the eaves as he waited for an answer.

"What do you want?" said Derek Miller.

"I want to know why you've been crank calling me," said Cullen.

Derek looked Cullen up and down. "You what?"

Cullen took the letter out. "You weren't very smart, Derek. You used your own mobile."

Derek shrugged. "So what do you want to do?"

"Can I come in?" said Cullen. "It's pissing down."

Derek leaned back against the door, gesturing for Cullen to

enter. He led him through to the living room where they first met months before.

"My parents are out," said Derek.

"I know," said Cullen.

Derek sat on a reclining armchair, looking worried. "What are you going to do with your information, then?"

"I could press charges," said Cullen.

"I could deny it," said Derek. "My phone got nicked. Some wee bastard from Wester Hailes nicked it from a club on Saturday night."

Cullen held up the report. "I got a trace done just to be sure. Seems like the wee bastard lives in this exact house, not in Wester Hailes."

"Aye, fair enough," said Derek.

"Why did you do it?" said Cullen.

Derek looked Cullen in the eye. "Who says I've stopped?"

"You've stopped," said Cullen. "There's a block put on your phone."

"Aw, man," said Derek, "I've not had any texts for hours because of you."

"You know, I thought a murder suspect on a case was making those calls," said Cullen. "I spent public money doing that trace. I didn't think it would be you." He tapped the envelope. "This is evidence related to the case. My DI might wonder why he's spent money on a phone search."

"Is your DI that Bain prick?" said Derek.

"Aye," said Cullen.

"Let him come at me," said Derek. "I'll sort him out."

"Quite the hard man, aren't you?" said Cullen.

"Harder than my brother," said Derek.

"Is that what you really think?" said Cullen.

Derek looked at the floor for a few seconds. "No, it isn't."

"You did it because you're angry with me over Keith's death," said Cullen.

Derek rubbed the tears out of his eyes. "It was his birthday on Monday. My parents took me to the cemetery with a bunch of flowers. We should have been going to the football tonight, me and Keith. It's Dundee in the League Cup at Easter Road. We should be watching the boys turning those pricks over but you got him killed."

Cullen held his gaze. "Derek, I didn't get your brother killed."

"Aye, you did," said Derek. "You weren't supposed to be in that flat."

"Keith died apprehending a suspect who was later convicted of five murders," said Cullen. "Keith had the bravery to hold the suspect on his own while I liberated a hostage."

"You're all the same," said Derek, his voice raised. "Total pricks."

"That's as maybe," said Cullen. "It's a risky business being in the police. Keith knew it and accepted the risk." He took a deep breath. "I once had a conversation with him about why we joined the police. We'd both worked for insurance companies in jobs we hated. Being a police officer is about doing something more than serving yourself."

"Is this my brother you're talking about or yourself?" said Derek, his face screwed up.

"Keith wanted to do the right thing," said Cullen. "He could be quite wild and it didn't always seem like he was committed, but he was desperately trying to get made a full-time DC when he died. It's a tough job. There are easier jobs in the police force — he could have become a desk sergeant in a quiet place in the country, for instance. But he tried to do the hardest thing."

"Aye, good on him," said Derek.

"I've had counselling to try and get over this," said Cullen. "I might not always have seen eye to eye with your brother but I got on well with him. As you say, I was responsible for his death. It was me that led us both in there. We should have waited for backup but we didn't. I have to live with that every day."

He paused for a few moments, letting the words sink in. "I have a new Acting DC working with me every day. She's very good and everything, but every time I see her, I'm reminded of Keith and the fact she's there because he isn't."

"What are you saying here?" said Derek.

"I can press charges against you," said Cullen. "You'll get a fine and maybe a court order. They might be harder than that."

Derek laughed. "They're not going to chuck me in jail because I made some calls."

"They might," said Cullen. "They were made to a serving police officer. They might want to make an example of you."

"I'm shaking here," said Derek. "You're really frightening me."

"Derek, I'm serious," said Cullen. "I'm offering you a way out of this."

"What?" said Derek.

"I think we could both do with someone to speak to about your brother and what happened," said Cullen. "You look like you're still hurt. I can help."

"What do you want from me?" said Derek.

"I want you to listen," said Cullen. "On the twenty-fifth of every month, we'll meet up somewhere and talk about Keith. If there's a Hibs match on we'll go and see it."

"That's it?" said Derek. "You're not a poof, are you?"

Cullen laughed. "No, I'm not. I think we both need to help each other."

Derek sat in silence for a few minutes, Cullen letting him think. "Fine," he said, eventually.

"Thanks," said Cullen.

"How will this work then?" said Derek.

"I'll call you," said Cullen. "I've got your number."

SCOTT CULLEN WILL RETURN IN

"FIRE IN THE BLOOD"

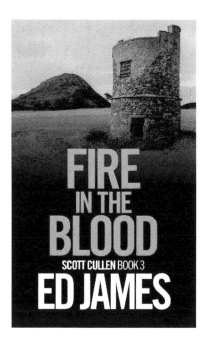

Out now!

If you enjoyed this book, please consider leaving a review on Amazon.

The third book in the series, FIRE IN THE BLOOD, is out now — keep reading to the end of this book for a sneak preview. You can buy a copy at Amazon.

If you would like to be kept up to date with new releases from Ed James, please fill out a contact form.

AFTERWORD

Many, many thanks for buying and reading this book. I hope you enjoyed it.

This is my second book and I've been lucky and not had "second album blues" — it's probably something to do with the fact that I'd originally written an outline of this in October 2010, though it's taken a lot of blood, sweat and tears as I've pounded away on a dying netbook on the train every morning and evening.

Scott Cullen will be back. There will be a sequel novel called FIRE IN THE BLOOD, of which I've written no words as it stands but I'm confident it will be out in a few months. Keep an eye on my blog or subscribe to my newsletter to keep up-to-date.

As with GHOST IN THE MACHINE, many of the settings in this book are entirely fictional. There is no Garleton except in my imagination (and hopefully yours now) — it's a lovely range of hills between Drem and Haddington, and you can go for a lovely walk along the ridge if you turn off the A199 at Barney Mains. The Pheasant pub in Haddington is currently boarded up and being turned into a style bar but it has a history in keeping with Jamie Cook and his mates. The band Expect Delays doesn't exist. Don't go shopping for Likely Laddie or Dunpender Distillery whisky. Finally, the town of Ravencraig in West Lothian is a fictional creation that will appear in STAB IN THE DARK.

Things that are real, though, include Balgone Ponds which is a really nice place for a walk — just hope you don't find a body in amongst the bushes or in the shack. The Burns poem is true (http://www.bbc.co.uk/arts/robertburns/works/ comin_thro_the_rye_alternate_version/) though Tommy Smith shares some of my theories, which are just theories.

The Clash song *Police On My Back* is mentioned, a cover of an Eddy Grant track off their much-maligned *Sandanista* album, though I prefer the live version on the late Joe Strummer's *Acton Town Hall* bootleg, soon to be officially released.

Thanks again go to C for the artwork and being the most critical of alpha readers possible — if only I could dedicate every book to her.

A huge thanks to Pat for beta reading and proofing — it really got me through the hard final straight of the editing process.

Also, thanks to everyone who reviewed GHOST on Amazon — seeing so many positive reactions to my debut got me through this.

This book is dedicated to my parents — I really appreciate their support over the years, especially through my wild years.

This book was greatly helped by the Thom Yorke solo album *Eraser*, the Global Communication ambient techno album, Biosphere's early work and, through the editing phase, the new Mumford and Sons album. Check them out.

One final thing, if you liked this, then please leave a review on Amazon — it really helps aspiring indie authors like me.

Thanks for reading it.

— Ed James,
East Lothian, October 2012

2014 Update note

I redrafted this in February 2014, bringing the style in touch with how it's evolved over the five Cullen novels. The word count went from 103,000 to 86,500 words, Bain's swearing was cut a bit and the action spread to three days. I added a couple of extra scenes to help the flow and cut out summary narrative. Hope you enjoy it.

Sincerest thanks to Rhona and Allan for the editing — this is as good as I can make this book without a page one rewrite...

— Ed James, March 2014

ABOUT THE AUTHOR

Ed James is the author of the bestselling DI Simon Fenchurch novels, Seattle-based FBI thrillers starring Max Carter, and the self-published Detective Scott Cullen series and its Craig Hunter spin-off books.

During his time in IT project management, Ed spent every moment he could writing and has now traded in his weekly commute to London in order to write full-time. He lives in the Scottish Borders with far too many rescued animals.

If you would like to be kept up to date with new releases from Ed James, please contact a contact form.

Connect with Ed online:

Amazon Author page

Website

OTHER BOOKS BY ED JAMES

SCOTT CULLEN MYSTERIES SERIES

1. GHOST IN THE MACHINE
2. DEVIL IN THE DETAIL
3. FIRE IN THE BLOOD
4. STAB IN THE DARK
5. COPS & ROBBERS
6. LIARS & THIEVES
7. COWBOYS & INDIANS
8. HEROES & VILLAINS

CULLEN & BAIN NOVELLAS

1. CITY OF THE DEAD (Coming March 2020)

CRAIG HUNTER SERIES

1. MISSING
2. HUNTED
3. THE BLACK ISLE

DS VICKY DODDS

1. TOOTH & CLAW

DI SIMON FENCHURCH SERIES

1. THE HOPE THAT KILLS
2. WORTH KILLING FOR
3. WHAT DOESN'T KILL YOU
4. IN FOR THE KILL
5. KILL WITH KINDNESS
6. KILL THE MESSENGER

MAX CARTER SERIES

1. TELL ME LIES

SUPERNATURE SERIES

1. BAD BLOOD
2. COLD BLOOD

FIRE IN THE BLOOD

EXCERPT

PROLOGUE

Alec Crombie tightened the sporran over his kilt and adjusted the tam o'shanter on his head. He wanted to look the part. He adjusted his bow tie in the mirror and decided he did.

He got his bottle of vocal spray and gave a couple of squirts. He cleared his throat and did a few exercises, passed down through generations of Crombies.

Fraser appeared through the door. "They're ready for you, Dad."

Crombie looked him up and down. "You could have bothered."

Fraser tugged his Dunpender Distillery polo shirt. "I'm just the cooper here."

"Yes well, I suppose you're right." Crombie made a final tweak to his bow tie, then got going.

Fraser led him through the distillery building, heading to the bar. "It was a great idea to open this."

"It was *your* idea."

Fraser held the door open. "Doesn't mean it's not great."

"Very true." Crombie patted his son on the shoulder. "It harks back to our family's proud ancestry."

He entered the large bar area of the distillery, already full of mailing list members. He smiled at a few familiar faces as he made his way to the lectern. A round of applause broke out as he climbed the stage.

He waited for the sound to die down, smiling all the time. "Thank you, thank you." He put his notes on the lectern and smoothed the paper.

He held his arm out and made a show of checking his watch. "It's not even noon yet, but I note a few somewhat ruddy faces in the room already." He held up the glass of whisky placed on the podium. "Sláinte."

Glasses all around the room were raised. "Sláinte."

Crombie took a drink, savouring the burn of Dutch courage. "As you all know, my distillery celebrates its centenary this year. The reason you're all here, of course, is we plan to launch an exclusive bottle to mark the occasion, accompanied by a crystal quaich and an engraved hip flask."

He looked around the room, noticing more than a few hands putting glasses to mouths. "Before we let you behind the magician's curtain, as it were, and show you the casks being opened, I wanted to say a few words."

He turned over the notes. "We are in the process of producing a book, marking our centenary. This will, of course, be available for purchase through our website and all good retailers, but I think it's important to dwell on the distillery's legacy for a while. Whisky is nothing without tradition, after all."

He flipped the sheet over, scanning the handwritten bullet points. "We can't quite pin the exact date the distillery was founded in 1912, so we've decided on the fourth of July in a show of solidarity with our cousins across the pond."

There were a few cheers from the back of the room.

Crombie held up his glass in acknowledgement. "Before we started on the whisky, our family used to run public houses in Gullane. We were noted for holding court, but also for our rich voices, passed down several generations from the seventeenth century to my own son, Fraser. People would travel from miles around to hear my grandfather orate — Burns, mostly. I still run the poetry recital group in Gullane."

He narrowed his eyes, trying to focus on the next point. He reached for his glasses, hands shaking as he put them on. "What's this got to do with whisky you ask? Beneath his public hostelry, my great-grandfather had an illicit still. He would serve its product at poetry recitals and after hours in the pub. The whisky soon became quite refined and Iain Crombie set this place up as a legal concern."

He beamed at the crowd. "I assure you that, apart from the days of the illicit still, this establishment has long since refrained from any lawbreaking."

A wave of laughter passed through the room.

Crombie took another sip of whisky. "In July 1912, Iain Crombie purchased a batch of malted barley. He reused the yeast he'd been cultivating for years, which we still use to this day. Of course, we don't know when the process began exactly, but the first batch of whisky was distilled and put in the pub cellar to mature."

"Fourteen years later, in 1926, the first bottles were sold." He reached down and retrieved a dusty bottle. "I tasted this batch when it was worth much less. This is now worth over ten thousand pounds."

He looked fondly at the bottle as he waited for the applause to die down. "My grandfather moved the company to these premises not long after. He converted the farm buildings into a medium-sized distillery and we have thrived ever since."

He held up his glass again, breathing in the aroma. "Dunpender whisky is softer and lighter than a Highland or Island and it's the product of one of the few remaining independent distilleries in Scotland. *Vehemently* independent."

He finished the glass and set it down. "Now, enough from me. I cordially invite you downstairs for some pomp and ceremony in our barrel room."

Crombie left the stage, leading the forty visitors down the stairwell into the rooms underneath the distillery, his son and a few other employees accompanying them.

He entered the large room and let the space slowly fill up, the low temperature noticeably rising in a short space of time.

Crombie playfully clamped his hand on the shoulder of a man standing by a pair of barrels mounted on racks. "Doug Strachan here has been with me since we were both wee laddies. We've produced some fine whisky over the years, as I'm sure you'll all agree."

Strachan held up a hand, bashfully staring at the floor. "The barrel on the left is made from sherry oak. It gives a nice clear finish to the whisky, almost like a vodka."

He held up a large mallet and held it against a stout wooden stopper stuck in the side of the barrel. "This is known as the bung. It keeps the cask whisky-tight, save for the angel's share, of course."

He smacked the bung with the mallet, before easing it out and placing it in the pocket of his overcoat. He knelt and sniffed at the exposed hole in the barrel, drinking in the aroma of the unblended spirit.

He held up a long copper cylinder on a chain. "This we call the dog." He lowered it deep into the barrel and allowed it to fill before pouring the contents into a clear glass bottle. He swirled the bottle and examined the golden liquid. "See how it looks nice and clean? There are no noticeable impurities. It's taken on the lighter colour of the sherry oak cask it's sat in for the last eighteen years."

Crombie gestured at the bottle with a flourish. "This is clearly a worthy candidate for the centenary edition blend."

Strachan replaced the bung before moving over to the second barrel of the pair. "This one is a darker bourbon cask, which will complement the softer sherry oak of its sibling when we blend them after dilution." He gave a cheeky wink to the crowd. "Of course, we will offer a few bottles of cask strength once they are blended."

He held his mallet up and hit the bung of the second cask. He hit it again twice, before leaning over to Crombie. "It's stuck fast."

Crombie grabbed the mallet and gave it a good few hits, before it finally slackened. He wiped his forehead with a handkerchief then beamed at the crowd. "I shouldn't be sweating given how cold it is in this room, but I hadn't expected any form of exertion."

Strachan dipped a second dog into the barrel.

It hit something hard.

He retrieved it and frowned — it was only filled a fraction. It danced about on the chain and spilled its contents onto the cracked flagstones of the floor.

Crombie whispered at him. "What's the matter?"

"It's hit something." Strachan picked up a torch and shone it into the barrel. "There's something in here."

Crombie's eyes nervously glanced at the crowd before he snatched the torch from Strachan. He shifted the light about, angling the beam to cut through the liquid. It shone on an object. He struggled to make it out.

He saw a human ear.

THE THIRD SCOTT CULLEN BOOK, FIRE IN THE BLOOD, is out now. You can get a copy at Amazon.

If you would like to be kept up to date with new releases from Ed James, please fill out a contact form.

Printed in Great Britain
by Amazon

62759420R00215